INSTRUCTIONS FOR BURNING THE WORLD

a novel

REBECCA GARDNER

Olive Ridley Press
(a Manta Press, Ltd. imprint)

Cover Design by Celia Winters
Cover Concept by Tim McWhorter

First Edition

Printed in the U.S.A.

For my sister, Maureen,
who has loved this book so much for so long.

Chapter 1

"Here's my theory," Dominic said.

Katie turned her face to the sun-drenched sky, closing her eyes and soaking in the warmth. "This should be good."

"My theory," Dominic repeated, "is that Mrs. Kozel is always three minutes late on purpose to get our hopes up. That way, when she strolls in, she's guaranteed to get a *reaction*."

Katie answered his expectant grin with an eye roll.

"Get it? Because she teaches chemistry? *Reaction*—"

"I get it, Dom. It's just stupid. Like all your puns."

He laid back on the hood of his mom's car, pillowing the back of his head on his arms. "Yeah, but I got a patented Katie Byrd eye roll out of it. I call that a success."

The metal of the hood was warm under Katie's palms as she leaned back on her hands and glanced down at Dominic. His straw-colored hair splayed against the practical silver of the car, and his beige skin was starting to flush from the sunlight. "I'm calling a ban on school-related conversation. It's Sunday. Don't do this to me."

"You like school."

"Doesn't mean I want to think about it on the weekend. Let me live."

It was still summer a week into September, and she wanted to hold on to that. The warm air and golden sunlight hadn't left, and the grass of the sledding hill in front of them was lush, the way it only got at the tail-end of summer. The kids running around the playground at the bottom of the hill were still in shorts and t-shirts. But Dominic and Katie's junior year of school had started, which meant summer would collapse into fall soon. Then winter would squeeze fall 'til it cracked into ice and bitter winds and too little sunlight. Summer hadn't fully ended, and Katie already missed it.

"We should go sledding this winter," she said, her gaze following the slope of the hill. "It's the only thing snow's good for."

"Sure, I'm game."

"Also, we should roll down the hill. Like, now."

He barked out a laugh. "Like kindergarteners."

"I'm serious." Katie stood, flashing him a grin over her shoulder. "Last one to the bottom eats farts." Before he could reply, she jumped over the concrete bumper, hit the ground, and rolled down the hill.

The smell of grass and flashes of sunlight spiraled around her as she tumbled down, laughing uncontrollably. Everything felt bright and sparking, like something in her chest unlocked and shook out, free and clear. It was the best she'd felt all week.

She won. She was lying in a giggly, panting heap at the bottom of the hill when Dominic tumbled down next to her. "Cheater," he managed.

"Fart-eater."

"Bugbreath."

"Fishface."

They both rolled onto their backs, faces to the blue sky. "That was a good idea," Dominic said. "That was fun."

"Right? I feel…" She waved a hand around, searching for the right words but settling for, "better."

Dominic snorted. "You do need to let go more, Byrd. You're all wound-up."

"No, I'm not."

"You so are. You're a creature of routine."

She turned her head, leveling him with a skeptical look. She'd just spontaneously rolled down the hill, thank you very much. But maybe he had a point. There was a difference between small risks, like rolling down a hill, where the worst that could happen was bumping over a rock and bruising your arm, and big risks. He was right—there wasn't room in her life for big risks. She made sure of it.

Katie gave in. "I guess so."

"It's not a bad thing. You just like reliability."

"Well, yeah." She folded her hands on her stomach, tugging the hems of her long sleeves over the backs of her hands. "I've had enough major shake-ups for a lifetime."

He smiled a smaller smile with softer eyes. Katie knew it well. Neither of them had to say out loud that she meant her mom's death—it was implicit. Sometimes Katie thought Dominic forgot what Katie had lost. Who she'd lost. She'd worked hard for half her life to be okay, and most of the time, it worked these days. Most of the time, she was fine.

But Katie could never forget. So, yes. She liked stability.

"Oh hey," Dominic said, eyes brightening as he shifted the subject, "speaking of things you like." He sat up and pulled something out of his pocket. Katie sat up to meet him as he held out a smooth yellow stone.

"That's cool." Katie tilted her head closer. The stone was translucent, perfectly round, and flattish, with a hole right in its center. "Where'd you get it?"

"I was on a run in the metro park and saw it at the edge of the path. It glinted at me. It called to me."

"Very dramatic."

"Isn't it cool?" He was smiling his easy, familiar smile now, turning his palm so the stone caught the light. "I thought you'd like it. It reminds me of those pieces of sea glass you have."

A strange emotion twisted in Katie's chest. Something between warmth and ache. "Yeah," she said. "It kind of does."

His phone buzzed in his pocket. Swapping the stone for his phone, Dominic read his texts and groaned. "Mom needs the car.

Ready to head back?"

Katie pushed herself up and started climbing the hill, Dominic at her side. "You should get a bike. Then we could bike places together."

"Yeah, for like two more months until it gets cold."

"I bike in the cold."

"And I forever fail to understand it. Especially with how much you hate winter."

He sounded weird, almost strained, the laughter gone from his voice. He almost sounded winded, except Dominic's idea of a fun Saturday morning was climbing rock walls, so they weren't nearly far enough up the hill for him to be winded. Katie glanced over, and sure enough, he was frowning. "You okay? You're all—out of it."

"Do you smell oranges?" he asked, furrowing his brow.

"Not really."

"I smell oranges. Like, a lot."

Katie shrugged. "Maybe someone down in the park is eating one."

He still looked perplexed. "Maybe I'm having a stroke."

"Oh my god, Dom, you're sixteen. You're not having a stroke."

"If I am, will you save me?" Now he grinned again.

"Dominic Gunn, if you think for a second I wouldn't have 911 on the phone before you hit the ground—"

"As I would for you. C'mon, slowpoke, I've got fifteen minutes to get home before I get a disappointed chiding."

They rolled down the windows and Dominic turned up his music—he liked Nirvana, like somebody's dad—and Katie leaned her head into the wind and let the sunshine fall on her face. She smiled. Everything always felt better in the sunshine.

Once she got home and kicked off her shoes inside the door, she headed straight to the kitchen to make her favorite jasmine green tea. Alex was there, arranging sliced cheese on crackers. Katie wrinkled her nose as she turned on the kettle. "You're gonna stink up the whole house."

Her brother shrugged, his hair falling in his eyes as he bent to watch the plate spin in the microwave. By the time Katie's water was hot enough, he was disappearing out of the kitchen with his stinky snack. "Hello to you, too!" Katie called after him.

"Yeah," he called back on his way upstairs.

Katie poured the water over the tea bag in her favorite mug and poked her head into the living room where her father and Tracy were sitting. "Please tell me I wasn't like that when I was thirteen."

Her dad peered at her impassively. "I plead the fifth."

"Ha ha. Also, has he gained another inch already? Because I know I'm short, but it's unfair that he's taller than me."

"Ah, Kate." Her dad shook his head. "You got my freckles, but not my height. Alex got my height, but not my freckles. Genetics are strange. I'm sorry."

Katie laughed, scrunching her nose. "Let's be honest, I got your freckles and Grandma's and Uncle Verne's all together."

"And then doubled," Tracy added.

Katie glanced at her stepmother, and Tracy smiled that careful smile she always gave Katie. She was curled up on the couch with Peaches on her lap. The brown tabby was only a few years younger than Katie herself and only ever wanted a warm lap to sleep on. "Peaches got comfy."

"You know her. I try to start working, and she gets in the way of the laptop."

"It's for the best," Katie's dad said. "You need to stop checking work on the weekends." He was about to continue, but was cut off by Skimbleshanks, their orange tabby, leaping into his lap.

Katie flashed her dad a grin, raised her mug at both him and Tracy. "Enjoy the cats," she said as Skimbleshanks kneaded his paws, trying to get comfy. "Now you're both trapped."

"A terrible fate," Tracy cooed, scratching Peaches behind the ears.

In her room upstairs, Katie dropped her bag on the carpet and stood in the sunbeam angling in through the window. The first couple sips of tea were perfect, so she lingered there, cradling her mug. Afternoon light glinted on the bowl of shells and sea glass pieces she kept on her windowsill, and Katie smiled against her teacup. It was like a little hello from her mom when the sun winked off the glass like that.

But the stillness and quiet highlighted how the freedom of rolling down the hill had already slipped away. Restlessness itched under her skin, taking its place. So, Katie set her cup of tea on the bedside table and tugged her yarn basket over from the corner.

Knitting helped the restlessness. It felt good to make things out of almost nothing. The needles in her hands were familiar and comforting.

Okay, maybe Dominic was right. She did like her comfort zone.

But what was wrong with that? She deserved to feel secure.

Batty, the third and youngest of their cats, slept at the foot of her bed, curled into a fluffy black-and-white circle. Katie settled carefully on the bed next to her and dug her current project out of the basket. Sipping her tea, she fell into the rhythm of knitting the orange sock already on her needles, letting the restlessness wriggle out of her chest and into her hands and out into the yarn.

Batty slept quietly the whole time until, as Katie finished turning the heel, she heard chattering start up behind her. She smirked. It was such a cute sound—the weird, alien-like chattering cats made when they were tracking something, a reflection on the wall or a bird outside, that they wanted to hunt but couldn't get to.

"What're you after, Batty?" she asked, turning to see if a fly had gotten caught in her window.

Batty still lay curled up, fast asleep.

Katie furrowed her brow. "Bats?" Then her gaze fell to the floor, to the golden square of sunbeam. To an orange stone lying there.

"What the *hell*." It came out as a whisper. She climbed off the bed and picked up the stone.

It looked just like the yellow one Dominic had showed her: about the size of a half-dollar coin, translucent and flat, with a hole right in the middle. Except this one was orange, not yellow. And it definitely hadn't been lying on the floor when Katie came in.

"What. The hell," she repeated, turning the stone over in her hand. It caught the sunlight, reflected it, flashed it in her eyes and made her blink.

Knitting was forgotten. Katie closed her fingers around the stone and hurried downstairs.

Tracy was on the couch by herself now, reading and petting Peaches behind her ears. Skimbleshanks had taken up residence as an orange-tabby noodle snoozing between Tracy's feet. "Hey Tracy?" Her stepmother looked up, and Katie held out the stone. "I found this in my room. I don't know if it's yours? Or Dad's? Maybe one of the cats got hold of it and was playing with it?" Because the thing had to come from somewhere.

Tracy craned her neck to see without moving Peaches, who was snoring softly. "No. It's pretty, though. Maybe Alex lost it?"

"Huh." Katie shoved it into the pocket of her leggings. It didn't look like something her brother would like, but then again, she found him increasingly hard to read. "Weird. I guess I'll ask him." She turned, ready to go back upstairs, but stopped. A familiar smell filled her nose out of nowhere. "Is—is Dad baking bread?"

Tracy smiled. "No, he knows better than to try baking without your help. He's making dinner, though. I hope stir-fry sounds good."

"Yeah." Katie scrunched her nose. It didn't smell at all like stir-fry. It smelled unmistakably like bread.

She went to Alex's bedroom at the top of the stairs and knocked on the door. "Hey, I need to ask you something." A long pause, in which she heard absolutely nothing through the door. He probably had his headphones in. She knocked harder. "Alex!"

Finally, he opened the door. Yep: earbuds in his ears, phone in his hand dangling at his side. "What?"

Katie held up the stone, wiggling it in his general direction. "Is this yours? Because I found it in my room, and if you were in my room, we're going to have *words*."

He rolled his eyes (almost exactly like she did, and she couldn't decide if that warmed her heart or annoyed her) and started closing the door even as he said, "No. Why would it be mine?"

"I'm trying to solve a mystery," she called through the crack in the door. Alex shut it without response.

Katie may have rolled her own eyes on the way back to her room.

She set the orange stone on her windowsill next to the bowl of shells and glass, eyeing it with growing suspicion. She grabbed her phone and pulled up her messages.

Hey Dom, remember that stone you showed me today?

Dom
ofc
why?

Katie took a deep breath, snapped a picture of the orange stone, and sent it.

This is in my room for no reason
I've never seen it before and it's nobody else's
I asked

Dom
byrd wtf???

I know
It's weird, right?

Katie tossed her phone on the bed and turned, pacing back and forth in the space between the bed and dresser. When her phone buzzed, she whirled around, bending over the bed, her long hair falling in a red-brown curtain over her shoulder as she opened Dominic's message.

Dom

> *I mean I think it's weird*
> *it looks just like mine & like where tf did it come from*
> *either of them?*

> *It's in my HOUSE*
> *How did it GET HERE*

Her hands were starting to shake. She dropped her phone again and paced over to the window, staring down at the stone. It lay there, like a stone should. It didn't do anything. But it freaked her the hell out.

If some random object showed up in her room, that nobody in her family recognized—yeah, that would be weird. The fact it was the exact same kind of stone as the one Dominic found *and* it showed up in her room with no obvious explanation—that was freak-out weird.

Maybe Dominic found this one too and forgot about it. Maybe at some point on the way home from the park, it fell out of his pocket and into her bag, then fell on the floor after she got home. That was possible. Convoluted, maybe, but possible.

She picked up the stone.

The second she touched it, she immediately smelled baking bread again.

But it wasn't just the scent. She smelled it and was sucker-punched with comfort. The building anxiety rushed out of her and all she felt was cozy, satisfied, and homey, like every time she kneaded bread dough or slid a loaf into the oven or sliced a freshly baked batch.

Then she remembered climbing the hill.

She grabbed her phone, ignored whatever Dominic's latest text message said, and called him instead.

"Byrd?"

"Hey." She turned the stone in her fingers, watching the way it flashed in the dimming sunlight. "Remember earlier when you thought you smelled oranges?"

"Yeah. And like, it kind of keeps happening."

"Has anything else weird happened? When you touch it?" He hesitated, and Katie huffed. "Dom, it's me."

"So," he started. "I keep tasting pencil eraser."

"Well, have you been chewing on your eraser? Because you do that—"

"No, I'm not, but I taste it anyway. Like it's not a bad taste—"

"Not to you," Katie muttered.

"But it's weird."

"I keep smelling bread," she said. "And I start feeling the way I feel when I bake bread." She heard him take in a sharp breath. "And earlier I thought I heard Batty doing that thing cats do when they're hunting, that chatter sound? But she was asleep, and Skimbles and Peaches were downstairs. But I swear to god I heard it, and then right after that I saw the stone for the first time."

For a moment, he didn't say anything. Katie sat on the bed, hunched over and staring at the stone in her palm. She could still smell bread. She closed her eyes like that could block it out, but it didn't.

"What the hell are these things?" Dominic finally asked.

"I have no idea. Maybe we should dump them somewhere."

The second the words left her mouth, light flashed behind her closed eyelids. Like how it had flashed in the stone when it caught the light. No. Not quite. It was exactly the way sunlight flashed through trees when their leaves shifted. Exactly. Katie knew that pattern of light. It was something she chased, something she loved. Dancing sunlight always made her heart right in a way she couldn't explain if she wanted to.

She saw it as she clenched her fingers around the stone, and that rightness swelled in her chest even as anxiety rose against it.

"No." Her voice came out low. "Never mind. I don't want to get rid of it. It feels…"

"Familiar." The quiet ring of truth in Dominic's voice told her all she needed to know. He felt it, too. "Like I used to have it when I was a kid, and then I lost it and forgot about it and then found it again."

"Kind of, yeah."

"But it just— appeared in your room."

She sat up straight and opened her eyes, blinking against the sensation of sunlight that wasn't there. "Okay. So, we'll—study them. Try to figure out what they are and where they came from. But…" Her gaze fell to the orange stone in her palm. She rubbed her thumb back and forth across the smooth surface. "I don't want to get rid of it. And it's not hurting anything, really. It's just… weird."

"Weird as hell."

She tilted her head, tilted the stone. "But it's making me curious. I want to figure it out."

"I wonder if they do anything else. Maybe we can run some kind of experiments. Like test them."

"Okay. So, the talented Mr. Gunn will come up with some experiments. Then he and the clever Miss Byrd will run them." That earned her a laugh. "Okay. I'm gonna… try to finish my knitting before dinner, I guess."

"Ever industrious."

She smiled despite herself. It broke up some of the tension in her chest. "More like distracting myself."

"Talk to you tomorrow, Byrd."

Katie hung up and set her phone on the bed. She petted Batty with one hand and held the orange stone in the other. It was such a simple, small thing to shift her this much.

For all its friendly-seeming feelings, she didn't quite trust it. She shut it away in her desk drawer for the night.

Chapter 2

When Katie put the stone in her pocket the next morning, she swore she heard that cat chatter sound again, even though none of the cats were nearby. The sound didn't come back on the way to school, but the stone kept distracting her. More than once during her first period history class, she pulled it out of her pocket, turning it in her hand. If she blinked too fast, she swore she saw sunlight flashing through trees.

And there was a new effect this morning. As she ran her thumb along the edge of the stone, a dry, tannin taste bloomed on the center of her tongue. It was the aftertaste of black tea. A few drops of milk, no sugar. The exact way her dad made a cup for anyone who was upset.

The things the stone made her sense were happy. Warm. Things that had always brought her comfort. But the fact it was able to do those things, and the way it had appeared in her room, passed beyond weird into the uncanny. If she lingered too long on those thoughts, her stomach began to sink. By the time the bell rang at the end of class, she was more than ready to get to chemistry and see Dominic. It was nice, at least, that she wasn't alone in this.

"That's a cool stone."

Katie turned around. It was the tall girl who sat behind her, standing with her hands shoved in her jeans pockets. What was her name? Katie smiled. "Thanks," she said, and the girl walked out of the classroom with her. "I actually just found it. It's cool, I guess."

"Huh." The girl reached up and ran her fingers through her short, dark hair. Melanie? Melissa? Katie was reasonably sure her name was Melissa something. She was also reasonably sure Melissa-or-Melanie was a senior. This elective history class was their first together. "Do you know what kind of mineral it is?"

Katie shrugged. "I don't know much about this stuff."

"I collect rocks and minerals. Yours is nice. Really clear. I've got one kind of like it, with that weird hole."

Something warm twinged in Katie's chest. She clutched her books tighter and looked up at the girl. "Really? My friend found one, too. Stones like this with holes in them can't be that common, right?" She pulled out the orange stone, flashing it as they walked. Her pulse beat quick in her fingers.

"Yeah. Adder stones. That's what they're called when they form naturally, like in rivers. But they're not usually gems like that. Although mine's solid iron, which is unusual too." The girl shrugged. "They're cool. Lots of folklore around them."

"Really?"

"Yeah. Like if you look through them, you can see into another realm. That they're magical or some shit." She quirked an eyebrow—it reminded Katie of a more subdued version of her own eyerolls.

"That's wild." Katie put the stone back in her pocket. If the stone could make her smell things and hear things, could it make her see things? More than the strange sensation of sunlight? "Have you ever tried it?"

"No. I don't believe in that stuff."

Neither did Katie until yesterday. "Maybe you should sometime."

The girl smirked. "Sure. This is me." She turned off into a classroom. "See you."

"Bye." Katie kept walking, books clutched against her sweater, heart thundering.

She slid into her seat next to Dominic as soon as she got to chemistry. He sat sideways in his desk, talking a mile a minute with Jordan Meszaros and crinkling something in plastic wrap. At first, Katie didn't interrupt. Dominic and Jordan had been friends since fourth grade—way longer than Dom and Katie had—but Katie'd never spent much time with Jordan. It always felt awkward butting into their conversations. But after a minute she nudged Dominic's chair with her foot, and he turned around. "Someone else found one."

"Foumb one wom?" His mouth was full of peanut butter sandwich.

Katie rolled her eyes. "One of those stones," she said under her breath.

"You know," Dominic said, crinkling the plastic wrap from his sandwich into a ball, "you roll your eyes gloriously. You're like the queen of epic eyerolls."

"Dom, are you listening?"

"Yes, Byrd. I always listen." He shoved the plastic wrap into his backpack and turned to face her across the aisle. "Who found it?"

"She's—I don't know her name. Senior, really tall girl. Thin, super pale—Melissa something?"

Dominic waved his hand around his head in a vague gesture. "Short hair?"

"Yeah."

"Mel Aspen. I know her a little bit. She's good people."

"You know everyone a little bit," Katie said. The bell rang, which meant they still had exactly three minutes, per Mrs. Kozel's routine. "She said something about folklore. That if you look through a hole in the middle of a stone, you can see into another realm."

Dominic raised his eyebrows. "You think—"

"We wanted an experiment," she said.

"Maybe during lunch?" His brow furrowed. "Although, I mean, what if Mel's right? What if we look through these things and get, like, transported to another dimension?"

She leveled him with a deadpan look. "Seriously?"

"I don't know, Byrd. They've already done wild shit."

He wasn't wrong. Katie rubbed her thumb against the outer edge of the stone in her pocket. "Maybe you're right. Not about dimensions, but if it's something really weird, I'd rather be safe at home to have an existential crisis."

"Tonight, then." His gaze cut to the side as more of their classmates filed in and the room began to fill. "We'll both look, then call each other."

"Compare notes."

"Right."

Katie nodded. "Okay. A plan. Good, I like having a plan."

But she also liked answers. On the way to her next class, the temptation to duck into a bathroom and look through the stone nearly swayed her. But she told Dominic she'd wait. And it was probably best to wait until she got home in case anything did happen. She still didn't trust the thing, for all it felt warm and familiar.

"Bonjour, Byrd." He flashed Katie a bright grin as she sat down at their lunch table.

"Do your cheeks ever hurt from smiling so much?" she asked.

"Never." He gestured with his slice of pizza. Katie watched a mushroom slip off onto the lunch tray. "I have a rare genetic mutation. Gives me extra good cheer."

"Like a mutant, or like a superhero?"

"Why not both?"

Katie fiddled with her lunch bag. She hadn't brought a sandwich, but all she could smell was oven-fresh bread. The orange stone pressed into her hip inside her pocket.

Tonight felt so far away. Maybe she could ask if—

Dominic raised a hand and called out across the cafeteria. "Hey Simon!"

Katie followed his gaze to a smartly dressed dark-skinned boy who started heading their way. "You know him?"

"Yeah. Simon Snow. Senior kid. Head editor of the literary magazine. He's cool."

A slim shadow fell across the table. Katie glanced back up at Simon Snow, who gripped the strap of his messenger bag and said, "Hey."

"Hey!" Dominic pulled out a chair. Simon folded his long limbs into it, adjusting his tie and setting his bag on the floor. "Can I do introductions?" Dominic grinned and cracked his knuckles. "I think I shall. Simon, this is Katie Byrd. Small but feisty. Genuine delight. Always complaining she's cold. Byrd, Simon Snow. General dapper fellow. Usually eats in the lit office but is gracing us with his presence today. He tolerates my shitty submissions to the magazine."

"They're funny," Simon said, shrugging one shoulder.

"Hey." Katie waved from her side of the table. "Nice to meet you."

"Likewise."

"How you've made it this far without knowing Simon, I can't imagine." Dominic shook his head in mock admonishment. "He's the coolest cat in the senior class."

Katie snorted. "You sound like someone's grandpa." She gestured to Simon's tie and cardigan combo. "You have a presentation this early in the semester?"

"Nah," Dominic broke in before Simon could do more than give a small smile. "Simon's always dapper."

Another shrug in response. "I like feeling put-together."

"No criticism meant," Katie said. "It's cool."

"This pizza is not to standard," Dominic rambled. "It tastes like pencil eraser."

Katie glanced up in time to see his eyes widen. He realized it wasn't the pizza, and Katie saw him realize it. She pushed on to a joke, to cover in front of Simon. "Maybe if you didn't chew your erasers all through class—"

"Byrd. Please." Closing his eyes, Dominic pressed a hand to his chest. "This is Simon's first day with us. We have to survive the whole semester. Don't turn him against me now."

"Unlikely. You're a mutant superhero, remember?"

That earned a chuckle from Simon.

Since she'd lost the chance to ask Dominic about it, Katie was going to wait until she got home to look through the hole in the middle of the stone. She really was. But she felt fidgety all through lunch. Her mind kept wandering to the stone in her bag, and the smell of bread didn't go away, and neither did the warmth it bloomed in her chest.

Towards the end of the period, when she went to throw her apple core, she lingered by the line of trash cans and recycling bins against the wall of windows next to the double glass doors that opened into the courtyard. The sun was high, shining warm and bright in a clear dome of blue sky.

Her fingers closed around the stone in her pocket. The taste of black tea bloomed on her tongue.

She wanted to know.

Holding the stone between her thumb and forefinger, she lifted it to catch the sunlight and looked through the hole in its center. A chill shuddered under her skin.

The hole in the center of the stone didn't show blue sky on the other side, even though sunlight glinted through the rest of it. Instead, through the hole, Katie saw trees. Trees with pale bark, weird patchy bark she'd never seen before, and the mist curling between the trees was almost purple.

Her hand jerked into a fist around the stone, and she leaned against the window. Why was her stomach dropping? Because— because—she lifted the stone again, looked again. They were still there. The trees. The mist.

Her hands started to shake even as that stomach-sinking feeling spread through her limbs and her head began to swim. No. No panicking in the middle of the cafeteria. She took slow breaths, forcing them deep into her belly, until her hands stopped trembling.

"Byrd?" She almost jumped out of her skin, whirling around to see Dominic at her shoulder. "Shit, sorry! I didn't mean to scare you. But you looked—"

"I was freaking out a little." Thankfully, her voice came out steady. "But I'm fine now."

"You know you one hundred percent can tell me if you're not."

"I know." She clenched her fingers around the stone in her fist. "It's—stuff about our experiment. I'll fill you in later?"

He held her gaze. That scrutiny was in his eyes, the keen perception that always hid behind his jokes and grins. "Are you gonna be okay? It's not a panic attack?"

Katie got those sometimes. Dominic knew about them—he'd been at her side through a couple. Of course he recognized the warning signs.

"It's not. It just…" She sighed, shoving the stone back into her pocket and reaching up to adjust the collar of her sweater. "I looked. It's messed up, and I freaked out. But I'm not panicking. Not really. I promise I'll fill you in when we're not—here."

Dominic's brow still furrowed, but he nodded. "Okay."

He turned to go back to the table. And maybe Katie was still weak from that spike of panic, or maybe she was desperate to not be alone in what she'd seen. Either way, she reached out and grabbed his wrist.

He turned back again, surprise in his eyes. Katie blinked. She had surprised herself, too. She let go. "Sorry. I didn't mean to grab you. Just—do you promise? That you'll look too?"

Dominic stared at her, hard. It didn't bother her. She was being really weird, and she knew it. But then he smiled, easy as ever. He held up one hand, all his fingers curled in except the little one, which he held out to her.

It was a silly kindergarten kind of thing, a pinkie-promise. But sometimes a silly kindergarten kind of promise was the purest kind you could make. Without pretension. Without judgment.

Katie smiled back and hooked her little finger around his.

He held her gaze a moment longer, his smile kind. Then he headed back to the table. Katie watched him go and took another deep breath, letting some of the nervous agitation in her stomach settle.

Waiting for Dominic to text her after school drove her up the wall, so she worked out the nerves by knitting. The feeling of yarn looping over her needles, building rows of stitches, and shaping something out of practically nothing was the kind of focus she needed. So, by the time her phone finally buzzed—with his incoming call rather than a text—she was only half-tense when she answered. "Hey Dom."

"Hey. So."

"So."

"What exactly happened to you earlier, anyway?"

She let out a rush of breath, bigger than a sigh. "When I looked through the hole in the middle, I saw… not what was actually on the other side of it. I saw these weird trees and mist."

Dominic laughed, tight and humorless. "Okay. At least I'm not alone."

Her heart leapt. "You saw it too?"

"Trees and mist. These like, pale trees, but the bark was patchy. White and almost greenish in some spots? And the mist—"

"Was purple?"

"Like a grayish kind of purple, yeah. Byrd, what the actual hell."

"I don't know, but it's *weird*. To put it mildly."

He made a frustrated noise. "We need more experiments to figure out what these are and why we found them. Don't you wonder if we found them for a reason?"

She hadn't. Or… maybe not consciously. She cut her gaze to the windowsill where the orange stone lay in her bowl of shells and sea glass, gleaming in the sunlight. It was familiar. It made her hear and smell and see things that felt—friendly. Like home. Like the things she liked most about herself.

"Where should we start?"

"Well," he said, "we know they make us smell things that aren't there. Or taste them. Have you tasted anything?"

"Tea. Not the kind I usually drink. The kind my dad makes when I'm upset." She stood and went to the window, touching a fingertip against the stone. "I see things, too, sort of. Not just through the middle of the stone. Like—almost like I'm picturing it in my mind, but I'm not doing it on purpose. It's always sunlight flashing through trees."

"I haven't seen anything, I don't think," Dominic says. "Besides through the middle. But in seventh period I swear to god I heard the wind chimes on our porch. Like, clear as day."

Katie tucked her hair back behind her ear and turned, pacing across her room. "Okay. So, let's make lists. Write down all the things that happen when we hold these. Give ourselves a couple more days and see if anything new happens." As she paced back the other way, she picked up her stone. The weight of it was starting to feel familiar in her hand. "I wonder if it would still happen if we switched stones?"

"Good idea. Let's swap tomorrow morning and see what happens. Then we can go from there."

"It's as good a place to start as any."

"Dom and Byrd, amateur metaphysical scientists."

Katie laughed. "If any dumb kids can figure this out, I guess it's us."

"We're not dumb, ma'am. We're both smart cookies."

"I know. I was being self-deprecating for comedic effect. Thanks for ruining it."

She heard the smile in his voice when he said, "Any time."

She sat back down on the bed, turning the stone in her hand. "Hey." She felt her expression soften. "Thanks, Dom. Really."

"I've always got your back."

"Yours too."

She hung up and left her phone on her bed as she went to the window. She laid her stone back in the bowl.

It was weird that she'd put it there in the first place. Nothing ever went in that bowl except the shells and beach glass. And she hadn't told Dominic, but maybe that was another reason the stone felt good to have, even as bizarre as it was.

It made her heart warm, just like the shells and glass. The pieces she kept as memories of beach vacations when she was little. When she still ran around in the sunshine with her arms bared. When her mother found the pretty pieces of smooth glass and gave them to Katie, their own shared little treasures.

She blinked hard as her eyes grew hot. Slowly, carefully, she pulled up her left sleeve until the light fell over the raised line of scarring running down the side of her arm, an angry memory of surgical staples. The patchy coloring of the rest of her skin that, while no longer puckered from burns, never quite healed back to even.

Nothing in her life had been shaped the same since her mother died. Not her heart. Not her family. Not even her own skin.

As her stomach plunged and her heart clenched, Katie tugged her sleeve back down and scrubbed at her eyes. Yeah. The stone was weird. Maybe she shouldn't trust it. But she'd always take anything she could get that made her feel okay.

Chapter 3

Katie had planned to talk more with the girl behind her in history—Mel, Dominic had said her name was Mel—and ask about the stone she'd mentioned, the iron one with a hole in the middle.

But Katie's focus was pulled too much by Dominic's yellow stone. They'd met before classes started and swapped them, and now his was tucked in her bag. She kept checking in with herself, but she didn't smell or hear or taste anything. Maybe this one didn't work on her. Or maybe it would do the same things to her that her orange one did.

But no. She didn't sense any of the things her stone made her sense, and she didn't feel that homey comfort and spark of joy it gave her.

Also, when did she start thinking of it as *her* stone?

She was half-dazed with distraction all the way to second period. Dominic was already in his seat when she sat down and shook her head.

"Nothing? Me neither." He sighed, slumping back in his seat. "Maybe it's not enough time yet. Let's not switch back until tomorrow."

"Good plan. If I can focus on anything else today." Katie dropped her chin into her hand. "I hate feeling like I can't solve something."

"Hey now." He wagged a finger at her. "No time for complaining. We *shale* prevail."

Katie met his shit-eating grin with a deadpan stare.

"Get it? Shale? Because stone—"

"I get it, Dom."

The rest of the morning passed without Katie tasting pencil eraser or hearing wind chimes. Maybe they really only did work on one person after all.

She shouldn't have skipped breakfast, though. Even after lunch, she felt… not quite lightheaded. But off-kilter. There was a funny dropping in her stomach that didn't go away, and whenever she walked between classes, she felt light on her feet in a way that was disorienting. Eventually she got a hall pass halfway through trigonometry and went to the nurse's office. A quick basic exam didn't uncover an obvious cause—no fever, no she wasn't on her period, yes, she'd eaten enough at lunch—so Katie laid down until the final bell rang.

She sat up carefully, but the half-dizzy feeling was gone. Finally. She thanked the nurse, lifted her bag from the chair across the room where she'd left it, and headed out to the bus.

Not halfway to the school doors, her step felt light, and her stomach dropped.

Katie stopped, moving to the side of the hallway to get out of the rush of other students. Why had it—

She squeezed her hand holding the strap of her bag.

It had come back when she picked up her bag. Which had Dominic's stone in it.

Hurrying was disorienting, but Katie still hurried to get out to the parking lot before Dominic boarded his bus. She barely caught him in time, calling his name across the pavement. The afternoon was windy and bright, and he turned, the breeze whipping his sandy hair across his eyes. "What's up, Byrd?"

"It's doing something," she said. "The dazed way I've been feeling? I think it's from this thing."

"Huh. It never made me—" His eyes widened. "No, it does. I didn't even think to mention it. I don't think I realized? But yeah, sometimes it makes me feel the way I do when I'm up high. Like on a cliff or the top of a ladder."

That was it. That was it exactly, the stomach-dropping mix of weightlessness and heaviness that had been disorienting her for half the day. "Ugh, I hate this feeling."

Dominic grinned and shrugged. "I love it. Maybe that's why I didn't pick up on."

"I'm gonna miss my bus. Text me if you notice anything." The parking lot was almost empty, and the first buses were nudging forward, ready to roll out. She hurried as fast as she could, thanking the bus driver when he let her on at the last second.

As soon as she was home, Katie pulled the yellow stone out of her bag and left it on the coffee table in the living room. Giving herself space from it, she went to the kitchen and made a cup of tea. Usually, she'd pick her favorite lemon green tea or the white jasmine tea she'd had earlier this week. But today her hand reached right for the basic black tea. She missed that tannin taste. She missed—

Katie snorted as she filled the kettle with water. She didn't miss her orange stone. That was ridiculous.

Still. It felt friendlier than Dominic's.

When her tea was ready, she returned to the living room, picked up the yellow stone, and looked through the hole in the center.

Yeah. Weird trees. Weird mist.

She didn't get that up-too-high feeling this time, but her tea, which was plain black tea, started to smell like oranges.

Furrowing her brow, Katie set the stone back down, sat on the couch with her feet tucked underneath her, and sipped from her mug until Dominic reported he kept blinking like sun was in his eyes, and he definitely heard that chattering sound that Sunflower, his family's springer spaniel, definitely did not make.

Katie didn't want to admit the relief that washed over her when they swapped their stones back in chemistry the next morning, and she shoved the orange stone into the pocket of her leggings. But the way Dominic's shoulders sagged in relaxation told her he was on the same page.

"This is annoying," she muttered. "I'm annoyed. I don't want to like this thing when I don't even know what it is."

"Mysteries on mysteries." Dominic rummaged in his backpack for a pencil. "I guess we have to keep trying things."

But as Katie sat at their usual table a few periods later, waiting for Dominic and Simon, someone else got there first. It was the girl from history class. Mel. She dropped her books onto the table and pulled a round piece of metal out of her pocket. "This is my adder stone."

It was iron, Katie guessed, like Mel had said, and there it was, a hole bored through its center. She finished chewing her bite of lunch, swallowing and imagining that she was swallowing the nervous fluttering in her chest at the same time. "That's right. I forgot that's what you called them."

Mel huffed. "Adder stone. Or hag stone. Whatever you want to call it." She plunked the stone onto the table. "Stones with holes naturally formed in them. Usually from water eroding in a specific pattern over time. Traditionally believed to prevent nightmares, protect against the evil eye, cure snakebite, or—" Mel tapped her fingers on the table next to her stone. "Let you see into other realms."

Katie's mouth felt dry. "Yeah. You told me."

"Do you have yours?"

Katie took the orange stone out of her pocket and placed it on the table next to Mel's as the other girl sat across from her.

"Right. Look how smooth and round they both are. You said you found yours just lying around, right?" Katie caught Mel's glance and nodded. "And I found mine in the gravel at the edge of my driveway. It wasn't part of my collection, and it's not my mom's, and it's not my downstairs neighbor's. Why would these be lying around like that?"

Already Mel's words were thrumming something warm through Katie's veins. Katie wanted answers, and so, apparently, did Mel. "I know. It's weird, right?"

"Yes, Katie. It's weird." Mel sat back in the crappy plastic chair and fixed Katie with a firm gaze. "Was there a particular reason," she asked, "that you asked if I've ever looked through it?"

Katie closed her fingers around her stone. "Yeah."

"And you friend who found one—"

"Dominic."

"It was Dominic?" Mel tipped down her chin. "Okay. Did you tell Dominic Gunn to look through his?"

"Yeah." A tension was forming between them now, practically crackling in the air. "Because I looked through mine first."

Taking the stone between her thumb and forefinger, Mel lifted it. At the moment that Katie saw Mel's clear blue eye through the hollow, she smelled an overwhelming wave of lavender. "And what happened when you did?"

"I saw trees," she blurted. "And this weird mist."

For a few moments, Mel said nothing. She just sighed this heavy sigh, closed the stone in her fist, and lowered her hand. She stared at Katie, and every inch of Katie prickled, anticipating. Finally, Mel said, "I saw it too." Katie's fingers loosened their death grip on her stone. Relief washed over her, and Mel's gaze fell to her fist, brow furrowed. "And I swear to god I hear things when I hold it. Like walking on gravel and—"

"Hellooo, ladies!"

Katie half-startled as Dominic approached their table. He

grinned his usual lopsided grin. "What've you got there?"

Mel uncurled her fingers, revealing the stone in her palm. "What did you see through yours?"

"Ah. So, that's where we are." He set his cafeteria tray down next to Mel and slid into the chair. "Let's actually leave that for the moment. Simon's coming. And I saw the same trees as Katie."

"You can tell him," Mel said as Simon joined the table. "He already knows about mine."

"About what?" Simon asked.

"My weird-ass rock." Mel gestured to Dominic and Katie as she began taking out her lunch. "These two are having the same experience."

Katie glanced at Dominic, at Simon. "Wait, why does he—"

"She's my best friend," Simon says.

"Since fifth grade," Mel clarifies. "I tell him everything. Like I wouldn't tell him some paradigm-altering shit."

"Oh."

"It's weird," Simon said. "Weirder now, if you two are going through the same thing."

"That," Dominic said, "is a dramatic understatement."

Mel shook her head. "I tried to do some research, but I'm hitting dead ends. Want to help? I'd love to know why this thing made me physically see a bison in my driveway."

"A *bison*?" Dominic asked.

"Yes. That was my reaction, too."

"We'd love to help," Katie offered. "We've started experimenting but haven't gotten far."

"I vote we discuss this outside school hours," Dominic said. "So, we can stop whispering. I hate whispering."

"Fair point. What about this weekend?" Mel leaned back in her chair. "I want to dig into this."

"That should work," Katie said. Dominic nodded.
"Okay. Cool."

And that was the end of it for the moment. The conversation

lapsed into banter and homework complaints, and everything was smooth.

Until the end of the period, when everyone began clearing out. Simon slipped off quietly, and Dominic made his effusive goodbyes as he hurried off to meet Jordan Mezsaros. Katie was picking up her books when Mel said, "Wait." She pulled a pen out of her jeans pocket, reached out, and grabbed Katie's left wrist.

A cold shock ran straight to the pit of Katie's stomach. She yanked her hand back, gasping, her heart already hammering. "Don't do that," she snapped, cradling her wrist in her other hand.

Mel held up both hands, her brow furrowed. "Jesus, sorry. I was just going to write my number on your hand so you can text me. So, we can update you this weekend."

"It's—it's fine." Katie blinked, fumbling to pull her phone out of her pocket. "I've got my phone. Just tell me your number." Who the hell wrote their number on their hand anymore? Her fingers shook as she entered Mel into her contacts list and took a few slow breaths.

"Are you okay?" Mel asked. "I'm sorry. I didn't mean to scare you."

"You didn't scare me." Katie cleared her throat, feeling her cheeks flush. God, this was so embarrassing. "It's fine. I just—I don't like people grabbing me. Or touching me, really. It's nothing personal—I'm sorry I snapped at you."

"No offense taken." Katie glanced up to see Mel's mouth pressed into a hard, thin line. "Well, yeah, I gotta go." And she left without another word.

Katie watched her leave and took a few more breaths, calming herself down. She tucked her hands inside her long sleeves and squeezed her eyes shut for a second. It was no big deal. It wasn't.

It wasn't.

Chapter 4

Despite leaving things rocky the other day, Katie's mood was bright after the twenty-minute bike ride to Mel's apartment. A good ride always perked up her spirits. She locked her bike to the bottom of the black metal stairs that zigzagged up the side of the house to the second floor as Mrs. Gunn's car pulled into the driveway, tires crunching on the gravel. She waved to Mrs. Gunn as Dominic hopped out.

"Look at that healthy glow in your cheeks," he said as they climbed the staircase. "No wonder you didn't want a ride. You're like a plant that just got watered." She rolled her eyes at him, albeit fondly, and knocked on the door.

A pale woman with shoulder-length dark hair answered, and Katie wasn't sure if she was Mel's mom or her older sister. "Hey, c'mon in. I'm Julia."

That did little to answer her question. "They're in Mel's room," Julia said. "Second door in the living room."

"Thanks, Mrs.—Julia." Dominic gave a cheeky salute. Julia laughed.

Mel's room was simple—bed in the corner, dresser covered in trays of rocks and gemstones, empty coffee cups nearly crowding a laptop off the desk. A bass guitar leaned against another corner, and a bookshelf was stuffed with paperbacks and thick reference books.

"Make yourselves at home," Mel said, digging in one of her dresser drawers. "My mom's leaving for work in a minute, so we'll be able to talk." Simon was already sitting at the foot of the bed, his back against the wall and long legs stretched out. Katie sat on the carpet with Dominic as Mel turned back to them and unrolled a large square of canvas fabric onto the floor.

"You're a genuine hobbyist," Dominic said, leaning into peer at the supplies. Magnifying glasses, square pieces of glass and white and black tiles, a handful of laminated cards.

"Yeah." Mel held out her hand. "Can I see your stones? There are a few tests we can do to figure out what they are."

Katie dropped her orange stone next to Dominic's in Mel's palm. "What sort of tests?"

"I'm better at rocks than gems. Don't trust myself to figure it out just from color and luster. That's professional shit." She held up one of the white tiles. "I'm gonna try a streak test. I can try the Chelsea filter, maybe a hardness test…" She furrowed her brow. "I could check the cleavage and fracture, but I'd have to break them."

"Don't." Katie said it before she even thought it. Dominic nodded his agreement. "It feels…"

"I get it. I wouldn't want mine to break either."

Mel's mother knocked on the doorframe and poked her head in. "Do we need anything from the store? I can stop on my way to work."

"A life purpose would be fantastic."

"They don't have that at the store. Maybe try Etsy?" She gave a little wave to the rest of them. "Have fun, kids. Don't break any windows or have any orgies." Mel gave her a thumbs-up, and she headed out.

Mel put on some music—some rock singer Katie didn't know with crunchy guitar lines—and started in on her tests. Simon picked up a dog-eared paperback from Mel's bedside table and started reading somewhere in the middle, jiggling one foot in time to the music. Dominic watched Mel work with a keen focus.

Katie wasn't great at long silences, at least not with other people. She took another look around Mel's room, tried to imagine her in here. Maybe she always put on this kind of music and played her bass along with it. It got good light—her window was big and faced the street, so nothing obscured the sun angling in against the wall. It was a good window to sit by with a cup of tea. Or, well, coffee, in Mel's case.

Around the time Mel huffed and went to dig a tiny hand-held blacklight out of her closet and shine it on Dominic's stone, Katie started scrolling through her phone. Mel was too in the zone to explain what she was doing, and unless she could learn what the process was, it wasn't holding Katie's attention.

"Yellow fluorite," Mel said, handing Dominic's stone back to him as Katie opened Instagram.

"What's that tell us?" she asked, glancing up.

"Not much yet. But at least we know what it is. Yours is trickier, Byrd, give me a minute."

Katie shrugged and went back to her phone. She swiped into her notifications—a friend request from Asha Sengupta.

Huh. Asha was a junior, too, but the only class they'd shared before this year was art class in ninth grade. All Katie really knew of her was her paintings, her appearances with the student council at assemblies, and her well-curated Instagram. Which Katie had been following for a while, admiring Asha's color-coded studyspo notes, but Asha had never requested to follow Katie's private account until now.

She was in first period history with her, though. And Asha was nice. They'd never hit it off in art class—Katie was quiet then, partly because she was bad at art and was miserable in the class, and partly because it was her first year back at public school after five years of homeschooling. She'd never really gotten back into the whole "properly making friends" thing.

It was just a social media follow. But maybe they could be friends now.

Katie approved the request, then tapped into her DMs. Asha had sent her a message, too.

"Why is Asha Sengupta DMing me?" she asked aloud.

Dominic leaned closer to peek at her phone. "Dunno."

"She's in our history class," Mel said, peering closely at Katie's stone through some hand-held tool.

"Probably something about homework." Katie opened the message, and all thought of homework vanished.

It was a picture of Asha's hand. Asha's hand holding a pale blue stone, round and flat with a hole in the middle. And beneath it, a short message: *Can we talk tomorrow?*

"No way," Dominic said.

Goosebumps prickled the back of Katie's neck. "What does she know?"

"What is it?" Simon finally shifted to the edge of the bed, leaning down to look.

Katie turned her phone so Simon and Mel could see. Mel went even paler than usual. Simon's lips parted in surprise.

"What in the genuine hell?" Katie asked.

"Ask her."

"No." Katie swiped out of the app and shoved her phone in her pocket. "I don't want to ask over text. Tomorrow morning after class."

Mel ran her fingers through her hair until it stuck out. "Well, for what it's worth, I'm pretty sure yours is fire opal. Like I thought." She held out the orange stone, and Katie took it, tucking it back in her pocket next to her phone. "But this just got—"

"Weirder."

Mel frowned and picked up her iron stone, turning it in her hand. "Well, shit, maybe she'll have answers we don't. Because I'm not getting far with this." The grumble in her voice told Katie she wasn't happy about it.

"Hey, you've gotten us farther than we were before," Katie said. "Maybe Asha's the next piece of the puzzle we need."

"Maybe."

Asha sat a few rows up from Katie in their history class. Katie tried to pay attention to the teacher the next morning, but she struggled to not stare at the back of Asha's head. Her homework had been half-assed because she could hardly think about anything except the fact that someone else had found a stone.

Her own stone had spent the night in the bowl on her windowsill again. That was its spot now, if it wasn't in her pocket, and Katie hadn't fully untangled the conflicting ways she felt about that.

The second the bell rang, she was up from her seat and at Asha's desk before Asha could even put her books back in her bag. "Hey. I got your DM."

Asha looked up. "Hi Katie." Her gaze drifted up. "Hi Mel. Can I talk to you in the hall?"

"Yeah," Mel said from above Katie's shoulder. "C'mon."

They huddled against a row of lockers. Mel stood with her back to the hall, shielding them from the rush of students. "So," she said, hands jammed in her jeans pockets. "Why'd you send Katie that picture?"

Asha's gaze danced back and forth between them. Nervousness creased between her brows. "I didn't mean to be weird. But—" She reached into the pocket of her cardigan and pulled out that pale blue stone. Katie's breath caught. "I found this a while ago. And… I thought maybe I'm just weird."

"Weird how?" Katie asked.

Asha bit her lip. "I saw you two talking that morning about Katie's stone. And I saw that it looked like mine. And then I had— I had this dream."

The first bell rang, but Katie ignored it. "About what?"

"I get really vivid dreams. I always have. And sometimes…"

She trailed off, shaking her head. "Well, in this one, you were there. And I told you how when I hold this stone, everything tastes like snow."

Katie's fingers scrabbled in her pocket, pulling out her stone. "I taste black tea," she said, staring at Asha.

Asha's gaze fell to the stone in Katie's hand. "Good," she said softly. "I'm not crazy."

"You're not crazy," Mel said. "But something weird is going on. I have one too, and so does Katie's friend." The final bell rang. Mel swore. "What lunch are you in?"

"First."

"Good. So are we. Come find us then and we can talk about this more. I gotta go, I can't be late again."

And Mel was gone, striding down the hall on her long legs so fast Katie didn't have time to say goodbye.

She met Asha's wide-eyed gaze. "Prophetic dreams?" she asked.

"I know. I know how it sounds. But it felt..." Asha smiled a hesitant smile. "It felt like it was safe to tell you."

There was something so fragile in Asha's smile. It was weird. She always seemed so pulled-together. Katie smiled back. "Meet us at lunch. We'll figure this out." And they both hurried off, late for second period.

Katie told Dominic in chemistry class because of course she did. She texted him with her phone under her desk. His eyebrows flew up, and he said "Well, shit," out loud, which made half the class snort in laughter and Mrs. Kozel level him with her best disapproving stare. Dominic clammed up but gave Katie a what-the-hell look. She could only shrug.

Until lunch, when they waved Asha over to their table.

"Welcome," Dominic said as Asha sat. "We're forming a club."

Asha raised her eyebrows. "You all have one." It wasn't a question.

Simon shook his head. "Not me."

"I do, though." Dominic leaned in closer as Asha took out her stone and set it on the table. "Do you see weird trees when you look through the hole?" She nodded, and he whistled low. "Well. How would you feel about joining our study group?"

"We're trying to figure out what they are," Mel said. "And where they came from."

"How did you find yours?" Katie asked.

Asha bit her lip, hesitating. "You would think it's weird," she said.

"Asha, we *see things* because of these stones." Dominic's voice was low as the cafeteria got more crowded. "We're not going to think anything about them is any weirder."

"Not about it. About me." With a deep breath, Asha said, "I have these dreams sometimes. About things that haven't happened yet. But then they come true." She hesitated again, looking around the table. Dominic was leaning in with his chin in his hand. Mel's brow was furrowed in concentrated attention. Simon had actually put down his pen and closed his notebook.

When Asha's wide eyes met hers, Katie nodded.

"That's how I found it. I dreamed I was swimming in the ocean. Way deeper than people can go. I couldn't see anything, but I could sense it. So, I kept swimming down until my hand touched the sand, and the stone was there. I picked it up, and then I woke up, and then…" She sighed. "It was there when I woke up."

"There where?"

"Right there in my hand."

Mel's eyebrows shot up. "And you don't think someone put it there?"

"Not after that dream." A kind of resolution passed over her face. "I know it sounds unbelievable. But I've had these dreams almost my entire life. I know how they feel, and I know when they're real. And I know this is real." Mel still looked skeptical—so did Dominic—but Simon gave a slight nod. "And when I saw Katie and Mel talking about the same kind of stones, it felt like a huge push. I know it's real, but I don't understand it. And I know I can't figure it out alone."

"I believe you," Katie said. "And I want to know what it means. We all do."

"Then let's all research." Mel leaned back in her chair. She ran her fingers through her hair and shook her head. "This shit is weird and I believe you dreamed about it, but my head doesn't go straight to—"

"Magic?" Asha offered.

"Or whatever. I'm into mineralogy and stuff, so I've figured out what the stones are all made from." She held out a hand. "Can I see?" Asha placed her stone in Mel's palm, and Mel turned it back and forth. "Maybe blue topaz? Or aquamarine? It's hard to tell just looking when these are all shaped and polished like this. I have tests at home I could do like I did for these guys." She held the stone up. "Can I borrow it? Or do you want to come by to help test?"

"I could come over," Asha said. "Is it weird that I'd rather hang onto it?"

"Pretty sure we're all starting to feel that way," Katie said.

Mel nodded, handing the stone back to Asha. "Okay. So, once this one's identified—Byrd, you're sciencey, right? You could check out the physical properties of the stones. Maybe there's some kind of reaction the minerals might have? In the right conditions?"

"Maybe." Katie nods. "I can do that."

"And I can deep dive into the folklore."

Asha lifted a hand to jump back into the discussion. "If you let me know what they all are, I can research the… um, metaphysical side. Crystals that are supposed to bring on visions and things." She shrugged when Dominic raised his eyebrows. "I know it sounds silly, but at this point…"

"No such thing as a silly idea." Dominic rubbed his hands together. "What if they're laced with something? I can Wikipedia some drugs. Maybe there's one that sets off hallucinations that are like, tied to memory."

"Drugged rocks?" Katie raised her eyebrows.

Dominic tsked his tongue. "No silly ideas."

"I'd like to help."

Katie looked over at Simon. It was the first thing he'd said since clarifying he didn't have a stone. His smile was tight, but his eyes were sincere. "The trees," she said. "That we can all see through the stones. Maybe you can try to figure out where they are. Maybe there's a certain region where trees like that grow."

"But he hasn't seen them," Dominic said.

Mel pulled her stone out of her pocket and handed it to Simon. His shoulders rose with a steadying breath; then he lifted the stone and looked through it. "Oh," he said.

"You can see it?"

"Yeah. It's… yeah."

"Do you sense anything when you hold it?" Dominic asked. "Byrd and I traded once and got some crossover sensations."

Simon furrowed his brow, lowering the stone. He was quiet again for a long moment. Then he said, "It feels… no, sounds like walking up your driveway. The gravel crunching."

Mel nodded, taking back the stone and shoving it in her jeans pocket. "Yeah. I hear that sometimes, too."

"Okay. So, Simon tries to find the trees." Dominic grinned. "You know, I like this. Coming together to solve a mystery. Feels good. Feels organic."

Rolling her eyes, Katie finally opened her lunch. "Glad we have your approval." But she smiled as she said it. Partly because it was Dominic, but partly because the progress was welcome. The closer they got to figuring this out, the better she'd feel.

Chapter 5

Mel

> *Aquamarine for sure*

Katie blinked at the message in the group chat. It took her a moment to realize Mel meant Asha's stone.

"The first rule of game night," her dad said, peering down his nose at his cards, "is no phones."

"Sorry." Katie shoved her phone back in her leggings pocket even as she felt it vibrate again.

"You can't abandon me here, Kate."

"I know, I know. Euchre is serious business."

"It *is*," Alex said. "So, keep messing up, Katie."

"Like I'd let you win."

It was her turn. She scanned her hand—she had a decent card. Setting it down, she glanced at Tracy to pass the turn along.

"Thank you," her father said. "You get to talk to Dominic all day at school. It's not so bad to talk to us while you're home."

"It wasn't Dom," Katie said. "New friend."

Her father raised his eyebrows. "That's good."

Katie gave a tight smile. She knew her dad knew she wanted more friends at school. It was still uncomfortable to talk about it. "Yeah," was all she said, and thankfully, he dropped it as the game continued.

By the time they wrapped for the night, Katie was yawning but restless. After saying her goodnights, she closed her bedroom door and opened her laptop, pulling up Google.

Aquamarine. A type of beryl—beryllium, aluminum, silicon, and oxygen. Toxic, but only when inhaled, so Asha was safe as long as she didn't start grinding the stone into powder. Katie's opal had silicon, too, but no other parallels jumped out at her. Dominic's— she checked her notes—no, fluorite was a completely different type of mineral. Different crystal structures, too. And Mel's stone was iron, which wasn't even a crystal.

Katie rubbed her eyes, frowning. Maybe she should wait until tomorrow after all. She was tired and there weren't any obvious patterns.

She pulled out her phone. It was getting late, but somebody was probably still up.

> *I'm not finding any patterns yet, but I'll keep looking*
> *Anyone having better luck?*

Mel

> *The problem w folklore is it contradicts*
> *Adder stones can protect from faeries or attract them*
> *Protect from witches or be used by them*
> *Jesus*

Dom

> *no I don't think he used them lolllll*

Katie rolled her eyes as she typed her reply.

> *So you think maybe it's fairies?*

Mel

> *No because I don't believe in faeries*
> *Personally I'm rooting for Dominic's research*

Dominic did not deign to reply. He was probably half asleep already. Katie sat back in her chair and rubbed her eyes again. It was a school night. She needed to sleep, too. The research would still be waiting for her tomorrow.

Winding down for the night was hard, though. Even once she was in her pajamas, she sat on the edge of her bed for a long while, staring at the orange stone on her windowsill.

She felt the way she felt on a clear summer day, when the golden hour rolled in and the brilliant sun shifted in dapples over her face, filtered by tree leaves. She had the urge to tip her face up towards the sun, even though it was eleven o'clock at night. And for all the nights were starting to get chillier, her hands were warm.

The stone almost glowed in the light of the streetlamps coming through the window.

She made herself lie down, and fortunately, sleep came swiftly.

In history class on Monday, Mel had dark shadows under her eyes and a large cup of gas station coffee perched on her desk. Katie sat down, raising her eyebrows at Asha, who was sitting next to her. "I thought you sat up in the front corner."

"I did, but nobody's been sitting here, and I thought it might be nice to sit together." She smoothed the skirt of her dress down her knees. "If that's okay."

"Of course."

"Thanks. And thanks for letting me sit with you at lunch. This is the first year since seventh grade I haven't had lunch with Malia and Rosie."

Katie raised an eyebrow. "Malia Headley?"

Asha nodded. "And Rosie Novak. My best friends."

Katie smiled until she heard Mel sigh. She twisted in her seat to see Mel hunched over her phone. "You okay?"

Mel made a noncommittal noise in response and shoved her phone in her pocket. "Up late researching. I'll show you guys at lunch."

And she did. Everyone had barely settled by the time Mel had her phone out and the browser app open. "Most of this is bullshit," she said, "but there's some interesting bits." She swiped into a new tab. "Most sources I've found say they're used for protection. Some say if the stone breaks, it means it did its job protecting you."

"From what?" Simon asked.

"Usually, faeries or witches or the evil eye. Maybe just general bad luck. Hell if I know. Also, more relevant." She switched to another tab. "Looking through the holes in them can let you see into other realms."

Katie caught Simon's eye across the table. "Have you figured out if those trees are real yet?"

He shook his head. "Nothing so far. Similar ones, but not exact."

"And the mist is weird," Dominic added. "It's purple."

"So, maybe it's not a real place," Katie said. "Maybe it's something—"

"A fae realm?" Asha made a face. "I mean, I believe in a lot of things, but I don't know…"

"No. But what if it's a total illusion? Dom, you're trying to figure out if there's some kind of drug involved, right?"

Mel took another long swig of coffee. "What possible reason could someone have for doing that, though."

"I don't know, Mel, it's just an idea."

"Well, if someone *did* make these to mimic adder stone folklore, this might be helpful." She ran her fingers through her hair, making it stick up in places. "There are trends across the sources. They're supposed to aid in some kind of second sight, and they're supposed to be protective."

Katie reached into her bag, brushing her fingers against her stone. The now-familiar thrum of warmth ran up her arm, and while she didn't outright smell bread baking, she felt an echo of the satisfaction she got whenever she pulled a well-risen loaf from the oven.

"Maybe that's why we're connecting to them," Asha said.

"Besides all the personal associations, they make sense to us. Maybe we're supposed to like them. To feel protected by them."

Mel mussed her hair again and looked down the table at Dominic. "Have you gotten anything solid yet?"

"Not solid." He crumpled his napkin. "Our lord and savior Wikipedia suggests it's definitely nothing with deliriants or dissociatives."

"Meaning?"

"Deliriants make you delirious. Like all confused and agitated. Dissociatives—"

"Make you dissociate?" Asha asked.

"Yeah. Kind of out of body, in a trance. And none of us have had anything like that happen, right?" A soft chorus of no's and heads shaking. "But I haven't found anything about a drug that like, specifically targets memories that make you happy."

Katie raised her eyebrows. "Huh. Yeah, I guess that is what the sensory stuff is associated with."

"It is for me," Asha said. "Either good memories or comforting things, or things that just feel like home. Like I'll hear water running for a bath or smell my mom's rasgulla."

"And my dad's tea," Katie added.

"Bison comfort you?" Dominic asked Mel. "You said you saw a bison." Mel shrugged, her arms folded.

But as the rest of the week passed, even Mel's skepticism and Simon's caution waned when their lines of research weren't coming to fruition. When Asha shared her findings on supposed metaphysical properties of the stones, the skepticism was minimal compared to before.

Asha 🪲

> *Yellow fluorite is good for understanding/logic, cooperation/harmony, & positive outlook*

Dom

    kdjcjfjx asha that's me to a t

Asha

    Fire opal is for passion, independence, moving past limitations, & healing

Dom

    byrd byrd byrd byrd
    do yours asha

Asha

    Haha
    Patience, sensitivity, speaking your truth
    It's kind of like Mel's folklore research, the meanings can vary, but these are pretty consistent ones.

Dom

    admittedly don't know you as well as I know byrd
    but that sounds right on

Katie smirked at her phone as she sat on a bench in the metro parks, taking a breather before heading home from her bike ride.

    You're not wrong, it's all pretty accurate
    Kind of like astrology though isn't it?
    Vague enough that you can say it's just like you

Dom

    idk byrd I think im being swayed by the metaphysics
    esp bc I can't find a drug that matches what's happening

Asha 🐞

> *Oh it's definitely not perfect, but you never know what might help!*
>
> *Iron was a little trickier to track down. Fewer witchy websites talk about it, haha*
>
> *But in general: protection, resilience, honor, determination*

Mel didn't respond. Katie was getting to know her better, and she guessed that meant it hit closer to home than Mel wanted to admit.

She swiped her phone open again and reread Asha's words. *Passion. Independence.* She wouldn't argue that.

Moving past limitations. Sure. She liked to find better ways to do things, liked to solve tricky problems.

Healing.

Katie swallowed.

She climbed back on her bike and started pedaling towards home. That one wasn't wrong, either. But she didn't want to dwell on it too much right now.

Simon hadn't piped up in the conversation. He didn't contribute much to the group chat unless it was specifically sharing his research. Katie hoped he didn't feel like he was butting in or anything. He might not have one of the weird stones, but any help was welcome. Besides, he was nice, if super reserved. She'd like to be friends.

Back home, as she put her bicycle away in the garage, her hand fell to her hip reflexively, reaching to touch the orange stone in her pocket, but nothing was there.

Her brow furrowed. Had she left the stone in her bag? She thought she'd brought it.

Once inside, she made a beeline for her room to check for it. Her father gave a hello as she passed through the dining room, where he had his laptop and papers to grade. "Kate, hold on a minute."

Twisting her mouth in frustration, she stopped. "What's up?"

There, held between her father's thumb and forefinger, was her stone. "I think you dropped this. Found it in the front hall." He smiled. "Wouldn't want you to lose your new trinket." And then, playfully, he held it up and looked through the center.

"No—" Katie's heart leapt, and she lunged forward. She couldn't let him see—

But he lowered his hand, puzzled. "I'm giving it back," he said. He held it out to her, all ease and normalcy, like he hadn't just seen things that weren't there through its hole. "Is this special?"

He hadn't. He was calm, except for the tinge of concern at her outburst. He hadn't seen anything.

"I like it a lot," she blurted. "Sorry. Weird mood." And she held out her hand, letting him place the stone in her palm.

"Understood. Believe it or not, I remember being a teenager."

"Right." She closed her fingers safely around the stone. "I'm gonna go finish my homework."

"On a Friday night? Okay, maybe I don't remember it as well as I thought."

She laughed, only half-forced, then turned and hurried through the living room and upstairs, heart beating hard in her chest.

The second she was in her room, she pulled out her phone and opened the group chat.

> *Okay so my dad was just goofing around and looked*
> *through my stone and he didn't see anything*
> *Simon you're sure you haven't found one?*
> *Why can you see the trees but he couldn't?*

For a solid two minutes—Katie watched the minutes click past on the screen—nobody replied. And then:

Simon
> *I was going to text you all as soon as I calmed down.*

And then a picture. Of a greenish, flat round stone lying in his hand, a perfect hole right through its center.

Chapter 6

Saturday morning was bright and clear, and Katie woke with Skimbleshanks curled against her shoulder the way he liked, Batty stretched out along the side of the bed, and Peaches a softly snoring lump between Katie's feet. "I'm gonna lose my socks, kitties," she muttered as she wriggled free, but Peaches kept snoring.

Now that Simon found a stone, the plan was to get together at Mel's, all bring their stones, and see if they could put their heads together and finally make progress.

But there were new messages from Asha from like seven in the morning.

Asha 🐞

> *Mel, is your mom home? If she is, we should meet somewhere else*
> *I had a dream last night. It gave me an idea. But I think we need privacy*

Mel 🔪

> *Yeah she's off work today*
> *How about the metroparks?*
> *Rockpoint's usually pretty empty*

A quick breakfast, then. The metro parks were farther away than Mel's place.

Downstairs, her father sat at the kitchen table, lingering over his tea and the newspaper. "Slept in?" Katie asked, rummaging in the cupboard and fridge for things to make breakfast. It was already past nine o'clock and his breakfast dishes were usually in the sink by eight.

"For once. It was fantastic. You're already dressed?"

"Yeah, I'm going to the metro parks with some friends today." She popped some bread into the toaster and got out the peanut butter. "Any fun plans for your Saturday?"

"Tracy and I are having dinner at the Paskos' house, remember? Can you be home by six or so to keep an eye on your brother?"

"Yeah, no problem."

"Thanks, Kate." He kissed the top of her head on his way out of the kitchen. "Have fun. Be safe."

It was perfect September weather when Katie headed out on her bicycle. The sunshine and the breeze felt amazing on her face. It was a long ride, but she liked a long ride, and the sun made it all the better.

She rode past the metro park's entrance sign, staying careful around the turns in the wooded road when the sidewalks disappeared, until she got to the parking lot at the Rockpoint picnic area. Another bicycle was already locked in the bike rack; across the green lawn, Asha waved to Katie from a picnic table.

They were alone. Most of the cars driving through the parks headed for trail entrances for all the morning joggers and dog-walkers. Katie smiled as she climbed on top of the table next to Asha, their feet resting on the bench. "Well, this is exciting."

Asha smiled and ducked her head. "Something like that."

"So, you had another one of those dreams?"

She nodded. "I don't know if we'll make any difference. But I think it's worth trying. It felt promising. Like a push in one definite direction."

Over in the lot, a beat-up red sedan pulled into a parking spot. Mel and Simon sat in the front seats. "Which direction?"

"Maybe the craziest one."

The car doors opened and slammed shut, and Simon and Mel strode across the grass. Mrs. Gunn's car rolled into the parking lot, pausing long enough for Dominic to climb out and say some cheerful goodbye, then drove off as he jogged to catch up to the others.

"Asha," Katie said, "if you're crazy, we all are." And she looked over at Asha, at the tentative hope in her wide, dark eyes. "But I don't think we are."

"Me neither."

"Morning." Mel set her coffee cup on the picnic table and rubbed her nose with the back of her hand.

"Is it time to alter our perception of reality?" Dominic asked.

"Again?" added Simon.

Katie peered at him. "You okay?" He was always quiet, but there was a new tension in his face.

He shrugged. "I'm not sure. It's overwhelming."

Katie took her stone out of her pocket, rubbing her thumb across its smooth surface. There it was, warm in her chest: the expansive happiness. "What's yours made of?"

"Moss agate," Mel said.

Asha nodded. "Stability and balance. Healing. Growth."

Simon turned to Asha. "So, what do we do now?"

"I don't know if it'll work. But the dream…" Asha trailed off, seeming to search for words. "It's hard to explain. And I know it sounds vague. Dreams don't translate into reality, and intuition isn't methodical. So, I can't give you proof. All I can tell you is that I believe if we look through our stones and say this phrase, we'll finally get answers." She shrugged. "And even if it's silly, I want to try."

"What do we need to say?" Katie asked.

"While you're looking through the center," Asha said. "Say 'draw me through the veil.'"

Mel shifted her weight. "Sounds like fae stuff." Asha shrugged again. Mel sighed. "It can't hurt to try, I guess."

"'Draw me through,'" Dominic said. "Doesn't that sound like we'll—"

"—get drawn somewhere?" Katie finished. Nervousness pricked at her, and she wouldn't be nervous unless part of her believed it. But hell, her stone already made her see and taste and feel things that weren't there. She was finding her ability to believe rapidly expanding.

"Maybe we're supposed to go there," Dominic said. "Like— whoever finds the magic stones is supposed to go to the forest."

"It's worth trying," Simon said. "If we get answers."

And Dominic nodded. Mel nodded. Katie took a deep breath, held up her stone, and looked through the middle. Out of the corners of her eyes, she saw her friends doing the same, but straight ahead all she saw were those trees and that mist right through the middle of her stone.

"On three?" Dominic suggested, pushing his voice bright.

"One," said Mel.

"Two," said Asha.

Katie wasn't sure who said *three*. All she had room for was the view through the center of her stone.

"Draw me through the veil," she whispered.

The stone thrummed against her fingertips. Like a string being plucked and vibrating along its length, something in her tugged or snapped.

She only had a half second to notice it before the picnic lawn was gone.

For a moment, everything was warm and dark and weightless. Then Katie blinked, and she was kneeling on the ground. Not the same ground. Instead of grass, a springy sort of growth cushioned her knees.

She lifted her head, the smooth edge of her stone pressing into her clenched fingers. The patchy-barked trees. The almost-purple mist hanging over the trees.

Her breath caught in her chest.

"Byrd."

Katie tore her gaze from the mist toward Mel's voice. She stood over by Simon with one hand on his back. He looked winded. "Come on." Mel's voice was strained, but even. "We need to stay together."

Across from her, Dominic stood up, his flannel askew and his eyes dazed. Asha had a hand on his elbow, guiding him to Mel and Simon.

Katie forced a slow, deep breath into her lungs and joined them.

"Well," Dominic said, with almost-convincing cheerfulness, "guess it worked, Asha."

"Maybe we can get back if we look through again," she murmured. Her cheeks were dusky with an uncomfortable blush, her gaze downcast.

Dominic's tone softened. "It's not your fault."

"We're here anyway," Mel said. "Unfortunately, who knows where the hell 'here' is."

The trees were tall, the branches and the mist high above them, but even though there was plenty of light, Katie couldn't see the sky. "No birds," she said. "Do you hear that?" No birdsong, no rustling in the undergrowth. No undergrowth, actually—just neat, close-growing groundcover clear through the woods.

"Do you think we're in any danger?" Dominic asked. "This place isn't exactly great for hiding."

Katie rubbed her thumb against her stone, furrowing her brow. "Why aren't I scared?"

"Because you're Byrd."

"Shut up, Dom, I'm serious." She glanced around at the others. "I'm freaked out because I have no idea how we got here or how we'll get home. Don't get me wrong, I'm…" She took another deep breath, fighting the tightness threatening to clench her chest. "I'm worried. But I'm not *scared*."

"It feels safe," Simon said. "Whether or not it should."

Mel's jaw set hard as she stared off into the trees. "I hate that you're right."

"Is it these?" Asha opened her hand, revealing her stone. "It's always made me peaceful. It still does, even though we're… here."

Mel ran her fingers through her hair and sighed. "Look, I get it. You're saying everything I'm thinking. But we still don't know where the hell we are or why these rocks brought us here. I vote we try Asha's theory and see if we can get back home. If that doesn't work, we need a plan."

From somewhere in the trees, a deep voice said, "We have a plan."

Now fear crackled through Katie's veins. Because the voice was deep and immense and did not belong to any of them.

Mel swore, Dominic swore, even Simon swore, and Katie whirled around to see the figure who appeared between the trees. Appeared was the right word because there was no way this— person? being?—could have sneaked up on them. He was huge, more like a mountain than a person, towering and broad and solid.

"Who are you?" Mel's voice cut hard. "Where are we?"

The person—though was he a person? He, or they, was way too massive to be human—regarded her silently. Katie's mind and gut railed against each other. Because her mind saw this person, with his heavy plated armor, at least ten feet tall, how he appeared out of nowhere, how he felt more part of the landscape than a person—her mind took that all in and screamed this was not normal.

But her gut. Her intuition. It wasn't afraid. It said stay, wait, listen, learn.

The juxtaposition put her on edge. Judging by the tension in everyone else's shoulders, they felt the same.

"I am Skiron," the being said. "And you have answered the call."

Something fluttered in Katie's palm as she held her stone. "These things," she said. "We found them. *We* found them."

He—Skiron—nodded. "And they have brought you here."

"Why?" Mel lifted her chin, her eyes sharp. "And where is here?"

Katie glanced over at Mel. In profile, her brow furrowed over the long bump of her nose, the serious line of her lips. It was probably stupid of her to be so bold to this mountain of a being, but her confidence was comforting.

"This is the veil between worlds," Skiron said. His voice was so deep and resonant, Katie almost felt it rumble through the ground into the bones of her feet. "And you have been brought here to help." His gaze didn't leave Mel, and as she stared back, her face softened. "It is not unwise to be cautious. Follow me, and I will explain." He turned and walked into the trees.

"We could still try to go home," Asha offered as they watched Skiron retreat. But she didn't sound like she wanted to.

"I want answers," Katie said. "That was the whole idea, right?"

Mel nodded. "We need them. Come on." She turned and followed Skiron into the woods.

"What happened there?" Katie murmured as they fell into step behind Mel.

"I'm not sure," Asha said. "But something did happen between them."

"Do you think it's actually okay?"

"I trust Mel," Simon said. "Either she's right, or she's being fooled. If she's right, I'm with her. If she's being fooled, I'll watch her back." And his long legs carried him past them, catching up to her.

They walked through the trees, past scattered ponds and pools of water. When they reached a clearing with a ring of tree stumps in the center, Skiron waited between them and the stumps. "You may sit if you like," he said. "I have much to tell you."

None of them moved.

Skiron's broad, square jaw was unmoving, but his forehead creased. "If it will make you more receptive, I will stand farther away." He strode to the other side of the clearing, right against the opposite edge of the trees.

Mel glanced at the others, then walked to the stumps. Katie followed right behind, and the others joined them.

They sat. Katie crossed her arms with her elbows on her knees, tucked into herself, and waited for Skiron to speak, every inch of her awake and alert.

"This is the veil between worlds," said Skiron. "I am one of its guardians."

"Okay, but what does that *mean*?" The words were out of Katie's mouth before she could think it might not be wise to sass a… guardian.

If Skiron was fazed, he didn't show it. "Earth is not the only world. There is another existing alongside it. This veil is the space between them, and we as the guardians ensure the worlds remain balanced."

"Whoa whoa whoa. Wait." Dominic leaned forward, eyes flashing. "You're talking parallel universes? Like for real?"

Skiron's eyebrows raised slightly. "That is a way to describe it. If that allows you to understand, then yes."

"This is wild. *Wild*." His voice rose with excitement. "There are theories—quantum physics—but—*seriously*?"

A confused crease formed between Skiron's eyebrows. It was almost funny. "I am serious."

Dominic sat back, biting his lip like he wanted to keep asking questions.

"It is true," Skiron said, "that sentient beings of both worlds are unaware of the existence of the other. This is as it should be. The worlds exist by remaining in balance. For beings of Earth to cross into Harath, or Harath to Earth, would ultimately create great imbalance." He sat straighter, if that was even possible. "We guardians tend that balance, and its health is reflected in the veil." He lifted one massive hand, gesturing at the mist curling around the treetops. "As you can see, the balance is not secure."

"The mist isn't supposed to be there?" Mel asked.

"No. Sometimes one world falls farther from the balance point than the other. When this happens, tears appear in the fabric between the worlds. They are small things, and we guardians repair them, among our other duties." His expression had been serious from the moment he appeared, but now it turned grave. "Now on Earth there are larger tears, growing into rifts. We have tried, but we cannot close these larger rifts. This mist has appeared as a symptom of that failure."

Softly, Simon asked, "Is that our fault?" Katie was surprised he'd asked a direct question, but also didn't get what he meant. She wasn't the only one looking at him in confusion, so he clarified, "Not the five of us specifically. But... humans. We're sort of messing up the planet."

"Try massively messing up the planet," Dominic muttered.

Skiron shook his head. "No. The humans' impact on Earth's climate has impacted our work as well, but it is not the source of these new rifts."

Katie turned her orange stone over and over in her hand. "Well... what happens if the worlds fall totally out of balance?"

When Skiron turned his gaze on her, it was heavy. "Destruction." She shivered. The words coiled in her gut. "It begins in ways familiar to you. Extremes in your weather. Then it would become stranger. Your waters would grow poisonous, your air insufficient. And if the rifts tear wide enough and the balance is lost, all things will break apart and crumble until nothing remains."

"Oh," Asha said softly.

"So, it is important that we maintain the balance and close the rifts."

Mel stood up. Jamming her hands in her hoodie pockets, she strode across the circle of stumps, squared her shoulders, and stared up at Skiron. "You said you can't close these new rifts."

He stared back at her. Katie watched them and saw whatever passed between them earlier cross Mel's face again. "That is correct. And that is why we seek your help."

"What the hell can we do?" Mel's voice broke in a way that twisted in Katie's chest. "We're just kids."

"You are more," Skiron said. "You found the sightstones. You used them to travel here. That demonstrates your worth to be vessels."

On Katie's other side, Asha tentatively raised her hand, like in school, then sheepishly let it fall. "Vessels for what?"

"For the guardians," Skiron said.

A strong pulse of warmth blossomed from the stone in Katie's hands and seeped into her veins, coming to sit in her chest.

"We believe if we channel our power through a being of Earth, it will tie us more firmly to the energy of Earth. This may give us a greater chance to close these rifts. We ask you to be these vessels and help us restore the balance of the worlds."

"What would we do?" Katie fidgeted with her sleeves, pulling them down over her hands. "If we become your vessels?" She caught Dominic's gaze. His green eyes were huge.

"When we discover a new rift, we will call upon you. We will take you wherever on Earth that rift is. There, we will use you as our focal point through which we channel our power. We are incorporeal by nature, which will allow this channeling." He gestured at his enormous form. "This body is one I chose and created for the purpose of meeting you, to be more relatable to humans."

Dominic made a weird noise in his throat. The twitching at the corners of his mouth told Katie he was holding in a laugh.

Yeah. There wasn't much relatable about Skiron's mountain-like physique.

"So, we'd be… tools?" Simon asked. "Puppets?"

"No. You should retain control of your body and mind at all times. We believe we will simply pass our strength through you as a focal point."

"It sounds like you're not sure," Simon said.

"That is true. We have never done this before, and we cannot guarantee it will be successful. But the rifts must be closed, and we believe this to be the best chance."

Mel sighed heavily. When Katie glanced over, she saw Mel's eyes were closed. "And this is real," Mel said. "This is actually happening."

"You know it is, Mel." Hearing Skiron say one of their names jolted Katie. It felt more real.

Mel turned back to the rest of them. Her eyes, the set of her jaw, were resolute. She's already decided, Katie realized. She's already decided she's going to do this.

"How does it work?" Asha asked. "What would it feel like?"

"We intend to align our own power with earthly reflections of it. So, we will use forces of Earth."

Dominic raised his eyebrows. "Such as?"

"Such as the wind, or the energy of growing plants. Each guardian will draw allies from earthly forces which resonate most closely to our own power, and then we will channel that power through you."

Katie fixated on Mel's steady expression. "Okay." Dominic and Simon and Asha all looked at Katie. "We have to, don't we?" she asked, and Mel's gaze flicked over to her, too. "If someone doesn't help them the world's literally going to end. At least we can try."

Skiron nodded. "All the guardians are prepared to meet you and attempt to seal the first rift. If all goes well, we will continue the arrangement."

"What the hell?" Dominic stood, grinning, his eyes bright. "Like Byrd said, fate of the world and all that. Plus, I kind of want to see what these other guardians are like."

Asha nodded, her hands twisted in her lap. "I'm nervous. But it feels right. The way my dream did."

From across the circle, Mel stared at Simon, her eyes soft. After a moment he said, "Alright. Let's do it."

Skiron returned to the edge of the circle. "The sightstones you found will be your link to your guardian. To activate the link, you will hold your sightstone, speak the name of your guardian, and ask them to cross the veil to you." He lifted one enormous hand and pointed at Asha. "The guardian who has chosen you is Zephyrus." His finger moved to Simon. "Yours is Ophion." And then Dominic: "Aerie."

His gaze, and his hand, landed on Katie. "Your guardian," he said, "is Nyth."

When he said the name, the stone—the sightstone—thrummed in Katie's hand. She took in a sharp breath, feeling more awake. The stone was warm, and she barely registered Skiron looking back at Mel and saying, "I, Skiron, am your guardian."

Katie looked down at her orange sightstone. It flickered in the light. It reminded her of laughter. It reminded her of—something. Something on the tip of her tongue. Something she could shape with that single syllable.

"Nyth," she whispered. "Nyth, cross the veil to me."

She was washed in a mix of sensations when the name crossed her tongue—sun-warmed grass and cartwheeling and the chatter of a hunting cat, sunlight flashing between trees—before the veil fell away around her. She passed through somewhere dark and hot. It was almost like when they traveled to the veil, but this was faster, a tugging in her gut and a sense of being yanked off her feet. Katie cried out, but the sound didn't go anywhere, and the next thing she knew something hit hard against her left shoulder and hip.

Her fingers pressed into the grass as she blinked her eyes open. No, not grass. That clover-like stuff in the veil. She was lying on her left side on the ground in the veil, but not in the circle of stumps. Somewhere else, where the trees grew closer together.

"Sorry."

Katie yelped, whirling around.

"Sorry!" the voice said again. A person—being—stood not far from her, hands on his hips and shoulders at an easy slope. "That was rough. Haven't done that for anyone but myself before. I pulled you to me instead of me going to you."

Katie stood up slowly, pressing her palms against her

thighs. Her gaze flicked over his weird clothes and weird hair, a true bright red that didn't seem to know which way it wanted to grow. But he smiled at her, a wide, easy smile on a golden face, and when he met her eyes, her breath caught.

It was like looking in a mirror. His eyes were exactly like hers.

"It's you," she said.

"Well, yes. I'm me."

"No, it's—" Katie held up her sightstone. "It's you. Nyth."

His smile broadened into a full-on grin. "Yes. That's interesting, hearing my name out loud in a human voice." Nyth looked down at his long hands, turning them back and forth. "Is this okay? It's been a long time since I took corporeal form. I tried to make something kind of like you."

"Yeah," she said. Her chest felt strange. "You're—you're really different from Skiron."

"Of course, I am. You're really different from Mel, aren't you?" His brow furrowed. "What's wrong? You're tense. Aren't you having fun?"

"Um, fun isn't exactly the word I'd—"

"I've been waiting so long to meet you. I wanted you to have fun."

"It's—I'm just overwhelmed."

Nyth tilted his head. "Really?"

Was he serious? "Yes, really." Hot irritation bubbled in her chest. "An hour ago, I didn't even know all this existed. Plus, I have to what, literally save the world? It's a lot to process." Her legs were still shaky, too, and her shoulder was sore. "And you pulled me here really roughly."

"It won't always be like that." Nyth stepped in closer. Katie realized he was almost the exact same height as her. Shorter than most boys. But then, he wasn't a boy. Wasn't even human. "I promise. I'll make sure I take care of you next time."

Something in his face really was familiar. Not just his eyes that looked like hers. Something else—a warm, friendly flicker.

She'd met him before. This was just the first time he had a face, name, body. She'd met him that day she'd picked up an orange stone from a sunbeam.

"What are you?" she asked.

"I'm Nyth. A guardian of the veil. Didn't Skiron tell you—"

"Yeah, he told us that. But what are you, really?"

And he seemed to catch her meaning. His expressive face shifted from puzzled to the easiest kind of smile. Nyth turned on his heel and strolled off in an arc, weaving through the thin trees around them. "An incorporeal being," he said, his voice ringing clear in the forest of the veil. "Old as the worlds themselves. I can be anywhere, and parts of me can be in more than one place. Making things happen. Making things move. Touching everything like sunlight." His pacing brought him back around to her, and he leaned in, grinning. "I always come back to sunlight," he said. "The sun and I are best friends."

Katie surprised herself with an easy smile of her own. "Me too."

He beamed at her. "That's good. Sunlight and sparks, that's us. And fire." Her skin prickled cold at the suggestion, but he rushed on. "Fire is the earthly force I connect with best. It's how we're going to seal the rifts."

Katie's tongue felt heavy, her mouth dry. "No." Nyth wrinkled his nose like she'd offended him, but she pushed on. "I'm not going to—play with fire."

"Not play with it. Use it. Channel it to do good."

"Fire isn't *good*." A familiar feeling was crawling up from the back of her mind, a kind of electric haze that warned her she'd be hearing screaming metal soon if she went too far into this. The sounds of the crash were always the first thing to resurface from the deep pool of trauma before panic wracked her whole.

She took a deep breath, trying to calm her growing anxiety. He didn't get it. "You guys aren't human. You guardians. But you know about human emotions?" Frowning, Nyth nodded. "You know about fear?"

"I don't think I've ever felt it. But I know what it is."

"Sometimes, humans get so scared of something they can't go near it without losing it." He didn't react, so she clarified. "Freaking out. Getting so scared they can't move or think."

"Oh." His hands landed on his hips. "And that's how you feel about fire?"

She nodded.

Nyth let out a huge, blustering sigh. "I don't want to make you scared. But that's the best way I know to close the rifts. We don't have much time to waste."

Katie's heart was in her throat. She tugged the ends of her sleeves down over her hands. "It's—it's really that bad?"

"The longer rifts stay open, the greater the risk to the worlds."

Squeezing her eyes shut, she tried to breathe evenly. They were talking about saving the world. She would survive a panic attack. She'd done it plenty of times before. The world wouldn't survive falling apart.

"Okay." There was no hiding the tremor in her voice. "We can try it. But I can't—I can't promise anything."

Nyth tilted his head. "It won't hurt you. The fire I use. I promise you won't get burned."

She shivered. Her left arm prickled.

He held out one hand to her, palm up. "Are you ready?"

Katie looked down at his hand. He had no creases in his palm.

She flicked her gaze back up to meet his. He smiled, carefree and confident as anything.

All she could do was her best.

She took his hand.

Chapter 7

She passed again through the emptiness. Nyth was true to his word—she landed neatly on her feet, blinking as the world rushed back.

They'd arrived in the middle of a wind-swept plain, all tall grasses and wildflowers, and Nyth stood at her side. It was beautifully sunny, but Katie's pulse was too quick, her breath too shallow. She tried to let the sun's warmth melt away the fear and turned with the wind, catching sight of Dominic. He was grinning, and in front of him was a tiny sprite-like person with a round face.

Dominic saw Katie and waved, still beaming. "Hey Byrd! You made it!"

"Yeah." That was all she could manage while fighting down the panic skittering under her skin.

"Did you see Aerie? She's so cool."

The tiny person—Aerie, the guardian who'd chosen Dominic as a vessel—turned her grin to Nyth. "This is amazing," she said. Her voice was stronger than Katie would've expected for her size. "Look at you!"

Nyth laughed, clear and bright. "I know! I'm like a human."

"Did you manifest a circulatory system?"

"No, that was too much work."

Aerie grinned. "Then not really like a human."

"Where's everyone else?" The question tumbled out of Katie, fueled by nerves. Dominic pointed over her shoulder.

Katie turned. There was Asha, further back on the plain. Katie only registered her for a moment before her focus locked on the person next to her. Zephyrus—it must be Asha's guardian Zephyrus—looked startlingly like Asha. The same heart-shaped face, round dark eyes, curved body. But changed, somehow. Elevated. It was how Asha might look in twenty years if she grew with perfect grace and a little ethereal otherworldliness. And Zephyrus was so tall, a couple heads taller than Asha, with hair that rippled down much longer than Asha's and a white dress that floated around her, the colors in its sheer hem shifting from white to gray to blue to green and to white again.

Zephyrus smiled, more with her eyes than her mouth. "Hello." Her voice reminded Katie of bells. "I am so glad we can all be together, now."

Nyth huffed. "Show-off."

Zephyrus moved smoothly as she and Asha walked closer to the others. Asha glanced up at Zephyrus a couple times, glowing with adoration. "I didn't expect to feel good about this," she said to Katie when they stopped, "but I do now. Don't you?"

Katie tried to smile. She wasn't sure she succeeded.

"It's so weird," Dominic said, still grinning. "Completely weird."

Katie wasn't surprised he was loving this. And Asha—she radiated peace. Guilt and jealousy tangled in Katie's chest as cold sweat prickled on her back.

Nyth clucked his tongue, catching her attention. "Business time," he said, "Skiron's here."

They turned. There was Mel, tall and sinewy against the wide sky, but next to her was Skiron, making her look tiny. He was like a monolith out here on the plains. "We need to start," Mel said. "Can't let this rift thing sit around forever. Where's Simon?"

Katie felt the ground tremble. She wondered fleetingly if it was the rift, but then the grasses near them grew taller, wrapping around one another in a tall, thick pillar of greenery, which split open as

Simon climbed out, disheveled and bewildered. The grasses and leaves wove together again, and Katie thought she almost saw a face among them as a voice that seemed to come from everywhere said, *We are here.*

"Thank you, Ophion," Skiron said. The bower of grasses receded into the earth again. Apparently Ophion wasn't taking a human-like form. "Vessels, there are several rifts. The others have not fully opened and will be sealed in time. For now, we will show you the rift that has already broken through the worlds."

He raised his enormous hands, palms facing ahead. Katie followed the direction of his arms and felt her gut shiver and twist when the air seemed to open and this—thing, the rift, appeared. It cut a jagged shape across the air, but it wasn't hanging in the air. It was like the air itself had split open and this purple-gray shuddering mass was seething through it. It made every fine hair on Katie's body stand on end. Asha gasped. Mel swore softly.

"It is an abomination," Zephyrus said. "We attempted to close it on our own, but it defied us. This has never happened before, and so we ask your help."

"Of course," Asha said, distantly.

"We will resume our incorporeal bodies," said Skiron. "We will still communicate with you, and through the sightstones you have, we will channel our abilities to close this rift."

One by one, they blinked out of sight around Katie and Dominic and the others. Katie kept staring at the rift. It was time. She had to use fire. Let Nyth use fire, really, but through her. Her heart thundered against her ribs as her palms started to sweat.

Nyth turned, stepping into her line of vision. "Hey," he said. "Do you trust me?"

A golden glow hummed through her veins at his words. She wished it was enough to soothe the anxiety. "I want to," she said. He smiled, then winked out of view. "You feel… familiar, in a way," she whispered.

She almost heard his clear laugh in her ear. *That's because we're made of the same stuff,* he said. His voice wasn't audible to her ears or a clear voice in her mind. It was almost like she thought the words herself, except she knew she hadn't thought them—they had dropped in from somewhere outside of her. *Ooh, that's weird,* she thought, and she felt a ripple from Nyth that reminded her of laughter. *So, you're telepathic, too?*

Not exactly, he said. *But that's close enough. Now let's focus.* Her heart leapt in a sick way, and maybe he could tell, because he added, *Remember, it's not going to hurt you.*

He could say that all he wanted. It wouldn't make her legs any less wobbly.

Mel and Simon walked forward, closer to the rift. They stood side by side and lifted their sightstones, palms facing the writhing gash in the air. Katie watched as Mel squared her shoulders and Simon furrowed his brow. Nothing shot out of their hands, no big bursts of light or anything flashy like that; but as they concentrated, thick vines grew up from the ground and started looping around the edges of the rift. Where they bound it, its shifting edges stilled.

It took a while, but Katie couldn't look away. It was as bizarre as the rift itself, watching the vines move of their own accord until the entire edge of the rift was bound.

The swirling purple-gray mass inside the rift shuddered and moved, pressing against one side of the vine border. It bulged, like it would break—but a crystallization began forming around the edges of the rift. Where it formed, the rift stopped its creeping spread. The swirling colors still pressed against the edges, but the crystal stayed unmoving.

Focus now, Nyth said. *We all play a different part in sealing this because we're all good at different things. They're holding it still so we can clear it. You and me, we're hanging back until the end. So, focus. Bring up all that heat in you.*

Katie thought she knew what he meant. She closed her eyes and turned her attention inward, feeling that soft warmth that glowed in her chest. The warmth was soothing, like summer sunshine. Heat without fire was good, was comforting, like baking bread and snuggling under blankets. Maybe they could use heat instead of fire. She could ask Nyth.

A huge sigh made her open her eyes. The rift was completely closed in by the crystallized border, vines still anchoring it to the ground. Mel was sweating visibly, and Simon looked frail, bending over with his hands on his knees. "Keep it moving," Mel said.

Dominic stepped into Katie's field of vision. He furrowed his brow in a moment of intense concentration, then grinned as a gust of air puffed out around him, ruffling his hair. At the same time, the shifting gray and purple colors in the rift blended together until it was a solid, unmoving gray. It looked brittle, now.

One step closer. Katie's head started to swim. She struggled to swallow with a dry throat, tried not to let the panic rise too high. She had to do this. She had to.

Asha came in next, lifting her sightstone and closing her eyes. Katie watched as the heat grew under her skin. She felt like everything in her that was Katie was evaporating and becoming nothing but heat swirling inside the shell of her body. Maybe it could even evaporate the fear. Maybe she could surrender to it.

Asha was still for a long moment. Then she let out a breath, and Katie saw a point in the center of the rift flicker. It rippled out along the solid surface, shimmering, until the solid gray cleared like mud settling out of water. When it did, the rift stopped being weird colors and became a window into the veil. Katie could see those patchy trees and the mist.

They've brought the edge of Earth and the edge of the veil back together, Nyth told her. *Now we seal it closed for good.*

It was time. Heat rushed in her ears. Her knees wobbled. She raised her sightstone with shaking hands.

I don't want to, she thought. Not at Nyth, because it didn't matter if she didn't want to. She had to. But still she thought, I don't want to, I don't want to, I don't want to. Please—

And then the fire leapt.

It sparked from somewhere near her sightstone in a hot flash. It caught the edge of the rift, making the crystallized border glow white, then melt and run towards the middle of the rift.

Katie couldn't breathe. Her heart slammed in her chest. She heard, not around her but back in a sharp corner of her mind, the sound of screaming, twisting metal. She couldn't breathe and her eyes blurred with tears and she felt everything flowing out of her, all the heat leaving her, and the white-hot melting border covered the entire rift until it glowed bright, brighter, and then faded. When it faded, the rift was gone, and Katie felt her knees buckle.

Her ears were ringing. The heat was gone, but her body still felt hollow. She swayed, tried to catch herself, but her feet wouldn't move. She fell back. Strong arms caught her. It was too hard to support her head—it lolled back, and she was looking up at Nyth. His brow was furrowed in concern. Her body was all pins and needles as her vision tunneled and blanked out.

Hands were stroking her hair. Katie started to open her eyes, but it was too bright, so she lifted her hand to shield her gaze and slowly blinked them open. Her fingers were clammy against her forehead.

Asha gazed down at her. "Are you okay? Don't be embarrassed. Simon fainted, too, and all of us are weak."

Katie had no idea if it was from the rift or the panic. At least she was awake now. She pushed her hands against the ground and sat up slowly. Her chest was tight, her hands and face all pins and needles, but the worst of the panic, the part that made her want to claw her way into a corner, was gone. Maybe passing out had helped. Like a reset button.

Still. It had been years since it had been this bad.

They were back in the veil. Simon sat next to Mel, looking dazed. Dominic crouched next to Asha, and he smiled when Katie met his gaze. "Jesus, Byrd, you scared me. You okay now?"

"Yeah." She so, so did not want to talk about it. Her stomach croaked. Run with that. Talk about anything else. "Am I the only one that's hungry?"

"Starving." Mel ran her fingers through her hair. "I feel like shit in general."

"It'll get easier in time," said a perky voice. Katie stood carefully, stretching her legs, and saw Aerie standing nearby. Had she just… popped in? She was smiling. "You did well. Rest and eat food and you'll be fine, no damage done. It just took lots of energy. It won't be quite so rough on you next time."

Mel shoved her hands in her jeans pockets. "How many more times do we have to do this?"

"We don't know," Aerie said. "Depends on how many rifts open, which depends on how quickly we figure out why this is happening and stop it." Her huge brown eyes were shining along with her smile. "When we find another rift, we'll let you know."

"How?" Dominic asked.

"Through your sightstones. Keep them close to you. They'll pick up a small vibration when we call for you."

"Okay. And how do we get back home from here?" Mel asked. "We ended up here by accident to begin with."

Aerie pointed to the stone in Mel's hand. "If you look through them and ask them to draw you to the veil, you'll end up here with us. Ask them to draw you home, you'll go back where you started." She wiggled her fingers in a little wave. "We're proud of you all! Get rest. We'll let you know when we need you again." And she shimmered out of sight.

"I'm never going to get used to that," Simon muttered.

"Are you kidding?" Dominic said. "I think it's awesome."

Katie turned to suggest they go the hell home, and then Nyth was right in front of her. She jumped, hand flying to her chest. "Sorry," he said. "Are you okay?"

"Yeah, I'm fine, I'm—" She met his gaze, and she could see it in his eyes. He knew it was more than the rift.

Behind them, the others were getting themselves together. Getting ready to go home.

"Please don't make me do that again." It came out a whisper.

Katie pulled her sleeves over her hands and blinked hard against the surge of emotions that had been triggered out. Fear tumbling over grief tumbling over the part that hurt too much to name. "Please."

Nyth nodded, his face serious. "It hurt you. Inside."

"Yeah."

"I think heat will work instead of fire. It'll take longer, but I don't want you getting hurt like this every time."

A shaky sigh escaped her. "Promise?"

"Yeah. I promise."

"Byrd?" She turned to see Dominic watching her. "Let's go home."

Katie turned back to Nyth to say thank you, but he was already gone. She took another deep breath and blinked her eyes clear. "How long have we been here? My dad and stepmom are going to be out tonight. We can all recharge at my place if you guys want."

"And reconsider our entire perception of reality? Sounds good," Mel said. "C'mon. I can squeeze you all in my car. Throw you girls' bikes in the trunk. Let's go home." She lifted her stone, muttered something, and vanished.

Katie looked at Dominic, whose eyes were wide. "Well, I guess it works," he said.

She lifted her orange sightstone, peering through its center. No magical visions through it this time. Please, she thought. Please just take me back to Earth. The center of her sightstone shone brightly, and the surrounding veil faded away.

Time apparently passed differently in the veil than it did on Earth. It was already after six by the time Katie let everyone into her house. "Alex?" No response, no annoying music from his room upstairs.

"He's probably next door," she said as everyone wandered behind her into the living room. "We're all clear."

Dominic wasted no time sprawling out on the floor next to the coffee table. Simon went to the big bay window, stretched out his long legs on the bench and leaned back, closing his eyes. Mel slumped across the couch, laying her arm over her eyes.

"Katie." Asha leaned against the wall behind her. "We should get some food."

Katie sighed. "Right. I'm pretty sure we have something I can pull together."

"I can help."

"Asha, go sit down. You look like hell." Katie shrugged. "No offense, since we all do."

"Right. Including you. It'll go faster with two pairs of hands, won't it?"

Despite the tired ache in her limbs, Katie felt the corners of her mouth tug up just a hint. "Come on then, let's do this fast. I'm starved." She called into the living room. "Nobody has allergies, do they?"

A chorus of nos. "Just nothing too spicy," Dominic called back. "You know what that does to my digestion."

There was leftover rice and chicken from the night before. "And we've got a bag of stir-fry vegetables somewhere in here," Katie said, digging in the freezer.

Asha opened the container of rice. "Can we heat the chicken separately from the rest of it? I'm a pescetarian."

"Oh, yeah, no problem." Katie poked her head into the fridge, clinging to the door handle. "Want some eggs instead? Are eggs okay?"

"Yes please. Thank you."

Katie popped the chicken in the microwave, and they threw the rice and the vegetables into a pan to stir-fry while Asha scrambled a couple eggs for herself. Katie's head was swimming, and the blue flames of the stove, which usually didn't bother her anymore, made her chest tight. The sick, post-panic-attack exhaustion was settling heavy in her on top of the sealing draining her.

The moment the vegetables were heated through, Asha got a pile of plates and forks, and Katie brought the chicken and the pan of stir-fry—and, as a thought at the last moment, a bottle of hot sauce—into the living room. "Food," she said. "Sorry for not dishing it out, but—"

"No formalities needed," Mel said.

Everyone ate, mostly in silence. Asha and Dominic didn't use the hot sauce, but the rest of them did, and the spicy tang of it on her tongue grounded Kate. Soon she felt her body steadying. She was still drained, but not so shaky.

"So," Dominic said, "that was something."

"Tell me about it."

He grinned. "Aerie was so excited to meet me. Can you believe that? They're like, nature spirits or demigods or whatever. And *she* was excited to meet *me*."

"Nyth, too." Katie remembered the excitement in his eyes, then the disappointment when she'd been uncertain.

"I had a lot of strange dreams leading up to today," Asha said. "But I didn't expect any of this."

"Did they start when you found your sightstone?" Mel asked.

Asha paused. "Yes, these did. I'm pretty sure Zephyrus sent them to me."

"That's the guardian who picked you," Simon said slowly. Asha nodded.

"Is it weird that I'm not surprised by everything?" Mel asked. "Like don't get me wrong, it's bizarre."

"Paradigm-altering," Simon said.

"Right. I should be shocked and I'm… not." Nobody responded. "It's just… when I met Skiron, I got the same feeling I get when I hold my sightstone. Like it's what I'm supposed to have."

"Or how we weren't scared when we landed in the veil," Asha said. "Even though we knew we should have been."

"Nyth said he looked a long time for a vessel," Katie said. His presence had been familiar. Like sunlight. "And that he picked me because I'm like him. Maybe that's helping."

"It feels like you're at home within yourself," Simon said.

Katie glanced up at him. Batty'd found him by now and curled into a white-and-black ball on his legs. Simon smiled his small, careful smile. "Ophion didn't talk to me in words. More like impressions." He scratched Batty behind her ears, making her chirp. "They told me things I can't find words for."

"Says the writer," Dominic joked.

That earned something closer to a smirk. "Like Katie said, they all picked us because we're like the things the guardians are drawn to." He paused again, his thumb brushing softly between Batty's ears. "Ophion said they're sort of spirits. Not quite the right word, but close enough. But they don't have bodies or genders or anything. Just their names and their powers and their natures."

"I keep thinking of Aerie as a she." Dominic furrowed his brow. "Am I being an ass, or...?"

"They don't seem to mind. Like it's irrelevant to them one way or another. Because they're not human, you know? Those things aren't important to them the way they are to us."

"That's how Zephyrus feels, too," Asha said.

Simon nodded. "And I think the sightstones carry some of their essence over for us. And they picked us because we remind them of their own essence. That's what's important to them. And that's why the stones are so comforting to have."

"You know," Dominic said, "I think that's the most words I've heard you say at once." Simon just shrugged.

When everyone finished eating, Mel helped Katie carry the dishes back into the kitchen. "Thanks for letting us come over here. It was a good call."

Katie started rinsing the dishes so they wouldn't get crusty. "Yeah. It's not like there's anyone else we can talk to about this stuff." The food, the conversation, their presence—it kept her from falling deeper into a painful hole in her mind. The longer she could cling to it, the better.

Mel fiddled with something in the pocket of her zip-up hoodie. A crease formed between her eyebrows. "We should be scared," she said.

"I mean, like Simon said—"

"No, I don't mean logically. Obviously, we should logically be scared. I mean…" She ran her hand through her hair again. By this point it looked more like a dark dandelion fluff on top of her head than hair. "We shouldn't get lulled by this. By the familiarity of them. There's still a lot we don't know. They implied we'll be safe, but we need to not be stupid."

Katie fidgeted with her sleeves. "Yeah. I guess so."

"I know so. I…" Mel swallowed visibly. "I don't really have words for how grounded Skiron makes me feel. But we're just pieces in this puzzle, you know? The world—both worlds—are at stake. We shouldn't expect them to be gentle with us."

"That makes sense." Agreeing didn't feel good. Her intuition squirmed in defiance of it. But Mel wasn't wrong. It was smarter to be cautious.

"Sorry, Byrd. I'm not trying to be a downer when we're already feeling awful."

"No, you're right. We need to remember the stakes." Katie wrapped her arms around herself, tight. "The whole world," she whispered. "And a whole second world. And they'll be gone if we don't do this. If we don't help."

She hoped to god that using heat would work instead of fire. Because she didn't have the choice to back out.

Chapter 8

School on Monday felt surreal. Walking through the halls, taking notes in class, being acutely aware the entire time there was a whole supernatural plane nobody knew about, not to mention an entire parallel world, and she'd spoken with the guardians who kept it all in check. That if she didn't help them, then every classroom, locker, crumpled wad of paper on the floor that missed the garbage can, and of course every person in the school, not to mention the rest of the world, would—cease to exist? Be swallowed by a void? Meet destruction as the earth itself crumbled? Katie didn't particularly want to know the specifics.

And the rifts didn't stop. The next one came on Tuesday, right as Katie was walking across the parking lot to her bus after school. Her sightstone buzzed on her wrist. She'd fashioned it into a sort of bracelet by looping two hair ties through the hole and sliding the whole thing onto her right wrist. Aerie had said to keep them close, and Katie figured she couldn't miss the next call this way.

She wasn't wrong. Her wrist bones practically rattled from the intensity of the stone's vibration.

At the same time, her phone vibrated in her pocket.

Mel

> *Come to the student lot*
> *I'll get us somewhere*

Katie turned on her heel and cut sideways across the bus lot towards student parking. She caught Dominic's eye as he came her way; a moment later, Asha peeled out of the crowd and joined them. A girl with long blond hair and a snapback—Rosie Novak, Asha's friend, Katie was able to match the name and the face now that she saw her—called after Asha questioningly. "I forgot I'm volunteering today!" Asha called back, waving. "My friends are giving me a ride. I'll text you later!"

Her cheeks flushed as she turned back towards the student lot, adjusting her bag on her shoulder. "I hate lying to her," she said.

"I mean, it's not really a lie," Dominic said. "You are volunteering for something, and your friends are giving you a ride there." And they climbed into Mel's car, where Simon was already in the passenger seat. "Quick thinking, Mel."

She shrugged with tense shoulders. "We can't vanish in front of the entire school."

She drove them a couple minutes down the street to the shopping plaza and pulled around to the back, where only a few employee cars were parked. Katie shrugged off her coat and her bag, leaving them in Mel's locked car, and finally lifted her still-buzzing sightstone. She heard the others saying it almost at the same moment: "Draw me through the veil."

Nyth was waiting, hands on his hips, when Katie landed in the circle of tree stumps. "That took forever."

Katie rolled her eyes. She caught a glimpse of Asha off to the side, blinking out of sight as Zephyrus swept her off to the rift. "School just let out. We had to get out of the crowd."

"Fair enough. Let's go."

Nyth held out his hand, still with that unlined palm. It was odd, but it suited him, somehow.

Katie's heart beat in her throat.

"You still promise?" she asked. She looked up from his palm to meet his gaze. "No fire."

His eyes were like hers, so she saw the flicker of frustration in them. But then he smiled and nodded. "No fire."

Relief surged through her. Katie smiled, and she took his hand.

He pulled her through that nothing-place, and when she landed, she almost fell forward down a steep, rocky slope. The wind was high and chilly, and she shivered as she noticed Dominic and Asha nearby. Simon and Mel popped into view down the slope. "Damn," Dominic said. "It's weird seeing us do that."

"Nyth?" Katie didn't see him but felt something like laughter bubble up near her.

"You looked really funny wheeling your arms like that." His voice was audible, near her ear, even though she didn't see him.

She smirked. "You could've warned me about the slope."

"I always like a laugh."

"Even if I end up tumbling down a mountainside?"

"Don't be silly. I never would've let you fall. C'mon now, wake up that heat. We're about to unmask the rift."

In the back of her mind, Katie remembered what she and Mel had talked about. That they should be more cautious. That they didn't really know these guardians.

Still. It was hard not to believe Nyth.

They started like last time: first Simon, or Ophion through Simon, brought up the vines that wound around the writhing edges of the rift, holding it in place. Katie watched the green creeping its way around the rift, nearly circling it in whole.

Focus, Nyth whispered.

And she did. Katie closed her eyes and felt the heat starting to build under her skin.

This time, less distracted by wonder, she felt flashes of familiar things in the heat. Something sparkled like sunlight on the surface of water. Something whispered like warmth rising from sun-drenched grass in high summer. Something flashed like the sun behind tree leaves shifting in the wind. Bits and pieces of the warmth of Earth, plucked by his attention, focused through her.

Her eyes fluttered open. A soft smile crossed her face.

Then her gaze drifted to the rift. All purple and gray, like the mist in the veil, but thicker and soupier and shivering against the vine border. And there was a spot—a spot—Katie furrowed her brow.

"What the—" Dominic edged down the slope, closer to the rift. "What is that?"

Katie's eyes kept dancing over it. She saw it, she knew she saw it, but her eyes weren't talking to her brain well enough. The most she could register of it was a blankness. Not white, exactly, and not quite static, but sort of like both. A tear within the tear that was the rift. And it was—

"Cold," Dominic muttered, stepping in closer still.

"Dominic," Simon said. It sounded like he was gritting his teeth. "You should—"

But then Dominic yelped, flinching back with wide, wild eyes. "Aerie!"

Nyth didn't say anything, but it was almost like he tapped her shoulder frantically. "Is she okay?" Katie called on his behalf.

"I think so. It felt—holy shit. That thing—"

"Shut it down," Mel growled. "Simon, push it faster."

And he did. The vines looped their way around the rest of the border, closing it off, and Mel and Skiron immediately started pushing the crystallization after it. The bit of void—that was all Katie could think to call it, was void, it looked and felt like nothing at all in a way that made her skin crawl—stopped its shuddering when the crystals stilled the rift, but it didn't go away.

"Can you still smooth it?" Asha asked Dominic.

He looked winded, but he nodded. "Aerie's... she's okay. She can still do it."

It took longer than it had before, and the pocket of void was the last bit to smooth over. It resisted, shuddering again as the rest of the rift blended into solid gray, but eventually it shrank and collapsed in on itself.

Dominic sat on the rocky slope as Asha and Zephyrus rippled the rift clear.

Focus, Nyth told her. We need to get this closed. So, Katie let the heat pour out of her. It warmed the edges of the rift, melting them, making them run in bright streaks towards the center of the rift.

It took a long time. Dominic said something, then Mel, and a twinge of annoyance shuddered through the warmth from Nyth. But Katie focused only on the heat pouring through her until the gash in the air was sealed and gone.

The heat trickled out of Katie's fingertips back into the world, and she swayed on her feet with the sudden exhaustion. At least this time she didn't faint. On shaky legs, she climbed down the hill to Dominic and helped him to his feet.

"What happened?" Mel asked.

He was looking more like himself now, but so tired. "When I got close to that thing… you know, she was getting close to it too. She tried to touch it and see what it was." He shook his head. "It messed her up."

Nyth materialized next to them, startling Asha. "How? She's already—" He wiggled his hand in a vague gesture. "Off. Didn't hang around."

Dominic furrowed his brow. "It… I think it scared her."

And Katie remembered what Nyth had told her the first time they'd met. How he'd never felt fear. Never had reason to.

"She's never been scared before, has she?" Katie asked. Dominic shook his head.

Nyth frowned. "This is no good."

"Will the rest of the rifts have that… thing, too?"

"That's the part we don't know. We haven't unmasked the next one yet."

Mel raised her eyebrows. "There's another rift already open?"

"Yes. But the sealings are still draining you too much. If we tried to close it right now, you'd all probably pass out before it was done." He laughed. "No good to us if you're unconscious, right?"

His laugh was light and clear, and Katie was reminded again of sunlight glinting on moving water. Still, something twinged in her chest. The guardians were letting them have a break because it was practical. That was all. It was smart to remember that. "Yeah. But it'll get easier, I hope."

"Bit by bit. Go home, Katie Byrd. Eat some food? Sleep? Those are the things that'll help, yes?"

"I can drive you guys home," Mel said. "The sightstones will drop us off where we were when we crossed over, right?"

"Right."

Mel nodded, lifted her sightstone, and flashed out of view. The others followed after.

Katie closed her fingers around her stone and turned to Nyth. "Hey. Thanks, by the way." He stared at her, eyebrows raised. "For not making me use fire."

Because yes, they were tools for the guardians, ultimately. But he could have forced her. And he didn't. And that meant something to her.

Nyth shrugged. "It would be more efficient. But you being too scared isn't gonna get a rift sealed. And it's not good for you, either, right? You should be sunny. I don't want to make you not sunny."

An honest grin broke across her face. The twinge in her chest softened. "Thanks, Nyth. See you next time." And she took herself home.

The next morning was a blur from too little sleep and too many worries. And Katie wasn't the only one—when everyone got to lunch, they sat around the table looking completely checked out.

"Well," Dominic said when nobody had spoken for a full

minute. "Yesterday was weird."

"Is Aerie really okay?" Asha asked.

"Yeah. Just shaken up." He shook his head. "It scared her. She's never been scared before."

Katie picked at her sandwich. "I wish they'd told us anything about it."

"They didn't know what it was," Mel said. "And that's unsettling too."

It was getting easier to read her friends. Dominic was an open book to Katie, and Asha was nearly as transparent. Mel didn't wear her heart on her sleeve like Asha, but her tells were growing clearer. The way she leaned on the table told Katie she hadn't slept enough last night, either.

But she couldn't read Simon. He kept his head down and wrote in his notebook, only glancing up occasionally, his expression unreadable.

It wasn't his quietness that bothered Katie. But she saw the others in classes every day. Mel, after meeting Katie's cats, started sending Katie cute cat memes, and Asha was so easy to talk to. She felt bad not knowing Simon as well. Sure, they'd only been secret superheros for a few days. But secret superheros had to be there for each other.

Especially if this was going to get even weirder, she wanted to know she could talk to any of them.

On the bus home, she got Simon's number from the group chat and sent him a text directly.

> *Hey! It's Katie*
> *Random question: how do you feel about zucchini muffins?*

He didn't reply until the bus was almost to her house.

Simon

> *I like zucchini bread. Never had it as muffins*

Any reason behind the randomness?

I'm gonna make muffins after school & I can bring some
over if you want!
Esp if you're feeling funky
Since this weekend was weird

Simon
Sure, sounds good

He followed up with his address. Katie sent an enthusiastic thank-you with a happy cat emoji.

Simon lived on the other side of town, past the mall. The houses over there were older than where Katie and Dominic lived, more mid-century split-levels and Cape Cods than the brick-fronted houses in her neighborhood. Big flowering bushes bordered Simon's front yard, and huge ferns hung from the porch ceiling. Katie grinned when Simon answered the door. "You guys like plants," she said. "Guess you were chosen well."

He gave her his signature small smile and stood back to let her in.

Sunlight streamed in through open curtains, making the house glow warm. Simon led her to the kitchen, where his mother was spooning something spicy smelling from a slow cooker into a bowl. "Hey there honey!" She flashed Katie a grin. "You must be Simon's new friend. I'm Tonya."

"Yep." Katie held up the muffins she'd bundled in a tea towel. "I'm Katie. I brought muffins."

"Mm, they smell good. And it's chili night, so this'll stay hot if you want any. Simon, give your sister a muffin. Excuse me, honey, I still have another hour of work." All smiles, Tonya leaned over and gave Katie's upper arm a friendly squeeze before heading down the hall.

Katie's pulse spiked at the contact, and her hands clenched. She felt one of the muffins squish under her fingers as she swallowed her panic. *Jesus,* why did people have to touch strangers? It was well-meant. It was friendly. She knew that. Katie took a slow breath and glanced at Simon.

He was getting plates from the cupboard. Good—he'd missed it. By the time he turned back around, Katie was smiling again. "One for each of us, one for your sister?"

"Yeah. She really likes zucchini bread, so this works out. Do you want any chili?"

"I'm good with a muffin for now." The chili smelled amazing, but her stomach was uneasy from the rush of anxiety. Better to get something starchy into her first.

Simon led her down the hall lined with photos of him, of two sisters, one younger and one older, including one where the older girl wore a graduation cap and gown, hugging a man who looked so much like Simon he had to be their father.

Poppy music came from behind one closed door in the hallway. Simon knocked and called, "You want a muffin, Darya?"

After a moment, she opened the door. Beads clacked at the ends of her braids as she tilted her head to peer up at Katie. "You're not Mel."

Simon held the plate towards his sister. "I can have friends besides Mel. This is Katie. She made zucchini muffins."

Darya raised her eyebrows. A smile tugged the corner of her mouth, and she took the muffin with a "Thanks" before shutting the door.

"She usually thinks I'm boring," Simon said as he opened the second-to-last door. "I used to be cool."

"My brother's the same. Now I'm even less cool than our dad." Simon's room was incredibly *him.* Dark blue walls, neutral bedding, everything neat and tidy. Succulents crowded a table under the window. Simon pulled out the chair at his desk, offering it to Katie, then sat on the bed.

"You have an older sister, too?" she ventured as he took a bite of muffin.

"Grace. She's living with our dad in Michigan while she's in college. These are really good, by the way."

"I really like baking. Mostly breads and pies."

"My mom doesn't bake much. But her chili is really good."

"I'll have to have some before I go."

Silence crept in between them. Katie stared out the window to not stare at Simon. Bushes and low-lying plants covered at least half of the back yard.

Honestly, she wasn't sure what to talk to him about. He was so quiet, and she didn't want to steam-roll him when the whole point of coming over was to get to know him better.

"So, you like to write," she said. He nodded. "You were writing a story at lunch this week? And you work on the literary magazine?"

"Yeah."

"That's cool. What kind of stuff do you write?"

He paused, brushing crumbs off his fingertips. "Mostly mysteries. I like the architecture of them. It's satisfying to map out. But writing good characters is the best part. Letting them grow throughout the story."

"I get that. That's sort of how a knitting project feels. But, you know, with yarn instead of words." She gestured to the succulents "You like growing things in general."

Simon smiled a wider, easier smile. Less controlled than his usual one. It looked nice on him. "I do."

"And you're good at it. All these plants look great. I had a fern once and killed it in like, a month." She nodded to the window. "What's in the backyard?"

Simon glanced over his shoulder. "The garden. It's winding down for the season now. You should see it in July."

"You work in it?"

"Mostly me, yeah. My dad used to take care of it. After the divorce, it just grew wild for a couple years before I started working it."

Katie leaned back in the chair. "I guess Oph—um, you were well chosen. For things."

He followed her gaze toward the open door. "Don't worry. I can still hear Darya's music, so she won't hear us. And my mom keeps headphones on when she's working."

"Gotcha. Then I guess Ophion did well picking you. Since you're into plants. That seems to be their thing."

"It's true." His eyes softened, and he turned to gaze out at the garden. "I used to play in the garden a lot when I was little. Dad had these big rows of vegetables. I loved sitting under the bushes and smelling how alive everything was. Ophion reminds me of how it felt under those bushes, when I could hear my dad singing in the lettuce patch and caterpillars crawled on my hands." He looked at Katie. "That was the first thing my sightstone did to me. Made me feel those caterpillars on the backs of my hands again."

Katie leaned her head against her hand. "Nyth is like that for me. He reminds me of how it feels when you roll down a big hill. Or the way sunlight flashes through trees or sparkles on water. Little things that are kind of part of me, they're part of him, too."

"You…" He stopped, flicked his gaze upward for a moment. He was piecing together his thoughts, she realized. Those were his long pauses. "You mentioned light. And Nyth's been using heat to seal the rifts. But he used fire the first time."

He didn't ask the question, but Katie felt it. She bit the inside of her lip and considered how much to reveal. He was her teammate, now. And hopefully her friend. "I'm scared of fire," she said. "Phobia-scared. Nyth said we could just use heat so I don't panic at every sealing."

Another pause. Then: "Do the others know?"

Katie shook her head. "Just Dom. He already knew. He used to invite me to his family's bonfires all the time, and after saying no a hundred times, I told him why." He'd never prodded her about it, though. Which she appreciated. There were some things she wasn't ready to tell even to him.

"You two have been friends a long time, haven't you?"

"Actually, only since the beginning of high school. But it seems like forever." She sighed. "But that's why Nyth has to work so slow. Should I feel bad about that? He didn't say it was a problem."

His usual brief pause before speaking, a thoughtful frown. "I think it makes some of the other guardians impatient. Not Ophion, but I can feel it echo through them. But if nobody has said anything, maybe you don't need to worry."

"Ophion is interesting," Katie said, steering the conversation away from her neuroses. It was starting to make her itchy. "They don't show up in a body like the others do."

"No. They feel better if they stay closer to the earth." He looked up at her, shrugging. "I understand why they stay in the plants and everything. But I worry like I stick out because of it."

Katie grinned. "Well, I stick out because my guardian makes special exceptions for me. So, we can stick out together." He returned her smile. "We can both be weird outliers. And we can also both go to the kitchen, maybe? I need to try this famous chili." And he laughed softly, and they went back to the kitchen together.

Chapter 9

At ten minutes to dinner on Friday, Katie's sightstone buzzed against the back of her wrist.

She swore under her breath, putting down her knitting. Fumbling under the blanket over her legs, she pretended to check her phone, then rolled off the window seat and headed toward the kitchen. "Hey Dad? Don't hate me, okay?"

He looked up from setting the table. "This isn't school-related, I hope."

"No. Um—I know it's almost dinnertime, but—" She held up her phone. "My friend Mel just texted me and asked if I wanted to go over there to eat."

"We're about to sit down, Kate."

Her sightstone kept vibrating against her wrist bones. "I know, I'm sorry. But this is a big deal! She's never invited me for dinner! She's standoffish to a lot of people, so like, a dinner invite is pretty significant." He hesitated, so she pressed on. "You're always hinting that I should have more friends. Look! Friend development!"

Her father sighed, a sheepish smile creeping onto his face. "Alright. But you owe me lunch together tomorrow."

"Deal. I'll make you noodles. It'll be great." She flashed him a smile and hurried to grab her bag and pull on her coat and a scarf. Keeping up the pretense but hating the wasted time.

"You're in a hurry."

"Well, you know! It takes a while to bike to her place, and I don't want to be late."

Katie left as quickly as she could and pedaled her bike down the street, feeling the incessant buzz of her sightstone. It didn't make sense to actually go to Mel's, and she didn't have time for that, anyway. She also shouldn't let anyone see her disappear into thin air. Her mind raced as her legs pedaled, the evening air—chilly by Katie's standards—stinging her face.

There was a spot in her neighborhood between two rows of houses where the trees grew thicker together. Like a mini-woods without going to the park. Katie turned her bike off the sidewalk and bumped over the grass between houses until she rode into the shelter of the knot of trees. It was getting dark, and she hoped the trees and the dusk would hide her enough as she pulled her sightstone off her wrist and drew herself to the veil.

Nyth was already there, pacing around the circle of stumps in the meeting place, when she landed. "There you are! It always takes you so long. What were you doing?"

"I was about to sit down to dinner with my family and had to come up with an excuse. Can't tell them I'm popping out to save the world, can I?"

He grinned. "Shame that you can't. Let's go." And he took her hand and whisked her away through the darkness.

Everyone was waiting when they arrived. "Sorry," Katie said. "Had to get out of dinner with my family."

"What was your excuse?" Dominic asked as Nyth shimmered out of view and Mel and Simon started working on the border of the rift. "We were halfway through, and I faked that Jordan and I volunteered to sell tickets at the football game tonight. Arianna's never gonna forgive me, I was supposed to help her with her math homework. My little sister," he clarified when Asha tilted her head inquisitively.

"I might've used you as an excuse, Mel," Katie called. "Sorry about that."

"It's whatever." Mel's voice was strained, and Katie didn't

bother her again while she was focusing. Especially because she noticed there was a wiggling pocket of void in the rift again.

Someone tapped on her shoulder. But when she turned her head, nobody was there. "Nyth?"

"Time to concentrate." His voice was not-quite-there near her ear. But she closed her eyes, felt his presence curl around her as heat began to build in her chest and spread out underneath her skin.

Maybe it would be easier if she let him in more. Like Asha seemed to with her guardian. Asha wasn't a wallflower by any means, but she often held herself close. Books clutched to her chest, hands resting on her purse strap, fingers playing with the ends of her hair. But at rifts, her steps had a grace and her posture an openness and power. Like Zephyrus.

And the light, the wild joy, in Dominic's eyes was something she'd seen before. It showed up the first time he free-climbed all the way to the top of his favorite rock wall; it was there after the first time he drove a long stretch of highway after getting his license. It was his roller coasters, tree-climbing, hell-of-a-good-run look. But it had a different light this time. Something of Aerie flickered behind his grin.

Nyth chose her for a reason. Maybe she couldn't let him use fire, but she could find their common ground.

It got intensely hot, channeling all this heat. Part of it was cozy, like burrowing under a pile of blankets in winter. Part of it crackled through her, dancing between her molecules the way sunlight danced between shifting leaves in summer. All of it was Nyth, sharing pieces of himself.

It was like parts of her sat up, taking notice and reaching out to touch similar parts of him. How her heart would pound and her blood sing through her veins when she rode her bike as hard as she could down a long stretch of path in the metro parks, sunlight flashing in her eyes as she sped. The rush in her chest when anger flared through her. Her cats' pupils expanding and whiskers twitching forward and muscles coiled when they prepared to pounce. Even, in a way, the endless rhythm of her knitting needles and the long stretches of looped yarn that spiraled off them the longer she knit, creating something out of nothing.

Something like laughter danced around her. *Now you're getting it.* The heat began to pool between her cupped palms.

The heat rising off asphalt in summer. A fox running low to the ground. Sparks leaping off the edges of a blazing bonfire—

Katie gasped, her eyes flying open. Her heart shuddered in her chest, and her throat tightened as her eyes dampened.

"Hey." Nyth's voice came audible again, whispered only for her to hear. "Hey, it's okay. I've got you. You're fine."

Katie couldn't feel cold with all Nyth's heat coursing through her, but she felt stiff now. She swallowed her anxiety and refocused.

The rift was fully encircled in vines now, and Mel pushed the crystallization along the border. The void squirmed, but that was okay, as soon as the border was stabilized it wouldn't be able to—

Even through all the heat Nyth was funneling into her, Katie felt a wave of cold wash over her.

Something was poking out of the center of the void.

"What the hell—" Mel leaned forward, visibly straining to help Skiron push the crystal further.

"What is it?"

It unfurled, dangling out of the rift. Katie's heart beat harder. It was like a vine, or a root, twisted at odd angles. And instead of green or brown, it was a grayish color, an almost leathery texture. But it was a vine. Three limp, thick leaves hung off it.

The crystallization snapped home. The border stabilized. The vine broke off from the pocket of void and fell to the ground.

Dominic wasted no time smoothing over the colors of the rift. Asha wasted no time rippling it clear, dissipating the void as well, until they could see the veil again. And Katie wasted no time turning the reins over to Nyth, letting him pour heat through her to seal the whole thing closed.

The strain of it made her sweat, especially as it dragged on for so long. The rift was halfway closed when Mel turned around, brow furrowed and hands on her hips. "Skiron wants to know what's taking so long," she called. "It should be faster than this."

A twinge of irritation plucked behind Katie's chest. "Is it an actual problem that it's taking a while?"

"I mean, no. But it shouldn't take this long."

"If there's no actual problem, then let me focus, okay?" And she let the heat and her own rushing blood become the only sounds she noticed, focusing harder and more pointed, so that if Mel—and Skiron—bugged her anymore, she didn't have to hear it.

Eventually the rift sealed away completely. The last of the heat slipped out of Katie, leaving her shivering but less exhausted than before.

Nyth materialized next to her again, his brow furrowed. Katie stared back at him, feeling cold now that his heat was gone.

"What the actual hell," Mel said. "Can someone—"

Aerie shimmered into view, already crouched and peering at the piece of vine. "It's dead," she said. "Ophion?"

They didn't see Ophion take form anywhere, but after a moment, Aerie looked up. Her eyes were clear and hard in a way Katie had never seen on her. "It doesn't exist," she said.

"I beg your pardon?" Dom said.

"It doesn't exist, Dominic. This vine doesn't grow anywhere on Earth or Harath."

Simon rubbed his forehead. "Then what is it?"

Aerie was staring down at the vine again. "We don't know." She frowned. "But we can try to find out."

"Can I help?" Katie offered. "I have chemistry this year. I could take a piece of it to the lab. See if I can figure out what it's made from."

"Yes." Aerie hesitated, then picked up the vine, snapping off the end of it, including one leaf. "Wrap it in something. I don't know if it can hurt you." Katie folded it into her scarf, careful not to touch it just in case.

Nyth leaned in over her shoulder. It made her stiffen, him coming so close, but more as a reflex than anything. She realized he was really warm, and it was kind of comforting. "These aren't normal rifts," he said. "They haven't been since that void first showed up. But this—"

"Is messed up." Katie nodded. "Okay. We'll see if we can figure anything out on the mundane side. You guardians will do better than us at the… mystical side?"

She said it with a hint of humor, and it landed. Nyth's tension shifted into amusement. "Yeah. We can call it mystical."

"Go ahead home," Aerie said. "The rift is sealed. Everything's okay for now. We'll all do the best we can to figure out what's going on."

"And I guess next time we'll try to be prepared for anything," Mel said.

"Unknown territory."

Nyth turned back to Katie, opening his mouth to say something, at the same time Mel turned and asked Katie, "What was your excuse?" Katie stared at her, bewildered, until Mel clarified, "Do you still need cover?" Nyth twisted his mouth in an almost comically annoyed expression.

Katie felt her cheeks grow warm. "Yeah, sorry about that. I didn't know what to tell my dad, so I said you'd invited me to dinner."

"Do you want to come over? It wouldn't be anything fancy."

"You don't have to do that."

"It's fine, Byrd. I want to." Mel's arms were crossed, but as Katie peered at her, the offer seemed genuine. "Both of you can come," she said to Dominic. "I'll make pancakes."

Asha's face lit up. "If you do, could I stop by in a while? I already had dinner, but I have something I made for everyone."

"You're all so sweet." Katie turned, surprised. She hadn't heard Aerie come closer. The shift in her tone was welcome. "It's nice that you're all friends now."

Katie glanced at Dominic, then the others. A smile bloomed on her face, warm and comfortable. "Yeah. That sounds good, Mel." She turned to Nyth. He still looked put-out about being interrupted. "Hey, you with the pout. You okay?"

The irritation flickered out of his face. "Was I pouting?"

She laughed. "For a demigod, you're not very self-aware. Yeah, you were pouting."

"Not really a demigod. Still, you—" His eyes cut to the side, towards Aerie; Katie looked but didn't notice anything she was doing in particular. But Nyth rolled his eyes and shrugged. "You kids go eat your food. We've gotta get back to work." And then whatever he'd been feeling flowed into an easy smile, and he leaned in closer. "Remember what you tapped into during that sealing," he said. "You're starting to get it. You just gotta let yourself flow."

Her smile mirrored his. "I will. It felt good."

Mel opened the door at the top of the steps a few moments after Katie knocked. "C'mon in." She held open the screen door, and Katie slipped inside. "The guys are already here. My mom's still at work, so we have the place to ourselves."

After hanging up her jacket and scarf, Katie joined them in the kitchen, which smelled like pancakes. Simon's plate was already cleared, and he stood from the small table so she could have a seat. Mel gave her a plate piled with syrupy pancakes, then leaned against the counter and ate one herself, plain, with her hands.

"The heck do you think Asha made?" Dominic asked.

"I have no idea," Mel said. "Knowing her, probably something adorable."

Simon scratched the back of his neck. "She's been leaning into getting to know our guardians, lately. It might have to do with that."

"It could also just be a nice, sweet Asha thing. She's the type to do cute stuff just because."

"Wanna place bets?" Katie pointed her fork, wagging it between the two of them. "Simon, ten on guardian-related? Mel, ten on mundane niceness?"

The doorbell rang. Mel said, "No bets," and left to answer it.

Everyone moved to the living room as Asha came inside. It was tight for five people at once, but Dominic sat on the floor next to the coffee table, and Katie sat with him, letting the others have the couch. Asha sat clutching a shoebox.

"So, what's this mystery surprise?" Katie asked, resting her chin in her hand.

"I've been thinking about rift sealings," Asha said. "The more I understand Zephyrus, the easier it gets for her to work through me. And well—" She opened the shoebox. Katie caught a whiff of something green smelling. "I had some hunches. So, I ran all over the city the past couple days to find things for these."

She lifted a small bundle out of the box. It was some kind of herb and white-and-pink flowers with wide-splayed petals, the whole thing tied with yellow string. "I made these for everyone. They're charms, sort of. The idea is that if we keep these around, they might help us understand our guardians more. And get more in tune with the things in us that are like them." She held the bundle out toward Dominic.

He took it and turned it gently in his fingers. "What is it?"

"Yours is rosemary and amaryllis. To keep your mind clear and your spirit playful."

A crooked grin caught his mouth. "That's Aerie for sure."

"And you," Katie said.

Asha turned to Simon next to her, handing him another bundle. "I got you comfrey and chamomile. Fortitude, I think, and nurturing. Or healing." He brushed his fingertips over the tiny yellow flowers, wordless but smiling.

Reaching past him to Mel, Asha gave her a bundle that didn't have any flowers on it. "It's juniper berries," she said, "and thyme. For protection, courage, and strength." Mel nodded, cleared her throat, and stared at the berries.

Then Asha gave Katie that tentative smile and held out a bundle of jagged-edged leaves and bright red poppies. This one had white cloth wrapped around the bottom of it, which was tied on with red string. "Only touch the covered part," Asha warned, and Katie took it carefully. "That's stinging nettle in with the poppies. To strengthen your will, and—" She hesitated, then finished, "—for release. And cleansing negativity."

Katie's heart pricked, even if the fabric wrap kept the nettle from pricking her skin. She remembered Asha mentioning her dreams, and the glimpses of things she caught in them. She wondered how much Asha might have seen. "Thank you."

"What's yours?" Simon asked.

"I left mine at home," Asha said. "But it's mugwort and sage. For my dreams, and for wisdom."

"I like it," Mel said, still looking at her bundle. "But what exactly do I do with it?"

Asha fidgeted, started to answer but then hesitated.

"Go on, Asha," Dominic said. "We're all supernatural superheroes here. Nobody's gonna think you're weird."

She relaxed a hair. "Maybe meditate with it. Hold it and try to feel the things in the world, or in yourself, that remind you of your guardian. Just now and then." Dominic quirked his eyebrows. Asha shrugged. "Other than that, keep it somewhere you'll be near it a lot. It wouldn't hurt if—" She hesitated again. Simon nudged his shoulder against hers, and she sighed and smiled sheepishly. "Katie, keep yours somewhere where it can get sunlight. Dominic, try keeping yours near your books. Simon, anywhere warm and safe. Mel, I know this is specific, but you should put yours in a ceramic dish with a lid. I may or may not have brought one in case you need it."

Nobody replied for a moment. Asha's cheeks flushed. Then Mel grinned—not her usual wry smile, but a wide grin. "Asha, you're amazing."

Her eyes lit up as Katie nodded. "Seriously. This might be just what we need." Maybe just what *she* needed. "Thank you."

Chapter 10

Katie put a small nail in the side frame of her window and looped the thread on her bundle of nettle and poppy over it, hanging the whole thing upside down. That way it would keep its shape better when it eventually dried. In the meantime, the sunlight beamed through her south-facing window most of the day, soaking the flowers and leaves in warmth.

No rifts came for nearly a week, which gave her the chance to plunge into her fall knitting projects. She's decided to make Dominic a sweater—he'd gotten a hat from her for the past two years for Christmas, and she wanted to up the ante. It was going to be a shade of yellow that she personally found hideous, but that Dom loved.

She'd also decided to make scarves for Mel and Asha and Simon. For Christmas, or for general winter-time generosity, if any of them didn't celebrate. It just felt right, considering everything.

Katie'd been knitting since she was ten, so scarves flew off her needles easily enough (though she'd picked something with tricky cabling for Simon because why make anything easy for herself). But Dom's sweater took more time and focus, and the week to breathe gave her the headspace to start making progress.

It was good. Knitting helped her get out of her head. It was easier to manage all the things built up in her chest when she could watch herself creating something out of nothing but her will, the movements of her hands, and some yarn. It was why she'd started knitting, and it helped now, too.

Still, no rifts didn't mean a total break from secret superhero duties. Katie registered a time slot in the science lab under the guise of working on an assignment, but instead she smuggled in the piece of creepy vine from the last rift. Wearing gloves, she sliced an ultra-thin piece and peered at it under the microscope. It had the right kind of cell structure for a plant: large and squarish, with a thick, porous cell wall.

Dominic had told her how to use the combustion chamber. He'd had that analyzing look when he'd told her—peering at her too intensely. She got it. She was going to be burning things. Not exactly her favorite activity. "Do you want me to help?" he'd finally asked. Hesitating, like he knew it would piss her off.

Which it did. "I'll be fine," she told him, even as anxiety writhed in her stomach.

It roiled now as she placed the rest of the vine in the chamber, checked the oxygen and carbon dioxide readings on the meter, and readied to light the torch. She was sweating, her heart pounding. The fire wouldn't be that much bigger than the stove burners at home, but it wasn't the stove burners at home. It wasn't something she'd worked to get used to. She was terrified to light it, and she was mad at herself for being afraid, at Dominic for pitying her, at the stupid vine from the stupid rift for stirring fears she thought she'd gotten a handle on.

She *could* handle this. She could do it.

Katie ignited the burner. The flame flashed, and she stumbled back.

It defied all safety protocol to not keep an eye on the flame, but she sank to the floor and sat leaning against the side of a lab table, eyes squeezed shut, forcing herself to breathe slowly and evenly as panic bubbled up in her mind, pulling sounds with it. Sounds of crunching metal. Sounds she didn't want to remember. She breathed and breathed and breathed and tried to let it wash over her without washing her away.

When she stopped shaking, she stood up, feeling sick.

She was supposed to check the readings again to see how they'd changed in the course of burning. It wouldn't give them exact answers, not with what was available in a high school lab and her high school knowledge, but it would narrow things down.

The problem was that the meter was blank. On, but blank. And the vine was gone.

Like entirely gone. Not even a piece of charcoal or a smear of ash. There was a sand-like substance at the bottom of the chamber, but it didn't even look like it had been burned.

They had the next rift that evening, shivering in a desert somewhere in the middle of the night. The rift wasn't the biggest they'd ever seen, but its border squirmed. A pocket of void yawned open, but nothing wriggled out of it. They still shut it down nearly as fast as the last one. Nobody wanted to wait and see.

Aerie and Skiron appeared in physical form back in the veil once the rift was sealed, and Katie told them what she'd found. "It didn't make sense. It didn't burn the way things are supposed to burn." If her tongue tripped over the sentence, nobody called her out on it. She still felt shaky and sick from earlier.

"We couldn't hunt down its origin," Aerie said. "It has to be crafted, somehow. If it doesn't grow naturally in either world, what other way could it have formed?"

"Could the rift have made it?" Mel tried. "Some kind of… transformation of something?"

Aerie pursed her lips thoughtfully. "That's possible. Rifts have never done anything like that before, but we all know now these rifts are different. That void—it might be able to corrupt things."

"Don't like the sound of that," Dominic muttered.

"We will continue to observe," Skiron said. "Please remain on your guard at every sealing."

The guardians left, and Asha turned to the others. "Now more than ever," she said, "we should keep trying to connect with them."

"The better we can work, the faster we can shut down rifts," Mel said. "Before more creepy shit crawls out of them."

Katie went home and got ready for bed, taking extra care to brush her hair thoroughly, to massage Skimbleshanks's little paws until he purred, to make her bed feel as comfortable and cozy as possible when she climbed into it. To calm herself. Because she was tired and wrung out from the panic episode in the lab, even now.

She couldn't let Nyth use fire through her. She couldn't. She had to connect with him another way.

Pretending everything was normal got harder. And weirder. September gave way to October, and the everyday stuff didn't stop just because Katie knew, now, about a whole other layer of reality.

Baking oatmeal cookies with her father on Saturday—his request, and mostly her effort, but a good time anyway—she felt Nyth's presence swell in the wave of hot air from the oven when she slid in a tray. Part of him was in heat, like he was in the way Batty pounced at spiders and the brilliant rush of energy that coursed through her blood when she stretched in the mornings, waking her sleep-tight muscles. She felt it every time she opened the oven. And her father didn't notice at all. Didn't know there was anything to notice.

She watched him lift fresh cookies from the baking sheet to the cooling rack. It was the weekend, so he was wearing his glasses and his old college sweatshirt with the sleeves rolled up. He chuckled when he broke one of the cookies, murmuring "Well now I have to eat it," casting a conspiratorial grin to Katie as he shoved the cookie in his mouth. She shook her head with a smile as she slid the next tray into the oven, feeling that burst of Nyth-like energy.

Who would have been her dad's guardian? In another world where the guardians chose fully capable adults for their vessels instead of a bunch of kids, would Nyth have chosen him?

Katie hopped up to sit on the counter and sampled one of the cookies. No, not Nyth. Her father was much more grounded than she was. He always had been. She was glad of it—it was the main thing that held their family together after her mother died. Maybe Skiron, she realized, surprised at the realization. Her father was so much gentler and more open than Mel, than how Skiron seemed. But there was that steadiness, that sturdiness, that air of protection. He was safe and stable and strong. And that was Skiron, wasn't it? Not just the mountainous height and stern expression.

"Where'd you go?"

Katie blinked. "What?"

Her father tilted his head. "You zoned out."

"Sorry." She grinned sheepishly. "A lot on my mind right now."

"Classwork isn't too much, is it?"

"No, I just think I might've taken too much on my plate right now. It'll sort out, eventually."

"Alright. If things start getting too hectic, you can tell me. I know I'm an old fart, but age brings wisdom, or whatever it is they say. I can always try to help you sort out your schedule."

Sorry, Dad, but I don't think you'd be able to balance mystical rift-sealings with chem group projects. "This is gonna sound out of left field," she said, though it was perfectly in keeping with her inner train of thought, "but I was wondering… I take after Mom, don't I?"

"Your freckles betray you as very much my daughter," he said. He didn't quite look at her. "But yes. She was sassy like you."

"Me? Sassy?"

"Is there another word you'd prefer for your eye-rolling habit?" He looked at her, then. Humor glinted in his eyes, but that shade of sadness was behind it. It hadn't ever gone away. It probably wouldn't ever. Katie knew how that felt.

But she wanted to stay in the happiness and warmth. So she stuck out her tongue, confirming his diagnosis, until he laughed and shooed her off the counter so he could start washing dishes.

Alex might've been chosen by Nyth, too, Katie thought. Or maybe Aerie. Tracy would belong with Ophion. And her mother…

Katie's memories from age eight and back weren't as clear as she wished they were. But from what she did remember, all sparkling laughter and cartwheels in the grass and races along the beach and happy hugs and tickle fights—yes. Her mother would've been chosen by Nyth, too.

Chapter 11

"Byrd!" Dominic grinned at her at the cafeteria doors. "Bonjour, mon amie! Do my eyes deceive me, or are you wearing three layers?"

Katie wrinkled her nose at him. "It's cold."

"Quit your bellyaching, you lizard. It's like fifty degrees." He fell into step next to her on their way inside. "Brought anything good for lunch today?"

"You'll have to find out when you get back from the lunch line."

He held up a lunch bag. "Surprise! I'm brown-bagging it now. Shockingly, after ten and almost a half years, cafeteria lunches are losing their magic for me."

Katie laughed as they sat at the table, where Asha was opening a container of grapes. "I'm shocked to the core."

Asha smiled, leaning her chin in her hand. "You're both so charming."

"Asha, you're sweet. For that, I'll give you a cookie." Katie handed over one of the pecan sandies she'd packed alongside her lunch.

Asha took a bite, and her eyes lit up. "That's really good. Did you make these?" Katie nodded. "You're a good baker."

Dominic leaned his elbow on the table, mimicking Asha's posture and batting his eyelashes. "You're an amazing baker, Byrd. Also, a true-blue friend. And your freckles are to die for."

A snort of laughter escaped Katie. "Shut up, you nerd. You can just ask if you want one." She passed him a cookie, which he shoved whole into his mouth with a grin.

Mel and Simon came to the table, sliding into their chairs. Asha smiled. "Hey guys." Simon nodded and Mel said hello, and Asha leaned her elbows on the table. "So, um. Now that we're all here, there's something I'd like to talk about together."

Batting his eyelashes again, Dominic said, "How jealous we are of Byrd's fabulous hair and pajama-glam fashion sense?"

"I gave you a cookie, asshole." She grinned. "You're not getting apple slices, too, so you can keep your eyelashes to yourself."

Simon smiled his small smile. "What did you want to talk about, Asha?"

She fidgeted when everyone's gaze turned to her. Lowering her voice, she said, "Okay, so I'd been getting this… impression from Zephyrus. It's not anything she told me, but I've noticed things when she's near me during sealings, or in my dreams, sometimes." She ducked her head and started peeling a grape. "You know how when we do sealings, we all act as these… conductors for the guardians' powers? Like we're focal points for them to channel their energy through."

"I get that," Katie said. She lowered her voice a smidgen to match Asha's; nobody was likely to hear them in the loud cafeteria, but it didn't hurt to avoid being blatant about it. "Nyth builds up all the heat he's going to use, and I feel it build up in me and then pour off me at the rift."

"Right. Well, the impression I've been getting is that there might be a more direct way for the guardians to use their power through us."

Mel furrowed her brow. "How much more direct could we get?"

"After getting these impressions, I stayed in the veil after the last sealing and asked Zephyrus to explain it." Asha started peeling another grape, not eating the first one. "She was evasive. I think the guardians might be handling us on a need-to-know basis, and I'm not sure this is something we needed to know. But she did tell me they think we could do what she called assimilation. The guardians would be able to join with us in our bodies and minds, and it would let them use their powers more directly. So, rifts could be sealed faster, which might be good if they start getting bigger, or if there are more of them too close together."

Simon leaned in on his elbows. "I felt that from Ophion," he said. "That something like that could be possible. But I only caught glimmers of it."

"How would that even work?" Katie asked.

Asha glanced up at the ceiling in thought. "Okay—So imagine the guardians are archers, and they use their bows to shoot their powers—the arrows—at the rifts. The way we're working as vessels right now, it's like we're standing on the other side of the room, holding their arrows. We have to bring one over before they can shoot. It uses up time and energy, and the whole thing is way less efficient. In assimilation, we'd be like quivers they could wear on their backs. No more walking back and forth, just arrows right there, ready for them. Faster, less wasted energy."

"But how would it *work*," Mel asked.

Asha shrugged, giving a ghost of a smile. "That much I don't know. I'm not sure Zephyrus does, either. It's not like anyone's done this before. But I think it has to do with being…" She let out a frustrated sigh, clearly searching for the right words. "Being bonded with them. Being close enough to let the assimilation happen."

"Because we're already like them," Dominic said. "I mean, we all feel that, right? And Byrd, didn't Nyth say something like that to you? He picked you because you're like him?"

Katie nodded. "I mean, that's why we're vessels. There's certain stuff in the world that they all work best with. And I guess something of that stuff is in us."

"The sightstones," Simon said. "They draw on our own memories, but everything they make us feel is connected to the guardians." His shoulders hunched a bit. "Don't you think?"

"They do." Katie slipped her fingertips under her sleeve, turning her sightstone on her wrist. "Everything it made me sense at the beginning, now I know those are all things that feel like Nyth."

"Hm." Mel stirred her lunch in its container. "That makes sense. And if it'd make the work go better, we should probably try for it."

"I don't know if we can force it."

"Not force. But we can all try to tune in more with our guardians. It's easy during sealings. They're right there with us, working through us. We just have to get even deeper on their frequency. But even the rest of the time, if we can figure out a way to get more on their level, it'd only help."

Simon tapped his fingers against the tabletop in a loose rhythm. "Maybe it would help with the big picture, too. If the guardians can do better work on each individual rift, maybe it'll bring them closer to figuring out where they're coming from."

Mel grinned. It made her face look surprisingly soft. "Shit, it's as good a plan as any."

"Now, we're well into the semester, and it's time to start the group project." Mrs. Kozel remained unfazed by the sighs and mutterings she got in response. "This isn't new news, people. Remember this project is twenty-five percent of your final grade, so even if you don't get paired with your best friend, please still make an effort."

Katie glanced sidelong at Dominic, who raised his eyebrows in response. They already had enough on their plates. Especially now that those weird vines were appearing from the rifts. Even without group projects, it was getting harder to focus on—

"Katie Byrd," Mrs. Kozel called, jolting Katie's attention back to the front of the room. "Victoria Chamberlain, Malia Headley, and Jordan Meszaros."

"Nice," Dominic whispered.

In the row beyond Dominic, Victoria Chamberlain jotted something down. Of course she was already organizing. She'd been on track to be their class's valedictorian since freshman year.

Katie's grades were good as a general rule, but not to the point of competing for that title. She'd had a few honors classes with Victoria, though. She could be standoffish, but she did good work.

Jordan and Katie had only ever been casual friends. Dominic was mostly all they had in common. But at least they were on good terms.

Malia Headley was the one Katie knew the least. But she was Asha's best friend, and she was friendly. Didn't seem the type to flake out and make everyone else do the work, which was about as much as anyone could expect from a group project.

After Mrs. Kozel read out the groups, everyone migrated around the room to cluster up. They didn't have long—Mrs. Kozel had only given ten minutes until the bell to pick a general topic for their projects. "Brainstorm specifics," she instructed as Katie sat sideways in the desk next to Jordan's, "and bring them back to your group tomorrow."

"Hi," Victoria said. She had her notebook out and a pen in hand. "Does anyone have anything they especially want to study?"

Katie shrugged; Jordan shook his head. Malia said, "I'm really into chemical bonds."

Victoria pursed her lips thoughtfully. "We could do something with intermolecular forces. Or maybe chemical reaction experiments? Comparing and contrasting different types of reactions?"

"I like that," Katie said. "And it sounds doable."

"Any objections?" Jordan and Malia shook their heads, and Victoria took more notes in neat penmanship. "Alright. Chemical reactions. Let's all come up with specific ideas and bring them back tomorrow. Either experiments you'd want to do or a hypothesis you want to explore, anything as long as it's specific. I don't want to do a half-assed generic thing, you know?"

"Agreed."

"Okay. Cool, thanks guys."

Victoria pulled out her phone, and Malia and Jordan started chatting. Katie glanced at the clock—still six minutes until the end of class. At least they'd been efficient.

Across the room, Dominic caught her eye and pantomimed a dramatic, choking sort of death. Katie wasn't sure if that meant his group was doing a project on poisonous compounds or if he hated his group.

School hadn't exactly been her top priority lately, but a group project could be good right now. Something mundane and lower stakes to keep her grounded. Nothing about it to trigger panic attacks or stir old emotional wounds. Questions, experiments, problems to solve that didn't have the weight of the actual world hanging on them. Maybe it would actually help.

Chapter 12

The rest of the day dragged hard. In trigonometry last period, Katie glanced at the clock above the door for what had to be the hundredth time. They still had almost fifteen minutes until the last bell.

As she lowered her gaze, her heart half-stopped. Her sightstone began to vibrate on her wrist. And through the door's glass window, Nyth waved at her frantically.

Katie shot her hand into the air.

Mr. Blumenthal peered over his glasses. "Yes, Katie?"

"May I use the restroom?"

"Be quick," he said grudgingly. Katie swept her notebook into her bag as subtly as she could as she stood up. Mr. Blumenthal squinted at her. "Is it necessary to take your things with you?"

Halfway to the door, Katie froze. "Yes," she blurted. "I need a tampon."

Someone in the class snorted. "Please be more mature, Mr. Welch," Mr. Blumenthal said, turning back to the blackboard. "Alright, alright." Katie turned on her heel and slipped out the door.

She moved out of the classroom's line of sight to where Nyth was waiting and whispered, "What are you—" Then she looked him up and down. "What are you *wearing*?" she finished.

"This?" Nyth glanced down at himself: blue-checked button-up shirt, bright yellow cardigan with floral appliques, black tights—not leggings, but tights—and red sneakers. The shirt was tucked into the tights. "I thought about things I've seen you kids wear. I wanted to blend in. Is this not okay?"

"It's…" Katie sighed. "It's fine. You're fine. Untuck the shirt, at least, and maybe people will just think you're a hipster."

Nyth began walking, untucking the shirt as he went. "What's a hipster?"

"Oh my god, Nyth, it doesn't matter. Why did you show up at school? I felt my sightstone."

"Because I knew you'd wait until your classes were over and apologize when you got to the rift. We don't have time for that today. Where's somewhere nobody will see us?"

Katie groaned. "Hang on, let me see if anyone's in here." They were about to pass a bathroom; she poked her head inside. "It's clear. C'mon in."

Nyth ducked inside behind her, then without another word, grabbed her hands and whisked her away.

They landed somewhere that reminded her of the metro parks. Maybe not their own, but something similar. They stood in a grassy field surrounded by trees, but through the trees on one side, she could easily see a parking lot dotted with cars.

Her heart squeezed. "It's so close to people."

"That's why we couldn't wait."

"Where's Asha?" Mel asked. She and Simon were already there. Dominic popped in with Aerie, who glanced off into the air with hard eyes before shimmering out of view.

"Don't know. But we gotta go." Nyth waved a hand, and the rift unmasked.

"Shit," Dominic said.

Katie agreed.

The rift was easily twice as large as any they'd seen so far. Wider than it was tall, it spanned across the grass, with a weird sort of bowing middle that snaked a tendril to the ground. It looked… wrong where it met the grass. The rift kept going down, further than the line of the ground. Staring at it made Katie's eyes strain and her head swim. It didn't help that dead in its center was a blank span of void. She looked away, meeting Nyth's gaze.

"Stay focused while they work," he said, his eyes blazing. "It's a mean one." He disappeared, and she felt his warmth rise around her.

Mel and Simon squared up, starting their work stabilizing the crackling border of the rift as quickly as they could. Asha finally appeared, immediately apologizing. "Sorry, I was taking a test—oh my god—" Katie shrugged, tried to focus on the heat building under her skin and between her hands.

Mel swore. The edge of the rift shuddered again, cracking through her unfinished crystal and shredding part of Simon's vine. She flung her arm towards it, like she'd thrown something, and a thick patch slammed over the crack.

A question bubbled up somewhere near Katie, not quite audible. *Are you sure we can't just use fire this time? This one's rough.*

She gritted her teeth and shut her eyes and tried to ignore him. She needed to focus, not to worry about—

"Oh my god—"

"What is that?!"

Her eyes flew open, and her heart leapt into her throat.

Some—*thing* was crawling out of the rift. Its leathery skin, the same grayish color as those creepy vines, rippled with muscles. It skittered with too many legs out of the cut in the air and down into the grass. Katie couldn't tell where its head was, but for a horrible moment it froze, like it was watching them. Then it ran towards Simon.

Asha screamed. Katie's heart slammed in her chest, knees buckled, and she stumbled backwards. With a grunt of effort, Mel grabbed Simon and pulled him away, used all her weight and all the momentum to throw him out of the creature's path, half-stumbling after him. It scurried past, turned too quickly, and headed for Mel.

In the moment Katie's heart was about to stop because they were in fact going to die, a flash of light burst from Mel's fist. The light shot up her arm and engulfed her body, and when it faded a second later, her jeans and sweatshirt were gone, replaced by dark pants and a dark shirt and gleaming armor that looked like Skiron's. She dodged the creature's charge, just barely. On the ground where she landed, a shining metal blade grew from the earth. At the top it formed a hilt, and Mel grabbed it and pulled a sword out of the ground.

"Holy shit, Mel!"

Mel didn't even notice Dominic's cry. "Simon!" she called as the creature doubled back toward her. "Get the border stabilized."

"Mel, I can't by myself—"

"Yes, you can. Trust me." The creature scuttled toward her, and with a grunt she swung the sword. It clattered alongside the creature's legs, and the thing let out an eerie shriek. "Just hurry and do it!"

Katie's pulse fluttered in her wrists, in her throat. "What is that thing," she said, her voice hoarse. Every hair on her body was standing on end as Mel's sword flashed in the sunlight.

I don't know, Nyth said. *I've never seen it before. Katie, this time—*

"I can't."

A rush of hot air like a breath on her cheek, and she heard his voice fully. "What if there are more of those things in there? We need to seal this fast."

"Maybe Mel can…"

But Mel was struggling even with one creature. That square strength of Skiron's was in her shoulders more than ever—he was there, he was with her, they assimilated—but she was still Mel, and she'd obviously never held a sword before. The creature tried to dodge around her to get at Simon, and she barely kept it back.

Simon was visibly sweating, pushing thicker and thicker growth of vines around the border of the rift. They closed over the cracks in Mel's work, wrapping them tightly. The vines began to bristle with flowers, tiny white and yellow things, and the edges stabilized where they grew. It took too long, but finally, finally he got it solid.

Dominic didn't miss a beat, rushing in, eyes blazing, to blast the rift solid. Asha stepped in, getting ready to ripple it clear.

Katie's breath still came ragged and shallow in her chest. She couldn't stop watching the thing, all its skittering legs, couldn't stop imagining the fire she knew she had to channel to get it closed.

She felt a sudden rush of heat under her skin. It reminded her of a hand taking hold of her chin and turning her face. *Focus.* But her knees were wobbling.

Mel cried out. Katie's gaze darted back over—Mel stumbling, hand pressed to her thigh. "Simon! Ophion, get it down!"

Things were happening too fast. Simon held one hand to the border, holding the vines in place, and reached the other hand to Mel. Roots shot from the ground, tried to encircle the creature, but it dodged them. Simon called, "I can't," and turned back to the rift as a crack wiggled free, sending fresh vines to tie it back down.

We need to do this now, Katie. We don't have time to mess around.

Her heart was going to burst. She couldn't breathe. Fine. *Fine.* "Fine!" she screamed, and she threw up her hands, and her body jerked forward as all the heat inside her charged out her palms and turned into flame.

It was so much more than the contained, controlled little flame of the stove burner she'd made a tentative peace with. It was so much hotter than the familiar and comforting heat of the oven. The sound of it swallowed her as the rift caught fire in a hot orange blaze that melted it all to glowing white and faded it away to nothing.

Everything rang white and roaring in her ears and eyes for a long moment. She couldn't feel her hands. Her face was numb. She heard one of her friends yelling but she also heard twisting, screaming metal, lurching in her ears until she felt sick.

Vaguely, as through smeared glass, she saw the roots come back up from the ground and catch the creature in a cage. Sweating and panting, Mel raised the sword and brought it down heavily once, and then again, and then the creature stopped moving. The roots sank back into the ground as the creature crumbled into dust.

Katie's hands pressed over her mouth. Her body shook. Her knees buckled again, and this time they gave, and she was kneeling on the grass, bent so far forward her forehead almost touched the earth, gulping for air. She felt hands on her shoulders and a rush of air and then the hands were gone, but someone was kneeling in front of her. "Byrd." Dominic's voice was soft. "Hey, Byrd. Katie." She felt something brush her upper arms, and she flinched. "Hey. Listen to my voice, okay? Come on. Sit up, look at me."

Her trembling hands moved, one after the other, from her mouth to press against the ground. She pushed herself up enough to tilt her face to meet Dominic's gaze. "Slow breaths, Byrd. All the way down."

Her chest spasmed as she tried to breathe deep. It rushed out too fast, too thin.

"It's okay. Listen to my voice. Just close your eyes and listen."

She did, feeling the scrambling inside her head, but also feeling herself behind it, trying to claw back to calmness. She breathed again, deeply, and this one stuck.

"Keep your eyes closed but look up. Like at the sun."

Her heart jerked, and she choked on a sob. A ragged, wet breath rushed in and out, but it was deeper in her belly now, not shallow in her chest. Her hands and face tingled, but she pressed her fingers in the springy grass of—of the veil, they were in the veil—and breathed, and she started counting backwards from 100 by threes.

When the dizziness had passed enough for her to sit up straight, she met Dominic's eyes. He looked wrecked. Katie let out a shuddering sigh, wiping her face with the heel of her hand. "Sorry," she said.

"You don't have to apologize. You know that." He raked his hair out of his face. "But, uh, that was the worst one I've ever seen you have."

She fidgeted with the ends of her sleeves, pulling them down over her hands. "Did the others—"

"Nyth took you pretty quick. I had Aerie bring me to you. Everyone else is at the meeting place. We can wait 'til whenever you're ready."

"Guessing I can't really hide this."

He grimaced. "Not so much. It's okay. Nobody's mad or whatever."

That wasn't the point, but she didn't have the energy to argue. "Let's just go, then," she said. It took a minute to get to her feet. Dominic hovered close enough she could've leaned on him but didn't reach out to touch her. He had learned early on not to do that.

They made their way through the trees back to the circle of stumps. Everyone else was there, kids and guardians. Including Nyth, who was managing to look both worried and pissed. Dominic must've told him to hold off.

"Okay," Katie said, sitting on one of the stumps. "So, what the hell was that?"

"We don't know," Zephyrus said. She stood with Skiron outside the ring of stumps. Ophion wasn't there—no, they were. Flowers sprung from the ground where Simon sat and curled protectively around his knees. "We know all things that live in both this world and Harath, but we do not know this beast."

"Like the vine," Asha said. "It's something different."

Katie furrowed her brow. Her mind was still sluggish, exhausted by the panic. "The vine," she said. "When I tried to test it, all it left behind were these… particles. Just like that thing did when Mel…"

"And since we know nothing about it, we don't know if more exist," Aerie said. "It might've been an anomaly. Or there might be more that are able to cross through any rift we're trying to seal."

"More seems likely." Nyth paced the perimeter of the circle. "The vine showed up more than once. Now this—rift beast. It's a progression."

"So, we have to be ready," Mel said. Her voice was rough, and she kept rubbing her thigh.

"Are you okay?" Asha asked. "I mean, didn't you… wasn't that assimilation?"

"Yeah. Good thing, too. Whatever that thing was, I couldn't have handled it alone. It spit acid at me or something."

"I am sorry." Skiron's voice rumbled into the surrounding ground. He somehow sounded even graver than usual. "I did not feel the pain." Mel looked at him. She didn't say anything, but her eyes cleared a little. Katie's gaze flicked over to Nyth. He was staring at her.

"I'll be fine," she said. He still kept frowning.

Mel stood up, wincing. "I kind of want to get home and patch this up," she said, gesturing to her thigh. "Is there anything the five of us can do about this beast thing?"

"No." Aerie shook her head. "If we don't know anything about it, there's no way you could. We'll let you know as soon as we learn something."

Katie remembered that she hadn't even left the school yet, back home. She still had to get home. Do homework. Pretend things were fine at dinner with her family. In the wake of a panic attack, it sounded beyond exhausting.

"Yeah," she said. "Let's go home."

Mel left first. She barely even said goodbye to Simon. He watched her go, frowning, then said his own goodbyes and left, too.

The guardians began to shimmer out of view, one by one. Nyth lingered, staring hard at Katie across the circle. She shook her head; he twisted up his mouth and disappeared.

Strangely, Skiron was the last guardian left. "Um…" Asha peered up at him. "Are you alright?"

"This is grave." His voice was softer than Katie had ever heard it. "We must do all we can."

"Of course."

And then he was gone. Asha turned to Katie and Dominic, wide-eyed. "Is he okay?"

"I wouldn't be able to tell." Dominic stood up. "But he has the right idea. Let's go."

Katie lifted her sightstone, something heavy settling in the pit of her stomach.

Chapter 13

The temptation to stay in bed and pretend to be sick the next day was overwhelming. Her body still felt tired, and the memory of so much fire so close to her skin kept dancing in the back of her mind, spiking her adrenaline before she'd even put her feet on the floor. But she did, somehow, though breakfast didn't happen, and her hair ended up in a ponytail instead of combed neatly down her back.

Dominic was there to meet her outside the buses, as always, but their small talk was stilted. Katie made her way to first period in half a daze, only to find Mel grimacing in her seat behind Katie.

"You okay?" Katie asked quietly.

"My leg just hurts." Mel didn't look up from her notebook. She wasn't writing anything.

"Are you sure? You seem a little…"

"Byrd. It's fine."

Asha slid into her seat, and they exchanged hellos, but before Asha could say anything else, Katie said, "Did you have something that treated it okay? If you want, I can see if—"

"Will you let it go?" Mel finally looked up. The shadows under her eyes were deeper than usual. "I mean, do you want to talk about how *you're* feeling?"

Katie felt her mouth pull into a hard line. She turned in her seat. Asha caught her gaze, widening her eyes and mouthing *What's wrong?* Katie shrugged, shook her head, and opened her book.

"Mel was rude as hell in first period," she said the moment she sat next to Dominic in chemistry.

"Well, nobody's dancing on sunshine right now. Yesterday was rough." The memory of the rift beast skittering out of the rift, trying to tackle Simon and Mel, sent a chill through her. "I'm sure she's gonna be fine. Just maybe, y'know, don't pry. She's private."

Katie lowered her voice a little more, enough for Dominic to hear her over the chatter of their classmates. "Yeah, well, this is something we all share. If she doesn't talk to us, who's she gonna talk to?"

"Maybe she doesn't want to talk."

"I guess."

The bell rang, and Mrs. Kozel started class. Katie paid attention, opening her folder to pass in her homework. Right after she'd put hers on top of the pile and kept passing it to the front row, her phone buzzed in her pocket.

Dom

    are YOU okay?

She frowned, typing back under her desk.

I mean yeah
Now
But this is why I didn't want to do that again
I knew I'd panic

Dom

    is it anything N can help w?

The mention of Nyth made her heart feel funny. A happy warm leap conflicting with a sinking dread. She'd hated the way he'd looked after the sealing yesterday.

Idk, maybe?

But he's busy, esp now
I'll try to figure it out on my own

And of course, because she couldn't get a break, Mrs. Kozel made everyone get into their groups for last ten minutes of class.

"Okay," Victoria said, down to business as always, "who wants synthesis?"

Nobody spoke up. Katie glanced at Jordan and Malia. One of them could have it if they wanted.

"Please." Victoria's tone went flat. "I swear to god, guys, don't make me assign it out like a teacher."

"I really want to do single replacement," Malia said. "I have this idea to test reactions using the periodic table to predict if they'll go single replacement."

"Okay." Victoria wrote it down. "Now who's taking synthesis?"

Katie stared across the aisle at Jordan, who stared back. She sighed. "I'll do it." Like it mattered. Like she was going to be able to care about this project at all, with everything else going on.

"Thank you." She noted it on her list. "Jordan, how do you feel about decomposition?"

"I can do that."

"Great. And I'll do double-replacement."

Silence settled in. Katie frowned at the twinge of guilt in her chest. She could try to care. If she completely flaked, she'd feel guilty about it, and the last thing she needed was more guilt. "So we can each fill out our project plans," she said. "And bring them to the next session and see how we can put it all together into a cohesive project?"

"Good idea." Malia smiled. "You know, I'm glad you're in our group, Katie."

"Thanks." That—that was really nice.

She stared down at her project plan worksheet, mentally running through options for her portion of the project. Or trying to. After a few seconds, her mind wandered. To rifts. To a gross creature skittering on too many legs. To fire in her hands—

"Earth to Katie."

She snapped her head up. Malia was holding out an orange sheet of paper. "Sorry."

"No worries. Here."

Katie took the paper. It was a flier with a cheesy-spooky drippy font and a cartoon ghost coming out of a house's window. "A Halloween party?"

"Yep. I do one every year. You're all invited." Victoria and Jordan had invitations, too. "Me and Rosie and Asha, we go all out."

"Asha's going?"

"Of course. So, you should definitely come. Costumes aren't mandatory but they get you bonus points."

A party. For Halloween, which she loved. Something normal. Something fun. Something without rips in the fabric of reality or her friends killing things with swords or panic attacks.

"Yeah," she said. "That sounds fun."

Malia grinned.

Katie was nearly asleep Friday night when her sightstone rattled her wrist bones under her pillow.

With a groan, she wriggled free from Skimbleshanks—who looked offended at her leaving him—and squinted at her sightstone in the dark. "Your timing sucks," she groused. But she jammed her feet into a pair of shoes, listened at her door to be sure nobody was in the hall, and then lifted her sightstone.

She landed in the meeting place. Asha flashed in at the same time, wearing purple-rimmed glasses and a chunky, oversized cardigan over her pajamas. "I didn't know you wore glasses," Katie said as Nyth shimmered into view.

"Contacts," Asha said, and then Nyth was taking Katie's hand and pulling her away.

It was dazzlingly bright daylight when they arrived with Asha and Zephyrus right behind them. Katie squinted in the sunlight at Dominic and Mel. Sand shifted beneath her feet, and an ocean rolled its waves up close, and thankfully there was nobody else in sight on the beach surrounded by steep cliffs.

Nyth was still holding her hand. How long had he been? He didn't look disappointed like he had last time. He gave her a small smile, then vanished as the rift unmasked.

It cracked a jagged line right above the waves. Simon appeared at the same time that Mel assimilated. They shared a look, then leaned straight into stabilizing the border with vines and crystallization. Katie firmed her feet in the sand and reached out to Nyth. She didn't have to reach far. He rose to meet her, and her sightstone grew hot in her hand, and the heat began to build under her skin.

But the border wasn't moving fast enough. A shivering pocket of void appeared right in the middle. Mel swore, and she and Simon pushed the border faster, but a bulbous, leathery head shoved out, followed by too many skittering legs, and then a rift-beast was on the sand. Mel pulled back, crouched, and shoved her gauntleted hand deep into the sand to pull out her sword; but by the time its blade flashed in the sunlight, another rift-beast shoved its head through the rift and crawled onto the ground.

"Keep going," Mel called. "All of you." She squared her shoulders, her hands strong around the hilt of the sword, and she lunged in.

Katie's heart beat in her throat. But Skiron was with Mel, and Nyth was nudging her focus back to the rift. She took a shaky breath as Mel cut into one rift-beast, slashing its side as it wriggled away, as she tried to block the second one, as it split open its mouth and tried to bite her, its too-many tiny teeth clattering along her armor as she dodged away. Katie breathed through the anxiety and felt the heat swell inside her, ready to channel into the rift.

Then Mel swore again, and the second rift-beast slithered under her sword and raced towards Katie.

Her heart leapt. She tried to twist out of its path, but her feet had sunk deep into the sand.

A strong, sudden gust of wind nearly knocked her down, and as she tried to dodge the beast, for a second, she caught sight of Dominic. He was wearing different clothes now, and the rift's swirling mass had already been stilled, and he was leaping into the air and making some motion with his hands, and that was all she had time to see before the rift beast slammed against her shins and she sprawled across the sand.

"Are you serious?" Mel swung her sword, then swore, leaping back as the beast's tongue lashed across her legs. "What's in these things?"

Katie gulped a trembling breath, wondered why the beast wasn't already on her, tearing apart her soft, unarmored, weaponless body.

Then she heard it shriek. Near her, but not on her. From up in the air, Dominic was shooting arrows at the second rift beast. She could barely see the arrows or the bow—they looked like glass.

Focus, Nyth said. *They're taking care of it. Just focus on the rift.*

Katie nodded. She gripped her sightstone, climbed to her feet on unsteady legs, and turned back to the rift.

Asha stood in front of it, knee-deep in the water. The waves lapped against her legs, then started to curl around her, and then a flash of light blocked all view of the rift. When it faded, Asha's clothes were gone, replaced by the same shifting dress Zephyrus wore. Asha raised both her hands, and as she did, the center of the rift rippled clear faster than it ever had before.

And now it was time. Katie thought back to that quiet candle flame inside her, and she closed her eyes and tried to let it grow. But a lightning bolt of panic shot through her, riding the tremors of the rift-beast's attack. No no no I can't, not yet. A twinge of frustration from Nyth; but then it vanished, and the heat in her rose again, then rushed out her hands towards the rift.

One of the beasts was already gone. Mel hacked into the other one last time, and it crumbled into the sand. The border of the rift glowed bright white hot, melted in on itself, and sealed away the rift.

Katie's heart beat hard as she met Mel's gaze, but she turned away when Dominic landed from out of the sky and held his arms open wide.

"Look at this!" He spun in a circle, showing off the light blue jacket with its high collar and what looked like, in the brief glimpse Katie had, embroidered wings on the back. He was beaming in a way he only did sometimes, when he'd had an amazing run, or beaten someone's ass soundly at chess or cards. A wild, loose, free grin that looked so at home on his square face. "This is incredible, Byrd, like a thousand percent incredible."

Katie smiled. Something in the flick of his hands reminded her of Aerie—was Aerie. That's what assimilation meant, right? "Coolest kid I know," she said. She couldn't feel Nyth anymore, now that she wasn't channeling all that heat through her body. The sun was bright, but she felt a little cold.

Asha came back from the water. The hem of her dress trailed behind her so that Katie wasn't sure where it ended and the seafoam began. "It's just… right," she said. Her voice was so calm and even, and her smile was so serene. "Like coming home."

Light flashed, and Mel was just Mel again, in shorts and a zipped-up hoodie. "Proud of you kids. But it's late, and we have school tomorrow. Get yourselves home safe." There was blood splattered on her neck and the side of her face. She half-waved, then disappeared.

"Do you think she's okay?" Katie asked.

"Tired. I mean, we're all tired. But seriously!" Dominic's grin was even bigger, if that was possible.

But Katie looked to Simon. He stood with his hands in the

pockets of his cardigan and stared out over the water. Asha stepped in closer and spoke to him, too softly for Katie to hear. Simon shook his head, but smiled at her, and Asha touched his arm for a moment before turning and coming back up the sand.

"Mel's right. We should get home. Even if I don't want to undo it." But she closed her fingers around her sightstone and when the light faded, she was back in her pajamas.

"Glasses," Katie mused. "Don't know why it's throwing me so much."

Asha was still glowing. "I've never seen you with your hair braided, either."

"Keeps it from tangling when I sleep."

"And keeps you looking impossibly adorable." Dominic sighed, then flashed back into his own clothes as well. He glanced at Asha. "Weird."

"Almost lonely," she said. "After they've gone."

Dominic met Katie's gaze. "Don't stay out too late, now," he said, in his best dad voice, which wasn't very good.

Katie forced a laugh. "I promise. See you guys tomorrow."

When Asha and Dominic had gone home, Katie walked down to the water. Simon sat now in the last stretch of dry sand, and Katie sat next to him, pulling her knees to her chest and leaning back on her hands. The sand was warm at first, then cooler as her fingers sank deeper into it.

"We should form a club," she said. "The Reluctant Late Bloomers Club."

He half-laughed, mostly just a little expulsion of air. "I can write the bylaws."

"We'll need a passcode and a secret handshake."

"I think we can make that work."

They fell into silence. It was that silence Katie was trying to be more comfortable with, that both Simon and Mel always settled into with such ease. She listened to the roll of the waves and watched the sunlight on the shifting water. A breeze ruffled her shirt. It was a cool breeze, and it only reminded her of how much colder she felt when she wasn't helping Nyth. When he wasn't helping her.

"What's wrong with us, anyway?" she asked.

Simon didn't answer right away. He took the pause he always took when what he wanted to say was important to him and he wanted to get it right. "I like a quiet life," he eventually said. "Like my garden. Gardens are slower and quieter than people. Maybe that's why I feel better there. I don't want to be in the spotlight. I don't like it. And…" He cleared his throat. "Sometimes it's still difficult for me to admit to myself that I'm really doing this. That all of this, this superhero kind of life, is real. So, if all I do is stand there and let Ophion use me as a focal point for their power, then I can keep myself distanced from it all. But if we assimilate…"

Simon leaned forward, resting his elbows on his knees. His hands twisted together. "I don't want to do the things Mel's having to do, or Dominic, now. Maybe I won't. Asha didn't do anything too… violent." He shook his head. "But I know if I assimilate with Ophion, it's all going to get more real. More personal. Because saving the world is kind of impersonal, isn't it? It's so abstract. But inviting a sentient force of nature to share your mind and heart, that's different. And I can't. Not yet. No matter how much I love Ophion."

Katie turned her head, leaning it against her knees to look at him. "I don't get that," she said. "I mean, I understand what you're saying. But for me—god, I want to be close to Nyth more than almost anything. It's like Asha said. He already feels like coming home and we haven't even assimilated. I want to help. I want to be stronger and better. But I keep stopping myself. I feel like a failure."

"You're not a failure."

"And you're not not ready. Like you said, your garden is basically your home, and Ophion is basically a garden. But both of us are stopping ourselves."

He finally looked at her. "I guess we have to figure out how to stop stopping, then."

Katie held his gaze for a moment. Then she looked out across the water again and lifted her hands in the air, splaying her fingers and making an explosion noise. "Gimme the epiphany."

Simon laughed. "Exactly."

She stood up, scattering sand as she went. "C'mon though. It's late—at least back home."

"I know." He was still watching the water. "I kind of want to stay a little longer."

Katie bit her lip, glanced up at the cliffs. "Are you sure? What if someone comes along and only speaks—I don't know where we are—Greek or something?" She tilted her head. "You're sure you'll be safe by yourself on the other side of the planet?"

He looked up at her, his eyes serious. "Do you think Ophion would ever let anything happen to me?"

Katie smiled. "No. I know they wouldn't."

"Goodnight."

"Goodnight."

As she was pulling her sightstone back into her palm, he said, "Take care, Katie Byrd. We'll get there, in time." She only nodded, then drew herself home.

Chapter 14

Katie knew her family was picking up on her mood. Her father gave her a wide berth, and Tracy followed suit. Alex asked her on Sunday morning if she wanted to join him in a video game—that was his version of noticing, of trying. Katie shook her head, said she just wanted to knit, and hoped it didn't hurt his feelings.

Her dad appeared in her doorway around one o'clock. "We were thinking of going out for lunch," he said. "Your brother, too. You want to come?"

She flashed him a smile. "I kind of want to lie low. But thanks."

He nodded, hesitated a moment, then went back down the hall.

Katie put down her knitting, listening to the sounds of them getting ready floating up the stairs. When the door closed, and she heard the car pull away, she got off her bed. After pulling on her coat and a hat, she went out and started walking.

It was chilly but clear-skied. The gentle warmth of the sunlight on her face was a welcome comfort. Katie wove through the neighborhood, circling blocks as her thoughts circled the same paths. How free Asha and Dominic looked after assimilating. How long it took them to close the rift because of Katie. The blood spattered on Mel's face.

Katie swallowed. The walking wasn't chasing the thoughts out. But it did feel better in her body than sitting still had. It always did.

She headed home when her stomach started grumbling for food. She had just turned the corner onto her street when she saw him, wearing a black sweater and jeans and sneakers. "That's better than your last attempt," she said.

Nyth grinned. "Aerie gave me pointers."

"No coat, though. Aren't you cold?"

"Katie. Look who you're taking to."

"Good point." She felt her cheeks stretching and realized she was grinning. If he'd be upset with her for pulling back again, he seemed to be over it now, and it was a relief. "I missed you. You didn't stay to talk after the last rift."

"I missed you too. We've been doubling down on work, trying to figure this all out."

"Is that why you're here?"

His eyes warmed. "Nope. Just wanted to come spend time with my favorite vessel."

"Aren't I your only vessel?"

"The one and only."

Katie angled her head towards her house. "I'm heading home to make some tea and noodles. You want to come? My family should still be out for a while."

"I would love noodles!"

"Do you even eat?"

"I can! Come on, show me where you live. It'll be fun."

They walked together back to the house. He turned circles in the entryway while Katie unwrapped herself. She laughed at him. "You can explore if you want while I make the food. I have cats."

"I love cats!" He grinned and dashed off down the hallway.

Katie boiled water and stirred in spices and sliced toppings, all the while listening to Nyth's distant exclamations that Peaches was beautiful or the couch was soft or Skimbleshanks liked him or there were so many books in that one room. He reappeared in the doorway, holding Batty, who Katie could hear from five feet away was purring intensely. "I like it here," he said.

She grinned. "I'm glad. Hey, I just heated water for some tea, too. Do you want a cup?"

"Yes please!"

"What kind?"

"What kinds are there?"

"Oh, you have no idea what can of worms you opened, asking me that." He stood next to her while she ran down her extensive tea collection in the cupboard, describing the different varieties. Finally, he said "That one" to a masala chai.

Katie made the cups of tea and portioned noodles and broth into bowls. "I hope you like it. I don't know what guardians of the veil usually eat."

"Not this. I'm excited! It's been a long time since I ate with a mouth."

She took a careful sip of her tea. "Then try some, doofus."

Without pause, Nyth swirled a huge forkful of noodles and stuffed them in his mouth. His eyes widened, and Katie almost choked on her tea. "Are you okay? Did you burn your mouth?"

He shook his head rapidly and said something too muffled by noodles to understand. She raised her eyebrows; he chewed, swallowed, then said, "This is delicious." Katie laughed, and they fell into silence, both eating noodles—though she blew on hers a bit to cool them, at first.

She watched him as they ate and sipped their tea. The afternoon sunlight was bouncing off the walls of the kitchen, and he almost glowed in it, the way it played off his golden skin and bright red hair. A glance told her the palms of his hands still didn't have any creases. He looked so human until she noticed things like that. He felt so human-sized, sitting here in her kitchen.

Nyth caught her gaze. His mouth was full of noodles again, so he raised both eyebrows questioningly—a really human expression. It was hard to remember what he was, right now. "Nothing," she said. "It's just surreal to be sitting in my kitchen with you, eating noodles."

"Well, I think it's great to be sitting in your kitchen with you, eating noodles." He slurped the last of his bowl and drank some of his tea. When he set the cup down, he turned it around a few times in one hand before saying, "You're not wrong. It's not exactly standard behavior for a guardian to have lunch with a human. But I wanted to come say hi and make sure you're okay after that last sealing." His eyes darted in her direction. "You've been soggier and soggier the past few days."

Katie caught the last of her noodles from the bottom of her bowl and ate them, to not have to answer right away. "I'm okay, more or less. We did what we had to do. And like, yeah, I wish I'd done it sooner, so maybe Mel wouldn't have gotten hurt." She stared down at the light reflecting on the broth left in the bowl. "But that's it. I'm not doing it again."

Nyth sighed noisily. "I was afraid of that. I'd hoped you'd be okay with it by now."

Something hot and cold at the same time jolted through her chest. "No, I'm not okay with it now," she said, glaring at him. She heard the sharp edge in her voice, but she didn't care. "I had a panic attack after that if you'll recall. Panic attacks do not equal being okay with it now."

"Yeah, I recall. That's why I'm here. But we don't know if this is gonna keep happening. If it does, sealing off rifts with fire is faster and easier. It might prevent—"

Katie pushed her chair back, the legs scraping the floor. "Do you think I don't know that?" She grabbed her bowl and his, turning sharply and taking them to the sink. "I'm not stupid, okay? I'm completely aware everything would be better if I could just get over myself." The bowls and forks clattered when she dropped them; she turned the water on too high. "But I can't."

"I'm trying to get you past it so we can do better."

She heard his chair scoot back and felt him walk up behind her. She raised her shoulder, blocking him, and poured too much soap into one of the bowls, grabbed the sponge, started scrubbing. "Well maybe I'm not ready to get past it."

"Okay, then why are you so afraid? You know I'd never let you get hurt. If you tell me why you're so scared, maybe I can—" He sighed. "You're getting water all over your sleeves, doofus."

"I don't care."

"What's the matter with you? Push them up." He reached down into the sink, shut off the water, and then her heart clenched as his fingers touched the hem of her left sleeve.

"Don't," Katie hissed, jerking her arms in close and stepping away from the sink, away from him.

Nyth stared at her, irritation melting into concern. "Why are you crying?" he asked.

Oh. She was.

She could hardly see him through the tears. "This," she said thickly, and she rolled her left sleeve up to her elbow. Her vision was too blurred for her to see her own skin, but she knew it, knew the too-pink and too-pale mottled coloring of her skin, the angry line from the seam of the skin grafts.

She heard Nyth's sharp, soft inhale.

He knew fire well enough to know what caused these scars.

Katie yanked her wet sleeve back down over her arm, pulling it almost to her fingertips. "So, no," she said. "No, I'm not okay with it now."

He didn't say anything. The wall clock was ticking too loudly. Katie stared at the sink, at the half-washed dishes, at anything except Nyth. Finally, he asked quietly, "How did that happen?"

Her heart was in her stomach. "That's nobody's business," she said, just as softly. "Not even yours." Her wet sleeves clung to her arms. It made her shiver. "My family's going to be home soon. You should go." He waited a moment, maybe expecting something, then shimmered briefly before disappearing.

Katie left the dishes in the sink and went upstairs, into her room, shutting the door and locking it. She tugged off the wet shirt and dropped it on the floor, then stood in the center of the bedroom, staring at her dim reflection in the mirror. Her eyes started to sting again.

Reaching down, she took hold of the hem of her next shirt, peeling it over her head. She yanked off her shorts and pulled off her leggings and stood, shivering, looking in the mirror, before finally pulling off the last layer, the thin tank top, until she was staring back her bare skin. All her bare skin. The scar that ran up her left arm, the discolored skin that trailed onto her shoulder, teasing at the side of her neck. Her left side, streaking partway across her chest, her back, her stomach. Her hip, her thigh. Healed, grafted, not puckered and distorted like when her burns were new, but scars all the same. Like a shadow hanging over half of her but trying to swallow her whole. The way the fire had tried to swallow her whole.

She shivered with cold, and with her tears, and when she tried to touch the scars on her stomach, she cringed and turned away.

She put on her two warmest long-sleeved shirts and yanked on leggings and then sweatpants on top, and then she crawled into her bed and pulled up the covers. Skimbleshanks was napping under the sheet, and he purred when she burrowed under the covers. Katie rested a hand on his warm side and turned her face into her pillow and cried.

Chapter 15

Six in the morning was dark and cold, and Katie's stomach was still heavy, and she hadn't slept much. It was easy to fake sick to her father. She stayed in bed, dozing and sharing the warmth of Batty and Skimbles curled up with her.

When she finally got up, it was late morning, and pale, clear sunlight flooded her room. She stood by her window, washed in the sunbeams, next to the bundle of poppies and nettle dried out in her windowsill. The sunshine felt like an apology.

Her day passed in a quiet blur of blankets and bad daytime television and feeling too heavy to even think. For a little while she worked on Dominic's sweater, but even knitting didn't feel good. It was early afternoon, still a few hours before Alex would be home, when she felt something warmer brush near her. Like a wave of heat when you open the oven door. Katie looked up. The sunlight sparkled extra-bright. "Come on in," she said, and Nyth shimmered into view.

"Hi," he said.

"Hi."

"I'm sorry I made you feel bad yesterday. And I want to make you feel better."

The corner of her mouth twitched to the side. "That's sweet. You can't fix it, though."

"At least let me try to cheer you up." His eyes were dancing. "I have something I want to show you. Something I know you'll love."

Katie peered up at him, scrutinizing the light in his face. "Okay," she said. "What is it?"

"Not what. Where. C'mere."

He held out his hands to her. His face was warm, his eyes shining. She took a deep breath and took his hands.

He pulled her away through the darkness and warmth, and when they landed, he said, "Don't open your eyes yet."

"Nyth, c'mon." But she kept them closed. There was wind, *warm* wind, brushing her hair over her shoulders and tugging at the hem of her sweater. The air was chillier than she liked, but so much warmer than home right now that she didn't even care. She rocked on her feet, feeling hard, uneven ground. "Where are we?"

He gently pulled her hands to turn her in another direction. "Okay," he said, stepping back beside her. "Open and look."

The sun dazzled her eyes for a moment, and then Katie gasped.

They stood on top of a red rock formation, a wide desert sprawling far below them. It rose from flat ground into more rock formations, sandy pale at the bottom striping to reddish at the top, rising and falling in uneven, strange shapes. The sky was a blue bowl above them, and below, nestled between the rock faces, greenish water squiggled through the rocks. It was bright and clear and warm and beautiful, and it made her heart beat faster.

"Where is this?" She felt herself smiling as she asked.

"Lake Powell. In your Utah. And Arizona, but we're in the Utah part. Lots of humans come out here, so I tried to pick an emptier spot." He leaned into her sightline. His smile was like the sunshine. "You like it?"

"I love it. It's gorgeous." She met his gaze. "It's very you."

It was apparently possible for him to smile even wider because that's what he did. "It's one of my favorite spots around here. Good energy. Lots of sun."

"Can we just sit and soak it all up?"

"Absolutely."

They sat on the rock, gazing out over the landscape. Katie took deep breaths of the clean air, letting all the good energy of the place fill her up. It did feel like Nyth, how expansive everything was, how she could see everything. It was so warm. Not only the sunlight and the breeze, but the entire presence. Nyth's presence. If she let herself reach out, she could almost touch it: that sparkling, shimmering, vibrant energy he embodied so well, that running-across-the-beach-at-noon feeling. But that hovered on the edges of something softer and quieter. She wasn't sure what it reminded her of. A little like burrowing into her blankets, snuggling one of the cats, perfectly warm and safe.

That quieter, gentler warmth seeped into her heart the longer she sat with him—it was a long time for him to sit still, but it felt like he wanted to, now—and started to feel like spring sunlight slowly melting ice. Everything gumming her thoughts and her chest started to soften.

She touched her left forearm. Through two shirts, she couldn't feel her scars, but she knew how they would rise and fall under her fingers. The ice melted a little more, and she opened her mouth and said, "I want to tell you how it happened."

When she looked at him, he was already gazing back at her, eyes steady. "Some people know parts of it," she said. "But nobody outside my family knows the whole thing. Not even Dom."

"Should I not say anything until you tell it all?" he asked.

"Probably. If I stop, I might not finish."

He held out one of his hands, palm up. Katie slowly laid her hand in his, trying not to wince at the twinge in her chest when his fingers brushed her wrist. And she looked back out over the desert because that made it the tiniest bit easier.

"Everyone knows my mother died when I was eight," she said. "And that my dad started homeschooling me for a long time after she died. Um, I didn't go to the school with everyone else. Dad taught me at home. It's a thing." Her heart was beating hard and fast in her chest. She wondered if Nyth could feel it through her hand.

He probably could. "And they know she died in a car crash. But I don't tell people details. I don't like to talk about it."

She swallowed. Her mouth was dry. But that soft, gentle warmth was still there. Nyth was supporting her more than just holding her hand. So she said, "I had a sleepover at my friend's house that night. It was my first one, and I was really excited, but when we went to bed, I got so homesick." She shook her head. "I didn't want to wimp out. But I got really miserable, so Emma's parents called my parents, and my mom came out to pick me up."

Involuntarily, her hand squeezed Nyth's. He returned the pressure and waited while she took a few slow breaths.

"She was talking and joking with me the whole way back, trying to cheer me up. She always—she was really funny, and fun. And I was starting to feel better. We were going to make French toast the next morning since I wouldn't get to have it with my friends. She— she said she'd teach me how to make it from scratch and everything." Katie stared hard out at the desert until it shimmered in her watery gaze. "I still can't eat French toast, you know?"

Nyth squeezed her hand. Her throat felt thick when she continued.

"There was—a truck. On the other side of the highway. It was— it was this stupid series of events, you know? The truck driver had a stroke. Lost control of his truck. The truck took the curve wrong and rolled onto its side and slid across the median and hit us." Her mother crying out, swerving hard to get out of its path, but not fast enough, and the scream of twisting metal and the bone-shuddering jolt and her seatbelt cutting hard into her ribcage as her body slammed to the side.

"And we were both still alive. But she was hurt. She couldn't move. The—door had crumpled in; she couldn't get her legs out." Katie's breath shuddered as everything twisted and climbed up out of her darkest places to roar in her chest. "She could turn around just enough to look at me. Her eyes—"

—were so big, so scared, blood on her forehead, but her voice was steady, urgent but steady and—

"She asked me if I was okay. I hurt a lot, but I could move. But I couldn't get my seatbelt unbuckled. It was jammed. She said—said we'd sit tight until the paramedics got there. Hold still so we didn't hurt ourselves more. I remember my stomach hurt from the seatbelt."

And then. And then, and then—her chest clenching, her hand clenching Nyth's, her voice not even remotely steady—"And then there was smoke. It smelled—so bad. And her eyes got more scared. She told me to get out of the car. I didn't—she was looking at me the whole time. I was crying. She said to try to wiggle out of the seatbelt. I couldn't, and she was—she couldn't move. And then—"

Fire running over her hands, Nyth's fire, not hurting her, but that was it, that was why, that was what pulled all this up, she had known it would, eight years of healing and therapy and processing and working so goddamned hard to get better and now, all of it, all of this—

"There was fire. Smoke and fire." Her words were short now, thick, warped by the tears she couldn't even try to stop. Her fingers hurt from clutching Nyth's hand so hard. "It came in her side first. She couldn't get out. It got me, too, but not all the way. The EMTs— one broke the window and cut my seatbelt and pulled me out. They couldn't get her. It—wouldn't have—it wouldn't have mattered—"

A keening sob broke out of her. She bent forward, curling in on herself, shaking. Nyth shifted next to her; his free hand came up to stroke her hair. It reminded her of how Mom used to touch it, and she cried harder.

For a while there was only the warm breeze and his gentle touch and Katie's sobs shuddering up from her core. But slowly they calmed—they always, eventually, slowly calmed, a little more easily now than they had a few years ago. And when they did, he started to talk to her, slowly, softly.

"This is important," Nyth said. "This is your forest fire."

"What," was all she managed, hiccupping and scrubbing her

face with her free hand.

"When I met you, I said you have fire in you. But what you don't get yet is that fire has more than one kind. There's fire that burns and destroys. That's the kind that hurt you and took your mother and makes you hurt like this now." His fingers pushed her hair back from her face. They were warm. "But another kind is healing. Protective. Hearth fires, that keep people warm and cook their food and help them survive." She thought she heard a smile come into his voice. "And there's the fire of creation. The fuel, the beginning of things, the drive that keeps you moving forward."

Katie wiped her eyes. Nyth's hand rested on the side of her head. "That warm thing you feel inside you, that's your fire, your fuel. That's the kind of fire you need to find in yourself." His hand left her hair. She heard him shift his weight. "Forest fires, when they come roaring through, yeah, they burn down the trees. But they also make way for new growth. New things."

Katie sat straighter and lifted her head. His smile was so gentle, his eyes so warm. Hearth fire, she thought. She swallowed, cleared her throat, and said, "I want to, Nyth. But actual fire in my hands brings this all raging up. And I—" She took a deep breath. "I think, if I had toughed it out that night, she wouldn't have had to come get me, and she'd still be here. Or if I'd admitted sooner that I couldn't do it, we would have been home before that truck even got to that part of the highway. And now I'm doing it again." She bit the inside of her lip and shook her head. "People are getting hurt because I can't get it together."

He stretched out his legs and sighed. "Look. With wildfires, sometimes it takes years for the new growth to come through. But there are some flowers that only grow after a fire. It's the only way the soil has the right nutrients for them to bloom." He tilted his head to the side. "You shouldn't have had to lose your mother. Especially not in a way that was so horrible. But you've grown so beautifully, anyway. You can grow through this, too."

A small smile grew on her cheeks. "That's—thank you. That

means a lot, from you."

"I'd rather all these things hadn't happened to you. But the fact that you're growing anyway says a lot about you."

Katie sniffled, wiped at her face and nose one more time. "The doctors," she said. "I was in the hospital for a long time. And I had to go back a bunch of times, for skin graft surgeries and stuff. But early on, they said—between the smoke inhalation and the burns— There was this one doctor who was in charge of my case when I was first there. I remember her telling my dad that I was healing way better than they'd ever expected. My lungs—even my—my skin. That part, she said, was practically a miracle." She let out a shuddering breath. "So maybe you're right. Maybe I'm built to—to live through it. To thrive anyway."

Nyth was quiet for a minute. He sat back and looked at her with a furrowed brow. "I wonder."

"Wonder what?"

He hesitated. Nyth didn't usually hesitate. His eyes burned into hers until she almost fidgeted under the intensity of his gaze. Then he said, "Have you ever wondered why we chose you kids as our vessels?"

A sharp, clear laugh escaped her. "Only constantly. We're actual kids, Nyth."

"I know." His gaze darted to the side, then he shook his head and said, "So, a while ago, we discovered the veil was thinning. It always does that from time to time. It has cycles like everything else. We work harder for a while, and it goes back to normal. But this time it was thinner, and we had a harder time fixing it. So, we pushed ourselves until we could repair it, but we ended up pushing ourselves too far." He held up one hand in a fist, then opened it, splaying his fingers. "We splintered. Put so much of ourselves into the work that we left pieces of ourselves behind."

"That can happen?"

"Apparently." He huffed a sigh. "We felt it. It kind of hurt. But then the hurt lessened, and we thought it was gonna be fine. And the veil was repaired, so everything seemed alright. But it didn't feel good, missing those fragments of ourselves, and the work had gotten harder since we splintered. So, we tried to find the fragments." He met her gaze, half a grin pulling at the corner of his mouth. "We didn't find any on Harath, but we found them on Earth."

He paused. Dramatically, she thought. Katie rolled her eyes. "Where, Nyth?"

His eyes danced. "In some human children. Children who had some qualities that reminded us of ourselves. The fragments must've tried to find the closest thing to home they could, and they ended up in these kids."

The light in his eyes was purposeful. Katie raised her eyebrows, pointing to herself. "Me?"

"You."

"I'm the fragment?"

"Not your entire existence, doofus. It's just in you, like the other fragments are in the other kids. That's why we can channel our powers through you in the first place. Because part of us is in you, somewhere."

"I—" That warmth in her chest, that rush in her blood. She didn't know how she should feel. She didn't know how she *did* feel. "Why didn't you take it back?"

Nyth cocked his head and leaned back on his hands. "We were going to. The veil started thinning again, and when we tried to fix it this time, we weren't making much headway. And then the first rift opened, and we couldn't close that at all. And we thought, hey, maybe it's because we're missing those pieces of ourselves. But we couldn't figure out how to get them back from you kids without hurting you—they're buried too deep in you. So, we came up with the idea of the vessels instead." He grinned. "It was mostly Aerie. She knows the most about humans. Came up with the sightstones and everything." He leaned forward again, elbows on his knees. "Anyway, I wonder if that's why you healed so well. You got hurt by fire, but the fragment of me in you knows all about fire and how to handle it. So maybe it helped you get better faster." He shrugged. "Maybe."

Katie stared at him, down at her hands, back at him. This was—"This is a lot," she said. Her mind raced to process it all, and her heart heaved up to try to contain it all. "I—why didn't you tell us this to begin with?"

"Uh, exactly because it's a lot. I mean, I wanted to tell you, but Zephyrus and Aerie said it would be too much, and then Skiron said we weren't going to, and if you think I'm stubborn, he's even worse." His grin softened to a warm smile. "But I'm glad you know. I always wanted you to know."

She took a heavy breath, clenched and unclenched her hands a few times, then looked back up at him. His eyes, the same as hers. His grin, instantly familiar. "It makes sense," she said. "The second I picked up my sightstone, I knew it was… familiar. I knew it was mine, somehow."

"Because it is."

The warm Utah wind skimmed back over the rock face again, stirring her hair. "You said the veil is thinning again," she said. "Are we at least helping?"

His mouth twisted into a flat line. "It's helping. But maybe not fast enough. It's still thinning, and the rifts keep coming. And now with those rift beasts, we think there's something else going on. You know all that mist in the veil? It's not normally there. It means the veil is weakening."

"So, what can we do to fix it faster?"

A wry smile. "Assimilation seems to be helping."

Guilt twinged in her chest. "I can't force that."

"I know. And I wouldn't want you to. But hey, maybe this is a step, right? Maybe now you can trust me more."

"I do trust you."

"But not all the way. Because you're still too scared. But Katie, I promise you, the fire I use through you will never, ever hurt you."

"I know." And she did. But it wasn't that easy.

He watched her for a moment longer. Then he stood up, shaking out his hands. "Well, that's more than enough heavy stuff for one day. C'mon. There are more spots out here I want to show you."

Chapter 16

Katie's return to school was marked by a cupcake waiting on her desk in first period. It was rainbow-swirled cake, with neatly piped white frosting that spiraled into a peak, with glittery purple star sprinkles scattered on top.

She looked over at Asha, who gave her a small smile.

"Thanks," she said softly.

Asha nodded. "I hope you're feeling better. Did you have that bug that's been going around?"

"Something like that." She couldn't put a cupcake in her bag, and she didn't trust the crush of the hallway between classes, so she peeled back the paper and took a bite. "Oh my god, Asha," she said through a mouthful of frosting and cake. "This is so good."

Asha's smile broadened. "Thank you." She folded her hands together. "And you've seemed… like you've had a hard time lately. I hoped it would cheer you up."

Being vulnerable was not high on the list of things Katie enjoyed. Still, Asha was sweet. "Thanks. It really does."

Mel slouched in just before the bell, coffee in hand. "Cake for breakfast?" she asked as she slid into her seat behind Katie, who made a noise of assent through another mouthful. "Glad to see you're back, Byrd."

Everyone apparently accepted a sick day at face value. Dominic was the only one who poked at it further, texting her under his desk in chemistry.

Dom

    did you need to hide a little?

Katie almost smiled. He always could tell.

                              Yeah. But I'm okay now

Dom

    stayed cozy in the nest?
    get it?
    because Byrd?

She did smile at that, even if she rolled her eyes, too.

If she was honest, she was still shaky, still soggy around the edges, as Nyth might have said. But the sun was extra-warm again, and she could feel him everywhere. In that sunlight, in the warmth of her blood. He was in the adrenaline rush that spiked in her blood when she missed a step and almost fell down the stairs, but didn't fall, so she could laugh at herself for her clumsiness. And every time, no matter what she'd felt him in, the image rose in her mind of sunlight flashing between trees.

Every time, it was like she was back on the beach, not at the lake but at the actual ocean, seven years old with her hair still wet from the water. The chill of the shade as she sat at the back of the beach with her mother, sorting together through the pieces of sea glass she'd found. Katie's father halfway to the water, holding Alex by the wrists and spinning him in circles, kicking up sand, both of them laughing in the sunshine. Everything full of comfort and home and happiness, tired from swimming but pleased by so much activity, the good kind of tired. And the sunlight, winking between the leaves of the trees overhead, shifting in dapples on her shoulders and knees, every point of light, a point of warmth.

Katie wondered if Nyth had been in that sunlight, even then.

The warmth helped carry her through the morning, and she was the first one to the lunch table when Dominic slid into his seat next to her. "Hullo, fishface."

"Hullo, bugbreath. I have a proposal." He pointed back and forth between them. "You. Me. Science museum. This weekend." He crinkled open his brown paper lunch bag and pulled out a sandwich. "I'm of the opinion we need a good old-fashioned Dom-and-Byrd adventure."

Katie smiled. She could use something mundane and fun to keep climbing up out of her sad, soggy pit. "I'm in. It's been forever since I went to the science museum. Do you want to invite the others?"

"Do you have potatoes in your ears? I said Dom-and-Byrd adventure." He frowned, just for a moment, as he unwrapped his sandwich. "So much of our lives have gotten eaten up by that stuff. And it's cool. And I love our fellow superheros. But I also love Dom-and-Byrd adventures. Strictly mundane fun-times."

"Okay." Katie pointed an apple slice at him. "You do know you just doomed us, though, right?"

"By assuming it'll be mundane?" He shrugged, his grin reappearing as Asha slid into her usual seat. "We're already doomed. Embrace it."

Saturday morning was bright and sunny when Katie rolled out of bed, talking back to Skimbles in chirps and meows when he made a racket. "Don't complain. You have the bed to yourself now, right? You and Batty both. And it's all warm where I was lying. Enjoy it."

But the sunny, clear sky was deceptive: today was shockingly cold for mid-October. It took nearly ten minutes of sitting in the Gunn family's warm kitchen with a plate of egg-on-toast for Katie to fully warm up again. Dom's mother had offered them the loan of her car to drive into the city, on the terms that Dominic stay in the right-hand lane on the highway. So, once they were ready, Katie ducked back out into the cold and curled up on the passenger seat, holding her hands to the heat vents as they blasted air that wouldn't be warm enough soon enough. "I hate this," she groused. The pleasure of the sunshine was being crushed by the bitter chill. "Every freezing day is a battle to keep my core body temperature from crapping out on me."

"Clearly, you're a reptile. Maybe while we're out we can pick up a nice terrarium for you. And a heat lamp."

"Shut up," she said, but she was smiling. He cranked up his music, *("Do we have to listen to Dave Matthews?" "My car, my rules." "It's your mom's car." "Technicalities.")* and they pulled onto the highway.

At the museum, they wandered together through science phenomena exhibits, all the fun gimmicky ones where they could play with magnets and stand in a spot where their hair stood on end (Katie's hair was too long and heavy to stand straight out, but Dominic looked like a sandy-blond dandelion puff). They played in the shadow room, where they made weird fun shapes with their bodies and watched their shadows temporarily superimpose on the walls; they caught a film about weather patterns; then they split off for a little while. Katie spent almost an hour in the biomedical area, exploring interactive and educational exhibits on prosthetics, stem cells, PET technology—it made everything in her spark and light up. Hospitals still made her queasy, but this—the research, the developments, finding better ways to help people and save them and make their lives better—this filled her with excitement every time.

When she was done playing with the endoscopic camera in a model stomach, she went off to meet up again with Dominic. She found him at the indoor tornado machine, a grin on his face and a glint in his eyes that managed to look totally relaxed and kind of wild at the same time.

After the museum, they found a soup-and-sandwich shop down the street and huddled at a front table to have lunch before heading home.

"So?" Katie slurped the last of the broth from her spoon. "Verdict?"

"On?"

"Mundaneness. Mundaneity? Whichever."

"Yeah. For a couple hours there, I almost forgot we're superheroes."

"Good. Mission accomplished."

Dominic leaned back in his chair, stretching and scratching his chin. It made a rough sound. His facial hair had used to be softer and finer, less obvious when he didn't shave. This year it had started getting coarser. "I might be able to actually grow a beard someday," he mused, as though reading her mind, and his gaze drifted out the window. Then he sat up straight, suddenly beaming. "Look!"

Katie followed the line of his arm. "That little brown bird on the parking meter?"

"It's Aerie."

"Wait, for real?"

"Yeah." His gaze was fixed outside, his grin a million watts. "She shows up sometimes as that little bird." He waved, and the bird—Aerie—fluttered over by the window for a moment before flying away. "Just saying hi, I guess," Dominic said, still grinning.

They finished lunch and headed back outside. Katie shoved her hands in her coat pocket and blinked against the wind. "It's funny," she said. "Like, obviously, the guardians don't have to focus on their work a hundred percent of the time. Because they're away from it for sealings, or Aerie popping by like that. How do they spread themselves out?"

"I'm sure it's something we wouldn't understand. Though I've gotten the impression us being vessels makes it easier."

"Maybe because of the fragments?"

"The who now?"

He was staring at her, completely puzzled. She felt her cheeks start to burn. "Oh. Yeah. I wasn't supposed to mention that."

"No, no, no. Now you've gotta spill. What are the fragments?"

Katie sighed and told him what Nyth had told her: that the guardians had lost pieces of themselves, and those pieces had ended up in them, and in Asha and Mel and Simon.

"And that's why they picked us as vessels." Dominic ran his hand through his hair; it immediately fell back across his forehead. "And that's why assimilation works, and why it feels so right. Because when we fuse with our guardian, for a minute they get back that fragment of them that's in—our soul?"

"Soul's as good a word as any. It's all woo-woo to me."

"That explains so much," Dominic said. "Like, so, so much. Like how—"

It sounded like thunder, if thunder were forming all around you instead of way off in the sky, and everything shook, and—

People screaming, running away, and a jagged rift opening in the middle of the street.

Katie's heart skipped a beat as the sightstone on her wrist began vibrating insistently.

Dominic pulled his sightstone out of his pocket, and it flashed brightly as he and Aerie assimilated. People were staring and pointing and shouting, both at Dom and the rift. Katie's skin jumped with adrenaline. Then a rush of warmth and a surge of concern came through her sightstone. Nyth was here.

"Shit, shit, shit." Dominic started jogging towards the rift, Katie at his heels. "How are we supposed to—"

Mel and Simon flashed in, Mel already in her armor. "Son of a *bitch*," she seethed, seeing where they stood. Cars screeched to a halt, people climbing out of them, staring agape or running or pointing and yelling. "Simon, let's get this closed down. Now."

He didn't bother to nod. They lifted their sightstones and got to work.

No time to worry about people's reactions or how they would explain this or why the hell a rift had opened right next to them. Katie turned to the rift, trying to block out their surroundings. It was a wild one, long and wide and jagged, its borders pulsing manically against Mel and Simon's work. Katie felt the weight of her sightstone in her palm, felt its heat. She felt for the candle flame inside her, felt for that fragment of Nyth somewhere inside, and opened herself, letting the heat glow brighter in her.

Please don't let any beasts escape. Not here. Not now.

Asha appeared next to her, eyes and nose red and cheeks streaked with tears. Her eyes widened, realizing what she'd landed in, then in a flash, she assimilated with Zephyrus. She flung out her arms towards the crowd of people. White mist appeared in the air, settling down like a gauzy covering over everyone. As it fell, people's eyes fluttered closed, and they slumped across the hoods of their cars or fell to their knees and then laid across the sidewalk.

"Asha!"

"It's okay," she said, sniffling. "They're just sleeping. And—and hopefully they won't remember. I'm not sure." She was focusing, trying to push the mist into as large a cloud as possible, not bothering to scrub the tears out of her eyes.

"Damn it!" Mel's voice was harsh. Katie glanced back and saw one of the blank void pockets forming in the rift. Simon and Mel strained with effort, rushing the solidification around the edge of the rift—but too slow. The head of a rift beast wriggled out from the void. And then its featureless front end split open in a long, jagged horizontal gash that Katie realized was a mouth lined with sharp uneven teeth. It leaned forward out of the rift and bit down on the border, stopping the line of spreading crystallization. Its leathery skin bubbled and burst, and it went limp and dropped to the ground, dissolving into dust.

Katie's breath caught, and a stream of rift beasts began pouring out of the rift.

Dominic began firing arrows. Mel swore. Simon yelled louder than Katie thought he was even capable of, and beneath the rift, the pavement cracked and shattered as thick, leafy vines surged up and encircled the rift, completely crystallizing the border when they touched it, closing the void. His outstretched hands flashed a bright light, and more of the vines wrapped Simon in a cocoon of green for a moment before peeling back, leaving Simon standing, breathing hard, wearing armor made of tree bark and woven vines.

His gaze caught Katie's. In the middle of everything, there was a glimmer of peace in his eyes. It made her stomach twist.

Relieved from the border, Mel turned and chased down the fastest rift beast, which skittered along the edge of the street, running over collapsed bodies of bystanders, to loop behind the others. She crouched low to the ground mid-run and slammed her hand against a broken spot in the pavement; when she stood and ran on, her sword was in her hand. Simon turned for a moment, the peace lost to hesitation.

He doesn't know what to do, Katie realized. He said so on the beach. He doesn't want to fight.

But there were too many beasts. He ran after another one, the living armor on his arm shifting its shape and extending into a dangerously pointed spear. As he ran past her, Katie saw the grim focus in his eyes. It was so different from the almost-thrilled focus in Dominic's as he landed an arrow in a third rift beast, then paused long enough to send a blast of energy at the rift and meld its shifting colors into solid gray. The rift beast lunged at him, red mouth cracking wide to bite, but Dominic leapt into the air and resumed raining arrows into the thing.

Stay calm, Nyth said. He must have felt Katie's pulse pounding. *They're protecting you and Asha. They won't let the beasts get to you. Just focus and let go and don't doubt.* Katie swallowed hard and opened back up to the heat rushing under her skin as Asha began rippling the gray screen of the rift into a clear window.

The candle flame inside her was growing, slowly coaxed into brightness. She could almost feel Nyth's hands wrapping around hers again, filling her with heat and light and power. Come on, sunshine. You and me. We seal it fast, make quick work of the beasts, then the others will barely know what happened. We can help them. We'll be amazing. I've got you. Trust me.

The rift was clear. Katie's pulse raced and the flame inside her grew, filling every corner, until it finally began to flicker in the orange stone in her hands. She saw the light in it, and that was all she could see. The edges of her vision faded away as the light enveloped her.

Katie didn't know what she had expected. It was so fast when she watched it happen to the others. But as the flickering light surrounded her, it changed from a soft candle flame to a roaring, crackling, too hot, too bright, too yellow white-hot like she was standing in the center of a bonfire and no, no, she gasped in a ragged breath, clutched something inside her tight, and the surrounding fire vanished as her sightstone fell between her fingers and clattered on the pavement.

Dominic landed two arrows in the neck of another rift beast. Mel's sword swung in a shining arc, and more beasts crumbled to dust. Simon was crying, visibly shaking, as he speared a second rift beast through the middle and killed it. Over the din, Asha cried out to Katie, asking what was wrong, why they weren't sealing the rift.

Katie's fingers shook as she bent and retrieved her sightstone. Her friends seemed far away. Her limbs were heavy, slow to move. She held out the sightstone and dropped her head and, still crouching there, let Nyth push heat through her and slowly melt the border of the rift and seal it closed.

She reached out a tendril of thought to him. Nothing. Not a glimmer, not a hint, not a blush of thought or feeling.

But the rift did close; and Mel took down another rift beast, and Dominic killed the last one, and Simon knelt on the pavement, clutching his arm, and Asha knelt in front of him and gently took his hand and sent a wash of healing rain over his wound.

Katie sat in the middle of the scene, the sleeping bodies of the bystanders and the shattered pavement and her friends drenched in sweat and spattered in blood and shining in the garments of their guardians, and she stared at the lifeless stone in her hand and listening to Nyth's echoing silence.

Chapter 17

Katie hadn't spoken to any of her friends since Dominic drove her home, and she'd barely spoken to him then. She didn't even try to reach out to Nyth. After the rift closed, he'd completely blocked her out, like supernatural silent treatment.

If she could've avoided everyone on Monday, she would have. In first period, Mel and Asha were quiet; in second period, Dominic was too cheerful in that forced way that not everyone could see through, but she could. All of it made her even more irritated.

Once everyone was at the lunch table and the awkward silence landed heavy between them, she said, "I know, okay? Can we please just not?"

Asha and Dominic both relaxed visibly and fell into easier chatter, once the elephant in the room was recognized. But Mel still stared at her, and Simon too pointedly avoided her gaze. His shoulders were tense.

"So, are they helping?" Asha asked.

"They?"

"The gifts I made for you guys. The flowers and things? Are they helping anyone?"

"Oh." Katie's heart sank. "Yeah. It really is." Mel lowered her brows skeptically. Katie ignored her.

Simon's voice was quieter than usual. "Anytime I'm near it, everything feels the way it's supposed to."

"You did good, Asha," Dominic said. "They're helping."

"Oh, good. I thought they would. And—some things are going better, so I figured they must be doing something."

"Helping us be more in tune with the fragments, maybe?" Dominic said.

Katie shot him a glare he didn't see. "Then what now?" Mel asked. Asha tilted her head curiously.

Finally, Dominic glanced over and caught Katie's look. "Oops." He laughed, and he at least had the decency for it to be a sheepish laugh. "You did say we weren't supposed to know about that."

Mel's gaze darted between him and Katie. "You two keeping secrets?"

Katie shrugged, turning to Asha. "Not on purpose. Even telling Dom was an accident."

"What are they?" Asha asked.

"Nyth told me it's the reason they picked us, specifically us, to be their vessels. A while ago, one time they were repairing the veil, it took way too much energy. So these fragments of their—their essences, I guess? Fragments of themselves broke off and got lost. So, the fragments got lost on Earth and wanted to get back to where they belonged."

"But they couldn't get back to the guardians," Dominic interrupted.

"Right. So, they eventually latched onto the closest thing they could find." Mel kept staring at her, hard. She glanced down at her hands. "It's why we're all so much like our guardians. It's because there's a piece of them somewhere inside us."

"That makes so much sense!" Asha blushed and lowered her voice as she continued. "I've always had those dreams. I never told people because I was afraid they'd think I was crazy. But if I have a piece of Zephyrus's essence in my soul, I've probably always been tapping into her without even knowing it."

"Byrd," Mel said, her tone weirdly even, "why didn't you tell all of us about this fragments thing as soon as you found out?"

Because the context was nobody's business. Because what's

between me and my guardian is between me and my guardian. But outwardly, Katie just shrugged and said, "Nyth told me in confidence. I didn't even mean to tell Dom."

Mel's mouth twisted. "So what, you found this out when you were just hanging out with Nyth?"

Katie had been tense all morning, but her shoulders went tight at Mel's tone. She straightened her spine. "What's wrong with talking to Nyth?"

"Nothing, but you've been weird lately. If you talk to him so much, I don't get why you haven't assimilated." And then maybe she saw the flash in Katie's eyes, how her jaw set, because she quickly added, "I'm not trying to guilt you."

"Sure, after this weekend I'm sure—"

"I'm *not*."

Katie glanced away, tried to reel herself in. "Assimilating isn't that easy for us. And since the last rift, I think if I try to talk to him about it, we're just going to end up fighting."

"Fighting?" Mel ran her fingers through her hair. "So, what, are you two besties or not?"

Katie bristled at the way Mel's voice lilted almost mockingly over *besties*. "You don't know everything, okay?" Her tone came out sharp-edged, cutting, and she regretted it instantly, here in the middle of the lunchroom, but something in her was twisting tight.

Dominic leaned his elbow on the table. "Hey, Mel. Cool it, okay? Whatever's going on with Byrd is between her and Nyth." His voice was calm, but Katie knew this tone, and she knew his eyes were flashing cold steel at Mel.

"I'm not trying to piss anyone off," Mel said. "But it's not just between her and Nyth. Rift sealings are compromised and we all know it." She spread her hands. "I don't want to be an asshole here. But you know this is hurting all of us. Simon never should have had to kill those things."

"Mel." Simon's voice was still soft, but it edged on desperate.

"No, Snow, you know it's true. But I don't know how to help

you, Katie, because I don't get you and Nyth. Or you and Aerie, Dom. It doesn't make sense that you straight-up pal around with them. And I really don't get what's keeping you from assimilating if you're so close to Nyth."

"And I don't even get how you assimilated with Skiron in the first place," Dominic said. The cold anger leaked into his voice, and Katie felt her shoulders get tighter. "Does he even have emotions? How are you even close enough to assimilate?"

Something snapped. Katie felt it in the air, saw it in Mel's face, felt Simon and Asha shrink back from it. Mel leaned across the table, eyes narrowing. "Then you don't know anything," she hissed, her voice quiet but angrier than Katie had ever heard her. "You have no idea. Do you even know what Skiron is?"

"Duh, he's a guardian—"

Mel pressed on. "He's a *guardian*. He could crush my stupid little human body into a pebble if he wanted to because he's that powerful, but he never would because he values me, he appreciates me, and that blows my mind, that this literal force of nature appreciates me. Do you get that?"

Katie's eyes stung and her chest burned. "Shut up, Mel. Someone's going to hear you."

Her eyes flashed. "Do *not* tell me to shut up." But she did lower her voice again as she turned her glare onto Dominic. "Do you get that? Do you get that the guardians aren't cute little bird-girls? They're forces of nature. Aerie makes tornadoes. She *is* tornadoes. Just because she comes to you looking and acting like she does, it doesn't change that. She's just as huge as Skiron." Dominic opened his mouth, but Mel was on a roll. "She's the entire sky, Dominic. You remember how big the sky was on the prairie? How it stretched forever? That's how big she is. And you give her no credit." She sat back, crossing her arms, breathing hard. "Neither of you."

Katie couldn't tell if she was more pissed or stung. "That's not fair. Nyth is different from Skiron. So is Aerie."

"But that's not the point."

It was a quiet voice. It was Asha's voice, and Katie turned to her, surprised. Asha wasn't looking up at anyone, but she kept talking. "Of course, our relationships with our guardians are all different because the guardians are all different. Nyth is emotional and expressive. Aerie's curious and conversational. So, it makes sense you'd relate to them on a more… friend-like level."

"Friend isn't even the right word," Dominic interrupted.

"But that's not the point," she said again. "Mel's right. The guardians are beyond anything we've ever known." Asha leaned in closer. "Think about the ocean. How deep it is, and how it's mysterious and frightening the deeper it gets. Or how the moon gives light, but it's also cold and distant. And it's much, much bigger than what it looks like in our sky. That's what Zephyrus is like. That's what they're all like."

Katie furrowed her brow. "I never thought of Zephyrus as cold."

"Mel said it right. They're forces of nature. They aren't human. It's okay to be close with them, but you should respect their power." She finally lifted her head. There was something so tired in her eyes, but still so calm. "There are things about Zephyrus none of you know. Things that if I told you, you'd be terrified of her. But she's still kind and loving and generous, too. They're not simple. And they're not human, either."

"We know that," Dominic said, but the hard edge had left his voice.

She looked right at him. "We can't even comprehend their might. And if you think of them as human, you'll underestimate them in ways that could be even dangerous."

Katie realized her hands were clenched tight in her lap. "Nyth would never, ever hurt me."

"No," Asha said. "He'd never want to. But he could if he wanted to. And that's an important distinction."

A heavy silence settled over the table. Katie felt the tension start to drip out of her. She fidgeted with the hem of her sleeve, not meeting anyone's gaze. Mel ran her fingers through her hair and sighed. Then Dominic leaned back in his chair, arms crossed, as close to Katie as he could get without touching her, and said, "Maybe you're right. That's something to think about. Sorry I got defensive." Katie was pretty sure he meant it.

She stared at Mel, at the slump in her thin shoulders, the weight hanging her head down. She thought about armor and swords and beheading rift-beasts, about having to wash blood out of a hoodie in the middle of the night. Katie had never had to wash blood out of her clothes after a rift.

Simon still hadn't said a word.

Asha hurried off just before the bell to meet Malia and Rosie, and Dominic went to throw away his trash. For a moment, it was only Katie and Mel and Simon at the table. Mel leveled her gaze on Katie. She didn't look mad anymore. Just tired. "You could at least apologize to him."

It was apparently possible for Simon to look even more uncomfortable, because he did. Katie bit the inside of her lip. Something hurt behind her eyes, like tears that wanted to come out, but she wouldn't let them.

She knew it was her fault he'd had to kill those rift beasts. She'd seen in his eyes how much it hurt him to do it.

But out of all of them, he should realize how she was feeling, too.

"Sorry I didn't have an epiphany." Her voice was flat, and she didn't look at Simon, but she felt him flinch at her words. Mel looked confused, but Katie swept up her things and left the cafeteria before Mel could say anything else. She heard Dominic call after her, but she didn't turn back.

She felt like an asshole the second she was out of the cafeteria, but there was no way she was going back. There wasn't time anyway; the bell rang. The next three periods were one long slog of guilt (it's not fair to be a jerk to him just because you're upset with yourself; he finally found something that felt right and you want to take that away from him?; you do owe him an apology, you messed up again) until, after the last bell, she risked missing her bus to stop by the yearbook office.

He sat hunched over a pile of papers on a desk, his cardigan draped over the chair behind him, and his tie loosened. It reminded her of her father. Seventeen, and he already looked like a professor. "Hi," Katie said.

Simon sat up slowly, rubbing the back of his head. "Hi."

"I'm sorry," she said. "For Saturday. And for what I said at lunch."

He stared at her for a moment. "You have a lot of stuff to work through, don't you?"

She sighed. "Yeah. Always, apparently."

"I hope you figure it out." He turned back to the papers.

"Simon."

She hadn't meant to sound quite so pleading. He turned sideways in the chair, and Katie sat on the table next to him, clutching her bag. "It felt shitty. Being left behind when everyone else assimilated. I told you—I felt like a failure. But it made me feel better that you were in the same boat. You know?"

Simon stared at his hands. "I wasn't betraying you. Honestly, I wasn't thinking about you at all. I was only thinking about Ophion, and about saving everyone. And that's why it happened."

Katie swallowed. "Yeah. I get that. I just—figured I owed it to you to explain myself."

"You did. Thanks, Katie."

She furrowed her brow. "Are we okay?"

He met her gaze. "I'm not mad at you, if that's what you're asking."

Katie licked her lips and glanced at the clock. She had maybe three minutes to absolutely book it if she was going to make her bus, and she didn't expect Simon to offer a lift whenever he left. "Okay. I'm sorry. I really am."

"I know. I'll see you tomorrow."

"Yeah. Have a good night, Simon."

"You, too." He turned back to the desk, and Katie hurried out, somehow feeling worse than she had before.

Chapter 18

She awoke an hour earlier than usual the next morning. Groggily sipping a cup of tea, she stirred together dough and slid a tray into the oven while she went off to get dressed and have breakfast. A container sat on her locker shelf all morning until lunch, when she sat at the table with Dominic and Asha and set the container at Simon's seat. Dominic raised his eyebrows, but neither of them asked about it.

When Simon and Mel sat down, Simon paused, then took the lid off the container and peeked at the molasses ginger cookies inside. He glanced at Asha, but she shook her head. So then he looked at Katie. She smiled.

"Thank you."

"You're welcome." Katie watched him eat one of the cookies, her chest tight. "I owe you a real apology. So, cookies. I'm really sorry."

Their friends kindly acted extra-interested in their own lunches while Simon said, "I know. We're okay. I just needed time to process."

"I get that."

He smiled, took out a cookie, and held it out to her. Katie's own smile bloomed. She took the cookie. And thankfully, they all fell back into their usual lunchtime rhythm.

A few hours later, at her locker at the end of the day, Katie was stuffing the books she'd need for homework into her bag when Asha sidled up next to her. "Hi."

"Hi."

Asha tucked her hair behind her ear. "Listen, I know things have been awkward lately. And I just wanted to tell you I think you're really brave."

Katie paused, giving Asha a puzzling look. "What do you mean?"

"I didn't say anything back then because it seemed like you'd rather nobody did, but…" She leaned closer, lowering her voice. "We all saw you have a panic attack when you used fire instead of heat. And you're the only one who hasn't assimilated. I can tell it's a lot harder for you than you tell us about, and it's really brave of you to keep trying even though it's so hard."

Katie frowned and zipped up her bag. "I don't see what's so brave about it. We don't have much of a choice. My problems don't matter much, compared to the alternative."

"Maybe. But it's easy, for me and Zephyrus. Everything she gives me feels like it's what I was always meant to do. And the thing is, if I didn't feel that way, I don't know if I could do it. If it scared me even to assimilate, I don't know if I could keep fighting." She shook her head. "Sometimes I wonder if I'm really as strong as Zephyrus thinks I am, or if I just lucked out and ended up with a guardian who doesn't push my comfort zone so much."

The hall was emptying. They were both going to have to hurry to the buses. But Katie closed her locker and looked Asha in the eye. "Those fragments found us for a reason. All our guardians are like us, in a way. You didn't get an easy pick, Asha. You just don't have the hang-ups I do."

Asha pressed her mouth into a firm line, brow furrowing. Then the expression cleared, and she said, "Do you want to come over on Friday? I'm baking a ton for Malia's Halloween party. We could bake together."

Katie blinked. "Um, yeah. I'd really like that."

"Awesome. We'll plan it. See you tomorrow, Katie."

She turned to go, but Katie said, "Asha." When she turned back around, Katie smiled at her. "Thanks. For what you said. It means a lot."

Asha smiled back. "Of course." She waved, already walking backwards, then turned and left, leaving Katie with a smile and a whiff of perfume.

But Asha was barely around the corner when Katie's sightstone buzzed against her wrist. Asha turned back, eyes wide.

"Bathroom," Katie said, and they ducked into the nearest one. It was empty, so without hesitation, Katie pulled her sightstone off her wrist and lifted it to whisk her off to the veil.

"Is the mist even lower?" Asha asked when they landed.

"Shit, I think so."

"It is." Nyth was already there, or had just popped in. Katie turned and saw him waiting. Tension prickled in her chest—they hadn't spoken since the rift in the city. When she'd failed again. When all she'd felt was his disappointment.

But they had work to do, so she held out her hand.

His mouth twisted a bit. "Actually, we're—"

"Where's everyone else?" Aerie cut him off, shimmering into view next to him.

"On their way, I guess." Asha unwound her scarf. Even with the mist creeping lower, it was much warmer in the veil than at home. "Um, why aren't we going to the rift?"

"Things are a bit complicated today." Aerie flitted her hands, motioning towards the circle of stumps in the meadow. "Go on, sit. We'll get everyone here."

Katie exchanged a glance with Asha, but they went and sat on the stumps. Aerie vanished again, and Nyth paced around the stump circle, hands on his hips. Then Mel, Simon, and Dominic appeared. It only took a second for their faces to turn confused. "Are we not sealing?" Dominic asked.

"I have no clue. But apparently, we're supposed to sit."

Then Aerie reappeared, and Skiron and Zephyrus. As was their custom, Ophion didn't appear in humanoid form, but tiny pink flowers grew up from the grass and bloomed all around the stump where Simon sat.

"So, the thing is," Aerie said, "that this rift is in Harath."

Katie raised an eyebrow. "Harath where humans aren't supposed to go?"

"Yes. It's actually been open for a while. We've been working around it as best we can and hoping that maybe if we fixed things up on the Earth side, it wouldn't be a problem." She glanced back at the other guardians, at Nyth still pacing. "But it's a problem."

Dominic leaned forward, elbows on his knees. "Can we even close rifts on Harath?"

"We must try," Skiron said. "The rift is growing, and soon we will no longer be able to mask it, nor protect Harath from its effects."

"Okay," Mel said, "so we try. Let's go."

"There's one more bit." Aerie fidgeted from one foot to another. "Harath isn't for humans. It isn't really suited to you. So you might have trouble there."

"What kind of trouble?"

"Well, the air is the main thing. It's a different proportion of gases. You'll be able to breathe for a while, but we can't stay there too long. And it isn't going to feel good."

Mel gestured vaguely. "Okay. Let's get it over with, then."

"Is everyone okay with that?" Aerie scanned her gaze over all of them. "Do you accept the added danger?"

"We don't have much of a choice," Asha said. "We can't let a rift stay open, no matter where it is."

"We just—" Katie had never seen Aerie hesitate so much. Especially not about a sealing. "We don't want you kids to be hurt."

Mel barked out a laugh. "Every sealing is dangerous now. We've already been hurt. Is it really that different?"

"It is to us."

"Aerie." Dominic caught her gaze and held it. "I promise. We're fine with it. Right?" And he glanced at Katie, and at Simon, who had been silent. She nodded at him, and so did Simon. "Right, then."

Aerie was still frowning. "Okay."

Nyth paced around to Katie. He looked down at her, his brow furrowed, and held out his hand. Katie's heart fluttered against her ribs. "No humans have ever been to Harath," she said.

"Nope."

"We'll be the first," Simon said.

"Well then. Let's see what it's like." And Katie took a deep breath, and she laid her hand in Nyth's.

He pulled her through the emptiness. It was dark and warm like always, weightless, a nowhere-place. It felt longer than usual. She felt her pulse beat hard under her skin.

And then daylight, and the blinking readjustment. Nyth still held her hand tightly, and the ground under her feet felt… different. Katie looked down. Something green was growing, but not grass. More like a cross between moss and clover, densely curling close to the ground in a thick, springy mat. She breathed in. It felt normal so far, but the air tasted different and felt cooler.

Her friends were there with her, standing at the top of a hill. The sky was peachy pink like sunset, but the sun was high in the sky. Clouds drifted across it, giant puffs of cotton candy. And below them—Katie felt her breath catch. Below them the hill rolled into lower hills, and down into a valley. It was full of flowers, red and yellow and pink and white, some with wide-splayed petals, some bunched tight. Past the valley, the further hills were dotted with trees, low-lying wide-reaching things with broad flat leaves that shone golden-green under the warm sky. Further out, the trees got thicker, growing into a full forest on the other side of the valley. When the breeze picked up, the flowers and the trees shifted, and Katie heard a soft humming. Like the flowers were singing.

"Oh, my god," Asha breathed.

"It's gorgeous," Dominic said, voice softer than usual. Mel blinked and wiped her eyes quickly with the back of one hand. Simon stared out across the valley, lips parted softly, transfixed.

"This is incredible," Katie said.

"So is Earth," Nyth said.

"I know. But this is—different. New. A different kind of beautiful." Then she furrowed her brow, cleared her throat. Her breath had caught in wonder a moment ago, but it was still catching a bit.

Nyth looked at her carefully. "Let's seal this quick and get you home," he said. "You kids shouldn't be here too long." And then he disappeared, and the rift opened in front of them.

It cut a jagged line across their view of the valley, angry purple and shadows. Goosebumps ran along Katie's arms even under her coat as around her, her friends shifted into their assimilated forms. Nyth nudged at her to start building the heat as Mel and Simon stepped in and began solidifying the border of the rift.

Katie paused first to shrug off her coat. She was getting clammy and sweaty, and it wasn't helping. Then she cleared her throat again, even though it didn't help the thinness in her chest, and held her sightstone and let Nyth begin to channel heat into her.

There was a focus and determination to both Mel and Simon's work today that surpassed their usual focus, which was saying a lot. She heard Nyth whisper near her ear. "Skiron doesn't want Mel to fight. Not in this air. Sooner we close it, the less chance of beasts."

"Makes sense," Katie whispered. She didn't much want to do more than whisper anymore. It was starting to feel like if she raised her voice, she'd run out of air even faster. She turned her attention inward, focusing on the rising heat, letting it carry her.

Then a cracking sound, and Mel swearing. Katie opened her eyes and saw a rift-beast wriggling out and sliding to the ground. Simon grunted and pushed the border until it closed, sealing off before any more could get through. Dominic fired two arrows, blasted the rift solid, then fired two more. All four glassy arrows landed in the rift-beast, sinking into its flesh, and making it shriek.

Katie tried to refocus, but it was harder. Everything felt delayed. Brain fog, making her sluggish. She sucked in another breath. She could breathe. There was plenty of air. But not enough oxygen in the air, maybe. Her hands were clammy, her head slow, and she felt how short her breath was getting.

Dominic had already fallen back, leaning on his bow with his head bowed. The arrows had slowed the beast, and Mel managed to land a couple hacks with her sword that crumbled it. Asha was rippling the rift clear, but it was taking a lot longer than usual. Then Dominic was falling to his knees, Simon coming to check on him, but even Simon was moving slowly.

"It's going to take even longer to heat the rift closed," Katie said. Her voice was thin.

Nyth's voice, next to her ear. "Can you go faster?"

She knew what he meant. And the immediate thought was: no. Still no. I couldn't two days ago. What makes you think I can now?

But her gaze drifted across her friends. Mel leaning on her sword, one hand to her armored chest, recovering from those sword swings. Dominic and Simon sitting together, taking slow breaths, Dom's head bent low. Asha finally clearing the rift, revealing the misty veil on the other side, her arms curling in to her chest.

Katie's heart pounded. Her palms went clammier.

"Yes," she said.

She lifted her hands, sightstone pointed forward. The heat rushed through her, hotter than ever. She closed her eyes and felt the fire erupt from in front of her palms and hit the rift.

She thought: I can't do this.

If I don't, they'll get hurt again.

I don't know how much more guilt I can take.

It didn't matter what she thought. The fire rushed on.

By the time she opened her eyes, she was shaking like a damn leaf, but the rift was closing in on itself, burning away in the sky. "Go back," Mel said, and Katie just had time to catch Asha's admiring gaze before Nyth pulled her away to the veil.

Back in the mist, she let herself fall to the ground, sitting hard and taking deep breaths. Her head rushed, and she leaned back, laid back in the springy grass. Nyth appeared next to her, bent over her, his brow creased deeply. "Are you okay?"

She nodded. Her hands were shaking, her heart pounding, and it was hard to tell how much was from lack of air and how much was anxiety. But she was here. Whole. Scared, but holding on. The air was cool, and her head spun with the sudden flood of oxygen, pins and needles in her hands and feet, her body recalibrating.

"Come here. You're—can I—" His hands fluttered over her, not touching her.

"Go ahead," she whispered.

Nyth reached down and wrapped his arms around her, pulling her half against him. He was surprisingly solid and very, very warm. Her left side was pressed against his chest, and even through the fog she was too aware of all the scars separated from him only by her shirts, but it was okay. With Nyth, it was okay.

"I could feel you." He leaned his cheek against the top of her head. "I could feel cells crying for oxygen. Pulling things from you. I did that. I made you do that."

"We don't have a choice." She pressed a hand against the grass, pushed herself up. Her head was less swimmy. "We have to stop them. And Aerie said the air wasn't so bad it'd kill us."

"Yes, it would have. In enough time. And even if we didn't stay that long, it hurt you. I hurt you."

Katie lifted her hands and closed them gently over his arm, which he hadn't moved from around her shoulders. "I'm okay, Nyth. You don't have to feel guilty."

"It's not guilt. I mean it is. But it's not just guilt." His words were muffled, spoken into her hair. Katie saw the others, finally, Aerie crouched in front of Dominic, lightly touching his face. Simon sat in the grass, surrounded by flowers as tall as him. Mel sitting on a stump across from Skiron, silent, staring into each other's eyes. And Asha, lying curled up in the grass with Zephyrus kneeling over her, drifting her graceful hands back and forth, murmuring over Asha.

"Nyth." Katie pulled herself up, turning to look him in the eye. "I'm okay now. Shaken up, but okay. I promise. You don't have to be scared."

His eyes widened. "Is—that's it? This is fear?"

She gave him a small smile. "When the people we love get hurt, we get scared for them. I'm guessing that's where you are."

"I'm sorry," he said. "For shutting you out after the last rift."

"I messed up again. I don't blame you for being mad."

Nyth leaned in, his eyes warm. "But you did it this time. Maybe we can assimilate after all."

Her chest twinged. She hadn't flashed back to the sounds of the crash like fire bigger than the stovetop always made her. And that was something. That was a lot. But she was still sick and shaky. She knew she couldn't promise anything. "You know we can't force it, right?"

"I know. But—I'm jealous. Of them. They've all gotten to, and we haven't."

Katie softened. "Your fragment. If we assimilate, you'll feel it again, won't you?"

"That's not the only reason I want to. I want to because it's you. But yes. The others—when they assimilate, it's the first time they've felt complete since we lost the fragments."

His voice was so wistful. Katie took his hands in hers. "Well, I did use fire. That's a step in the right direction."

"Byrd?" Katie glanced over and saw the others standing, Mel facing her, the guardians beginning to leave. "They've got stuff to talk about. Let me get you guys home."

Katie stood. Nyth didn't let go of her hands. "Nyth. I'm okay. I swear to god." He finally let go, staring at her hard, and finally shimmered out of sight. Katie turned to face her friends. All of them looked worn out. Mel nodded, and they went home.

Chapter 19

Asha lived in one of the big builder houses in a cul-de-sac a few streets behind Dominic's house. Katie didn't even make it all the way to the front door before Asha opened it, calling, "Come on in! I have tea going."

The house was warm, and something sweet-spicy wafted down the hall to where Katie hung up her coat and scarf. She wandered into the kitchen, where Asha stirred a pot on the stove. "Thank you for making tea," she said. "It's cold as hell outside."

"I know. I don't think it's been this cold before November since I was little."

"Right? Maybe it's part of what the guardians told us about. The worlds being under strain because of all the rifts." She leaned in closer to the pot. "Masala chai?" she asked. It smelled like cloves.

"More or less. Doodh cha, technically." Asha crinkled her nose playfully. "Thank you for not saying 'chai tea.'"

"I know at least that much." She leaned on the counter and took a whiff of the steam rising from the pot. "It smells amazing. What's in it?"

"We do ours with ginger, cloves, and cardamom. And milk and sugar, of course. I like using orange pekoe. There are mugs in that cabinet there, if you could get some?" Katie got a couple mugs— pretty, cream-colored stoneware ones—and Asha filled them with frothy, milky tea. "Don't think I'm weird, but I like mine with puffed rice." She took a container of puffed rice from another cupboard, sprinkled some in her mug, and scooped it up with a spoon. "It soaks up the tea and gets so cozy and tasty."

"Pass that rice. I need to try this."

They settled at the island, perched on stools, and stirred rice into their tea only to scoop it back out again. Asha was right. It was both cozy and tasty, and the tea was perfectly spiced.

"Nobody else home?" Her voice echoed faintly off the high ceilings.

"Chandra's in middle school, so she gets out later. Plus, she has honors choir after school today. And my parents won't be home from work for a few hours." Asha smiled. "So, we can talk freely, if we want to."

Katie sipped her tea. "You mean about what happened yesterday?"

"Or anything. But yeah." She leaned her chin in her hand. "It was so beautiful there."

"I know. If there was enough oxygen, I'd convince Nyth to sneak me back over for a visit. See some more places."

"He wouldn't." Katie raised her eyebrow, and Asha stammered, "Well—I mean, not now. Not anymore."

"Yeah, I guess not. He was really shaken up."

"You don't know the half of it."

Katie watched Asha over the rim of her mug as she took a long sip. "Asha. What do you know?"

She looked sheepish. "Um. Don't tell them I told you this. But I had a dream last night about the guardians. They were fighting about it."

"About Harath?"

"About us going there. Nyth and Ophion refused to ever take us there again. After seeing us fall apart, it was like they couldn't bear it. And… Zephyrus and Aerie were arguing that even though it was awful to see us hurt, if more rifts open then they don't have a choice. There's a greater need. But they would never leave us there long enough to cause any lasting damage." She stared into her mug.

"Skiron surprised me. I would've thought he'd side with Zephyrus and Aerie, no question."

"So would I."

"He didn't, though. He didn't say much, but I caught a bit of what he was thinking. He's been bonding with Mel so much that seeing her in pain hurts him. That it's bad enough when she's fighting rift beasts, but at least he can help her with that. He can't make there be more air."

Katie's fingers tightened around her mug. "Do you think it was just a dream?"

Asha shook her head. "I think Zephyrus let it slip through. It's not the sort of thing she'd show me on purpose."

"That's weird. She always seems so in control."

"She usually is. But they're all stressed by the rifts, and by not having found the source yet. Maybe it's distracting her enough that she's missing things."

"That's not great. The guardians missing things." Katie sipped her tea, nearing the bottom of her mug. "But I think I know what you mean. Nyth I are getting closer. And it's almost like that's— kind of distracting him. He was so scared yesterday when he saw what happened. And jealous."

"Jealous?"

"Of you all, and the other guardians. He really wants us to assimilate."

Asha bit her lip. "Do you think you will?"

"I mean, I finally could stand to use fire to seal the rift. It sucked, but I handled it. That's at least a step in the right direction." Her tea was gone, now, and she ran one finger around the rim of the mug. "I hope so. I want to know how that feels. Coming home, that way."

She felt Asha watching her. "Come on," she said. "Mugs in the sink. I'll grab my phone and we can get this baking started."

Katie followed Asha through the dining room and living room, with their vaulted ceilings and well-placed furniture, and into the smaller, cozier family room. As Asha got her phone from the couch,

Katie peeked around the coffee table. In the corner, curled up in a fluffy dog bed, was a snoozing Boston terrier with graying fur. "Twinkle," Asha said. "She's not the brightest candle, but she's sweet. She's getting old and mostly naps now."

"Peaches is getting like that, too."

"That's the brown tabby, right?" Asha asked as they headed back to the kitchen.

"Yeah. Skimbleshanks likes me more than she does, but we've had Peaches the longest." Peaches had always liked her mom the most, but Katie's heart clenched when she thought of saying it.

Asha opened all the recipes she'd bookmarked on her phone and directed Katie to the baking cabinet for supplies while she got ingredients. Mixing bowls, measuring spoons and cups, spatulas and baking tins soon cluttered the island. On the counter, Asha lined up flours and sugars, cocoa powders, eggs, and everything else next to a copper Kitchenaid stand mixer.

"I'm not great at like… cupcakes and stuff," Katie warned. "Or decorating."

"Don't worry. Baking is baking, right? And I'm going to be doing most of the decorating tomorrow before the party. C'mon, let's start the sugar cookie dough since that's got to chill before we bake it."

Asha rolled up the sleeves of her cardigan as they got to work. Katie kept her sleeves down. But it was nice, sifting flour and sugar with Asha.

"Have all your dreams been getting weirder?" Katie asked. "Or was that one with the guardians an exception?"

"Well, they're not usually like that. But they've only gotten stronger since Zephyrus and I assimilated." She frowned into the bowl of the mixer. "You do think you and Nyth will assimilate, though?"

"Depends whether I can get my shit together."

Asha glanced over at her. "I've been trying not to ask. But you—"

"—clearly have some problems." Katie's fingers twitched, wanting to pull her sleeves further down over her hands. She tried not to.

"I wasn't going to say it quite like that."

"It's fine. Being vague about it hasn't helped any." She bit her lip. "Something—really bad happened when I was little. Fire reminds me of it. Viscerally. It triggers memories from it, but also… feelings, I guess? Like a big complicated knot of feelings. And I've been having trouble separating the two. So, there's part of me that still doesn't trust Nyth, not completely, and I don't think we'll assimilate until I figure out how to let that go."

"Dark nights of the soul getting really dark?"

Katie half-laughed. "Exactly."

Neither of them said anything for a moment. Asha started the mixer, and its whirring was too loud for soft, vulnerable conversation. Katie watched sunlight shift on the wall until the mixer stopped and Asha said, "Do you know who Sarah Williams is?"

"The name sounds familiar. Is she in our year?"

"No, she's—oh." Asha laughed. "There is a Sarah Williams in our year. But no, not her. The poet."

"Oh. Then no."

"She wrote this poem I love. Simon sent it to me. It's called 'The Old Astronomer, To His Pupil.'" Her eyes were soft as she patted the cookie dough into a disc on a piece of plastic wrap. *"Though my soul may set in darkness, I rise in perfect light; I have loved the stars too fondly to be fearful of the night."*

"That's really pretty. It sounds familiar."

"It's a famous line. The astronomer is dying, and he's telling this student he mentored, who he loves, not to cry over him because there's still so much more to see." She wrapped the dough slowly, carefully. "We walk in darkness a lot," Asha said, and Katie looked back at her, at the softness in her eyes. "Sometimes it's just because it's night. Sometimes it's because we can't stop covering our eyes with our hands. But there's always light. If you look up, you see the stars."

"You just have to stop staring at your own hurt, I guess."

"And sometimes that's hard. But the stars are always there for us." She turned to Katie, leaning against the counter. "They're far away, though," she said quietly. "Zephyrus is so far away. Even when she's inside me, in my dreams, she's far away. Like the bottom of the ocean, or the moon. I love her, and she loves me, but she's elusive. Nyth is like… he's everywhere." She bit her lip, lowered her eyes. "You're lucky your light is so close."

"I never thought about it that way." Katie glanced down at her hands fidgeting with her sweater cuffs. "You know, I don't think I've ever heard anyone else say they love their guardian."

"But we all do, you know? We all love them. And they all love us. That's part of the problem, part of why we're feeling all mixed up. It's because we've gotten them all mixed up. They love all of creation, and each other, but they've never really loved a person, not like we do. And they don't know what to do with the fact that we came into their world and got mixed up in their essences and now they can't help but love us just like we can't help but love them." She fidgeted with the plastic wrap, frowning. "Zephyrus can sense something is wrong. She's not letting me know what it is, and that's fine, I trust her judgment over anything. But I wish I knew. Because it's something big and it's something to do with all of this and I just…" She took in a slow, deep breath, the kind of slow deep breath Katie knew all too well, and she blinked too many times too fast. "I'm sorry, I'm talking too much."

Katie shook her head. "No. You're talking just right."

Asha glanced back up at her, this time with a weak but genuine smile. "I told you we were more alike than you thought." She bit her lip again, making her thinking face. The cookie dough was forgotten. "Remember the time I showed up to a sealing, and I was crying?"

Katie felt her stomach drop. "Shit. Asha. I'm so sorry, I was so focused on myself that I never asked—"

"It's okay, Katie."

"No, it's not okay. I don't get a pass to be a crappy friend. I'm sorry."

Asha twisted her fingers together. "Then I accept your apology. I only mentioned it because… I was crying because I'd been in the middle of a therapy session when they called us. I go every week. And I had to pretend I was going to the bathroom and then just not come back, and I knew there would be fallout from that, and it got me all stressed, so I was crying about it."

Her chest felt heavy. "I'm sorry."

"It's all right. I promise." Asha's fingers unfolded, instead fidgeted with the hem of her skirt. "It started around the end of eighth grade. I know a lot of teenagers get… moody." She made air quotes with her fingers, almost rolled her eyes. "But it didn't go away. And after a while, instead of just always feeling bad, I couldn't feel anything anymore." She paused, took a slow breath. Katie didn't say anything, gave her the space. "Can I show you something?" Asha asked, and her voice was small.

"Of course."

Slowly, being careful to only move part of the fabric, Asha pulled up the skirt of her dress, exposing part of her upper thigh. Katie took in a hiss of breath.

There were lines of pale scars there. Not messy, accidental scars like her burns. Neat, precise lines.

"I didn't start until things got really bad," Asha said, lowering her skirt again. "When I couldn't feel anything anymore, that was the only thing I did feel. That's part of why I started seeing a doctor. The therapist, and a psychiatrist too." She half-smiled. "It's funny. My mom's a psychiatrist. But she didn't realize what was happening until I was pretty far gone. I think it's easy to miss things, sometimes, when they're right under your nose. And I worked so hard to hide it all."

Katie hesitated over her question. "Do—do you still—"

"I've been clean for ten months." She smiled. "I'm lucky, I guess. I still have bad patches, but I have more support to get out of them. And Zephyrus… she helps. She really helps. Everything about her, everything she makes me feel about myself, is so beautiful and wonderful. I'm… connected, now, to the world, and to the immensity of everything. And that helps, somehow."

"I had no idea." Katie shook her head. "All this time, and I didn't even notice."

"I hide it pretty well. Even Rosie and Malia didn't have a clue until I told them." Asha tilted her head, her dark hair sliding over her shoulder. "You've been in therapy too, though, haven't you? The way you talk about this stuff sometimes, I can tell."

"Since I was nine."

Asha's mouth fell open. "Oh. I'm sorry."

"It's funny. Not even Dom knows that. I mean, he knows I've been in therapy. He's ridden out panic attacks with me before, so he knows that… stuff is going on. But he doesn't know how long it's been." She smiled. "Nyth does. God, Nyth knows everything."

Asha's sad expression melted into a soft smile. "That feels right, with you two."

"Yeah. It really does."

They gave each other weak smiles—but genuine ones—and turned back to the baking. For a while they worked quietly, the sugar cookie dough in the fridge and a rich chocolate cupcake batter coming together. Eventually Asha said, "You'll assimilate."

A startled laugh escaped Katie. "You sound so sure."

"I am sure." Asha's eyes were warm like always, but they were also serious. A different kind of serious than they'd been when she'd been talking about her depression. "Katie, I know I don't know any of the details, but anything that lands a nine-year-old in therapy must be horrible. And whatever that was, you've come all this way. You glow, you know? You're this… sparkling light. Everyone can see it, even when you seem like you're being rained on. And that's what Nyth is like. You're both made of the same kind of sunlight. You're going to get there."

Katie blinked hard so she wouldn't tear up. "Asha," she said, "nobody gives you anywhere near enough credit."

Asha smiled, and they got back to baking.

And really, Katie hadn't given Asha enough credit, either. She'd thought she was almost transparent in her feelings, but there was so much under the surface Katie had missed. Depths she couldn't fathom. Like the ocean.

Like Zephyrus.

Chapter 20

Deciding on a Halloween costume had rapidly slipped to the bottom of Katie's list of priorities. Last-minute efforts a couple hours before Malia's party were the best she could do. She had a black cat sweater she always liked wearing this time of year, and she was pretty sure there was a pair of seldom-worn orange tights buried in one of her drawers. She was digging for them when her phone rang.

"Do you have a costume?" Dominic asked when she answered.

"Nope. I'm gonna wear my cat sweater."

"Alternately, I'm furiously making something out of pillowcases as we speak. Want to do a buddy costume with me?"

"Depends. Is it good?"

"Byrd. You wound me."

"I'm going to wear my sweater just in case. But yes. Make me a costume. I'll wear it if it doesn't suck."

"You're too kind. I'll see you in an hour."

It turned out well for a quick job with pillowcases. Dominic was grinning in a white sack over a black shirt, a big felt letter *S* stitched haphazardly to the chest. He held out a gray sack to Katie; it had a letter *P*.

"Salt and pepper?"

"You're pepper, of course."

"Of course."

"Here." He held out a metal colander to her. Katie stared at it until he put a second colander on his head like a hat; then she laughed and followed suit.

"These are cheesy as hell."

"That's the idea, bugbreath. That's the idea."

Her hair was possibly going to get caught in the colander's holes, but that was a problem for later. Dominic blared a goofy Halloweeny playlist, all Monster Mash and spooky scary skeletons, on the way to Malia's house, which was near Asha's. As Dominic found a parking spot, he glanced at Katie. "You nervous?"

"Why would I be nervous?" Then she realized she was twisting her sightstone around her wrist. Nervously.

Their eyes met.

"We always have to worry about it now," she said.

"Getting called to a rift?"

"In the middle of anything. Did you know—" She bit her tongue before spilling about Asha skipping out of therapy. She'd kill someone if they blabbed about her own therapy sessions, so she couldn't do that to Asha. "I mean, we could slip out fine. But Asha's best friend is throwing this thing. It'd be hard for her to just disappear."

"We'll figure it out if it comes to that. We can cover for her, yeah?"

"I guess so."

"Right. Now let's go get spooky."

A woman in a mummy costume—Mrs. Headley—answered the door with a smile. "Come on in! Salt and pepper shakers? That's so cute. Food's in the kitchen, games are back in the rec room, and bathroom is down the hall. Just stay on the first floor, please."

It wasn't a jam-packed rager or anything (it really couldn't be with Malia's parents home), but the first floor was crowded with kids in everything ranging from black T-shirts to seriously dedicated costuming. The big dining table in the kitchen was covered in the tombstone cupcakes and ghost cookies Asha had decorated—and damn, she really was a good decorator. At one corner of the table, a generous platter of veggies and hummus was cheekily labeled

"Potion of Protection Against Death" in contrast to the more sugary offerings.

Further back, the rec room had actual bobbing for apples, a small table with cards for an in-party scavenger hunt, and an oversized checkers board with tiny white and orange pumpkins serving in place of the traditional red-and-black pieces. "Holy shit," Dominic said over the music being pumped at a pervasive mid-volume into every room. "Asha wasn't kidding about Malia and her family going all-out for this."

"Where is Asha?" Katie asked.

"Of course you'd be pepper."

Katie turned around and smiled at Mel, who was wearing a black T-shirt with skeleton bones printed on it. Simon was wearing his usual dapper clothes, but his tie today had jack-o'-lanterns on it, and he was wearing a headband with ghost-shaped boppers coming out the top, which lit up when he turned his head. Katie laughed. "You guys look great."

"I usually wear this to pass out candy to trick-or-treaters," Simon said, catching her laugh and gesturing at his headband.

"It's adorable."

They did another lap of the first floor—people dancing or hanging out talking in the living room, clustered in the entry hall with cups of bright-green soda (which was just regular lemon-lime soda with food dye), snacking in the kitchen, a few people attempting to bob for apples or peeking at scavenger hunts in the rec room. Asha was nowhere to be seen, but they found Malia and Rosie dancing at the side of the living room. "You guys made it!" Malia said, beaming.

"You both look amazing, holy shit."

Malia was a phoenix, with gorgeously applied makeup and red-and-gold feathers around her face and on her shoulders. Rosie was a fairy, with painted wings, her hair tied up in two buns streaming with ribbons, and enough glitter to permanently infect the carpets. "We like doing group costumes when we can. Wait 'til you see

Asha's—she's a mermaid."

"Of course she is." Mel smiled one of her half-smiles. "Where is she, anyway?"

"Making one more cupcake run. She baked everything and has one last batch to bring over."

"Asha made all those?" Simon asked.

"Isn't she amazing?" Malia grinned at Katie. "You helped, didn't you?"

Katie held up her hands. "Just the baking part. She did all the decorating. I'm no good at that stuff."

"We're gonna start the scavenger hunt when she gets here. Did you guys get anything to eat? There're sandwiches, too, if you don't just want sugar. Make yourselves at home!"

They wandered back to the kitchen for sandwiches, Katie's arm resting against her bag on her shoulder. As they were approaching the table, she felt a vibration against her arm. Her heart leapt, the alertness sitting up straight like an anxious watchdog. In a rush, the pressure of so many people around them, of excuses needing to be made, rose in her mind.

Then she realized Mel was putting a sandwich on her plate, and Simon and Dominic were chatting casually. It was just her phone in her bag vibrating from a notification. She let out a shaky breath, shimmied her legs to try to work out the sudden jump of adrenaline, and checked her phone. A text from her dad, Halloweeny emojis and *Have fun!*

So, she ate a sandwich with her friends and laughed with them and tried not to be on constant alert.

She was in the middle of pouring herself a drink when she caught sight of Victoria across the snack table. "Oh, hey! I didn't know if you were coming."

Victoria didn't frown, exactly, but she sure as hell didn't smile back at Katie. "I didn't think you'd be here either."

"Yeah, Dom and I figured out a last-minute costume."

"So, I'm guessing your lab report is done?"

Katie paused. Victoria's arms were crossed, her fingers digging into her elbows. "Um."

"Yeah, that's what I thought." The blond girl shook her head. "You know I was actually excited you're in the same group as me? You're smart. I figured you'd actually contribute."

"What—" Katie set down her cup, feeling herself bristle. "I'm working on my part." Her tone was edging sharper but whatever, Victoria was being rude.

"Everyone was supposed to attach their lab reports to the shared doc by Thursday. Everyone did except you. Did you even do your experiments yet?"

"I said I'm working on it. I'm sorry it's a little late, but we still have—"

"It's not just this, Katie. All your stuff has been late or half-assed." Victoria leaned closer, lowering her voice. "This project is worth a quarter of our grade. A quarter. Don't bomb all our grades for the semester just because you don't care."

"It's not that I don't care—" She cut herself off with a huff. "Look, I said I'm sorry, okay?"

Victoria half rolled her eyes. "Then get your part done. We're getting tired of worrying you're going to screw this up for everyone."

That stopped Katie's irritation cold. "We?"

"You think I'm the only one annoyed about this? Malia's too nice to get mad, but Jordan's pissed, too."

Katie furrowed her brow. "He's never said a word."

"Listen, Katie. I'm a direct person. If there's a problem, I'll tell you. Jordan Meszaros is as non-confrontational as they come, but trust me, he's upset about it too." She quirked an eyebrow. "If you don't believe me, ask Dominic Gunn."

"Dominic?"

"Hey." Mel sidled up next to Katie. "What's the issue?"

Katie glanced at Victoria. "No issue. We were just—"

"Byrd, I was by the sandwiches, not in another room. I heard what you were just." She turned a cool stare on Victoria. "A confrontation at a party? Cliché."

Victoria's expression faltered. She dropped her arms to her sides, mumbled something that might have been "Sorry," and turned and went into the living room.

"You didn't have to do that," Katie said. Her voice came out quieter than she meant it to.

"Yes, I did. She was being an ass to you." Mel turned to Katie, gesturing with a pack of cigarettes in her hand. "Wanna come with me?"

"I don't smoke."

The responding eyeroll gave Katie's own eyerolls a run for their money. "I wasn't offering one. You're what, sixteen? I meant you can come out and chill with me if you want. Cool your head. While these nerds are playing." The guys had migrated to the rec room for a game of pumpkin checkers while Victoria was tearing Katie a new one.

"Almost seventeen," she muttered, following Mel out the back door and taking the colander off her head. She suddenly felt stupid in it.

They went to the end of the driveway, well away from the house, which was courteous on Mel's part. Katie had bundled back up in her coat and scarf, but Mel had only her zip-up hoodie on over her T-shirt. "Aren't you freezing? It's like forty degrees."

Mel quirked an eyebrow. "Exactly. It's only forty degrees." Katie groaned, and Mel's mouth tugged up, too, in a half-smile. "I like this weather. But you're more bundled up than anyone else. What are you, cold-blooded?"

"Dom does call me a lizard."

She laughed, chasing a soft billowing cloud of smoke.

Katie peered up at her. "I didn't know you smoked."

Mel shrugged, rubbed her nose with the back of her hand. "I know it's gross, but whatever. We all die someday." She flicked ash off the end of her cigarette and frowned. "I've really needed them sometimes, lately, more than just wanting them."

"Well, things are… weird, now."

Mel nodded, furrowing her brow as she pulled in an inhale, then glancing sidelong at Katie as she let it out. "Don't think I'm condoning it, though. You're too cute to smoke. It'll fuck up your skin."

Katie laughed. "Don't worry. I'm in no danger of starting."

She cleared her throat, her cigarette dangling between two fingers. "You good?" She inclined her head back towards the house. "After that. With that girl."

"Oh." Katie hunched her shoulders, shoving her hands deeper into her coat pockets. "Yeah. Like… I'm pissed that she was rude to me. And in the middle of a party."

"Seriously."

"But she also wasn't wrong." Katie bit the inside of her lip. The edge of her sightstone pressed into her wrist bone. "I've been slacking on that project. And it's a huge part of our grade."

Mel leaned back her head, gazing at the night sky with half-lidded eyes, and let smoke curl out of her mouth as she spoke. "Like you said, things are weird. Our priorities can't be normal anymore. We have bigger shit to worry about."

"Yeah, but that doesn't mean I can just…" Katie pulled her hands free to gesture in front of her. "Let stuff slide when it affects other people."

With a shrug, Mel flicked off the last bit of ash and stubbed her cigarette out against the bottom of her chucks. "I guess it's about figuring out the balance."

"I'm not great at balance," Katie muttered, thinking of Nyth and the way he leaned into extremes.

"Really? You seem…"

"Organized? Controlled?" She let out a laugh. "I've made myself be on purpose. Kind of had to."

Mel's jaw was set as she stared at Katie, but her eyes were kind. "You'll figure it out, Byrd. Just be kind to yourself."

By the time they made it back inside, Simon had soundly beaten Dominic, to Dom's chagrin. And when Asha arrived right after, shimmering in blues and greens and gold and white, her hair in waves and crowned with a headband of twisted blue silk and seashells, Katie joined everyone in exclaiming over the beautiful falls of her skirt that represented her mermaid tail, then helped her unload jack-o'-lantern cookies and witch-hat cupcakes onto the table.

Asha peeked up at her through false lashes and thick gold eyeliner. "You doing okay?"

And Katie knew what she meant. She smiled. "Yeah. This party's a good distraction."

"The Headleys know how to turn up."

And Katie laughed, and they went to find their friends.

The guardians didn't call them during the party. It was good luck, and by the time Katie crawled back into Dominic's car, her cheeks hurt from laughing and smiling, despite how much colder it had gotten outside since she and Mel stood in the driveway. And she and Victoria had given each other a wide berth of mutual understanding, which didn't hurt.

But as soon as Dominic turned on the car, and Katie put her chilled hands up to the heat vent, she just felt plain tired.

They were quiet on the ride back to Katie's house. "I'm wiped," Dominic eventually said. "It's not even that late."

"It's because we were half on alert all night," Katie said. She leaned her head on the window and watched the streetlamps go by. "Constantly waiting for something to happen, when you don't know if it's gonna happen—it keys up your nervous system. So now that we don't have to be all keyed up, we're crashing."

He glanced at her, then back at the road. "Are you okay?"

"Yeah. Just tired." Then, after a moment: "Has Jordan said anything to you about me?"

"How do you mean?" Which was an evasive enough answer that she knew he had. She leveled Dominic with a deadpan gaze until he sighed. "Yeah, he has. About the chem project."

"Why didn't you tell me?"

"Because he's my friend, and he asked me not to, and because it would've just upset you."

Katie stared out the windshield, watching the streetlamps roll by. "Are you keeping up with your project?"

"Yeah, but ours is more collaborative than yours, so it's not like it'll fall apart if I don't do my part. At least one person is annoyed with me because I'm not totally pulling my weight, but—Byrd, we're trying to save the world over here."

"I know. I know that." She sighed, slouching in her seat. "I'm just… tired."

Katie looked back out the window, watching the lights pass by the car. After a few moments, Dominic turned his goofy Halloween playlist back on. Out the window, snowflakes began to fall.

Chapter 21

After seeing Asha's decorating skills at the Halloween party, Katie invited her over for another baking party.

> *Hopefully with less emotional angst*
> *But you've gotta teach me how to pipe frosting like that*

Asha was on her way when Dominic texted, eager to hang out, so Katie asked him over, too. He agreed in a heartbeat.

"I'll be no help with the baking," he admitted as Katie let them all into the house. "But I'll be great help reviewing them after they're made."

"Truly essential." Katie smirked. "How on earth would we ever get along with you."

Alex came home from the neighbor's not long after and found them in the kitchen, drinking hot cocoas and mixing butter and sugar for the buttercream frosting. "Can I have some of the cake?"

"Cupcakes. Alex, this is Asha. Asha, you remember my brother Alex."

"Nice to meet you. Sorry, my hands are covered in sugar."

Katie slid into a chair next to Dominic at the breakfast table. "But hey, Asha, you have to let me do most of the mixing for the batter. You're basically doing everything for the frosting. I'm gonna start feeling guilty."

"Fair enough."

Alex made himself a snack—his microwaved cheese-and-saltines, which Dominic praised as ingenious—and disappeared into the living room. Moments later, the sound of his current favorite video game started up.

"So, my vote," Dominic said, "is that after the cupcakes, we go sledding. A bunch of guys are going to the hill at the playground tonight."

"It's gonna be dark in like an hour."

"It's a park, Byrd, there's plenty of lights."

"Do you have sleds?" Asha asked, scraping the sides of the bowl.

"I think we have one in the garage here," Katie said.

"And someone will have extras at the hill." Dominic leaned back in his chair. "Or at least a bunch of garbage bags to slide down on."

"To increase the probability of broken bones? Alright, I'm in. Sounds fun. And if I'm hiking my way back up the hill over and over, I'll stay reasonably warm."

"That's the spirit."

Katie drank the last of her cocoa and watched as Asha finished with the frosting. "We need to do this more often," she said. "Just hang out. Do something with our lives besides homework and world-saving. Like Halloween was fun."

"Not gonna lie, homework's gone by the wayside for me." Dominic shrugged. "But you're right."

"Oh, me too. I like this. Should we do another baking day with Simon and Mel? Holiday cookies, maybe?"

"I feel like Mel would be less down for cookies than the rest of us would. A game night, maybe. Or, oh—Dom, text them, invite them sledding tonight."

Katie turned to put her cocoa mug in the sink, then froze. She met Asha's gaze, then Dominic's. The sightstone on her wrist had begun to vibrate.

Dominic pushed back his chair. "So, we're going sledding

now," he said. "Asha, want to put your bike in the trunk? In case it's a rough one and you want to just go home?"

"Okay. Katie, can I put this in the fridge?"

"Yes. I'll go tell Alex. The sledding thing, that is."

They moved quickly, with the ease of practice. Katie ducked into the living room. "Hey Alex? We want to meet some of Dom's friends to go sledding before it's too dark. Can you let Dad know?"

"Sure."

"If anyone tries to break in and steal you while I'm gone, Dad's old softball bat is in the coat closet. Just whack 'em a good one and then run screaming down the street."

"Will do," he said, not glancing away from his video game.

She spun and hurried back into the hallway, where Asha and Dominic were already getting into their coats. Katie pulled on her coat and grabbed her scarf and hat and mittens in a wad. No time to put them on, but someone would be suspicious if they saw Katie left them behind.

They got Asha's bike into the trunk of Mrs. Gunn's car faster than Katie thought possible, piled in unceremoniously, and Dominic headed out. The snow hadn't stopped since Halloween night and had piled up fast. The streets weren't even fully plowed yet. "I'm not gonna go all the way to the sledding hill," he said. "It'll take too long in this snow." Instead, he drove to the nearest shopping plaza and pulled around to the back, where only the employees' cars were parked. After a quick glance to ensure nobody was in their line of sight, they all took out their sightstones and pulled themselves to the veil.

Nyth was already waiting for her, crackling with impatience. "No time to lose." His golden-brown eyes burned into her.

She met his gaze and took his hand, and he whirled her away.

They landed in a snow-covered field under an overcast sky. The rift was already unmasked, a harsh slash above the ground. It shuddered, its edges shifting.

"It's so active." Katie clenched her hands into fists. "Let's close it."

"That's the way." Nyth grinned, then disappeared.

Simon was alone in front of the rift, already wearing the vine-and-moss armor of Ophion, trying to stabilize the border. It kept shifting, getting away from him.

"Where's Mel?" Dominic asked, a gust of wind settling around him as he assimilated with Aerie.

"Don't know." Simon squared his shoulders. "But this thing feels like it's going to explode. And it's too close to people." And then Katie realized where they were: the Rockpoint picnic area. Only a thin line of trees separated them from the picnic table where they'd first gone to the veil together.

With a flash of white light, Asha assimilated as well, trading her coat and boots for Zephyrus's illusion-hemmed dress. Katie felt for that small fire in her heart, let it grow, and let the heat began to build in her cupped hands, let it start to work its way all through her. She would be ready. Her heart pounded at the thought of fire in her hands again but using it at the rift in Harath hadn't broken her. She could do this. Nobody would get hurt again because she hesitated.

"Sorry!" Mel appeared just in front of Katie, barefoot in sweatpants, but in a flash assimilated with Skiron. "I was home with my mom, she was on her way out and wouldn't stop talking to me—Jesus, look at that thing."

"I need help," Simon called. "It keeps breaking off the border."

"It's getting those holes," Dominic added, circling around to flank them. "Watch it."

"Alright. Let's close it down."

She and Simon leaned into it, pressing the border further around the writhing rift. At Asha's feet, the snow swirled in slow circles, rose to pass through her upturned palms. Dominic stood to the side, eerily still, his glasslike bow and arrow aimed at the center of the rift. Katie felt them. She felt the strength of the guardians in them echoing through Nyth, their power, their focus. So she gripped her sightstone hard and let the warmth rush into her body, fill her, rise with the thundering of her heart.

The blank pockets of void gave a heave and started to spread. "Not this time," Mel growled, and she grunted as she pushed a long line of crystal along the border. But one void hole shot out an arm, shattering the border above it. Mel swore, but even as she leaned back in, the void grew larger, and something began to emerge.

It crawled out so much more purposefully than the rift-beasts, not skittering with too many legs but deliberately climbing out, its long, thin arms reaching, long, clawed hands grasping at the vines around the rift. It pulled its head and shoulders out. Its skin was the leathery grayish of the rift-beasts, but its shape was humanoid; and it lifted its head, which had no nose or mouth but eyes dark as a moth's and rimmed in red and white, and it looked straight at Mel.

Asha cried out. Dominic fired an arrow, but the creature tumbled forward out of the rift, and the strike barely grazed its back. Leaving Simon to finish the border, Mel drew her sword from beneath the snow and swung towards the creature. It rose to meet her, its clawed hand striking her face and knocking her to the side, sending her sword's arc away. Blood from her nose peppered the snow.

Katie's sightstone in her hand was burning.

She hated it. Whatever it was. Wherever it came from.

We'll send it back, Nyth said. *We'll burn it away. We won't let it hurt them.*

Mel struggled to her feet, coughing and wiping her nose on her sleeve. The creature cocked its head at her. The bottom half of its face split open in a wide red mouth, and it gave a rattling hiss. Then it turned and lunged toward Dominic. Mel leaped after it, slicing into the back of its leg. It shrieked and threw itself to the ground, away from her, and rolled until it slammed into Dominic's shins. He fell, dropping the arrow he was nocking. "Shit—" Before he could get up, the creature rolled over, rose up, and slashed its claws across his chest.

"Dominic, I'm almost there," Simon shouted. Vines curled

more tightly around the rift.

"*Shit—*"

Mel rushed in, sword singing toward the creature. It spun around, one long arm shooting up. It grabbed Mel's wrist, and Katie saw her eyes widen as it held her and flung its other hand towards the rift.

A long crack broke from the void, tearing through the vines and ruining half of Simon's work.

With a yell, Mel threw her full body weight into the sword. Skiron's strength was in her shoulders, and she forced her sword down to bite into the creature's shoulder, cutting deep. It howled, a ragged sound that tore the air, and it lifted a leg and kicked her in the stomach, knocking her away.

Mel lay winded on the snow, Simon sweating and swearing as he tried to repair the border, Dominic struggling to his feet, Asha's hand visibly shaking as she pulled a storm of snow up from the ground, readying to try to blind the creature.

Katie's heart slammed against her ribs. Her palms were clammy until the heat burned it away. It didn't matter that she was scared. She felt Nyth's presence so much closer than ever, almost brushing against her own mind. And she saw with him. She saw Skiron's desperation, Ophion's confusion, Aerie's racing thoughts, Zephyrus's growing fear. And Nyth's heart sang with hers. Help them. Help them. They need us.

Asha blasted the snow cloud at the creature. The flakes glinted tiny and hard, and the thing winced and shook itself, backing up closer to the rift. It stood, craning up to its full height, tall like Zephyrus but so much thinner and wilder. Dominic and Mel were both getting back on their feet, but the thing raised both its arms high, and with a sickening sound, three more arms burst from each of its sides.

There wasn't time. It was so fast. All eight arms shot out, lengthening, reaching, and the icicles Asha was pulling up from the snow shattered as eight clawed hands grabbed around her back and arms.

She cried out. The creature pulled its arms in, lifting her off her feet and yanking her back towards it.

"No!" Katie saw firelight glint off Mel's rising sword, and then all she saw was the fire itself.

It was like in the city. Not just fire in her hands, like in Harath. But all around her. Inside her. All she could hear and see and breathe and wait, wait, it was still too much—

She gasped. The fire faded. Just like in the city, she'd pulled back before she and Nyth could assimilate.

She didn't have time to register Nyth's sting of disappointment. Because she saw Dominic struggling to pull an arrow and Mel's knee buckling under her as she tried to lunge forward, Simon fighting to wrap the creature's legs in vines to hold it in place, all while the thing crawled backwards into the rift, holding a pale and gasping Asha.

Nyth was still so close though. When he nudged her to lift her hands, she did, flinching as fire leapt from her sightstone. It sailed over Asha's head and scorched down the creature's back. It opened its mouth in a red, howling shriek.

Just let go. Just let me work. Please.

But they couldn't seal the rift yet, not before it was cleared. And they were too slow. They were too slow.

The thing's hiss turned into a wide-open mouth, a red circle like an open wound, rimmed in rows of jagged teeth. And before Katie could do anything else, the thing snapped its head down and sank those rows of teeth right between Asha's shoulders.

Asha's eyes widened. Her lips parted, letting out a small, surprised sound. She looked up at Katie, at all of them, and looked so confused.

And then the pocket of void in the rift shuddered and jerked open wider, and the creature and Asha were sucked back into it fast as blinking.

Katie stared at the rift. Something in her, and something in Nyth, broke.

"No." Mel's voice cracked in the sudden silence. "No!" She leapt up, stumbling towards the rift; but its edges began to collapse in on itself, and it shrank until, by the time she reached it only seconds later, it was only a small point of bright light that finally vanished. Mel's mouth moved, but no sound came out. Her breath shuddered through her. She fell to her knees, still clutching the hilt of her sword as its blade sank into the earth. She leaned her head against her forearms and went still.

The field seemed infinite, empty, and with Asha gone their four small figures standing alone were helpless.

It was like a reflex, the way the guilt swelled in her chest, pressed into her throat, burned tears into her eyes. Katie reached for Nyth, the way she reached for his presence in sunbeams. And he was there. He hadn't left her. But all she felt from him was emptiness and aching loss.

Mel stood up. Even with her head hung low, Katie could see the blood drying on her face. "Back to the veil," she said, softly, and she vanished.

Nyth felt far away. So Katie lifted her sightstone and whispered the words that would take her away from this horrible field.

Chapter 22

They all landed in the meeting circle. The mist was hanging lower than ever. Dominic slumped onto the grass, leaning back against a stump, his hand clutching his chest. Katie went right to him and gently pulled his palm away, ignoring the tremor in her own hands. "Let me look at this."

His breath was shallow. "Thought you'd call 911 before I hit the ground," he joked, voice thin.

"Shh." He was trying to lighten the mood, but it only twisted the knife in her heart. She held back his hand, frowning at the blood on his palm, and shifted the shredded part of his jacket to try to see the wound better. Her breath came in sharp: the gashes were wide and deep, and the edges of them were tinged a whitish green that made her ill. "Damn it."

"Is it that bad?"

Katie looked up. Mel sat on a stump near them, rubbing her knee slowly. Simon stood next to her, gaze on Dominic but eyes far away. "We need Asha," Katie croaked.

"I might be able to help." Simon blinked, and Katie noticed his eyes were dry but there were tear streaks down his cheeks. "Can I try?"

"Yeah, of course." Katie moved away, and Simon took her place. He sat for a moment, concentrating. Then he splayed his hand over the wound and closed his eyes.

Dominic stared down at Simon's hand, and after a moment he

looked up at Katie and Mel. "D'you smell that?" His voice was softer, more gentle than usual. "It smells like trees do in the rain."

When Simon pulled back his hand, he said, "I can't heal them, but the poison is gone. I'm sorry I can't do more."

"Don't be," Mel said. "You're doing exactly what you should."

"Do you want me to do anything for you?" He looked at her, brow furrowing.

"No. I mean, not now. We need to figure this out first." Her eyes were glittering, cheeks flushed, jaw tense. "Let's—okay, let's get out and talk with the guardians face to face." And she did, squeezing her iron sightstone til it flashed, leaving her barefoot in her sweatpants again. She sat on the grass, rested her elbows on her knees, and hunched forward, rubbing her forehead with one hand.

Dominic and Simon separated from their guardians as well. The surrounding air shimmered. Skiron appeared first, his face grim; Aerie materialized sitting on the stump behind Dominic, and she peered down at his chest with her tiny mouth twisted into a frown.

Next to another stump, Katie noticed a humanoid figure sitting in the grass. Their hair was made of long, loose, swaying leaves, like a weeping willow's, and their skin was oddly textured and had knots and branches and tiny leaves growing off in some places. Ophion, embodied, their eyes dark and sad.

Then Nyth appeared in front of Katie, his eyes wide and the corners of his mouth tight. It hurt—it broke her heart. He stared at her for too long, but Katie couldn't look away.

She knew. She knew if she'd let them assimilate, this could've turned out different.

But he just let out a shuddering breath, so human in its fragility, and sat next to her.

"I realize you humans are not aware of this," Skiron said, "but we…" For the first time, at least as far as Katie knew of him, Skiron was searching for words. His face, usually so steady, looked more human for the worry furrowing his brow and the lost look in his eyes.

"We, as guardians of the two planes, have always been. We have always existed, at least as long as these worlds have existed. In all that time, we five have always been together. Our work draws us out across the worlds, but we stay in the same… place. Not a physical space, as you humans occupy, but a shared place all the same. For one of our number to be taken from us to places and fates unknown is not only distressing for our worry for Zephyrus—and for her vessel, Asha—but because this is a thing that…" He twisted his mouth and sighed, and his shoulders bowed. "It should not… be."

And Katie realized Nyth had never been alone. However long the guardians had been here—as old as the Earth—they'd never been apart. He had no idea what loss was.

No wonder he'd never understood.

Mel's head was still bowed, her long neck making a pale curve. "And we don't know what that thing was that took her," she said, her voice muffled as she talked toward her lap.

"Mel." Skiron's voice rumbled low. "Your hands."

Katie glanced at them. Mel's fists were clenched white-knuckle tight. She slowly uncurled them, revealing deep red imprints from her fingernails marked into her palms. "Sorry." Her voice was barely more than a whisper. She cleared her throat, then said more clearly, "But we don't know what that thing was, do we?"

"No. We have never seen its like before."

"I have a guess," Ophion said in a voice that was low and soft and rustling.

Skiron nodded. "Please."

"All of you, our vessels, know now that long ago we lost fragments of ourselves when we stretched ourselves too thin. The pieces lost on Earth are now in you, but something is still missing. More fragments of our essences may have been lost in Harath as well. We guardians, myself especially, know every living thing that walks or swims or flies or crawls or slithers in all the places of the two planes, and there lives no creature with the strength to overpower one of our own." Raising both hands, Ophion held them palms-up. The palms looked like moss. "I think our adversary has a peculiar advantage."

"It found the fragments," Simon said quietly.

"Or at least some of them. Perhaps it only found a piece of Zephyrus, which is why it took Asha while they were merged."

Katie glanced at Nyth. His brow was furrowed, his mouth drawn in a hard, thin line.

"Could something just absorb them like that?" Katie asked, glancing at the other guardians.

"You all did," Aerie piped up. "And you didn't even realize it happened. If someone else found them—someone—mystic enough to get a sense of what they were—"

"We have a real problem now," Nyth said, pushing himself to his feet. He started pacing, weaving between the stumps, almost but never quite bumping into everyone. "We don't know if we can close them without Zephyrus. And since we still, *still* haven't figured out why they're happening, we don't know if they'll keep coming. We can only keep them masked for so long before they get too big, and the veil starts to break down."

Katie kept trying to catch his eye as he paced, but he never looked at her.

With her head bowed, Mel rubbed her fingers against her scalp, slowly curling and uncurling her hands, long thin fingers mussing her hair. "So, we need to find Asha and Zephyrus. Not just for our own sake, but for…" She interrupted herself with a sound halfway between a sigh and a wheeze of laughter. "For the sake of the world. Both worlds."

Even though he was sitting straighter than Mel, Skiron's shoulders were still rolled forward, and when she looked over at him, Katie saw that crease between his eyebrows. "That is correct."

"Unfortunately, I don't think there's much you kids can do to help," Aerie said.

Simon's voice came soft and strained. "Except figure out what to tell Asha's family."

Katie twisted on her stump to look at Nyth. He'd paced out to the trees and was leaning on one with his forearm, staring out into the veil. The mist was swirling just above his head. "Nyth," she said. He turned at her voice, even if he didn't meet her gaze. Fear and anger danced together in his eyes, and grief bowed his shoulders.

"We can split our duties as best we can," Aerie said. "Try to cover Zephyrus's areas. It won't be perfect. There's gonna be gaps. But I think we can keep things from completely tumbling apart."

"And also search for Zephyrus, and Asha," Ophion said. They smiled a little. "It is a benefit of being noncorporeal in our true forms," they said to the kids. "We can be many places at once."

"There are limits. But we can do it."

"We will be stretched thin," Skiron said. "As Aerie said, our work will be imperfect, and the worlds will feel it. But I am hoping we can fend off the worst until we find our lost one." He passed his gaze over each of them. "We will let you know how things progress. Open communication is vital, now."

Katie looked at him, at Aerie, Ophion, at Nyth who came back over to stand near her. "Asha told me something," she said. "She had a dream about all of you arguing. After we sealed the rift in Harath. She, uh… she said she was pretty sure Zephyrus didn't mean for her to see it. Like it kind of bled over." Skiron's face went stonier, and Katie thought maybe she was getting to know him better when she suspected he was masking his embarrassment. "Do you think—" She glanced up at Nyth. "Missing your fragments. Maybe she was already being pulled too thin? If she let stuff slip through that she meant to keep secret, that's kind of a big deal. And maybe that's why that thing was able to take her, if she was already weakened."

Nyth twisted up his mouth, fingers tapping against his hips. "Maybe," Aerie said. "We've been stressed by it, but not enough for that. Not unless whatever took them is on our level."

"Maybe it is." Nyth paced off again, shaking out his hands at his sides. "It better get ready, then. I'm about to burn something down."

"Of course you are." Aerie climbed off her stump and leaned down to kiss the top of Dominic's head. It was so sweet and human that it caught Katie by surprise, but Dominic just closed his eyes and smiled. "We'll take care of the mystical part. You kids take care of the human parts."

"Someone has to tell Asha's parents something," Simon said again.

"We will." Katie caught his gaze. "We'll figure it out, Simon." His countenance didn't soften at her reassurance. Fair. It was paltry reassurance, and she knew it.

Dominic watched their exchange, then tipped his head up and murmured something to Aerie. She nodded and shimmered out of view, returning a few moments later, and she started helping Dominic to his feet.

Skiron stood, towering over them. He was looking at Mel, but his words seemed for them all when he said, "Guard yourselves, children. We do not want to lose anyone else." And then he was gone.

Simon pulled Mel to her feet. Katie got up and followed Nyth, who was pacing away. "Hey." He turned to her. When he finally met her gaze, she wasn't prepared for the intensity in his eyes. It was beyond anything she'd seen before. And whatever she'd meant to say—an apology, a plea, an explanation—died on her tongue.

"Stay safe," was all he said.

Katie wasn't sure if the fear or the anger burned hotter in his eyes.

He and Aerie vanished. Ophion briefly took Simon's hands, then melted into the ground in a wave of grasses and leaves. Simon looked into his palm. An acorn lay there.

"What's that for?" Mel asked, leaning against Simon's side.

"Hope," he said. "It means we should still hope."

Chapter 23

It was dark as Dominic drove Katie home in silence. He didn't even turn on music. Katie watched the yellow glow of streetlamps passing and tried to swallow the tangle of grief and guilt sitting heavy in her chest. It was a too-familiar feeling she wasn't eager to sink into.

"Hey Dom?" Her voice felt rusty. "What were you talking to Aerie about before we came back?"

"I asked her to come get Asha's bike." His gaze didn't waver from the road. "And take it back to the veil."

"What? Why?"

He cleared his throat. "I just thought, what are we gonna tell her parents?" He fidgeted, hands tightening on the wheel. "If it's not left behind, maybe everyone can hope she went somewhere on her own. They might not—" He cleared his throat again. "They might not assume she's dead right off."

Katie's stomach dropped. "Oh my god."

"You know that's what we're looking at."

"Because she would call home if she could. And she wouldn't leave her bike unless…"

Dominic sighed thinly, his shoulders hunched forward. "I just don't know what the hell to actually say."

Snow swirled in small, glittering flakes beyond the windshield. It kept piling up. In this part of Ohio, this close to the lake, snow wasn't uncommon this early, but Katie couldn't remember it ever getting this deep before January, if at all. And the snowflakes, so fluffy and soft that morning when they'd talked about sledding, had turned tiny and hard. Katie watched them flash through the car's headlight beams, and she realized the only thing they could say about Asha.

"Nothing," she said. "We say nothing."

"What the hell, Byrd? We have to tell them something."

"Okay, then, which lie do you think will help? We said bye while she was talking to a stranger at the gas station? We saw her get pulled into a van? You're right, it's—it's more merciful to just say we split up at the sledding hill and she was fine. It's the same as hiding her bike." She saw the tension in his jaw, saw his hands knuckling white on the wheel. "Look, we can still get her back. Let them keep a shred of hope while we have it, y'know?"

He didn't say anything for a while. The tires crunched over the new snowfall as they neared his street. Katie didn't say anything as Dominic pulled into his driveway and put the car in neutral.

They sat there for a long moment in silence. Talking had been better. As soon as they stopped, everything rose in her mind, her chest, her throat, shoving up behind her eyes and making them prick hot. She could hear Dominic breathing thinly.

Finally, he said, "I still can't believe she's actually gone." He looked up. "Shit. Sorry, Byrd, I meant to take you home. Guess I went autopilot."

"It's fine." She twisted her fingers together under the edges of her coat sleeves. She swallowed against the sick weight inside her. "Look. Dom. We're going to get her back."

He laughed. There was no humor in it. "You sound so sure."

"I have to be." She blinked hard. If she started crying now, she'd never stop. "If I'd just been able to—"

Her words stopped short, her heart twisting. Katie lowered her head, clenching her fingers in her coat cuffs, but Dominic said nothing. Usually, he'd ask what she meant. Or pick up on what she meant. He'd say, you're not blaming yourself, are you?

But he didn't. He just kept staring at his hands on the steering wheel.

"We have to get her back," Katie said. "So we will."

"Shit."

His voice was so small. Katie thought of going home and telling lies to her family, lying in her bed with all this weight in her heart while Dominic laid in his bed, his chest cut open and his brightness gone. She said, "Can I stay over at your house?"

He hesitated. "You never sleep over. You're all particular about your bedtime routine. And you don't even have an overnight bag."

"I'll live. I've lived through worse." She managed a weak smile. "C'mon. We just have to pretend everything's okay through dinner, then we can have a nice meltdown when everyone goes to bed."

He closed his eyes. "Yeah. Okay." He turned off the car.

The inside of the house was bright and warm. Mr. and Mrs. Gunn were as nice as always, but tonight it hurt. Their spaniel, Sunflower, kept jumping on Katie's leg with excitement, and Dom's little sister Arianna quipped from the kitchen that Dom could've taken her sledding, too. Katie smiled like a mannequin, stiff and plastic. When Dominic asked if Katie could stay for dinner, and Mrs. Gunn said, "Of course, sweetie," Katie texted her father with shaking fingers and made sure the message sounded normal.

Dinner was a nightmare. Anxiety and guilt and shame roared in the back of her mind, in the hollow of her chest, to the point she could barely swallow Mrs. Gunn's roasted chicken and potatoes.

So, she tried to cope. She clenched and unclenched her toes, counted her peas, did everything she'd learned in therapy to redirect the patterns in her mind and cue her body that she was safe, and slowly the anxiety abated. Her stomach still felt heavy, but she could at least focus.

Dominic, though. His jaw was too tense, his eyes glassy, his fingers tense against his fork.

After dinner, while Arianna helped her father with the dishes, and after Mrs. Gunn had said of course Katie was welcome to stay the night, especially so nobody had to drive again in all this snow,

Katie followed Dominic when he paced down the hall to his room. "You okay?" she asked.

He shook his head. "No. I can't—I don't know." He stared at the wall, his shoulders so tight Katie could see the rise in them. "Let's—let's get you some blankets."

She helped him carry some from his room and the linen closet out to the couch. While Katie arranged them to her liking, she heard him talking to his mother in the hall. When he came back, he had a pair of pajama pants for Katie.

And then he stood there, that same glazed detachment in his eyes. "Hey. Dom." He looked up, startled by even her soft voice. "Your chest. Simon said…"

"Right." He nodded, blinked hard. "I should go take care of that. I'll—I'll be back."

He disappeared down the hall to the bathroom. Katie sat on the edge of the couch. Arianna had gone to her room, Dominic's parents had bundled up to go walk Sunflower before bed, and for the first time since they came to the house, everything was quiet.

She curled forward, dropping her head into her hands, and let her breath come out ragged. Just a little. Before she imploded from the grief making its home in her chest.

Katie lost track of how long she sat there, which was what made her realize Dominic was taking way too long. She sat up and wiped her damp eyes. Were the wounds worse than they thought? Worry prickled in her mind, so she got up and went to knock on the bathroom door. "Dom?"

He didn't answer, and that scared the hell out of her. She opened the door.

He was sitting on the closed toilet lid, hunched over with his hands on his knees. His t-shirt was off, exposing his wounds, and a bottle of peroxide and some cotton balls were scattered across the counter next to an open first-aid kit.

He was shaking.

"Dom. Hey." Katie knelt, peering up at his face. The second she saw his eyes, she knew. He wasn't keeping the panic at bay. He didn't know how. "Deep breaths, Dom. Way down deep." He squeezed his eyes shut. "Do you want me to count them?" He nodded, so she did. Slow and easy. "Breathe in, two, three, four." He sucked in a thin breath. "Breathe out, two, three, four." The air shuddered out of him. So, Katie kept counting, kept her voice even and steady, until his breathing evened out, too.

He sat back. He looked wrecked. His eyes were red, and his face pale and Katie had never, ever seen him look like this. The angry gashes on his chest didn't help. Images roiled up in Katie's mind of the riftling's long, clawed hands closing hard around Asha, and she felt everything rising in a wave. But Dominic needed her. She took a slow, deep breath of her own, feeling her belly expand, letting it out slowly. Then she put some peroxide on a piece of cotton, handed it to him, and said, "Those are pretty nasty for a sledding injury."

Dominic's voice came out shaky, but he managed to speak. "You're a hoot. A real hoot, Byrd."

"Byrd. Hoot. It's the least I can do."

He actually almost smiled at that.

Katie sat back against the wall as Dominic dabbed peroxide over his wounds, wincing. He looked exhausted—Katie understood that all too well—but he looked calmer, at least. He grimaced when he wiped his wounds clean, and as he threw away a cotton ball, he asked, "Do you remember how we met?"

"Of course I do."

"No, I mean, do you really remember?"

His voice still sounded thin, and his hands were trembling as he opened a package of gauze. So, Katie leaned in, opened the gauze for him. Relief washed over his face. "I can hold while you tape?" He nodded, so she knelt next to him and carefully pressed the square of gauze over the gashes. It didn't quite cover the whole mess.

She still hadn't answered his question, and he was still shaky. She started talking in a smooth, even voice. Even and smooth for him to ground himself in. "It was freshman science class. Very first day. You asked me why I was wearing a scarf in August."

"I'd never seen you before. I thought maybe you'd moved here from Florida or something and eighty degrees was cold to you."

"It was a lightweight scarf, thank you very much." She held the gauze in place, her hands much steadier than her heart. "I was scared and self-conscious about coming back to public school. I was hiding in my scarf. But you asked me, wasn't I too hot? And you know, I was."

"You were sweating. I said, it's a cute scarf and all, but why make yourself uncomfortable?" His words started coming more freely. He finished taping down the gauze.

"It was nosy of you, but you meant well. And you were right." She had been terrified to be in classrooms, so close to so many other people, so afraid her shirt would slip or her sleeve would ride up and someone would see everything wrong with her. But the scarf *had* been too hot. And was it worth that discomfort for the minuscule chance the collar of her shirt would ride too far to the left? So, she had taken it off. And she had felt better. She'd been scared. Her stomach had clenched. But she felt cooler and could focus better on the lesson, and focusing took her mind off her fear.

Dominic didn't know all of that. Still, even now, for all he knew about her panic and her loss, he didn't know the details. He didn't know about her scars. They were a tangled blend of shame and guilt and grief she hadn't managed to crack open to him yet. But he'd helped her without even knowing he'd done it.

"You need another piece of gauze," she said. "There's still exposed scratches."

"Thanks," Dom said. Katie opened another piece, pressing it in place next to the other. "Seriously."

"It's the least I can do. There." He got it taped down, and Katie withdrew her hands and stood as he reached for his shirt. "All cleaned up and bandaged."

"Thank you, Byrd," he said again, tugging on his shirt. "For helping."

Katie took a few deep breaths as she started packing things back in the kit, sweeping up used supplies and throwing them away. "You did most of the work."

"I'm just glad you're here." His voice was soft. Katie glanced up. Most of the near-panic was gone from his face, so she relaxed a hair, then turned back to closing the kit. "When did you start homeschooling, anyway?" Dominic asked after a moment.

"Third grade."

"Right." He still hadn't stood up. "Where'd you go before that?"

"Ridge Heights Elementary."

"Me too. Hey, you know, we could've been in the same class. Remember at all?"

Katie looked back over to meet his gaze. His eyes were damp. More than damp. She softened. "No. But we're friends now. And that's what matters."

"I'm glad. I just—I wonder if we ever met before."

"Well," Katie said, turning to him, "all I know is one minute you said maybe I should take off my scarf, and an hour later I was having lunch with you and a bunch of your friends, and I've never wanted another best friend since." She smiled a quiet smile. "And that's what counts."

"Yeah." He sniffled. "Byrd." His eyes were still wet. "These things want to take us."

"I know."

"I don't want to lose you. Not like Asha." The waver in his voice broke her heart as he said, "I'm barely keeping it together here as it is."

Katie crouched next to him again, folding her hands gently over his. "But you are keeping it together now. Even if only barely. And that's what counts." She squeezed his hands. "And you're not going to lose me."

He stared down at her hands around his. Clumsily, he twined his fingers around hers. "The guardians don't even know what those things are. We don't know what they're capable of."

"You're not going to lose me." She tipped her head to the side. "We're Dom and Byrd, right? No creepy beasts can split us up. We'll stick together through this no matter what happens."

"To the end?"

"To the very end." She held up one hand, her small finger extended. "I promise."

The corners of Dominic's mouth turned up, looking so much better, so much more at home on his face than the tight grief and panic. He linked his pinkie finger around hers. "Pinkie swear it?"

"Pinkie swear it."

They heard the front door open and close, heard his parents' voices and Sunflower's happy whines. Dominic held Katie's gaze for a moment, then slipped out of the bathroom.

Katie changed into the pajama pants, brushed her teeth with some toothpaste on her finger, then went back to the living room. The lights were off except for one lamp on a side table, and the house had quieted. "Mom and Dad went to their room," Dominic said. He was sitting at one end of the couch, holding a pile of blankets in his lap. "Is it…" He tried to smile. "Is it okay if I sleep out here? On the floor? I just don't want to be alone right now."

"Me neither."

She climbed onto the couch while he arranged the blankets and snuggled into his nest. After a minute, she turned onto her side to look down at him. "Do you feel better?"

"My chest? Yeah, you helped."

"Well, that. And also—not that."

He shrugged. "Yeah. I do. I mean, it's still there. But I don't feel like I'm about to die anymore."

"It was a panic attack, you know."

"I wondered if that was what it was. Jesus, Byrd, how do you handle that shit?"

"Practice."

"That's not funny."

"It is if you're me." His eyes still looked pained, though, so she said, "Sorry. I'm glad you're more okay now."

"Okay enough to sleep, at least." Dominic got up to switch off the light, and then Katie heard him lie down fully under his covers. "Night, Byrd."

"Night, Dom."

The room was dark and still, and Katie stared at the bookshelf across the room, breathing slowly, trying to will sleep to come. But every time her eyelids grew heavy, she saw the riftling's face, and she jolted and clutched the blankets in her hands. She didn't want those things in her nightmares.

She reached out for Nyth. He was upset at her at the same time he was scared for her, for all of them, for what would come next. Fear and anger and grief—god knew Katie was an expert at that combination.

But when she tried to find him, he didn't reach back. He was there in the world like he always was, but he didn't answer her. Didn't send her his warmth. Didn't whisper that it was okay.

It took all the strength she had left not to cry. But he was right. It wasn't okay.

She closed her eyes, trying to let her mind go blank, when she heard Dominic say, "Why did your dad decide to homeschool you, anyway?"

Katie opened her eyes again. He was watching her. "Why?"

"Yeah. I've known you forever—okay, I mean a few years, but basically forever—but there's still a lot I wonder about you, Byrd."

She rubbed her thumb against the nubby texture of the blanket. "It's a long story. It was when my mom died."

His face fell. "Oh. Shit, I'm sorry, I didn't—"

"It's okay." Katie's stomach felt heavy, her chest tight. No way she could tell him this. Not now. Not when she'd just— "Hey. I'll tell you someday, okay?"

"Okay."

Katie wiggled one arm free of the blanket and let it hang down the side of the couch. She tapped Dominic's shoulder with one fingertip. "I promise."

In the dimness of the room, she heard him sniffle. Then his fingers closed around hers. "Goodnight, Byrd." And she closed her eyes, waiting for sleep to come.

Chapter 24

Morning came bright and blue-skied, and for once, the sunshine felt cruel. Katie rode home from Dominic's with her heart in her stomach.

Because Asha was gone.

Because the guardians were fractured.

Because maybe none of it would have happened if she'd been able to assimilate with Nyth.

The way he'd looked at her in the veil yesterday haunted her. Grief and fear tangled up in anger. Anger at her.

Her thoughts looped as her legs pumped as she flew too fast down the side of the road, slush spraying her legs, heart pounding from effort and from anger of her own. At him. At herself. At everything.

She tried more than once to reach out to Nyth. Every single time was like hitting a cold stone wall.

Just before she turned onto her street, she veered off between two houses, bumping through snow down to the knot of trees in the middle of her neighborhood. She left her bike lying on the ground, her breath spilling thick clouds into the air, as she yanked her sightstone off her wrist and held it up. "Draw me through the veil."

She landed near the meeting place, her breath still coming hard. The mist seemed to be drifting lower than the last time she'd been here. "Nyth." He didn't show up, so she turned, calling louder. "Nyth, come on. I want to talk to you."

Nothing but silence. Anger twinged hot in her chest. "Quit being a baby," she shouted. "I know you can hear me. Quit ignoring me and talk to me. *Nyth!*"

When she turned again, he was standing there, hands on his hips, mouth twisted into a scowl. "You know, I have work to do."

His words weren't playful, so neither were hers. "Can we just talk?"

"About what? What am I supposed to say?"

Katie waved her hands at him. "This! You! You're pissed at me when you know I can't force assimilation to happen."

He spread his arms. "What do you want me to tell you, Katie? Do you have any idea how much your indecision is costing us?"

Her cheeks burned. "Of course I do. You don't have to be such a dick about it."

"Zephyrus—" His voice cracked. It was such a human thing to hear. Nyth stepped closer to her, and his voice dropped. "You know as well as I do that if we'd worked together, we would've had a chance of saving them. But you pushed me away."

Katie's heart lurched into her throat. But he wasn't saying anything she didn't already know.

"I'm sorry," she said. "You know how much this is gutting me."

"Yeah. I do." His eyes darkened. "It's the same for me."

"I want to change it." The tension was rising, coiling in her body. "But I can't."

He shook his head. "That's not true."

"Yes, it is."

"I know it's hard, but—"

"No, you *don't!*" Something cracked in her. Everything rushed under her skin, all the tears she didn't let herself cry last night transforming and boiling up into the words that spilled out. "You can't know. You're not human, Nyth, you can't die like we can, you never had a mother—you can't possibly understand this." Her face was hot, her fingertips tingling. "And so I'm sorry, okay? It's not fair to everyone, but it's not fair to me either. It's not fair that I have to wake up every day knowing it's my fault people I love are hurt, or missing, or dead—" The words stopped hard on her tongue. Her stomach lurched.

Nyth furrowed his brow. "Wait, which thing are you upset about? Losing them? Assimilating? Your mother?"

"It's all the same, Nyth."

"No, it isn't."

"Yes, it *is.*"

He made a frustrated noise and wheeled away, pacing off in a circle. Katie called after him. "You think I don't want to make this happen? I just can't, Nyth."

"Can't," Nyth's mouth twisted around the word like a curse. "Can't, can't. All you're saying is you can't. But you can." He stalked back up to her. "There's a fragment of me stuck inside you, and it ended up there because we're the same."

"That doesn't mean—"

"It wouldn't just help everyone else if you'd let yourself do this. It'd help you, Katie. It would set you free. You blame yourself for your mother's death and it's holding you back in everything. But you won't let go. Because you don't believe you deserve to be free."

He looked so sure of himself, his hands on his hips. Incandescent rage crackled under Katie's skin, simmered up into her chest. "How dare you?" The words seethed out of her mouth. "You have no idea what you're talking about."

Nyth rolled his eyes, pacing away again. "Enlighten me."

"Screw you!" He spun back around to glare at her, at her words, and something hot and dangerous glinted in his eyes. It spiked a strange fear in her heart, but her anger was hotter. "Do you have any idea what I was like after the accident? Once I was stable enough to be kept awake, to see my family, to go home? My dad had to home school me for six years. I barely talked. Nobody could touch me. My brother—he was five years old, and I gave him a black eye when he tried to hug me." She yanked up the sleeve of her coat, brandishing her scarred arm. "Because I couldn't stand anyone touching this."

"That's not what I'm—"

"My dad and my therapist made me go back to school when I was eleven. That lasted all of two days. Know why?" Her throat felt thick; her words sounded thick. "I tried to wear my coat all day. To hide my scars. So nobody would ask me what they were and I wouldn't have to tell them I killed my mom." Tears blurred her eyes. "My teacher made me take it off, and I had a panic attack in the middle of the classroom. And the next day, I was so angry at her I took her scissors from her desk and shredded the cushions on her chair. Called her things I wouldn't repeat even now." The memory of it burned in her, hot shame and rage and grief.

Katie wiped her cheeks. "That was my life, you jerkass. For years. And now I go to school, and I have friends and I've learned how to handle my panic attacks—I've worked so hard to let myself be free again. But I know my limits. And this—this is too much."

And he was still staring at her like she was completely crazy, his mouth twisted in a scowl. Katie stared back, breathing hard, adrenaline rushing under her skin. "That's a bunch of bullshit," he said. Katie didn't know he even knew any swear words. "I can see into your heart, Katie, whether you like it or not. And whether you like it or not, you can do this."

He turned and stormed off. It was such a human thing to do, Katie might've laughed if she hadn't been so furious. "You have no idea what you're talking about," she shot at his back.

In an instant, he whirled to face her. "Maybe not. But I do know you're letting yourself stay hurt. And I'm not gonna watch you do it anymore."

And then he was gone, and the veil around her was empty. All Katie could hear was the blood rushing in her ears and her own heavy, angry breaths.

She took herself back to Earth and rode around her block five times to get the rest of the anger out of her system. Her leggings were ruined from the salt spray, and tears froze in streaks on her face, but by the time she put her bicycle in the garage, she wasn't furious anymore. Just sick to her stomach from everything.

The house was warm, but her nerves jangled as she hung up her coat. She heard her dad in the kitchen, and she really didn't want to— "How are the Gunns?" he called as she tried to sneak past.

Katie shoved her clenched hands into her sweater pockets. "Good. They're good." She didn't sound even remotely normal, and she knew it, and at least she could tell him about one piece of her misery. "Um, Dad… Asha didn't make it home last night after she was hanging out with us. Did she… did she come here or anything?"

"… No, no, we haven't heard from her."

"Okay. Thanks." He appeared in the kitchen doorway. Katie dropped her gaze. She couldn't look at him right now. "I think—I need to keep busy. Can I have the kitchen? To bake?"

"Of course." She still couldn't look at him, but she could imagine the line between his eyebrows, his concerned frown.

He gave her space. He'd learned years ago when it was best to give her space.

Tracy must've been in the living room because Katie heard her dad murmuring something in there. She turned on the fan in the vent hood over the stove to block it out and started pulling things from the cabinets.

For a while, it helped. Kneading dough always helped. She was rougher with the dough than she usually was, smacking it onto the counter more than she needed to, but it made her feel better. But then the dough was under a tea towel to rise for an hour, and she was restless again.

She took a shower, finally got out of her wet leggings, cleaned her room, and tried not to think about the rest of the day stretching ahead of her. How the hell was she going to fill the hours? How could she stand being alone?

When the dough was risen and shaped and slipped into the oven, she texted Mel.

Are you home today?

Mel

Where else would I be

Katie frowned. Wanted to be annoyed. But she remembered Mel's bowed head, her fingernails pressed into her palms so hard they left marks.

I'm gonna come over

She didn't even check her phone again before she headed out on her bike. She just went—the bread wrapped in the tea towel and tucked into her bag—and was more mindful of the slush this time.

When Mel opened the door, Katie held up the bread like an offering and said, "Can I come in?"

Mel stared at her for a moment. "You're ridiculous, Katie Byrd," she finally said, stepping back. "Come on in the kitchen, I guess." Katie unwrapped herself from her coat and scarves, then followed.

Mel stood by the kitchen window, almost silhouetted by the last of the daylight. Cold air snaked in through an inch of cracked-open window. Mel's shoulders hunched forward, her collar bones making deep shadows on her chest above the neckline of her sweatshirt, the same one she was wearing yesterday. She was smoking and leaned down to blow the smoke out the window.

Katie held the wrapped loaf of bread against her chest and asked, "Why are you doing that?"

"Because I don't want to put on clothes to go outside and my mom hates it when I smoke inside. I'm compromising."

Her voice was flat, so Katie didn't push it. She unwrapped the bread and set it on the kitchen table. Mel glanced down at it, then back up at Katie. "Why bread?"

"I needed to keep busy this morning." She shrugged. "Thought you could use some. It's homey. Comforting."

Mel stared at her a little longer, then flicked her cigarette ash into an empty coffee mug on the table. "Thanks."

The silence made Katie itchy, so she glanced around the kitchen. She hadn't looked around much when they'd all been over here for pancakes. "Those are pretty," she said, gesturing to a line of three pictures of lavender and sunflowers. "Julia likes lavender?"

"Not really," Mel said. "I do. And sunflowers are my favorite."

She snuffed out her cigarette in the bottom of the coffee mug, shut the window, and got butter and a knife. "So," she said, sitting at the table and scooting a chair out for Katie with her foot, "you brought me bread out of the goodness of your heart."

Katie sat, tucking her feet under the chair. "I could give you advice instead of bread, but I suck at advice. Mostly, I can't stand the idea of being alone today."

Mel didn't answer. She blinked hard and ripped off a piece of bread.

After a long silence, she said, "And you didn't call Dominic?"

"I saw him earlier." Katie shrugged. "He... I love him. But he doesn't get it."

"What it feels like to be a monumental fuck-up?"

Katie lifted her gaze. The shadows under Mel's eyes were deep and dark. "It's not your fault."

"Isn't it? It's my job to protect you guys." Katie opened her mouth to reply, but Mel shook her head. "I don't want to talk about this. Seriously. Let it go, Byrd."

"Okay. Fine." She turned her gaze back down and smeared way too much butter on her piece of bread.

Several minutes of tense silence later, Mel ran her fingers through her hair and said, "I'm not trying to be an asshole. I just don't have the energy to pretend everything's okay when it's not, you know?"

"Yeah. I know exactly what you mean."

Mel stood up, taking the butter knife and plates to the sink. "That… thing." Katie could feel the chill in her words. "If more of those show up like the rift beasts did…"

A twinge tightened Katie's chest. "Hey. Mel. We're all—we're all getting stronger. The guardians are gonna figure out what's happening. We're gonna be okay."

The corner of Mel's mouth twitched upwards. "Wow. You weren't lying about your terrible advice." She rubbed her nose with the palm of her hand. "I want another cigarette, but my mom's gonna kill me if I smoke a third one in here today. Can you wait while I put on sweatpants and then sit outside with me?"

"Sure." She wrapped back up in her extra sweater, her coat, her scarf, her hat, while Mel put on a coat and sweatpants over her running shorts.

They went out, the screen door banging behind them, and clanged down the metal staircase to sit at the bottom. Mel flicked on her lighter, lit her next cigarette, and sighed out a plume of white smoke. Some of the tension eased from her face. "So." She glanced sidelong at Katie. "You don't seem to be doing so well yourself."

Katie's face burned. She knew what Mel was referring to. "I'll be fine."

A snort of laughter escaped Mel. "You're a terrible liar, Katie Byrd. And I'm about as good at comforting people as you are at giving advice, but you've got to figure out your shit."

"I know."

She bowed her head, running her fingers through her dark hair, leaving it sticking up all over. "We have no idea what they can do to us. If they'll take more of us."

"I know," Katie said again. Her voice was small. Her chest was tight.

Mel stared at her, hard. Then she flicked away the butt of her cigarette into a terracotta pot next to the stairs and said, "C'mon, Byrd."

Katie hesitated. "Nyth and I fought." She hugged her arms

around her knees. She couldn't meet Mel's gaze. "Because I couldn't assimilate. Because if I had…"

Her heart lurched in her throat. And maybe Mel could tell because she didn't push anymore.

They sat in silence, Katie shivering and Mel smoking. It was snowing again; the wind kicking up. "I can't stand this," Katie managed through gritted teeth. "Not doing anything."

"What the hell can we do?"

And there, shivering on the metal steps, her heart heavy and her guilt raging, a shot of clarity pierced through the miserable fog. "Do you have any jars? I have an idea."

Chapter 25

"You sure this is going to help?" Mel asked as they drove toward the metro parks.

"No. But I'd rather try than just sit around and wait."

"I know." The snow had picked up, thick billows of tiny glittering snowflakes that threatened a whiteout, and traffic moved slowly. "It's making me sick to do nothing."

She turned up her music, and they drove on in silence for a while. The further they went, the more the silence rankled in Katie's chest. Finally, she said, "I know you don't want to talk about it. But maybe you should."

"Byrd—"

"I mean it, Mel. You keep everything all stopped up in your chest. That's not good for you. I know."

Mel let out a huff. "It doesn't matter."

"Of course, it does."

"No, it really doesn't." Her voice got clipped. She flicked on the turn signal, taking a turn carefully. "I already told you. It's my job to protect you guys. That's what matters, not what I feel."

"That's bullshit." Katie crossed her arms and stared hard at Mel, watching the older girl's jaw tense. "Dominic fights, too. And if it's your fault, it's my fault for not assimilating yet."

Mel shook her head. "That's not what I mean."

And Katie wanted to crowd in on her. Wanted to ask what she did mean, then. But she bit her tongue. Mel needed space. Kind of like Simon did. Space to unfold her tangle of thoughts and feelings.

Her restraint paid off when Mel said, in a softer voice, "It's not just about fighting. It's part of who I am. It's why Skiron's fragment chose me." Her long fingers gripped harder on the steering wheel as they turned into the metro parks, creeping between the tall trees toward their destination. "I've never known what I want to do with myself. With my life. I've always felt directionless, and it's always made me feel like shit."

They were pulling into the Rockpoint parking lot. Katie uncrossed her arms and folded her hands together in her lap. She watched Mel as she parked the car and then sat there, staring at her hands on the wheel. Something soft had come into the line of her mouth and her brow.

"When we landed in the veil that first time, and we were all lost. I spoke up. I stood up. And for the first time, it finally felt like I was doing something right. Doing what I should." Her hands slipped from the wheel and fell to her lap. "The first time I held Skiron's sword... I don't like killing things. But I like that I can spare Simon and Asha from having to. And I like knowing I can look out for you all."

She finally met Katie's gaze, and Katie's heart clenched. Mel was tall—almost as tall as Simon—and so controlled and cool. But she was eighteen. And she looked it, then. Not a leader or a warrior. Just a kid.

"It's bad enough to have lost Asha and Zephyrus. That's killing me. But knowing on top of that, knowing that even the one thing I finally felt right doing, I still messed up... It sucks."

And the clench in Katie's heart released, melted warmth through her chest. She reached across the console and laid her hand against Mel's elbow. "You're just a kid, Mel," she said. "Like all of us."

Mel blinked rapidly, her eyes shining, before she looked away and took the keys out of the ignition. "Yeah. I know."

They stepped out of the car into the biting cold air, Katie carrying the bag with her supplies in it. They didn't say much more as they crossed the picnic area, wading through a foot of snow. The silence felt even heavier when they passed the tree line. This was the clearing from the last rift. This was where Asha had disappeared.

Katie's heart dropped. But she kept going.

"What exactly are you trying to find?" Mel asked as Katie crouched and started digging through the snow in the spot where the rift had been.

"I'm not sure. I'm going to collect a soil sample from here and then one from out in the picnic area and see if there's anything funky about this one."

"It's the weekend. No lab at school."

"I know. But I'm not even sure what I'm looking for, so I'm going to have to improvise, anyway." She made it down to the dead grass below the snow and dug into the dirt. It was cold, but not frozen yet. "Thanks, by the way. For driving me out here."

"No problem."

Katie managed to scrape up a decent scoop of dirt, which she dumped into the cleaned-out jam jar they'd brought. When she was done, she kicked the snow back over the hole. Her fingers were like ice even through her gloves, and the wind and tiny, hard snowflakes that wouldn't stop swirling around her made her cranky, but at least the digging was keeping her warm.

They stopped in the picnic area on the way back to the car, where Katie repeated the whole process, scooping the dirt from there into a different jar and marking the bottom of it with a permanent marker to distinguish it from the other. Then they piled back into Mel's car, shivering and shoving their hands against the vents as the heater coughed to life. Mel wasn't wearing gloves because of course she wasn't; her fingers were pink and pale as she pressed them to the vent.

"Any obvious change?" she asked.

Katie peered at the two jars of dirt. "Not to the naked eye. Now I just have to figure out how to test them."

"You're a smart cookie. You'll figure it out." Her fingers tapped the steering wheel as she put the car in reverse and backed out of their parking spot. "I have that mineralogy test stuff at home. If there's some bigger pieces or bits of stone in there, we could examine them." Mel glanced over. "We can invite the others over if you want."

Katie nodded. "I'll text them."

Back at the apartment, Mel spread a big square of canvas on the living room floor and brought out some of her supplies from her room. She disappeared to make a pot of coffee while Katie started sifting through her soil samples.

Both had a bunch of little pebbles and tiny fragments of plain-looking, usual rocks. Nothing out of the ordinary for the most part. But the sample from the rift area had an abundance of another material. Still small, but darker in color, long chips with skinny grooves in them and an almost diamond shape on the short ends.

"Hey Mel," Katie called. "There's something."

Mel came back in with a cup of coffee and sat cross-legged on the floor, squinting at the pieces of mineral in Katie's hand. "Good. We can start figuring out what they are. You want anything to drink? Or there's still half that loaf of bread."

Katie shook her head. "I'm fine. I just want to figure this out."

They tested the hardness and the streak color of the mineral, and Mel was examining the luster of it when Simon showed up. He accepted a cup of coffee and curled up on the couch, watching Mel and Katie work with barely more than a hello. But his presence was gentle and calming, and Katie felt better with him there.

By the time Dominic arrived, Mel had checked out the angles of the breakage. "I'm pretty sure it's hornblende," she said. By now, she had her reference book open on her lap. She'd flipped through pages, occasionally stopping to pore over a section, before she settled on this one.

"Never heard of it," Dominic said.

"You should learn." Katie leaned back on her hands. "Don't you want to be an earth science teacher?"

"Yeah, but that's like, weather and biomes. Not geology."

"It says it's usually found in igneous rocks," Mel said. "Which is weird. There's mostly sedimentary rocks where we live, and that's all I found in the sample from the picnic area."

"Igneous." Katie wracked her brain for science class facts. "Those are the volcanic rocks, right?"

"Yeah. I mean, it doesn't have to be from a volcano itself, but magma's involved." Mel furrowed her brow, peering closer at the page. "If this formed naturally here, it would've had to have formed pretty deep."

"And maybe the rift pulled it up somehow?" Simon offered.

"Maybe. Or maybe the rift created it somehow."

"So, they're leaving some kind of signature." Katie picked up some of the pieces. "Aerie said there was a molecular shift the rifts left behind. Maybe this is the result."

Mel ran her fingers through her hair. "I have no idea how this would just form like that. But hell, we already know the rifts are weird."

"The guardians probably know about it, right?" Dominic asked.

Katie furrowed her brow. "I don't know. If they do, I guess it wasn't important enough to bring up."

"Or it doesn't answer any questions."

"We can tell them next time we see them. If they already know, no harm done. If they don't, maybe it'll help."

Simon gazed into his coffee cup. "Anything we can do to help."

Katie frowned.

This wasn't enough. What they were doing. How they were trying. Simon was still staring like he wasn't really seeing the coffee in his cup, his silence heavier than his normal pauses. Dominic was still trying way too hard to pretend he was okay, an almost-glassy desperation in his eyes and behind his smile. Mel was still rough-voiced, like she'd smoked way too much last night and barely slept. And Katie—

Didn't have time to try to analyze how she felt because her

sightstone vibrated against her wrist.

Mel swore, Simon tensed, and Dominic snapped his head towards Katie, meeting her gaze.

God, she wanted to cry.

But she swallowed the lump in her throat, and they all lifted their sightstones.

Her feet didn't even touch the grass properly before Nyth was there, grabbing her hand and whirling her away. When she landed at the rift, the snow came nearly to her knees, and the wind was bitter cold.

Nyth didn't materialize. They hadn't spoken since their fight.

Naked trees clattered their branches along one side of the gulch they stood in. At the top of the hill on the other side was a guardrail. "Where are we?"

Mel stared up the hill at the road above them, her jaw set hard. "On the other side of the highway, right behind my house." She assimilated with Skiron without hesitation, Dominic and Simon right behind her.

"Could it be a coincidence?" Dominic asked as Skiron, through Mel, unmasked the rift.

"I'm not keen to wait around and find out."

It was smaller than usual, but its edges were jagged, shifting eerily. "C'mon," Mel said, and she and Simon started stabilizing the border. Dominic nocked an arrow. Katie let the heat rise in her, pulse pounding.

"We still don't even know if we can clear it without Asha," she whispered.

Nyth's voice was audible next to her ear. "We have to try."

At least they agreed on that.

A pale crack appeared across the rift, as jagged as its border. Simon and Mel pushed harder, but it split open and widened. Mel leaned in, pushed the line of crystallization almost to the full edge of the border—but the void cracked wide open, shooting down and shattering part of the edge.

"Damn it." Mel crouched, drawing her sword from the earth. "Simon, keep pushing that border." She raised her sword, planted her feet, and readied herself right in front of the rift.

The void broke open further, sending out cracks that undid half of Simon's work, and a gnarled gray hand slithered out.

"Not today," Mel growled, and she lunged forward and drove the point of her sword straight into the void.

A shrill shriek cut the air, and Mel stumbled as her sword propelled back out. The void exploded, shattering the border of the rift, and a riftling pulled itself out and tumbled to the ground. Its shoulder was broken open, oozing pale liquid. It crouched, lifted its head, and bared its pointed teeth in a hiss.

Vines and leaves shot up from the ground to encircle the rift, Simon straining to stabilize it. Mel swung her sword as the riftling jumped toward her. Dominic leaped into the air with his bow, one of his glass-like arrows cutting down from above and landing in the riftling's open wound, making it howl.

"Almost there," Simon called.

Sparks danced over Katie's fingers. Her sightstone flickered like the heart of a flame.

Mel dodged the riftling's claws and swung the sword at its back, but it launched itself forward, slamming its gangly arms around Mel's legs. She cried out and tried to strike it, but it rolled over, and her blade bit the earth. The riftling began crawling backwards, dragging Mel, and her sword fell out of her hand.

"Don't let it through, Simon!" Katie yelled, dashing forward.

Simon whirled around, saw the riftling, and his eyes widened. "Mel!"

"Stay focused! I've got it!" Katie kept the heat growing in her hands as she sprinted closer, curving around the riftling, which was making poor pace with how hard Mel was kicking and struggling. "Nyth, please," she begged, and she lurched forward and grabbed the border of the rift.

Vines bent under her fingers and crystals cut into her palms as the heat building in her shuddered out into the rift. Katie's body jolted, her vision swimming and her stomach plummeting, but she didn't let go as a wave of flames rippled over the surface of the rift and into the body of the riftling.

It shrieked; an unholy rusty sound that made every hair on Katie's body stand on end. But the rift—it was a clear window into the veil, except for the shivering void the riftling was crawling backwards into.

Mel beat it around the face, a fierce, hard precision in her punches that were both her and Skiron. Two more arms erupted from it sides with a bone-crunching sound and braced against the ground while its main arms dragged Mel. Katie stumbled back from the rift, panic spiking. She'd shoved out all the fire she'd let Nyth build up. She felt his frantic tugging at her attention. They had to start over; they had to—

Then the riftling stopped and shuddered. It took Katie a second to notice the pale arrow sticking out of the base of its neck.

Mel took the window. She grimaced, her face stony like Skiron's, and punched the riftling square in the throat. It gurgled, its grip going slack, and she wriggled free. One powerful kick of her boot into the middle of its face, and the thing slumped back into the rift, the pocket of void closing behind it.

Nyth materialized in front of her, taking her face in his hands. "Katie. Are you okay?"

She blinked, forced her vision to focus. She was as exhausted as she'd been after the first sealing. "I grabbed the rift," she said.

"Yeah, doofus, you did."

"We still have to close it."

His brow furrowed. But she knew he knew she was right. "Sit down at least," he said before shimmering out of view.

Katie sat in the snow. It was freezing, but warmth pressed at her back. She mumbled thanks to Nyth and leaned her arms on her knees and held her sightstone toward the cleared rift and left the heat flow through her, from whatever fragment of Nyth lay buried in her heart, through her sightstone, into the world, until the rift's edges smeared and glowed and the whole thing was sealed away.

Katie turned to see Mel slowly getting to her feet, barely upright, before Simon grabbed her and pulled her into his arms. He held her too tight—Katie saw Mel's face twist in discomfort—but she returned the embrace. "I'm okay," she said. "Snow. Calm down. I'm okay." But her hands trembled against his back.

Square pink palms appeared in front of her face. Katie blinked. Dominic had un-assimilated. He stood in front of her, frowning, and held out his hands. She took them, and he hauled her up.

Everything tilted briefly. She closed her eyes. "That was stupid."

"You're lucky it didn't kill you or something."

"Yeah, well, Mel's still here."

Mel squeezed Simon's hands, then turned and crouched, digging through the snow. She shoved her fingers into the cold, hard earth, plunging wrist-deep before tearing up a crumbling handful of soil. Dark flakes of that mineral—hornblende, that shouldn't be able to form here—caught the light in her palm.

"It happened again," Katie said.

Nyth reappeared next to her. "What did?"

Mel held out her hand, showing him the hornblende. "We just found some of this at the site of the last rift. And it's here, too."

"Do you guys know about it?" Dominic asked. He'd let go of Katie's hands but kept glancing at her with shadowed eyes.

As if reading his mind—and hers, or maybe her body language and the way her knees were weak—Nyth slipped his shoulder under Katie's. It was so damn cold out and he was so damn warm and she was so, so tired. She leaned on him as he peered at the hornblende and said, "The rifts are changing the physical plane. Leaving a mark."

"Or whatever's causing them is." Katie jumped at Aerie's voice—she was very suddenly next to them. Simon and Mel huddled in closer. "This is good work, kids." She poked at the pieces of rock.

"I'll try to do more investigating. For now—you go home. Rest. Stay safe."

"What about you?" Dominic asked. His voice was thin. The cheerful bravado was falling. God, it hadn't even been twenty-four hours since Asha and Zephyrus had been taken. Katie felt sick.

Aerie frowned. "We'll be okay. These riftlings, they're corporeal. I don't think they can touch us when we're not physically manifested."

Nyth's fingers dug into Katie's upper arm. She winced. When she glanced at him, his eyes were haunted.

"Nyth?"

"Aerie's right. Go home and rest. Especially you."

All of them—it was heavy on all of them. Simon looked like he might crumble. Mel looked like she wanted to cry. And Dominic's smile was so far away Katie couldn't see a hint of it.

He nodded, let out a shaky breath. "Okay. See you, kids." And with a little furrow in her brow, Aerie took his hand and winked them away.

Mel let the hornblende fall to the snow. "Make sure she gets home okay," she told Nyth. And then to Katie: "If you pull a stunt like that again, I'll kill you." But her eyes were wet, and her voice had a ragged edge.

Katie just nodded.

Nyth's arm tightened around her, and then the warm darkness of the in-between place closed around them, and then Katie landed in the veil right next to the stumps in the meeting circle. She sank onto one and dropped her head into her hands.

Nyth crouched in front of her. She could feel the warmth radiating off him. The tension, too. Everything they'd said to each other, all the anger from before, still lingered. And apparently neither of them knew how to breach it.

"Are you okay?" he finally asked.

She dropped her hands and fixed him with a look. "Are *you* okay?"

That same hollowness was heavy in his eyes. "It tried to take Skiron." His voice was small. "It's hard enough now without Zephyrus. Can you imagine if we lost anyone else?"

"We'll be careful."

"No, we won't. We can't afford to be. When the rifts open, we have to seal them. When the riftlings come out, we have to fight them." He shook his head. "And it's true, you know."

"What is?"

"The only reason Asha's gone is because she merged with Zephyrus. You kids are in danger because of us. Because these things want us, and they can only take us when we're part of you."

Katie grabbed his hand. It was warm as ever, almost hot, and it soothed the ice in her fingers. "Don't think like that. If everyone wasn't assimilating, the first rift beast would've killed us all. You're protecting us every time. You give us a fighting chance."

Something so soft and warm came into Nyth's face. "I'm really old, you know. I've been watching humans come and go and crawl all over this earth for ages. It's crazy that one little human would offer to comfort me. Absolutely crazy."

Good thing I'm your favorite human, Katie thought. And she knew it was true, but she didn't say it out loud. It still felt weird. So instead, she let him squeeze her hand and take her home.

Chapter 26

Mel 🌻

Malia & Rosie are putting up posters for Asha. They asked if we want to help

Katie stared at the text for a solid minute, her heart heavy, before responding.

Did her parents call the police?

Mel 🌻

I don't know
But they want to put up posters
I said I would but I don't want to speak for you

Of course I will
Just let me know when

She set down her phone and stared at her plate of eggs. Breakfast had lost its appeal. Which was unfortunate because she'd felt like a poorly wrung-out dishrag since the last rift. Grabbing a volatile portal between worlds wasn't the smartest thing she'd ever done.

But the riftling hadn't gotten Mel. Or Skiron.

"Kate?" Her dad appeared in the doorway, his sweatshirt sleeves rolled up and his hands in his pockets. His whole posture felt too deliberately casual. "How's it going?"

Katie knew exactly how depressed she looked. "It's… going. Um. Some of us are going to put up missing person posters today. For Asha."

The particular crinkle that formed between his eyebrows was one Katie hadn't seen in a long time. He started to say something, then stopped, then tried again. "I hope you know you can talk to me. About anything you're feeling." He shrugged. "Awkward dad stuff, I know, but it's true."

And she really, really wished she could. She wished she could tell him everything, let him take care of things, let him fix it. But that wasn't the way things were. So, all she said was, "I know." And all he did was nod and back out, giving her space.

She got up, put her plate in the fridge, and headed upstairs. Getting dressed and putting things in her bag helped her feel more focused, and when Mel offered to pick her up soon to meet the others, she was ready.

Simon and Dominic were already in the car. Katie slid in the backseat next to Dom. "Is it just us?" Katie asked. "Helping them?"

"No," Simon said. "Some of their friends will be there. I got Robson and Miranda—they're from the magazine—they're helping."

"And Jordan is meeting us," Dominic said. "And a couple people from when I used to run track. We'll have lots of hands."

"I feel bad to make them come all the way out when we know these won't do anything."

"But it might help them," Katie said. "To feel less helpless. And that's something."

"Yeah." Simon nodded. "It's something."

Rosie and Malia met them at the same shopping plaza Dominic had parked behind before the rift where Asha was taken. Rosie looked angry—Katie didn't know her well enough to know if it was genuine anger at the thought of someone hurting her friend, or if that's what worry looked like on her. Malia was quieter, her eyes too big and her hands fidgeting. "I thought we could split up," she said, handing photocopied fliers to everyone. "Some of us can do the plaza, some can do the residential streets, maybe the mall and the metro parks."

Simon's and Dominic's friends were arriving, climbing out of cars. "We can do residential east of the school," Dominic said, taking a stack of fliers. "Maybe get a few more on the west side."

"Okay." Malia's breath clouded in the air.

Rosie frowned. Her lips were chapped. "Thank you for helping," she said, and she didn't sound angry for all the tension in her face.

"Of course," Katie said. "We all love Asha. We're going to find her."

Rosie nodded, her forehead softening the smallest amount before she turned to give fliers to the others.

Back in the car, Mel said, "You sound really sure of yourself, Byrd."

"I have to be. We have to get her back."

"But how?" Dominic asked. "We have no clue how."

"Yeah, and the guardians are working on that. We're damage control for the humans, right? And keeping people hopeful is the best thing we can do right now." Her chest was heavy. Maybe it always would be, now.

"I just…" Mel shook her head. "Can't pretend, I guess."

"I'm not pretending anything. But this is something we can do." Her eyes burned. She blinked hard. "We need to *do* something."

Nobody said anything for a moment. Mel tapped her fingers on the wheel. "You're right. Thanks, Byrd."

They parked at the end of a street and climbed back out. "Let's split up." Mel passed the fliers and rolls of tape around to them all. "Two of us can head north of the main road, two of us south. Do… let's say down to Linda Drive. Then come back to the car and we can warm up and drive a little further."

"I'll go with Katie," Simon said.

Dominic furrowed his brow slightly, but Mel just said, "Okay. Come on, Dominic," and turned and headed up the next street. He sighed and went after her.

Katie and Simon started down the road, pausing to tape the first flier to a telephone pole. "I know you probably wanted to go with Dominic," he said, ripping off a piece of tape. "But they're…"

"We're closer to Asha than they are," Katie said. "I get it. I'm glad we're together."

They walked and worked mostly in silence. Katie was freezing, even by her standards. November in Ohio wasn't warm, but it was never this cold this soon. The icy snow still hadn't let up, and the sidewalks were only partly shoveled and salted. They made slow progress.

"I wonder if they're following us," she said.

"The others?"

"No. The rifts. Yesterday, that was by Mel's house. And that rift that opened in the city? Dominic and I were there that day. We were there when it opened. And the one where—where they took Asha? Did you recognize where we were?"

He shook his head. "No."

"I didn't at first. And—with everything that happened, it wasn't really important then. But it hit me later. It was right next to the Rockpoint picnic area in the metro parks."

"Where we all first went to the veil."

"Yeah."

Snow crunched under their feet. They stopped in front of another telephone pole and began to hang another flier. "If they're following us," he said slowly, "that makes them even more dangerous. It brings them closer to people."

"And our families."

"Right." Simon smoothed a piece of tape at the top of the flier. He stopped, his hands on the pole, and stared at the flier. Asha's smiling picture, above the description and contact information. His mouth pulled tight, and his eyes grew damp and he leaned on the pole, his breath spilling out in a shaky white cloud.

Katie's heart ached. "We're getting her back, Simon. I swear I won't let them keep her."

He shook his head. He wanted a hug, Katie knew. She had spent long enough not hugging to have gotten good at telling when people wanted to. And she couldn't, quite. Not yet. But she laid her hand on his back and rubbed up and down gently. He visibly relaxed, and when he closed his eyes, a tear ran down his cheek.

"I know we have to get her back," Simon said. "We have to if we want to protect everything. But we don't know what she's feeling, or if they're hurting her, or… anything. And not looking for her is killing me."

And Katie knew this wasn't enough. Waiting for answers wasn't enough. Not when Dominic was having panic attacks and Simon was crying in the snow and Mel was tearing herself up. Katie taped down the bottom edge of the flier, and she quietly made a decision.

Simon sighed. He stepped away from the pole and wiped his face. "I think we can get one more on the next street before we go back," he said.

"Okay. Let's go."

They walked over to the next street, squaring their shoulders against the wind. "How's Mel holding up?" Katie asked. "She's seemed—you know."

"It's killing her. She's blaming herself."

"That's bullshit. It's nobody's fault. None of us were prepared for that thing, not even the guardians."

"Still. That's what she does."

"Maybe this will help."

"I hope so. What about Dominic?"

Katie shook her head. "Nothing really bad has ever happened to him before, to be honest. He has no idea how to cope with it."

"So, it was an excellent idea to leave them alone together."

Katie laughed, almost startling herself. "Maybe they'll make each other see sense. Come on, let's get this last one up and head back. There are a lot more streets to do."

When they got back to the car, Dominic and Mel were already there, shivering while Mel smoked. The sight of Mel's goosebump-covered bare neck reminded Katie of her knitting projects.

"Hey Simon, Mel. You want to stop by my house before you head home? I have gifts for you."

Mel turned back to them. "You got us gifts?"

"I made all of you gifts. I've been needing to keep myself busy in our downtime."

Dominic hesitated. "Did you make one for Asha?"

Katie nodded. "Yeah. I'm gonna keep it safe until she's home."

Nobody said anything. Mel finished her cigarette and said, "I'm curious now. Let's go."

Dominic's sweater was just shy of being done, but the scarves for Simon and Mel were finished and wrapped in tissue paper. When they got to Katie's house, she ducked inside to grab them while the others waited in the car.

She passed her father on her way back out. "Leaving again?" He looked at her quizzically.

"I'll be right back. Mel and Simon are in the car, so I'm giving them the scarves I made them real quick."

"Am I ever going to get to meet these new friends?"

"Soon. I promise."

She came up to the passenger side and handed Simon and Mel their gifts through the windows. "You can wait until you get home, if you want."

"Not a chance, Byrd. I'm opening this now." Mel ripped back the tissue paper, and Simon smiled, following her lead.

Mel's face softened when she unfolded the deep red scarf. Simon still smiled, gently and fondly, taking off the scarf he was wearing and putting on the steely blue one Katie had made him. But Mel touched her scarf, running her fingers over the yarn, which Katie knew was extra-soft. She'd spent several nights looping its softness over her fingers as she stitched it into the tight, warm pattern.

"You made this?"

Katie tilted her head. "Did I never tell you that I knit?"

Mel met her gaze. She looked tired—exhausted. She didn't smile, exactly, but her face was kind as she said, "Thank you," and buried her hands in the soft knit.

"It's beautiful," Simon said. "Thank you, Katie."

She smiled, her heart warm. "You'll get yours soon," she said, ducking her head to look across at Dominic. "It's not a scarf, and it's taking longer."

"Hey, no worries. Seriously."

Katie jammed her hands deeper into her pockets. "Get home safe, guys. I'll see you soon." And she hurried into the house as the wind kicked up behind her, whistling through the trees.

Chapter 27

The fact that they had school the next day felt like an insult. Like a cruel trick from the universe. But they did. Asha's empty desk next to Katie's burned a hole in her attention all through first period.

And chemistry class didn't help. They spent the period in their groups to have a last planning session before the presentations in a couple days, and as Victoria and Malia and Jordan pulled out their phones to share their documents so far, Katie went cold.

Victoria arched an eyebrow. "Is your part done yet?" she asked Katie.

She'd meant to do it this past weekend. Instead, she'd spent the whole time trying not to lose herself. Trying to keep her friends from spiraling into despair.

"Not yet," she managed. It came out like a croak. Malia caught her eye across the desks—her dark eyes were wide and sad and sympathetic.

"We were supposed to—"

"Did you hear about Asha Sengupta?" Malia asked.

Victoria's face fell. "Yeah. I'm really sorry. You're close, right?"

Malia nodded, blinking hard. She jerked her chin toward Katie. "Katie was the last one who saw her."

Victoria's perfectly glossed lips parted in surprise. "I'm sorry," she said again. "I didn't know."

"I'll get it done today," Katie said. "I promise."

So, she did. Mrs. Kozel got her a slot that afternoon, and Katie stayed after the last bell to finish her piece of the project. Mrs. Kozel had to supervise her lab time, and it took a few tries, tinkering with the proportions and conditions each time. The longer it took, the more restless Katie felt. She wanted to be out, home, doing something that mattered, not this.

But she tried to focus. Quartz sand, water, and sodium hydroxide. Eventually she got a hydrated silica. The same sort of material her sightstone was made of.

Not exactly. Opal could be synthesized in a lab, but on a scale of both time and resources Katie didn't have. Still, it was fascinating despite her impatience: observing the synthesis, the way multiple materials came together and created something new. It felt like Nyth. It felt like the best parts of herself.

She needed that reminder right now. She needed to remember she had agency.

Just because she'd screwed up didn't mean she couldn't fix it.

That night, once everyone went to bed, Katie sneaked a votive candle and lighter from the hall closet—they kept those and flashlights in there in case of blackouts—into her room. She dumped her bowl of stones and shells onto her bed and set the emptied bowl in the middle of the floor. Kneeling next to it, she set the votive inside, making sure it was steady. Her hair fell over her shoulder when she leaned in; she quickly swept it back, wove it into a fast braid.

Her hands were clammy. This was different from Nyth's fire. No promise she wouldn't get hurt.

She pressed her thumb against the lighter's flint wheel, but not hard enough. It didn't light. Her breath came out in a shaky rush. She tried again—nothing. Too hesitant.

Turning inside, she felt for that spark. Not Nyth's fragment, but the candle flame that was only hers. She pressed her thumb again. This time she heard the soft click, and when she opened her eyes, saw the flame dancing above her fingers.

Part of her wanted to cry. But she lowered her hand and turned the lighter enough to set flame to the candle's wick. It caught, and she let the lighter extinguish.

Katie breathed deeply, counting her breaths, and held the lighter in her cupped hands, feeling it cool. She watched the candle flame dance, yellow and orange and whitish blue at its center. She watched how it shifted and moved, wavered, and grew and shrank. She watched how it lit up a little circle of golden glow in her dark room, warm and soft and gentle. Like a tiny hearth.

Slowly, she slipped her sightstone off her wrist. She nestled it against the lighter between her palms.

"Nyth," she whispered, in the quiet of her bedroom, with the moonlight behind her and the candlelight before her, "Nyth, cross the veil to me."

At first, nothing happened. Then, in the dancing yellow light, he shimmered into view, sitting across from her.

"We should whisper."

Nyth nodded.

Katie stared at him across the candle flame. The shifting light moved shadows across his face, but his eyes glowed warm. She supposed hers looked exactly the same.

"I'm sorry," he blurted, barely keeping his voice down.

"I'm sorry, too."

She stared at him a while longer, him staring back. She was probably—*definitely*—keeping him from important work, but it wasn't like he was leaving, either. "You know I love you, right?" He tilted his head at her words, his forehead creasing. "Even when we're pissed at each other. Even though I'm messing up. It makes no sense. You make no sense, really. But I do."

Nyth moved his jaw weirdly, like he was rolling words in his mouth. "I do too," he said. "Huh. Oh."

"That's no small thing, is it? To be loved by a guardian of the veil?"

"No. No small thing. I don't know if I've really ever loved

anyone except the other guardians." He scrunched up his nose. "That's why I miss you all the time. Even when you're being difficult."

"Do not start."

He almost grinned.

"Listen. We can't keep waiting. We need to look for Asha."

"We are. I promise, we're working—"

"No, I know," Katie interrupted. "I mean us. Us humans. We're just waiting around, and it's killing us." She squeezed her hands around her sightstone. "I want to capture a riftling."

Nyth's eyes widened, gleaming in the candlelight. "Are you serious?"

"Yes. I don't know if we can. But maybe Skiron or Ophion can make a cage from the rocks or the tree roots or something. Just to hold it here long enough for you all to try to figure out what it is and where it's coming from."

He furrowed his brow. "That's reckless." But the corner of his mouth turned up when he said it.

"Maybe. But I'm sick of waiting." She lifted her chin. "And I don't want to wait for another rift, either. Let's bring them to us."

The lifted corner split into a grin. "I told you," Nyth whispered. "Fire in you."

Katie leaned closer. "I'm not gonna keep watching my friends kill themselves over this. You in?"

His eyes danced. "Yeah, sunshine. Yeah, I'm in."

The consensus was to the tune of "this is a horrible idea, but we agree it's better than doing nothing," and they decided to bait another rift in the same spot as last time. Dominic borrowed his mom's car to give Katie a ride to Mel's, Simon met them there as well, and they all walked together over to the woods on the other side of the highway, deeper in than before. It was still snowing, that same tiny glittering snow that felt like ice, and the wind rattled the branches of the trees and stung their faces.

"At least there's less snow under the trees," she said. "So, we don't have to wade through knee-deep drifts."

"Only ankle deep," Dominic mused.

They found an area where the trees were slightly closer together. "Might be more sheltered from the wind here." Mel tugged down her scarf to breathe warmth onto her fingers. She was wearing the scarf Katie had knit for her.

"Let me try something." Simon's gaze went distant for a moment; then Katie looked up, startled, as the bare branches above them wound around each other, lacing together more tightly. The scrubby bushes below the trees twined together as well, and all of it shielding them a bit more from the wind.

"Did you do that?" Dominic asked, grinning.

"No. But I did ask Ophion to do it."

"Genius."

"Well," Mel said, "I guess now we wait."

"If these things are following us," Katie said, "we should be pretty tempting all together like this."

After a moment, Dominic reached one hand inside the front of his coat and pulled out a thermos. "Anybody want hot cocoa?"

"Are you serious right now?"

"Obviously, Byrd. It's cold as balls out here, and we don't know how long we'll be waiting. And I like hot cocoa."

Mel laughed, and Simon grinned. Then Katie felt something like a nudge at the back of her shoulder. Nyth, sending her a question. Yes please, she answered, and soon after her feet and hands got warmer, and the wind felt less biting.

"Whoa." Dominic's eyes went wide. "Did anyone else feel that?"

"I think Nyth is helping us out," Simon said, glancing at Katie.

She nodded, smiling.

"Hopefully this works quickly, and he won't have to worry about it too long," Mel said.

After a second of stillness, Simon said, "I do and I don't. Hope that. But at least if they do find us, we'll be expecting it this time."

"Exactly."

Katie was holding Dom's thermos now, taking a couple small sips. She stared out into the trees, feeling the light thrum of adrenaline keeping her ready for a rift to crack open, and she suddenly, profoundly, wanted her mother. She wanted to curl up on the couch with her father on one side and her mother on the other and Alex on the other end, watching a movie, with Mom playing with Katie's hair. She reached for that moment, nine years ago now, but as close and tactile as yesterday. Then her mother faded, and Katie's side was cold, and she gasped a small breath as her eyes stung. Then she squeezed her eyes shut tighter as she faded away, too, leaving Alex at one end of the sofa and her father at the other, a wide expanse of emptiness between them.

No. No, we won't let that happen. It was her thought, a desperate self-comfort, but she felt Nyth whisper near her as she thought it.

I'm not just a guardian of the two worlds, he told her. *I'm your guardian. I'll protect you.*

"Hey Byrd, you done?"

Katie opened her eyes, the air stinging against their wetness. Dominic tilted his head, peering at her, half-smiling. She knew that look. "Yeah, sorry," she said, smiling at him and handing back the thermos. He held eye contact a moment longer, then turned back to conversation with the others.

They stood out in the trees for over an hour. Thank god for Nyth and Ophion's help, or they'd've been popsicles. Everyone was antsy, and Katie had the nagging worry that this had been a stupid idea. But they kept waiting.

In the middle of Simon telling them—finally, after most of a semester—some of the details of the story he was working on, a tingle of warning ran up Katie's spine. Simon fell silent, and everyone glanced out past the knot of trees. Further out in the woods, something purplish rippled in the air.

"That's our cue," Dominic said.

In answer, Mel pulled out her sightstone and assimilated with Skiron. Simon and Dominic followed suit, and Katie fell into step with them as the branches parted and they crossed the snow toward the emerging rift.

The air cracked open with a noise like thunder, and the rift slashed open in midair. "Ready, Simon?" Mel asked. He nodded. "Remember, don't worry about holding the border. Just be ready for me to get it in position."

Dominic nocked an arrow. Mel drew her sword from beneath the snow. Katie's heart beat in her throat.

Please trust me, Nyth whispered.

She did.

A pocket of void yawned wide open in the rift, but no riftling emerged. Instead, rift-beasts poured out, one after another after another. Mel's sword flashed as she swore. Dominic was immediately in the air.

Katie backed in close to Simon as Mel cut through the beasts to one side of them and Dominic rained arrows down on the other side. "Don't worry," she told Simon as rift-beast blood splattered across their knees. Her heart might be in her throat, but it was beating steady. "I'll never make you fight them again."

His eyes went so soft at that, that Katie almost missed the spindly arms reaching out of the void.

"Mel," Simon called.

Her only answer was a string of curses as she hacked through another rift-beast. They'd only just stopped scuttling out—there were still two more on her, three on Dominic's side. Two—one fell with an arrow in the back of its head and crumbled into dust on the snow.

The riftling climbed out of the void, its limbs bent at odd angles as it crouched on the snow. It lifted its head, its inky eyes locking onto Simon and Katie.

"Guys," Simon called again, his voice pitching up.

Katie stared back at the riftling as Dominic dropped another beast and Mel winced back from one that bit her calf. Its eyes bored into hers, and its face split open in a wide red grin.

She wasn't scared of it.

She was pissed.

The candle in her chest was burning brighter. It was a lantern, a hearth, a bonfire. Her heart beat steady, and with it, she felt Nyth.

"Get behind me," she told Simon. And her fingers closed around her sightstone.

And the bonfire wasn't only inside her, but around her. Bright hot white but not afraid, not afraid, because this wasn't the fire that had chased her all her life. It was heat, and it was light, and it was transformation and motion and everything that was Nyth.

This was his fire. This was *her* fire. Every cell inside her sang *yes* and *good* and *here we are, we, we, we.*

When the flames fell away, she was wearing different clothes. The bitter wind didn't touch her. And Nyth was with her. In every space, every drop of blood, in the fire that burned in her chest. Woven through her own mind and heart and breath. Something deep inside her, so deep she hardly knew it was there, almost cried with relief.

Every little bit of her that felt like sunshine wrapped itself in every little bit of Nyth that felt the same. Every corner of them both sang together in joy, in confidence, in love.

She grinned. So did Nyth.

They were home.

Mel killed the last rift-beast on her side and gaped at Katie. The corners of her mouth trembled, and then she smiled. Her brow smoothed, her jaw softened.

The riftling hissed, sprouted new arms from its ribs with a sickening sound, and shot them out at Mel.

One smacked hard against her elbow, breaking her grip on her sword and half spinning her around. In an instant, the arms closed around her, whipping her back toward the riftling.

One of the boys shouted, "No, *no!*" Katie's heart jumped as Nyth poured fire into her hands and she, or he, both were of the exact same mind, they flicked it out like a whip and seared a line down the riftling's back. It howled in wild pain, and Mel struggled, but the arms held her fast. With a raw wheeze, the riftling opened its red-rimmed mouth and bit into the back of her shoulder.

Mel gasped. Her eyes went wide. She was looking up and out, straight at Simon, when her eyes seemed to stop focusing.

Simon lunged forward, shouldering past Katie. The riftling's two main arms held Mel tight, but the other six shot out toward Simon. He dodged them, twisting like a leaf in the wind, and was within feet of Mel when the arms snapped back and slammed him against Mel's side. The riftling's mouth was already open, ready, and it bit through the vine-like padding on Simon's shoulder.

Blood roared in her ears as Katie dashed around to the side, trying to find an opening, but Mel and Simon's limp forms blocked the riftling's entire body. "Do something!" she cried, Nyth's panic clawing up in her throat, and Dominic fired an arrow that grazed past Simon's head to slash down the back of the riftling's shoulder. But it was already climbing backwards into the rift, using four of its spindly arms to push itself in. Katie sprang forward, hands blazing, and grabbed one of the arms, all of her desperation and Nyth's funneling together into a blast of flame that crumbled the riftling's arm.

But it was already in the rift. Its shriek of pain faded as it jerked back and tumbled backwards into the void. Mel and Simon's head and shoulders disappeared inside. Katie dropped the fire and grabbed Mel's leg, but it jerked Katie towards the rift. Her fingers clutched, aching from effort, but there was a huge tug. And then Katie was standing in front of the rift holding Mel's boot, and Simon and Mel were gone. The edge of the rift crumpled in on itself, and in the time it took Katie to realize that all that was left of them was a boot, the rift closed and disappeared.

Every inch of her was trembling. She was clutching the boot against her chest, shaking, and with her, within her, Nyth shivered like a candle flame guttering in the wind.

Gone.

They're gone.

Katie's breath hitched as her own grief caught onto Nyth's and both swelled so enormous in her chest that all she could do was hold Mel's boot and stare at the spot where the rift had disappeared.

And then Dominic was there in front of her, and it was more Nyth and Aerie than Katie and Dominic, but they slumped against each other. Dominic wrapped his arms around Katie, and she leaned into him and felt his chest heave as he let out a ragged sob, clinging to her.

The wind was blowing sideways, the tiny snowflakes prickling the side of her face, and Katie wasn't cold, not with Nyth, but the wind cut through her, anyway. Her forehead pressed to Dominic's chest. She stared down at the boot in her shaking hands.

Chapter 28

They sat together in Katie's room. It was dark now; Dominic had been there all afternoon, and they had barely spoken.

Nyth and Aerie had been there for a long while, off and on. They flickered in and out but never physically manifested. They were needed too much in the world to put that much of themselves in Katie's room. They were the only guardians left now, as the wind howled outside the window and ice patterns formed thick on the glass.

But they were there as much as they could be. Even if Nyth's presence felt like a wisp of itself.

Only the small bedside table lamp was on. In the dimness, Batty lay purring on Dominic's lap while he absentmindedly petted her.

"It's not over," Katie said. Her voice felt hoarse.

"I know," he said. "We're going to get them back. All of them. We have to." His voice was thick. He was starting to cry.

"Dom. Come on." Her own voice was weak, thin. Unconvincing. "We have to keep it together."

"I know. I am." He sniffled and wiped his eyes. "But I kind of think this is worth crying over."

She bit her lip. "Yeah. You're right. I'm sorry."

"I couldn't handle it," he said.

"Handle what?"

"If they took you." God, she had never seen him look like that, not even when Asha was taken. His eyes were still wet, brimming, and his nose was red. She'd never seen him cry so much as he had lately. His hand twitched away from Batty to rest on his knee. "I'd lose it, Byrd. I'd lose my shit."

Katie closed her eyes and took a slow breath. Her own gut was swirling with a mass of feelings, fear and guilt and grief. So she didn't try to hide the quaver in her voice, but she opened her eyes and laid her hand over his. "No, you wouldn't. You're Dom. You're good and strong, and if you lost me, I know you'd come find me."

His eyes widened at the ease of her touch. It softened the edge of pain in his face, just a little. And he smiled, just a little. "Not like you."

"What's not like me?"

"I'm not strong like you, Byrd."

She stared at him for a moment, considered saying no, you don't hide in your clothes, don't lock yourself in your room to cry. But she thought, you also have never lost anyone. You never had to learn how to be strong, not this kind of strength. I did. And I worked hard for it. And the thought made her warmer. "Hey. You won't lose me, remember? We're Dom and Byrd, and no matter what, we'll go to the end together. Right?"

Dominic lowered his gaze. He was gritting his teeth or maybe chewing the inside of his lip. Wordlessly, he held up one hand, small finger extended. Katie felt pressure in her chest and hot dampness behind her eyes as she linked her finger around his.

He lowered his head and pressed his forehead against hers. She closed her eyes and leaned into him, feeling a warmth like the way Nyth held her hands in his own, the way he put that gentle nurturing, safe kind of fire in her chest. And when she felt Dominic shudder with another repressed sob, she only closed her hand around his and waited for him to come back. She was strong, he had said. And she knew she was. So she would be, for both of them.

It was hard to sleep that night after Dominic had gone home. Katie sat on her bed in the dimness until all three cats found her.

Her heart echoed with cold and loneliness, and not just because of Simon and Mel. Because she'd felt it, now, that click when Nyth's soul locked into place with hers. After that, how could she not feel lonely when he wasn't there?

But he was. He was always there. He was in the swish of Batty's tail and the rumble of Peaches's purr. Katie lit a candle on her bedside table, and he was in that, too. Pieces of him, like the piece of him in her own spirit. But still him.

It was a little better. And she would take even a little bit right now.

When midnight had passed and she still couldn't sleep and staring into space was only making her feel worse, she shifted Skimbleshanks gently off her lap and went to the closet and pulled down the shoe box from the top shelf.

She'd gotten a diary for her seventh birthday and started writing every single day. After the accident, there was a gap from her time in the hospital. The next entries after that were in an even clumsier hand than before, as she regained her mobility. Plus, she'd been left-handed before the accident, and when it was so hard to even move that arm, she'd relearned how to write with her right hand instead.

Katie skimmed over those pages. She didn't need to relive that time right now. There was something else she needed.

When she was nine. When she'd started therapy, not only for her broken body, but for her head and her heart.

Katie meant to only read certain entries, but she found herself taking in all of them. Not just her post-therapy journaling, but a movie she had seen and liked, a game she had played with Alex. The day Peaches's brother, Mister, had died, far too young, less than eighteen months after Katie's mother had died, and it had felt so much worse because of it. And then the day they adopted Skimbleshanks, and all the pointless little entries about lying cozied up in one of her clumsy blanket forts, with Skimbles curled against her right side, reading and feeling his little kitten body purr into her ribs. Learning to bake. Learning to knit. Riding her bike again, birthdays, a trip to the museum.

The entries were short, and they flew by, swelling her heart and sometimes making her eyes prick hot and wet. But the long ones were the ones she had come for. Post-therapy, spilling her tangled agonies onto the page. Trying to sort out some kind of order, some kind of healing, from a trauma she was too young to even begin to know how to process.

She read each and every one of them. And slowly, over the years over the pages, she watched herself claw her way back up to healing. To being better. To the sunlight again.

She read all of them, not skipping one, because she needed to remember that she could do this. She had done it before. She was here. She was alive and full of her own fire.

There were a few old diaries collected in the box. She'd fallen out of the habit a couple years ago and never picked it back up. The last third of the most recent diary was still blank. A pen lay in the box.

The blank pages felt like an opportunity.

Katie clicked open her pen and wrote.

Fire hurts because I got burned and because it took you from me. The burns still hurt because I got them when I lost you. I don't want anyone to see them because they're ugly, and because they remind me I'm here and you're not, and that still makes me feel like I'm cracking in two.

Things she'd worked out in therapy already. But resurfacing, so she had to process them again.

Fire in my hands, even sealing fire, was too close to that loss. And it's missing you and it's guilt and it's triggering. I can hold it now. I realized if I'm made of fire after all, maybe I should try to give off light and warmth.

But it took too long. And now they're gone, and it's my fault.

Just like you were.

It sat heavy and sick in her chest, but she didn't cry. Determination began to burn through the heaviness. Her hand kept moving.

I couldn't save you then, and I might never forgive myself for that. But I still believe I can save them now. I want to fix this. I want to save them. No matter what.

Chapter 29

Katie got maybe two hours of sleep that night. She drifted onto and off the bus numbly, binder clutched to her chest. Dominic was waiting for her, like always. He looked like hell.

"I don't want to be here," was how he greeted her. His voice was thin.

"Me neither." Katie took a deep breath. "Presentations are today. In chemistry. After that, we can leave."

A ghost of a smile lifted his mouth. "Do my ears deceive me, or is Katie Byrd suggesting skipping school?"

She turned a deadpan gaze on him. "Let's be honest. We have more important things to do."

He nodded, shoving his hands in his jacket pockets. "We should meet with them," he said, clearly meaning Nyth and Aerie.

"After second period, we'll go. We'll figure this out."

First period was horrible. Not only was Asha missing beside her, but Mel was gone behind her. Katie hugged her arms around herself and kept her sightstone in her palm the entire time. It thrummed gently against her skin with its own quiet, warm pulse. Nyth was with her, even if he had to be spreading himself thin across the worlds, trying to cover the gaps Zephyrus and Ophion and Skiron had left behind. He was still with her.

In chemistry, she took advantage of Mrs. Kozel's habitual lateness and went straight to her group the second she walked in.

She didn't get a cheery welcome. Malia always looked sad and heavy, since Asha had disappeared. Jordan looked tired and resigned. Victoria's mouth was set in a hard, disappointed line.

There'd been updates to their group chat that Katie hadn't seen until too late. They'd be trying to plan the actual presentation part. Katie hadn't responded.

But after she'd read her journals last night, she'd kept working. She set the binder on the desk. Jordan raised his eyebrows.

"I know I dropped the ball," she said. "So, I went through everyone's reports and looked for common threads."

Malia tilted her head. "How come?"

"We could get up there and each present our parts and let that be that. But Mrs. Kozel will be more impressed if we're more intentional about it. If we have a unifying theme or message, we'll probably get a better grade."

Victoria's posture had been guarded, her arms crossed. Now she leaned onto her desk, peering at Katie's binder. "I like that. What did you find?"

"Why did we choose chemical reactions in the first place? We all agreed we were interested in it." She flipped to some pages she had flagged. "I think we all let hints slip in our lab reports. Jordan, you talked about how understanding the pieces that make up the whole can teach you more about the whole. Malia, you framed your experiment as wanting to see how basically moving one element's place changes the entire structure. And Victoria, you focused on how changing reaction kinetics changes the reaction itself."

Arching an eyebrow with something close to a smile, Victoria asked, "What about you?"

"For me, it was all about the catalyst. Reactants. What it takes to cause the change." She turned to the notes she'd jotted down the night before. Her handwriting was messier than usual, but the notes were still clear. "We all dialed in on different aspects of change. Which is what chemical reactions are. They're just changes. But how they happen, and why they happen, and what results from the change—those have so many possibilities. If we deliberately frame our presentation as an exploration of change, it'll feel intentional."

Malia smiled. It was small, but genuine. "I like that. It's simple, but it ties it all together."

"Makes a good framework," Jordan agreed. "Instead of us just standing up there and reading four different reports."

Across the aisle, Victoria tilted her head, thoughtfulness in her eyes. "I like it. It's good, Katie."

It was good knowing she'd managed to turn something around. That she had some small measure of control.

That she could fix something.

The presentation went fine. Jordan stumbled over his words a bit, and Katie had mixed up her index cards and started in the wrong place at first, but Malia and Victoria were great, and everything came together. And as she listened to Victoria giving their summary at the end, even that last sliver of grudge worked its way free and out of her system.

Maybe her parents were too hard on her when she didn't get A+ grades. Maybe she wanted to go to med school, and her pristine 4.0 was actually important. Hell, maybe she'd wrapped up too much of her identity in being a top student.

It didn't matter why she'd been as hard on Katie as she had. People usually acted the way they did for a reason. Katie knew that intimately.

When the bell rang at the end of class, she caught Dominic's eye. They walked together out of the classroom, down the hall, around a corner out of sight, and then pulled out their sightstones and went to the veil.

Katie shivered when they landed. The veil was colder than usual, and the light was pale, like the sun was barely in the sky. The mist curled down to the grass now, making it hard to see through the trees.

"Nyth?" Katie called, but he was already shimmering into view, Aerie not long behind him. It was the first time they'd been with them in physical form since—

Nyth didn't hesitate. He hugged Katie so hard it hurt a little, but she didn't mind.

"Thank you," he whispered.

"I'm sorry it took me so long."

He pulled back and squeezed her hands, and they turned to the others.

"We found something," Aerie said. Her eyes were hard and focused. "There's a desolate part of Harath, not unlike Antarctica here on Earth. There's a—thing there. Not a rift. It's like the void pockets of the rifts, but only the void."

"Just—void?"

"A crack split open right into it." Aerie looked at Nyth, who kept shifting his weight. "We found it from those mineral pieces. Tracked down spots with sudden new mineral populations, and there it was. We think if we go through it, we can get to where the riftlings are, and maybe everyone they took."

"Then let's go," Katie said.

"That's what I said!" Nyth shot Aerie a look.

Aerie shook her head. "We need time to prepare. You know that. But it'll be soon," she assured Katie and Dominic.

"Tonight," Katie said. "If not now."

Aerie frowned. "That's cutting it close, but we can make it work."

"Are you sure we can't go sooner?"

"No, Katie. We need to prepare."

But Nyth caught her gaze, and she saw her own exasperation echoed in his eyes. "Okay. Alright. Tonight." She softened her expression. "But—Harath."

"You'll only be there a minute this time. You'll be safe."

"No, I meant—how is it? Earth is feeling strain, isn't it? How's Harath?"

"About the same." Nyth shook his head. "It's only a matter of time, but there hasn't been another rift yet, so they're holding up better. Except the desert where this void portal is. That's even drier and more empty than ever."

"Then let's keep it that way. And let's get our friends back. Tonight?"

"Tonight, unless we can't get things ready in time."

Dominic scratched the back of his head. "Do you want to go back to school, Byrd?"

"About as much as you do."

"So, no."

She managed a smile. "We should probably both go home and take naps. I'm guessing you slept about as much as I did last night."

"If you mean none, then yes."

Katie reached out her hand, little finger extended. Dominic hooked his around hers, holding her gaze. Then he took Aerie's hand, and she whisked him away.

Nyth stayed, his presence warm next to her. "I can take you home," he said, and she nodded as he reached out and took her hands.

The house was quiet, with her dad and Tracy at work, with Alex at school. It was dim, too. The weather was only getting worse, thick gray clouds blocking the sun and spiraling icy half-snow, half-hail that was already a few feet deep.

Nyth lingered. Katie lit candles in her room, casting the room in a soft, warm glow. Skimbleshanks looked up from the pillow. Batty yawned. Even Peaches was there, curled in a neat brown-tabby circle at the foot of the bed.

"I can't stay long," Nyth whispered.

"It's okay."

They sat facing each other on the bed, petting the cats. How strange, to have a guardian of the veil between the worlds sitting on her bed, scratching Batty's chin. But how not strange at all, now.

Nyth held both his hands out to Katie. She took them, soothed by the warmth of them—and something else. A pulse.

"You've never had a pulse before."

"First time for everything."

"Why?"

Nyth looked down at their hands. "You have a heartbeat. So I want one, too."

It was so simple and sweet that it made her eyes sting hot. "It's comforting."

"Good. I hoped it would be." He frowned. "I'm kind of jealous. Of humans."

She wasn't prepared for that. "What is there to be jealous about? You're a guardian. You're way beyond us."

"Yeah, but you humans get to choose your own fate. I'm bound to my duties. I don't have as many choices."

Katie squeezed his hands gently. "Where's this coming from?"

He huffed. "I wanted to go to Harath and to that portal the second we knew it was there. But Aerie reminded me we can't. We're the guardians. The only two, now. We have to take the world's balance into consideration. So, we have to set up some stopgaps to hold things over until we get back."

"That's what she meant by preparing."

"Yeah."

She tilted her head. "You've never seemed bothered by that before."

Nyth smiled a wry half-smile. "Getting close to you has changed a lot in me."

Katie didn't know how to answer that. So she held his hands and felt the warm candle flame in her chest.

His face went blank for a moment; then he shook his head. "I have to go. Aerie needs me."

"Go on. I'll see you tonight." He smiled at her, then vanished.

The candle blew out when he disappeared, and Katie was left with Batty staring wide-eyed at where he'd been a moment before.

Chapter 30

She slept for a while, if not well. When she woke up, it was early afternoon, and everything was still quiet.

In the empty house, Katie kneaded together a bread dough, pressing the warmth of her hands into the dough. She let it rise, then baked it, then tore off chunks while it was still hot and ate them with butter and blackberry jam.

She took a long, hot shower, and afterward she stood in her room, staring into her closet. Choosing what to wear felt heavy on her shoulders. Silly. It didn't matter. Yet in some ways, it mattered more than ever.

She closed her fingers around the long sleeve of a black shirt with thin blue stripes. It was the shirt she'd worn the first day she met Nyth, when she first saw the veil, when her life changed. It was too thin to wear by itself in this cold. She pulled on a thermal shirt over her tank top, then tugged the striped shirt over it. Black leggings, black shorts, warm boot socks she'd made for herself when she was first learning to knit. They were lumpy and uneven, but the yarn was good. And they were hers.

Less than an hour of knitting, and Dominic's sweater was finally done. She should block the pieces before stitching it together, but she wanted to give it to him tonight. The small warps and tugs in the seams could be a sign of love.

And before she knew it, everyone was home, and it was dinnertime, slurping home-made chicken soup and sharing thick slices of the bread Katie had baked, with it dark outside but warm and bright inside, with idle conversation and questions about next semester; with all of it, Katie's heart grew so full it hurt.

She found herself clinging to the threads of the evening: the way Tracy's shoulders sloped when she washed the dishes, Alex crossing his feet when he settled on the love seat with a book, the particular creaks on the staircase when her father climbed it. She lingered over how the carpet felt when she laid across it, the small pressure of Batty's feet climbing onto her back, the warmth of Peaches plopping between her ankles, the tickling of Skimble's whiskers when he nosed against the side of her face, begging to be petted. She rubbed his cheeks and stroked his shoulders, and when he looked at her with his big yellow eyes, she could almost imagine he knew everything and was trying to remind her of her strength.

"Dad?" she asked.

With her face turned to the side, her cheek against the carpet as Batty curled up on her back, she saw him in the doorway to the dining room. He smirked. "Did you switch to a catnip shampoo?"

"Can I go hang out at Dom's?"

That worried crease came between his eyebrows. "Not tonight. It's already getting late. And the weather's bad. I saw three different accidents on my way home."

Her heart sank. "Okay."

It was okay. She had a magical stone that could transport her to another world. She could sneak out.

But she'd wanted an excuse to say goodbye to her family.

Just in case.

Eventually Batty got up for some cat business or another, and Katie was able to wriggle free from Peaches. She went upstairs, switching on only her bedside lamp in her room. It was warm but dim. She could hear the wind shaking the window.

Her phone buzzed.

Dom

> *told my mom I'm going to yours*
> *if you tell your dad you're coming to mine I can pick you up*
> *halfway*

> *Dad already said I can't go out tonight*
> *I can just meet you in the veil*

Dom

> *okay so*
> *let's be real*
> *we don't know what's going to happen tonight*
> *can I please drive you like we're hanging out like normal*
> *and listen to my music that you hate*
> *it'll help*

Her heart clenched. He wasn't wrong.

> *I'll meet you on the corner at 10*
> *<3*

She curled up downstairs on the armchair with her knitting. Her dad and Tracy watched a movie, and for once, Alex hung out with them. He was on his phone the whole time, but he stayed. Katie felt for her hearth fire in the warmth of her family together, felt for her spark in the project growing off her needles. Let them stay with her. Let them carry her.

When Alex got up at the end of the movie to head upstairs—probably to hole up a game until an obnoxiously late hour—Katie reached out a foot and poked his knee with her toes. "Hey. Thanks for hanging out.”

He caught her gaze and looked at her funny. “Yeah,” he said.

“You want to go sledding on Saturday?” The question was out before she even consciously thought it. “I bet the sledding hill’s all iced over.”

“So, you can crash onto the jungle gym at the bottom and break all your bones?” Their dad peered over his glasses. “Doesn’t sound wise.”

Alex cracked a grin. “Sounds cool, though. Sure.” And then he was gone, up the stairs, and Katie let out a deep breath.

“I mean it,” her dad repeated. “Be careful. The last thing I need is both of my children in full body casts.”

“We can use a two-person sled and I’ll sit in the front. Take all the damage if we crash. Then you’ll only have one child in a full body cast.”

It made her shiver a little, the thought of being laid up in a hospital bed. The old, sick memories of her recovery from the accident made sure of it. But it was a smaller shiver than it used to be, and it didn’t steal her away from the moment.

That felt good.

Tracy smiled her small smile. “See, dear? She’s thought of everything. They’ll be fine.”

And Katie smiled back.

She bent and kissed both their cheeks. Their eyebrows were raised when she stood back up, but looking at them too long was going to start to hurt, so she simply said, “Love you,” and turned and hurried upstairs.

How did one prepare to leap into the unknown and drag their friends and the guardians of the worlds back to safety by means still undecided? She found herself standing at her window, staring at the bundle of poppies and nettle tacked there. It had long since dried out, and as she’d grown closer to Nyth, she hadn’t needed to draw on it to help her as much. But it had absorbed a lot of love over the weeks she’d had it. Love and determination and strength.

Rummaging through her desk drawers, she found a little drawstring bag and carefully put the dried bundle into it. It crinkled. The thought of it crumbling made her ache, but tonight was the last night she'd need it, and she wanted it with her.

On the windowsill, her hand lingered on her treasure bowl. There were the pieces of beach glass from her mother, and the burned-down candle stump from when she'd lit a candle to call on Nyth. Any token of love, of strength, would remind her not to be weighed down. She placed the candle and a piece of beach glass in the bag with Asha's gift, tied it shut, and put it in her shoulder bag.

That was everything, then. Katie stood in her room in the dim light of the streetlamp outside. Skimbleshanks had found her by now. He mewed softly at her. Katie smiled, feeling her eyes sting, and picked him up and held him close, his small head resting on her shoulder. She closed her eyes and petted him one more time, his purrs trembling through her collar bones. "I have to go save the world, buddy," she whispered against his fur. "And that includes you."

She held Skimbles until the house grew quiet and still, and the night closed around them in full. Then she crept downstairs as silently as she could, put on her boots and coat and scarves, and slipped out of the house, locking the door behind her.

Her heart beat quick. She'd never sneaked out before. But maybe that was why it was so easy: nobody expected her to.

The sidewalks weren't well-cleared, and the wind was icy and sharp. Katie shuffled down the block to the corner with her arms wrapped around herself, grateful when she saw Dominic already waiting there in his mother's car.

The car was warm when she climbed inside. She buckled up, and Dominic turned to look at her. "Ready?"

"Almost." She pulled his sweater, folded tightly, out of her bag. "Your present. I finished it earlier today."

Dominic's eyes softened as he unfolded the sweater. "It's my favorite color," he said.

"Yeah, that's the idea."

In the dim light from the streetlamps, Katie couldn't be sure if his eyes were damp. Suddenly he shucked off his coat and his flannel shirt, throwing them in the back seat. A laugh startled out of Katie as Dominic carefully wiggled into the sweater, pulling it into place over his t-shirt. He grasped the steering wheel, his hair a messy halo.

"Okay," he said. "Let's go."

They didn't talk much on the way, but he'd been right. His music, the drive, the warmth of the heater and the little bag of beloved treasures she carried all brought her back to herself. The line of his shoulders was less tense. It was time to fix things. She was ready. They were ready.

He drove them out to the park with the sledding hill. The tires crunched and slipped on the snow—the parking lot hadn't been plowed. "Are you gonna be able to get back out?" Katie asked.

He was more himself now, too, his eyes sparkling like they normally did. He grinned without humor. "Might not have to worry about it."

"Oh my god, Dom."

"There would be perks if we fail. No more exams. No more having to clean my room."

Katie rolled her eyes. "Well, I'm not going to not save the world just so you don't have to clean your room."

"Talk about a buzzkill. Alright, then."

She dug in her bag for the dark chocolate she knew was somewhere at the bottom. "Before we go to the veil—you want some?" She held out the chocolate to him.

This time, his grin was genuine. "Bless you, Katie Byrd. We're about to face the end of the world, and you think to bring chocolate."

"Chocolate makes happy hearts, and happy hearts make us brave."

"You should do that up in needlepoint. Then give it to me so I can hang it on my wall."

"Deal. When we get back, I'll start learning needlepoint."

They each ate a few squares of chocolate, watching the snow blow past. Katie put her bag on the floor of the car, taking out the little drawstring bag. She could feel the dried flowers, the glass and candle, through the fabric. She tied the strings around one of the belt loops on her shorts, hoping it would carry over with her when she assimilated.

Then Dominic said, "Well, I guess we go."

Together, they lifted their sightstones.

Chapter 31

The veil was as misty as it had been the night before. Katie and Dominic stood under the trees, staring out into the haze. And then Aerie and Nyth were there, watching them, not saying anything, not needing to say anything.

Nyth held out his hand, and Katie took it.

Where they landed in Harath was warmer, dim, stark. Only a few low scrubby plants grew as far as Katie could see. But she didn't look far. The void was in front of her, and it held her attention.

It was like nothing else. Not like a rift. Just a blank space in the air. Her eyes registered it as solid white more than anything, but she didn't think it was actually white. It was hard to look straight at it long enough to be sure.

Nyth still held one of her hands, Dominic holding the other. Her gaze met Nyth's, the fire in her heart leaping. She closed her eyes as he vanished, leaving behind his corporeal body and swirling in to meet her, nestled against her heart and her mind.

When the bright light of assimilation faded, she was still holding Dominic's hand, although now he was in his high-collared jacket, Aerie nowhere to be seen. Katie felt Nyth's purpose beating like a heartbeat alongside hers. They were ready.

"Hey." She waited until Dominic looked at her to continue. "When we get back from this, I'll tell you everything, okay?"

"Everything about what?"

"About when my mom died. And why I was homeschooled.

And—everything." She twined her fingers between his. "I promise."

He tilted his head, his mouth softening. After a moment, he said, "Okay."

Together, the four of them turned back to the void. "Well," Dominic said, "here goes everything." And hand-in-hand, they stepped together into emptiness.

There was nothing. Katie couldn't see anything, feel anything, no sound or light or echo of sensation. She couldn't feel Dominic's hand in hers, couldn't breathe, could barely even feel Nyth still with her. It wasn't dark or bright, just nothing, nothing in a way that overwhelmed human sense, and her mind crackled with the first spark of panic.

But Nyth's mind pressing against hers, trying to help her, to lead her. She let herself sink back, let him guide them. There was a point of light. It was tiny, or maybe just far away. She couldn't tell. It got bigger, slowly. She was dying, maybe. She didn't think her heart was beating. But Nyth was there. Nyth was with her, and he was clawing them through the nothingness, closer and closer to the light, whatever it was.

Then she was moving, and her heart jolted awake, and her lungs gasped in air, and she felt Dominic's hand in hers again.

They were—somewhere, in between places, and something like wind buffeted their bodies, streaks of light streaming past them in wild colors. Katie wasn't sure if it was too noisy to think or so silent it deafened thought, but she was holding onto Dominic, and Nyth was with her, so she turned her face toward whatever was coming.

From the streaks of light, gnarled arms with long-fingered hands, faces with moth-black eyes and wide, split-faced mouths with tiny teeth appeared. Riftlings crawled out and tumbled alongside them. Spindly arms reached out, grabbing, trying to find purchase. Arms, too many arms, slammed around Dominic. His hand was wrenched out of hers before she could pull him back. He screamed something, but they pulled him away, and he disappeared in the light. Katie's heart clenched as she felt Aerie slip beyond

Nyth's sense.

"Nyth!" Katie shoved away grabbing hands, tried to orient herself. Arms closed around her. No, they couldn't have her, too. She was the only one left; Nyth was the only one left. And then she felt something in her mind slip, felt heat rush out of her body, and suddenly she saw Nyth being pulled up and away from her, gray hands clutching him. He was looking back at her. "Nyth!" He disappeared into the light, and the rushing and the riftlings tumbled into each other, and Katie saw black.

Slowly, she became aware of pressure against her left side. Ground. She was lying on the ground.

Katie sat up with a gasp. Too fast—it made her head light, and she had to bow back down until the spinning stopped.

She sat on hard-packed earth, surrounded by trees. It wasn't the veil, or at least not the veil as she knew it. The ground was too bare, and the trees weren't quite right. But it wasn't Earth, either. The same way Harath had instinctively felt different, she knew this wasn't Earth.

Or Harath.

She didn't know where she was. And she was alone.

Katie opened her clenched fists and found her sightstone lying in one of her palms. Its flickering dance of light was gone. So were the deep blue sleeves that covered the backs of her hands when she assimilated with Nyth. She checked herself—she was back in her own clothes.

Slowly, she lifted her sightstone and looked through its center.

Just trees. Not the trees of the veil, but the ones surrounding her. Katie closed her hand.

Unlike the veil, there was no mist here, and the trees didn't grow quite as close together. No matter which way she turned, she couldn't see a path or a clearing. Only more trees and more dusk-like dimness.

Katie tilted back her head and gazed up past the trees. The sky was inky-dark, a beautiful lush nearly black blue. And it was full of stars. More than she'd ever seen. More than even out in the desert at Lake Powell. They crowded the sky, gleaming and flickering. They made her think of Asha.

Her heart sank, heavy in the pit of her chest.

Asha was gone because of her. Because she had hesitated. Mel and Simon had been taken because she'd wanted to bait the riftlings. And now—this had been her idea, too. And now Dominic and Nyth and Aerie were gone.

So many people gone because of her failings. Just like her mother.

This was why she stayed so long in her comfort zone. Why she played it safe. Didn't shake things up, no matter how much the restless fire in her heart wanted to blaze. But it was too late. She'd made her choices, and now everyone was gone.

Katie opened her eyes, hot tears spilling down her cheeks. "I'm sorry," she whispered to the stars. The fire inside her was barely more than a candle flame, guttering in the wind.

She wiped her face and took a shuddering breath. She'd felt the moment when Nyth undid the assimilation. He'd let himself be taken alone instead of her being pulled along with him. In that last moment, in that last glimpse of his face, she hadn't seen any fear. No worry. Just determination.

He hadn't let her go only to save her. He'd let her go so there'd be someone left to finish the job.

Maybe her inner fire was small and sad and tired. But it was still there, and so was she. She still had to try.

Her gaze shifted across the sky, high above the dense forest. There was a place where the stars clustered especially closely, trailing along the sky like a pathway.

Katie put her sightstone in her pocket, stood up, and started to walk, following the stars.

It was too warm for her coat and scarf, so she took them off and folded them over her arm. She kept walking until she lost track of time, following the trail of stars winding high above the trees. Her mind turned through memories, beach glass from her mother and learning to knit and meeting Dominic, Nyth's passion and spark, Asha's kindness, Simon's steadiness, Mel's caring, the way all the guardians, every single one, had somehow come to love these little humans. All the things that had brought her to this moment.

And after a while, she saw a clearing ahead. A clearing with something in it.

The closer she got, the better she saw it. It wasn't a clearing after all, but the end of the trees, opening out into a wide expanse of desert. The object past the trees was a low platform made of stone. And on it lay four figures.

Katie's heart beat in her throat, but her feet didn't slow. She walked right up to the platform and sucked in a breath and tried not to cry again.

They were lying in a row, eyes closed, expressions soft. All of their hands were folded below their breastbones, and their sightstones laid on the backs of their hands.

Each sightstone was cracked clean in half.

Her friends looked the way they had when they'd been taken. Asha's wool skirt and tights she'd been wearing the day she'd baked cupcakes. Mel had on the jacket and gloves, Simon the boots and coat they'd worn the day they baited the riftlings in the woods. And Dom.

Katie knelt next to the platform. Dominic was on the end, wearing what she'd seen him in not that long ago, his jeans and sneakers and that ugly yellow sweater.

Her pulse was quick, but as she watched, she saw his chest slowly rise, then fall. And his face—there was color in his cheeks, a soft flush of circulation.

They were alive. All of them were alive. She checked, watched their breath, felt their cheeks. "Hey." Katie shook Dominic's shoulder, then Mel's. "Guys. Guys." They didn't wake up, just kept breathing so slowly, lying still.

Katie rubbed her eyes with the heel of her hand. They were so still, she'd known, or at least half-known, they wouldn't wake up.

But they were alive. Whatever the riftlings had done to them, however they'd stolen the guardians, it hadn't killed her friends. From what felt like years ago, Katie remembered something Mel had said. How in folklore, seeing stones broke after they had protected the bearer.

She sat on the edge of the stone platform. "I'm sorry," she said. "For all of it. Every time I hesitated. Every time you got hurt because of me." She took a deep breath and let it out shakily. "I wish I'd been a better person. Someone not so messed up. I wish…"

Katie's gaze fell to Mel's face, to the tiny crease between her eyebrows. Practical, burden-bearing Mel. Mel who blamed herself every time the rest of them got hurt. But it wasn't Mel's fault. None of it was. She'd always done her best, but she couldn't control everything.

Something twinged in Katie's chest.

"You shouldn't blame yourself so much." She looked down at her hands. "Sometimes… sometimes our best isn't enough, and that's not our fault." She swallowed the lump in her throat. "And even when you can't do your best—when it hurts too much to even try—"

She reached over Mel to touch Asha's hand. She watched the rise and fall of Simon's chest.

"Then you do better next time."

Katie closed her eyes.

She remembered sunlight shifting through leaves, smooth pieces of beach glass, her mother's smile.

She remembered crying in her pajamas, headlights on the highway, the scream of twisting metal.

It hurt. God, it hurt.

But the pain wasn't the only memory. More than the pain, more than the guilt, there were cartwheels and laughter and love, love, love. Those would always be there, more powerful than that terrible night. And forgiving herself wouldn't make her forget her mother.

It's okay, she whispered to herself, to the eight-year-old girl inside who wished she could turn back time. It's okay.

It's your forest fire.

If before she'd had a candle inside her, now it grew bigger, warmer, brighter. A leaping orange fire crackling in a hearth. Something plucked at the fire, coaxing it off in one direction. Katie turned her head, turning with the fire, towards the desert.

The ground was the same as it had been under the trees. Bare earth, hard-packed. But further out into the desert, sharp dark shapes rose from the ground. Pieces of a now-familiar mineral.

The heat of the desert pressed against her. The fragment of Nyth still inside her rose against it with something like a laugh.

Turning back to her friends, Katie laid her coat and scarves between Asha's and Simon's knees. She took a deep breath, let it out in a shudder. "I can't take you with me," she said to them all. "I wish I could. I'm tired and I miss you." She swallowed the tightness in her throat. "But I'm not stopping. And I'll bring you back." Her gaze fell on Dominic, and she thought of all his trust, all his support, and she dug down deep into that strength. "I'll bring all of you back, or none of us."

With one last look, she turned and walked out into the desert.

It was already warmer than it had been under the trees, even under the cool night sky. The path of stars scattered out across the sky, no longer clearly pointing the way, but that was fine. Katie approached the pieces of hornblende half-buried in the desert earth.

Igneous rock, she remembered. It needs magma to form.

She began following the hornblende out into the desert.

It was scattered, some pieces smaller and some larger, though none as tiny as the ones she'd dug up back on Earth. They weren't in a clear line the way the stars had been, but they definitely headed in one direction. Katie pressed on through the night, walking between the mineral deposits, the fire warm and clear in her chest.

It was beautiful, how the fire glowed when she didn't try to smother it. When she didn't try to hide it away in her comfort zone, in safety, in security. Safety and security went out the window the moment she first took Nyth's hand, and finally she was rising to meet it.

Walking alone out under the stars, Katie grinned.

She walked longer across the desert than she had through the trees, and that was saying something. The desert was absolutely flat. It made it hard to tell how far she'd gone. She lived in a place full of trees and buildings everywhere, things to mark where you'd been and where you were going. This desert had none of that. But as she walked, the sky grew lighter, and the sun began to creep above the horizon. And when it did, it silhouetted something in its glow.

Katie walked, watching the sky blaze orange, feeling the temperature rise as the stars slowly winked out in the brighter light of the sun. The thing ahead was a mountain. And the mineral deposits were heading straight towards it.

She picked up her pace, and the day cracked open around her until the sky was bright and pale, the sun rising high, the mountain a clear, dark shape on the horizon. It was the only thing she could see anywhere in the desert, but more importantly, it looked like it was made of the same stuff. And that was the best answer she had. So, she kept on toward it.

Before long, under this sun, her feet were boiling inside her boots. Eventually she stopped and tugged them off, just to get some air on her feet. The relief was immediate. Then she peeled off her socks, and the air was such an enormous relief that she tugged down her shorts and pulled off her leggings, sighing when the air touched her skin.

She paused for a moment, her fingertips resting lightly on the tops of her thighs. If there was one good thing about all this, one tiny silver lining, it was how amazing it felt for sun and wind to touch her skin for the first time in years.

The feeling of her scars under her hand, and the memories they dredged up—none of it felt good. But it was okay. She could carry it.

She pulled off her striped shirt, too, a little sadly. But two layers were much more bearable than three.

Katie put her shorts back on without the leggings, then her socks, rolling them down to her ankles to keep her legs bare, and then her boots. She carried her shirt and leggings balled up in one hand, and she started walking again.

The longer she walked, following the mineral deposits towards the mountain, the more the fire inside her grew bigger and brighter. She could feel that last piece of Nyth in her, really feel it like she never could before, that something that had been with her since she was very small. How she'd always felt like the sun was her best friend. How she could play outside as long as she wanted without getting sunburned. How, the summer of the accident, earlier in the summer, they had all gone camping, and the fire had felt friendly for the first time in a way it never had before when she roasted her marshmallows and apples. How the doctors had said she'd held on remarkably long in the burning car, how she had healed remarkably fast, lungs and skin alike.

He'd been with her since then, since she was small. He was with her all the years she hid. He was in the restlessness that never totally went away, the curiosity that always pushed her to solve problems and puzzles and find a better way, and the volatile emotions that made her lash out at her brother and father, and the anger and impulsiveness that made her slash her teacher's chair, and the spark of determination that never left her, even though it got buried for a long time. And he was still with her now. She'd never been alone. Not really. And she wasn't alone now.

It was his restlessness tangled up in her own determination that made her keep moving forward. And so, eventually, the mountain began to loom larger. It made her walk faster.

Time didn't seem to be passing normally, and once it was high overhead, the hot sun didn't move any further in the sky. She had been walking for hours, days, weeks, hell if she knew. How far could the mountain be? She wiped sweat off her forehead and noticed the sun, for all its fixed position, felt less harsh than before. Dim, foggy clouds were hanging low in the sky, stretching all the way to the mountain. They blocked the sun, but the air itself stayed warm, and the further she walked, the hotter it got.

Katie shoved her sleeves up to her elbows in exasperation. She pulled a hair tie off her wrist and tugged her hair into a ponytail as she walked, then carried on with more air on the back of her neck and her balled-up clothes swinging in one hand. A fine sheen of sweat covered her skin, and her shirt was stuck to her back, and she wanted lip balm. God, she wanted a lot of things. A big glass of water and a cool breeze instead of a hot one. Nyth by her side for real instead of only the fragment of him echoing inside her. Dominic with her, Mel and Asha and Simon up and fighting, all the guardians helping them, none of this to be happening at all.

But what she wanted didn't matter right now. All that mattered was walking 'til she got to that mountain, and then she would find something. Because if there was nothing there, then there was nothing anywhere, and whoever had put her friends on that stone slab meant her to walk this desert until she died. And Katie Byrd had no intention of dying anytime soon.

But as the mountain slowly, finally loomed larger and closer, as she could tell it was definitely made of the same dark rock, she didn't think that would be the case. The air was heavier and hotter. And she was beginning to suspect it wasn't just a mountain.

The flat, packed dirt gave way to uneven, rocky ground with a gradual slope. She considered dropping her leggings and shirt—having nothing to carry would be easier. But she said, "No. I've lost enough. These are my favorite leggings." And the absurdity of it made her laugh. She tied the shirt around her waist, then the leggings, knowing she was being ridiculous, but not caring. She kept walking, more carefully now.

The mountain loomed over her now. She had to crane back her neck to look up to the top of it. The slope steepened; she felt it in her thighs, in her calves, even though she couldn't see a change until the ground suddenly gave way fully to the rocky mountain surface. And then the incline was too steep to simply walk. She had to start climbing.

Katie looked up the mountain. She took a deep breath, thought of Dominic, and reached for a handhold.

Now the aches and strains in her muscles were in her arms, her chest, rather than her ankles and low back. The incline wasn't so steep as to force her to climb straight up—she was more crawling, using her hands to brace herself and keep from toppling backwards. Her fingers started to feel raw from scraping against the rough stone. Her breath came heavier, sweat running down her back, the middle of her chest, her temples. It was getting almost unbearable. The reptile had had too much sun. Katie stopped climbing, breathing hard, and leaned against the side of the mountain as she stripped off her thermal shirt, leaving herself in just her tank top. She didn't mind leaving this one behind, she realized, so she folded it and laid it on the rocks that were hot to the touch. God, she wanted a glass of water. She kept climbing.

Walking with her legs mostly bared hadn't bothered her because she didn't have to look down at them and didn't have to see her scars. Now as she reached up for handholds, the scars on her left arm came into and out of her line of sight in a regular flow. Something about it felt weird. It took her a few minutes to realize that what felt weird was that she wasn't upset. The reminder of loss on her skin was not important right now. All she was thinking about was getting to the top of the mountain so she could somehow save her friends and find the guardians. And that realization unknotted a nearly lifelong ache in her chest, and Katie smiled, grinned, laughed to herself alone on the mountainside.

The climb didn't take as long as the walk had, but it was still too long. Her shoulders and arms were aching, her knees and ankles hurt, her fingers were cramping from gripping so much. Her fingernails were chipped and her knees bruising and her hair sticking to her forehead with sweat. Her lips were chapped, and her throat hurt every time she breathed in. But the little drawstring bag tapped her hip with each movement of her leg. She remembered the way the light in her bedroom window looked falling across the bundle of poppies. Nyth's courage burned alongside her own. She kept climbing.

The clouds hung heavier now. Katie swallowed with her dry throat and pulled herself up another foot, and then another, and then another. And then her hands found level ground, and she hauled herself up, and the climb up the mountain ended as she finally stood shakily on the flat surface at the top.

Her heart was pounding, and not only from the climb. The flat surface rimmed the top of the mountain, and inside, down below, lava and fire swirled. She was right. It wasn't just a mountain.

Katie walked the perimeter of the volcano's mouth, catching her breath, feeling the incredible heat on her skin. The desert below was flat and empty in all directions. She couldn't see the forest she'd walked through anywhere on the horizon. This was the place, then. Whatever that meant.

She turned and looked down into the volcano. Her legs were so tired. She wanted to sit down. Instead, she reached into her pocket and pulled out her sightstone. It lay in her palm, hot and flickering with the light of the volcano. Then she shook the drawstring bag until the crumbled pieces of the flower bundle from Asha felt into her hand over the stone. Katie closed her fingers around it all, barely, and looked back down into the lava, into the fire swirling above it.

It was heat, and it was light, and transformation and motion and Nyth, Nyth, calling to her from inside her heart, from somewhere far away. A brilliant burning flame, and a small, scared voice trapped in shadow.

The flame inside her leaped higher, grew brighter, blazed like a bonfire. It was part of her, through her bones and sinew, in her blood, fueling her breath. She felt Nyth all around her, and she felt him crying out for her.

The fire in the volcano flared higher, circling in a way fire wouldn't normally. Reaching for her. Calling.

Katie held the stone against her chest and took a deep breath. Then she bent her knees and jumped and fell headfirst into the volcano's heart.

Chapter 32

As Katie fell, clutching the stone to her chest, the fire inside her reached out to meet the fire around her. Nyth, the bit of him still clinging to her, flared around her, shielded her, made her part of the flame. It felt like assimilating when her body should have been incinerating. And she felt flames streaking from her body as she closed her eyes and plunged into the inferno below.

Everything was hot and white for a moment, blinding and searing, and then the brightness began to dim. Katie stood still—she was standing, she realized, on solid ground. And so she opened her eyes.

Flames still twisted around her, but they were the flames she knew, the same fire that enveloped her when she assimilated with Nyth. They flickered and parted before her so she could see the trees.

She stood in the veil. She knew that pattern of bark on the trees, and the mist heavy in the air. It was thicker than ever before—she could only see a few trees before they vanished into the purple-gray shadow. But a light glowed faintly in the distance, so she started walking towards it.

Sparks fell to the ground around her as she moved. She felt her hair swaying out behind her, one with the flames licking off her arms, her legs, her back. The fire was with her; she was not alone.

The glowing light grew brighter, and as it did, the mist thinned. Katie realized it was sunlight, and a clearing among the trees. She was nearly to the tree line when she saw the huge tree at the far end of the clearing, thicker and wider and older than any of the other trees in the veil. She saw a figure seated there. Her pace stayed steady. Her heart beat in time with her footsteps, and the flames that were part of her fanned out in time with her beating heart.

She stepped into the clearing and stared across it. The roots of the large tree had burst from the ground, twisting around each other to form an uneven seat. On it sat a person who looked just enough like Nyth to make Katie take in a surprised hiss of breath. But he was too pale, too long and thin in the limbs. His hair was red, but a paler red than Nyth's, and his eyes weren't like hers. They were darker, heavy-lidded.

He was lounging on the seat of tree roots, his back against the tree trunk and his chin resting on his hand. He smiled when she stepped into the clearing. "I knew you wouldn't stop until you found me," he said, "but I didn't expect you so soon. Or quite so…" His gaze fanned over the fire around her. "Impressively."

If not for the fire holding her, Katie might have shivered. She took a few steps closer, stepping into the weak sunlight. "Who are you, and what did you do with the guardians?"

He laughed. "Good. At least there are still some surprises." He smirked at her, shifting his hand so the side of his face rested in his palm. "I'm Nyth."

Katie physically recoiled. Her hand reached instinctively for her sightstone, but her fingers found two pieces. Cracked clean in half, protecting her on her journey through the fire. Her heart clenched. "No, you're not."

"Oh, don't be stupid, Katie. You know the guardians can take on whatever physical form they want." He shifted his weight, leaning back fully against the tree. "You're partly right, though. I'm not just Nyth. I'm all of the guardians." He frowned. "Well, minus one stubborn little piece you insist on clinging to."

Her heart was skittering in her chest. "If you're really all the guardians, then where are the riftlings? Who sent them to take you?"

"We did."

She shook her head. "The guardians didn't send the riftlings. They didn't even know what they were."

He shook his head. "Not the guardians you knew. But we were split, remember? Fragments of ourselves scattered across Earth and Harath. The pieces on Earth found you, but the ones on Harath weren't so lucky." He writhed his fingers on one hand. From among them, like a magic trick, a little bundle of red poppies and nettle appeared. "Those parts of ourselves stayed alone and cold for a very long time."

Her gaze was stuck on the poppies. "Don't do that," she said.

He spun them in his hand idly. "We're not perfect, you know. We ought to have been. Would've made things easier." He smiled at her again. "But you've known that. You've seen Nyth's temper. You've seen us in fear, in resentment. We're capable of anger, doubt, malice. Making mistakes. The fragments we left on Harath were born of confusion and desperation, and they never found cozy homes to nestle into, so that part of us just got more and more desperate. More and more isolated. Over the years, we were able to steal bits of energy from Harath until we had enough to slip that pocket of void between the veil and the worlds. We knew the rest of ourselves would never let that go untreated."

"Could you… could you just drop those?" Katie asked, still staring at the flowers in his hand.

He tilted his head. "Do they bother you, sunshine?"

The nickname jolted her out of the haze of confusion. "Don't call me that." A stronger wave of fire rippled off her back. "Not— like this."

He narrowed his eyes. "We made the vines to test if we could breach the rifts. We made the rift beasts as practice and sent them on ourselves. And when we were strong enough, we made the riftlings to bring ourselves home." He leaned forward. "It hurts to be pulled too thin, and it hurts even more to be shattered. We were sick of hurting. So, we got the rest of ourselves back, no matter how hard we resisted." He frowned. "Again, except for that bit left in you. Nyth really is an annoying bastard, aren't I?"

"I don't believe you." Katie stepped in closer. "The guardians protect the two worlds. They wouldn't pull themselves away from that on purpose and let it all fall apart."

"Wouldn't we?" He raised his eyebrows. "You're mostly a good person, Katie Byrd. What did you do when you were burned?"

Unbidden, flashes of memory rose in her mind. Burrowing alone in her blanket forts. Alex's black eye. How she yelled and sobbed when her therapist told her that she ought to go back to school. The horror in her teacher's eyes as scissors flashed. Not letting her father hug her for years.

"Stop it."

"You know first-hand that things aren't that simple. Sitting alone in the dark for years, split off from your full self, does unpleasant things to you."

"So, you're whole now. So, it's fine now. So, why are you still—"

"Fine?" He stood and tossed aside the poppies. He was taller than Nyth, though not by much. Imposing all the same. "I want my last piece back. And you can give it to me freely, or I can take it by force."

"If you're the guardians," Katie said, unclenching her hands, "then I know you care about me. And the other vessels are still alive. You wouldn't hurt me to get back Nyth's fragment."

"I didn't have to kill the other vessels because the riftlings neutralized them." He spread his arms. "Do you see any riftlings here? We're giving you a chance to give it up. We want to be complete. Let us do that, or we'll do what we need to make it happen."

She stared at him, at the angles of his face and the tense corner of his mouth, and she realized what she didn't want to realize. She swallowed, and then she said, "No. Because you're not going to go back to holding up the two worlds, are you?"

"I don't know." He shrugged, lolling his head to one side.

"There's so much we don't get to do, pulling all those strings. There's an entire cosmos I could explore."

"And let Earth and Harath fall apart?"

"Maybe."

Katie narrowed her eyes. "That's bullshit."

His eyes flashed. "What?" His voice was so cold it almost raised goosebumps on her bare arms, even with the flames.

"You heard me. You don't get to screw over an entire planet just because you're hurting."

"You dare tell us what to do?" He strode in closer, and the line of his shoulders looked so much like Skiron even though they were slight, and the depth in his eyes looked so much like Zephyrus, and Katie really grasped for the first time that he wasn't just Nyth. It really was all the guardians, all tangled up in one. When they, this not-Nyth, spoke again, the cold edge of their voice felt like the slice of a sudden wind, like Aerie's precision. "You're an incredibly presumptuous little girl."

She lifted her chin. "I'm not giving up Nyth's fragment. Not like this."

Too many things flickered across not-Nyth's face for her to read. The light of her fire flickered in their eyes. "Fine," they said. "Then we do it the hard way."

Their mouth twisted in a scowl, and then the air between them changed, like a sudden cold front slipping down. The ground trembled, and Katie saw sharp pebbles burst up from the earth. The guardians' eyes were shining and their figure still as stone as roots erupted from the ground behind them, wreathed in twisting flame, glittering with shards of ice. And all of it swirled around itself and rushed around the guardians and straight at Katie.

Her heart was in her throat. Katie flung up her hands, fire licking off her arms and flaring out, arcing in front of her. The whirlwind of pointed roots, glittering ice, sharp-edged stone and flame met her barrier. It broke past, but it was weakened, and bits of earth and charred wood fell around her feet harmlessly.

The figure of the guardians seemed to vibrate before her in the meadow. "You dare?" they said. "You dare use a fragment of ourselves against us?"

"It's what I have," Katie shot back. "And it's not just Nyth's fire. It's mine, too."

"Our spirits belong to ourselves!" Not-Nyth lifted their hands, fingers splayed and palms towards the earth. Their jaw was set with firmness, their eyes blazing, and they lifted their hands slowly.

The ground trembled beneath Katie. Tree roots tore up from the earth, flailing and tangling around her ankles, curling around her knees and thighs. Above, the boughs of the trees thrashed in a gust that swirled down around her, whipping at her hair, making her eyes water, trying to flicker out the flames. She poured more of herself into them, and they still burned even as a slab of stone rose from the ground behind her, hitting hard against her back, pinning her against it like a target. She heard rushing—it was the blood in her ears as her heart pounded—and it was more, water rushing from the pools and ponds around the veil, all rushing towards them. The guardians' hands were raised, a deepness flashing in their eyes, and their Nyth-like figure was no taller but seemed so immense as all the waters of the veil roiled together behind them and rose like a wave. Katie opened her mouth to call out, but then the water rushed toward her, and she gasped in a breath instead, just in time before the wave slammed against her.

It kept rolling, pinning her hard back against the rock, her legs twisted in roots. Her head knocked against the rock, made her dizzy, and she'd run out of air soon, and she remembered the reverence in Asha's eyes when she spoke of Zephyrus, and she finally, truly, understood.

She gathered the bonfire inside her and felt for that fragment of Nyth that still rested in her heart, the part of him that didn't want to give up; and she pushed it out, letting heat and light run through her body. A wall of flame burst around her, a solid thing, pushing back the water and the wind, and she gasped in a few breaths, her shaking hands grasping the roots around her thighs. They tightened against her skin. Katie closed her eyes, took another deep breath, and felt the fire leaping off her strengthen. Then she lifted her head. "You're going to tear the veil apart."

"We'll do what we have to."

"Ophion," she said, "this isn't what you're meant to do, and you know it."

"We're as old as the moon," not-Nyth said in an even voice, staring back hard at her. "How can you know what we're meant to do?"

"Simon's told me about you. And I see you in him. Your life. I see it in Simon's eyes. I see it in you. That's what Nyth gives me— I can light things up and see them. And I see all of you clearly, now. You're not meant to hurt, Ophion. You're meant to heal. To grow."

"So, we should grow from our pain." And the guardians' eyes looked so much like hers, then. She saw Nyth shining through. "Is that what you did? No. You locked yourself away for years, rotting in your own grief and self-loathing. You have no place to tell us how to be."

"I know I did that," Katie said, her throat tightening. "And I know I shut people out. And maybe I needed to, then, to start healing. But you can't do that forever! When what you're doing starts hurting more than helping, isn't it time to find a new thing to feel?"

A softness passed over not-Nyth's face, that tenderness she'd seen in Nyth's face only a few times. And when they stepped towards her, the slab of rock slid down from her back, and the roots didn't squeeze her legs quite as tightly. And it was Nyth, such Nyth, looking into her eyes and standing so close. "I want the fragment of myself back," he said. "I want to be whole. Can't you understand that?"

"Of course I can. But I can't give it up. Not when I know you'd abandon the worlds. Not when I can feel you. The part of you that's still in me doesn't want to give up."

He reached out and touched her cheek, and Katie flinched back. But it was gentleness in his hand, and warmth, Nyth's warmth that she knew and loved and felt inside her own heart even when he wasn't there. "I don't have to take it back by force," he said. "I don't want to take it back by force. Do you even know how strong you are, Katie, to face the might of all the guardians? Even my fragment alone wouldn't be enough to protect most humans. It's who you are, how powerful you already are." His hand left her cheek and caressed her hair, stroking through the flames that licked off her without burning her. "It's this fire that's always been in you, even before my fragment found you." His eyes were soft now, so soft. "You could come back to me," he said, and his voice was barely more than a whisper. "Come back, sunshine. Assimilate with me one more time, and then you'll never have to go away again. I'll be complete, and we'll be together forever, and we can both have what we want. Everything will be alright."

She stared back into his eyes. He was so sincere. And—there, just there, just barely enough to see—so afraid.

"No," she said. Her gut turned over. "No. I won't help you abandon the worlds."

A fierceness flashed across his eyes, and he stepped back sharply, something quick and clear coming into his face. "Of course you won't. You're human. That's why you're so stubborn. I've studied you, all the humans, watched you, seen how you live. The same mistakes, over and over."

"And how is it any different from what you're—"

"And we're bound to protect your world, all for the sake of your selfish mistakes. There are billions of you. *Billions.* Do you think we care at all about you? About one?"

Katie narrowed her eyes. "Aerie," she said, and a flash of recognition passed across the guardians' eyes. "Aerie, that's not what you really think of humans. I know it's not."

"Assuming, assuming, you keep assuming you know—"

"I know because you love Dom." The words came out heavy,

spilling hard into the air between them, and Katie saw the guardians' eyes widen, lips part, a softness in the mouth that was all Aerie. "You love Dominic Aaron Gunn more than anything. You love to fly with him and sit inside his mind. You love him so much you follow him as a bird. None of the other guardians spend so much time following their vessels, not even Nyth with me. You love him so much, and that's why you didn't kill him when you took back your fragment.

"And Zephyrus? You love Asha. She's everything you are. You're part of each other, always have been. And Ophion, I see how much you love Simon every time he assimilates. The way that plant armor curls around his body is like you're holding him. You hold him steady. You keep him safe."

"Stop," they said, and they stepped back from her, a hardness setting in their jaw.

"Skiron. You're—" And Katie laughed, actually laughed, a strange sound to her ears in this moment. "I see you in Mel all the time. I didn't understand at first, but I do now. You love her, too, in your way. All of you, you love us all." She shook her head. "And it's not just because we carry the fragments of your spirits, and it's not because you needed us to close the rifts. You'd've loved us anyway for who we are. Like we love you."

And she looked into Nyth's eyes—they were Nyth's eyes now, exactly like hers—and pushed her hands down towards the ground. Fire fells in waves from her palms, burning away the roots, and she stepped towards the guardians. "It's okay to be afraid," she said. "And lashing out because you're hurting doesn't make you a bad person." She stepped in closer, and the figure of the guardians stepped back, but she narrowed the distance, reaching up and taking their face in her hands, gently, so gently. "But when you're hurting yourself? That's when the place you're in is bad for you. And that's when you need to change. To grow. To let go."

"You don't know what it was like," not-Nyth whispered, eyes wide. "Being so alone for so long. No warmth. No life. No touch.

No movement or freedom or peace."

Katie smiled, and when her eyes crinkled up from smiling, she felt a few tears sneak down her cheeks. "Yeah," she said. "Yeah, I do. And you know I do."

Not-Nyth lifted their hands, curled them hard around her wrists, tried to pull her hands down. The fire licking off her skin shivered around not-Nyth's hands as well, binding them to her instead. "What—"

"Do you remember, Nyth?" she said, and when she spoke his name, she saw something change in his eyes. "Do you remember what you said to me when I told you how my mom died?" He stared back at her, wide-eyed, with those eyes that looked exactly like hers. Katie leaned in and rested her forehead against his, hands cradling his face. "This is your forest fire," she whispered, and she closed her eyes.

The fire inside her shivered, rushed under her skin, hotter than hot, and burst out, out, surrounding them, shooting out throughout the veil, burning hot, white hot, white and hot and searing, and Katie felt the tears on her cheeks dry as the guardians' hold on her wrists became gentler. Then the brightness filled her, and then everything was gone.

Chapter 33

After a wildfire, the earth sleeps awhile. The life that burned down settles into the soil, feeding it rich new nutrients. The seeds sleep until they're fed. And then, slowly, with rain and sun and the nutrients born of the burning down, the seeds begin to wiggle their way towards the surface.

It seemed to Katie Byrd that she had slept for a long time. The earth cradled her, warm and safe, as worms turned the soil and the decaying ash of burned trees fed the seeds lying asleep alongside her. So, when she blinked her eyes open and saw red poppies swaying above her, she wasn't surprised at all.

Her body felt heavy as she turned her head, moved her hands, blinked into daylight. Slowly, she sat up in the grass. Something was warm. She tipped her head back, looking above her. Sun. She felt the sun on her face, shining down from beyond the trees.

The trees with the patchy bark. The grass springing under her fingers. She was in the veil, but a veil like she hadn't seen before. No mist, and past the poppies growing around her, tiny yellow flowers covering the ground.

And there. Just over there. Four shapes in the grass in the middle of a circle of stumps.

Katie stood on legs that felt strong but clumsy. She stumbled and ran her way across the meadow, crashed to her knees, and grabbed Dominic's hand, squeezing it tightly as a smile broke out on her face until her cheeks hurt.

He made a soft noise and furrowed his brow. He lifted a lazy hand and rubbed his eyes. Then he opened them, and he saw her, and his eyes widened, and he said, "You did it?"

Then from past Dominic, Asha sat up, and she saw them, and she said, "Katie? What happened?" And Katie laughed and burst into tears at the same time.

Simon woke, pressed himself up to sitting, found Mel and shook her until she woke. The moment her eyes opened, he hauled her up from the grass and hugged her so tight she wheezed, "Snow, Snow, come on, I can't breathe." Then, when he let her go, they both saw Asha. Simon's eyes shone wet, and Mel's mouth fell softly open. Her eyes widened, her brow scrunched, and they both reached out and pulled Asha to them. Asha let out a small squeak and raised her eyebrows back at Dominic and Katie. Dominic laughed, and he pulled Katie by the hand, and they crawled over and leaned in. Katie was on the outside, one arm around Simon's back and the other around Dominic's, and Mel caught her gaze from across Simon's arm and her smile was so beautiful it made Katie's heart almost too full to bear, and in the middle of it all Asha protested, "I love you, but I'm smothering a little." They leaned back so she could get air, and she started crying, too, crying and laughing and grabbing Simon's hands and gazing up at the sun like she thought she'd never see it again.

At the same time, they all felt it. They all turned. And they all saw their guardians standing in the meadow, smiling down at them.

And Katie knew Aerie was propelling herself forward, latching on to Dominic; she knew Simon twined his hands in Ophion's while flowers twisted their vines lovingly up his arms; she knew Mel went and stood in front of Skiron and he bowed his head and Mel leaned forward to lean her forehead against his massive chest; she knew Zephyrus brought herself in all her glory down to the grass and cradled Asha like a child, murmuring words of apology and love. But she didn't pay any of it any attention, because Nyth was waiting for her.

She went to him. She held out her arms. And he fell into them, holding tightly to her, his face bent into her shoulder. "You're okay," she told him, arms wrapped close around him. She felt his heart beating against her chest.

When he pulled away, he took her hand. They walked together into the trees, leaving the others to their reunions.

"I hurt you," he said, quietly, under the dappled light.

"I know." She squeezed his hand. "I forgive you. I understand."

"I don't. Understand, that is." Nyth shook his head. "How can you forgive me so easily?"

"Because I know what it's like to hurt people I love." She smiled, poked one finger against his chest. "And because we're part of each other. I know what you were feeling. And I know how sorry you are."

"You still have my fragment."

She nodded. "I can tell, now. I can feel it like I couldn't before."

"You'll keep it, then. I'm not going to hurt you anymore."

Katie tilted her head. "Won't you… aren't you…" She bit her lip. "Won't you feel incomplete? If all the other guardians have their fragments back, but you don't?"

And Nyth smiled like sunshine, like laughter, like golden mornings. "The parts of me that aren't with me are with you. Getting to stay with you? I could never feel incomplete."

Katie had no idea what to say to that. She simply smiled back, holding his hands, and listened to the leaves rustling softly overhead for a long moment. She wanted to take this warmth, this glow, this wonderful feeling in her chest and keep it safe forever.

She knew what was coming, and she didn't want it. But she was human. And part of being human was learning how to let go when it was time. So, she led him by the hand back to the meadow, and back to her friends and their guardians.

Everyone was standing together now. When they saw Katie and Nyth returning, everyone turned to look. Zephyrus stepped away from Asha and crossed the grass in long, graceful strides to meet them. She was so tall, Katie had to crane her neck back to look up at her.

"Thank you," Zephyrus said, in a voice like running water and bells.

Katie didn't know what to say. *You're welcome* was too mundane for what had happened. But she smiled softly, and she thought Zephyrus understood what she meant.

"Are the worlds safer now, then?" Mel asked.

Skiron nodded. "We can sense them from here. The tears are mending themselves. We will need to do more mending as well, but all is falling back into balance."

"Thanks to you," Simon said, staring at Katie.

"Thanks to Nyth," Katie said. "He saved me from the riftlings. If he hadn't, we never would have made it here."

Asha was still smiling like she couldn't stop, but it wasn't quite reaching her eyes anymore. "So, no more rifts," she said. "That's... that's good."

"It does mean," Ophion said, in their soft leaf-rustling voice, "that we will not need to call upon you anymore."

Mel ducked her head. "Right. It's good, though. Needing us meant the world was broken. And now it's fixed."

Dominic was staring at Aerie with sad eyes. Simon held Mel's hand and didn't quite meet anyone's gaze. And Katie felt her heart aching when she looked back at Nyth.

His eyes—like hers—were sad. "I don't want to."

"Neither do I," Katie said. "But I think—I think this is goodbye."

"For now," said Aerie. She looked at all of them, something sparkling coming into her face. "Only for now. Remember who we are. We're everywhere, and in everything. You can always find us. And we can always find you."

Katie squeezed Nyth's hand. He got to stay with her. That was what he'd said. And she felt it, felt the piece of him, still in her heart, fluttering alongside her own personal flame. The piece of him that would never leave.

"You'll always have a home to come to," she said.

And it cracked her heart clean in two, knowing she would never assimilate with him again. Never again feel his mind pressing against hers, feel his heart getting all mixed up with hers. Never feel him fill her hands with fire or direct her feet or keep her warm, even in the coldest snowstorm. But he would still be with her. And he would always be in the world. And she could always, always find him.

It was too much to say. But she saw it all in his eyes, and she knew he understood.

"Will you be okay now?" she asked. "You wanted—you were so frustrated. By limitations."

He reached up and tapped her nose, then her cheeks. Almost absently. "Your freckles," he said. "They're like little sunspots."

"Nyth."

"I'll be okay. We will." He lowered his hand. "Something did heal when you burned it all down. Something feels mended, now. And even if it's hard sometimes, I don't think we'll be stagnating like that again." He grinned. "And if we do, I know who to call."

Katie caught his hand, holding it between her own. "Okay."

Her friends stood with their guardians. Katie stood with Nyth. The veil surrounding them was warm and bright, safe and glowing, green and full of flowers. Nyth held out his hand, and she took it. Her breath caught in her throat, and one last time, Nyth pulled her through the veil.

And then she was standing in the snowy parking lot. Nyth was still there, holding both her hands, his face so warm and full of love. "Don't forget," he said. "I'm always here." And he leaned in and kissed her forehead, burning hot against her skin. Then he looked into her eyes, said, "I'll see you around, sunshine," and his hands pulled at hers. She reached out, trying to follow; but his hands slipped away, and he faded, and he was gone.

A shaky breath escaped her, clouding the night air. She blinked, hard, eyes hot and damp. Then she turned to her friends. Mel wiping her eyes with the heel of her hand. Simon swallowing hard. Asha's gaze downcast, face soft and still. Dominic meeting Katie's gaze, his face telling her he was feeling everything she was.

"What time is it?" she asked, because she didn't know what else to say.

Dominic pulled his phone out of his pocket. It was still there, after everything. "Half past midnight. Felt a lot longer than that."

Asha tipped back her head. It was starting to snow again, but this time in big, fat, soft flakes that drifted down lazily. "What do we do now?"

Simon took her hand. Katie wrapped her right arm through Asha's left. The pinched tension between Asha's brows faded.

"We go home," Mel said.

She took Simon's other hand. Katie reached out her left hand, reached for Dominic, and he found her, holding her mittened hand. They walked together towards his car, the snow falling all around them, and Katie didn't feel cold at all.

About the Author

Rebecca Gardner has been writing, in varying degrees of quality, her whole life. After winning various regional awards for her short stories as a child, she turned her adulthood towards writing books about fantastical things happening to big-hearted people.

She lives in Pennsylvania with two cats and an ever-growing collection of charming mugs. *Instructions for Burning the World* is her debut novel.

Acknowledgements

No book makes it to this point without incredible support, and I give my everlasting thanks to all those who've supported me:

Tim McWhorter, Emma Bailey, and everyone else at Olive Ridley and Manta Press. This book would still be a pipe dream living on my hard drive without you. Thank you to Julie McWhorter for your enthusiasm and encouragement.

Jeremy Jusek, poet and friend, who pushed me to submit this book and gave invaluable feedback on earlier drafts. (I know I don't always agree with your suggestions, but they always make me consider things in a new way, and this book is better for them.)

Maureen, my sister, who read this book in its very first draft and immediately fell so in love with these characters and their stories. I don't think anyone will ever know how much you've been the engine of this book.

The Words Are Hard cohort, the Little Reds, and all other writing partners, feedback friends, beta readers, and fellow wordsmiths— every writer needs a community, and I thank you for being mine. Celia, Jenna, Julie, Kate, Katie, Sarah, Victoria: you Get Me. I love you all.

And love and thanks to Kiersten, Ari, Brian, Marie, Kevin, Alec, Rachel, and Steve, for being the steady shores against which my day-to-day thought-oceans may fling themselves. We are better because of our friends.

***L*OOKING FOR MORE THRILLING *Y*OUNG *A*DULT BOOKS? *C*HECK OUT THESE OTHER TITLES FROM *O*LIVE *R*IDLEY *P*RESS AND *M*ANTA *P*RESS, *L*TD.**

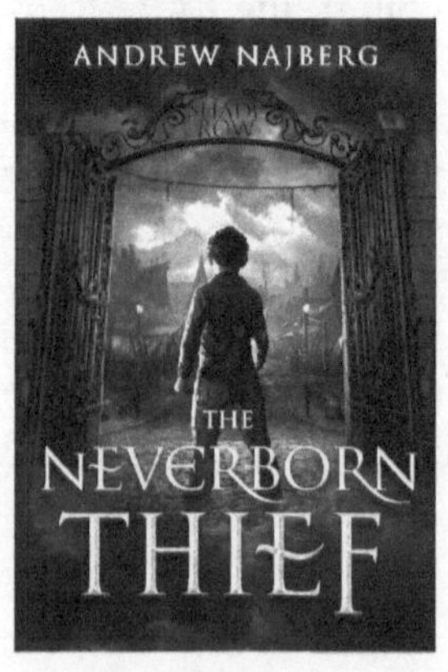

9 781958 370216